THE ZION
CHRONICLES
BOOK 5

D0547484

THE ZION CHRONICLES • BOOK 5

THE KEY TO ZION

BODIE & BROCK THOENE

TYNDALE HOUSE PUBLISHERS, INC.
CAROL STREAM, ILLINOIS

With love and respect
The Key to Zion
is dedicated to Papa,
an example to his children
of the righteous man
of Psalm 15.

He will be the sure foundation for your times, a rich store of salvation and
wisdom and knowledge; the fear of the LORD is the key to this treasure.
Isaiah 33:6

Visit Tyndale online at www.tyndale.com.

TYNDALE is a registered trademark of Tyndale House Publishers, Inc.

Tyndale's quill logo is a trademark of Tyndale House Publishers, Inc.

The Key to Zion

Copyright © 1988, 2006 by Bodie Thoene. All rights reserved.

Cover illustration copyright © 2006 by Cliff Nielsen. All rights reserved.

Authors' photo by Joe Dillon, Tuam, Co., Galway, Ireland. All rights reserved.

Designed by Dean H. Renninger

Edited by Ramona Cramer Tucker

Published in 1988 as *The Key to Zion* by Bethany House Publishers under ISBN 1-55661-034-3.

First printing by Tyndale House Publishers, Inc., in 2006.

Scripture quotations are taken from the *Holy Bible*, King James Version or the Holy Bible, *New International Version*,® NIV.® Copyright © 1973, 1978, 1984 by Biblica, Inc.™ Used by permission of Zondervan. All rights reserved worldwide. www.zondervan.com.

Library of Congress Cataloging-in-Publication Data

Thoene, Bodie, date.
  The key to Zion / Bodie & Brock Thoene.
    p. cm. — (The Zion chronicles ; bk. 5)
    ISBN 978-1-4143-0106-8 (pbk.)
    1. Israel—Fiction.   2. Jerusalem—Fiction.   3. Jews—Palestine—Fiction.   4. Palestine—History—Partition, 1947—Fiction.   5. Israel-Arab War, 1948-1949—Fiction.   6. Religious fiction. Icsh
I. Thoene, Brock, date.   II. Title.
  PS3570.H46K49 2006
  813'.54—dc22
                                                                200503237

Printed in the United States of America

17   16   15   14
9   8   7   6   5   4

PROLOGUE

The lights of ten thousand Roman-legion campfires winked like a new galaxy clustered on the slopes of Mount Scopus. Smoke drifted lazily skyward, half obscuring the bloodred moon in an ominous mist.

An occasional cry echoed through the courtyard as a mother discovered her sleeping child had died or a son reached out in the darkness to touch the frail form of his father and found him cold, unable to answer. Moans of those trapped in nightmares from which they would never awake punctuated the blackness of the Temple courtyard.

Eli bar Yehuda sat with his back against a pillar beneath Solomon's Portico and stared across the Court of the Gentiles. All around him lay the last defenders of Jerusalem—those who had been fortunate enough to escape to the Temple when the first Roman legions had breached the third wall surrounding the city. These last days were only a reprieve from death, at best.

Eli touched his hand to the gnawing pain in his stomach. Perhaps it would have been easier to die quickly by the edge of a sharpened sword instead of enduring this slow crucifixion of starvation. The Romans, Eli thought, had been in no great hurry to pursue them or storm the gates of the Temple. While they roasted the sheep of Jewish shepherds over their fires, hunger had already fought and won their battles against the Jews for them. Those defenders who did not die of starvation behind these sacred walls would be easy enough to finish off when the last battering rams of the Roman army crashed through the gates.

Eli clutched the long iron key he had used to lock the seven gates of the Temple nearly two weeks before. There was no key that would ultimately lock the conquerors out, he knew. Since that time, the daily sacrifice had ceased. There were no more animals to offer on the altar before the God of Israel. There was only Israel herself, broken and bleeding before Him.

"Why have You abandoned us, O Lord?" he asked with a quiet, trembling voice. "Tomorrow even Your Holy of Holies will be desecrated. Do You not see?"

Only the moans of the hungry answered him. He caressed the key that had been his responsibility for nearly ten years. By evening tomorrow it would be in the hands of men who had no love for the treasures it shielded.

Eli stood slowly and braced himself against the pillar. The Temple seemed to spiral downward around him. He rubbed his hands across his eyes and staggered over the sleeping bodies of those who remained. Carefully he picked his way through the living and the dead to the steps that led to the highest pinnacle of the Temple wall itself. Step by step he forced himself to climb the cold stone stairway, pausing to rest against the rough wall a dozen times.

"Who is there?" an urgent voice called as he neared the top of the wall.

"It is Eli bar Yehuda, keeper of the keys," he answered breathlessly.

"What do you want?" the gruff voice replied. "Your keys will not help us now."

Eli did not answer. Instead he sat on the battlements and stared in despair at the devastation below. "God has forsaken us!" he cried at last, his eyes scarcely able to comprehend the thousands of crosses that lined the road to the Temple gate.

"Every day that we hold out behind these walls, the Roman pigs crucify another thousand," the sentry growled. "Soon there will be no one left to murder. No one left for them to rule in Israel. Who will lock your precious Temple gates then, Gatekeeper?" The Zealot's voice was full of derision.

The anguish of finality weighed down Eli's spirit, and he cried out like the son who had found his father dead without a word of comfort or a sweet farewell. His voice echoed across the Valley of Kidron and surrounded the crosses that forested the hillsides around the city.

Eli staggered to his feet and held the key high above his head. "Oh, God! All is lost. All is ended." His voice cracked.

Then, throwing his beloved key toward heaven, he shouted, "Henceforth, almighty God, be Thou the guardian of the key until Your people return to Zion forever!"

PART I

Blood and Fire

Out of blood and fire Judea will fall.
Out of blood and fire it will be reborn.
ANCIENT PROPHECY

DAWN AFTER DEATH

Rabbi Shlomo Lebowitz rose stiffly from the bed, where he had finally fallen asleep only a few hours earlier. He was still dressed, and his aged feet ached inside his shoes. He put a hand to his head in confusion as he glanced around the unfamiliar room and tried to piece together the events of the night before.

"*Oy,*" he whispered hoarsely. "So, this old man is losing his mind?" He coughed loudly and blinked hard as he stared down at the silent radio on the table. He flicked a light switch, but the room remained in soft, predawn gloom. "*Oy!* The electricity is gone, *nu,* Shlomo."

Suddenly memories of the long night flooded him with a hollow dread that caused him to shake his head. He groped for the bed and sat down slowly, then reached to switch the knob of the radio back and forth in a fruitless attempt to bring it to life.

Down the hall, his grandson, Yacov, slept peacefully in the bed of Professor Howard Moniger. The boy knew nothing of what had happened to the convoy that had carried their good friend the professor and Rachel Sachar, Yacov's sister, into an Arab ambush just this side of Hadassah Hospital.

The rabbi put his hands over his face in despair. There had been no word of how many had survived the attack, no word of Rachel or the professor. Grief and horror had come to the old rabbi as he listened to the radio reports through the long hours of the night. And then, as though God Himself could bear no more, the lights had flickered off and the radio had groaned and fallen silent, leaving Rabbi Lebowitz to worry and wonder until a merciful sleep had come to him.

Now he stroked his beard and stared disconsolately at his scuffed shoes. He laid his hands in his lap and studied the swollen knuckles and age-spotted skin. "Once these hands were young," he whispered, "and strong with hope." He touched the corner of his eye. "And once these eyes opened to the joy of my youth."

He lowered his head in defeat. "No, I have lived too long. Too long. To see the innocent die thus." A single tear escaped and clung, unheeded, to the gray beard of the old rabbi. "Better I should die, God. Better You should take an old man, *nu*, instead of those with hope and joy left to spend."

Minutes passed slowly as the room lightened with the morning sun. Still the old man did not move. *You brought our Rachel back to us from the grave to die once again? I cannot believe such a thing. I cannot.*

The door creaked slowly open, and Yacov entered, followed by a large bony dog. "Grandfather?" asked the boy in a sleepy voice. "You are up early." He rubbed his eye that had been injured while fleeing from pursuing Arabs. "Rachel and the professor? Did they come home last night from the hospital? I would like it if Rachel would fix pletsls for breakfast."

The old man shook his head. "Not this morning. No, Yacov. Not—"

"Grandfather?" Yacov stepped toward him.

"Put the dog out, boy." He turned his face away. "I have fixed you breakfast these eight years. One more morning will not harm you. *Nu!* Put the dog out and we will have our morning prayers."

Yacov nodded, adjusting his yarmulke and tugging at his nightshirt. "My sister is not home yet?"

"No," the old man said in a controlled voice, "not yet."

"She is coming home?" Yacov's voice sounded small and vulnerable. "And the professor?"

Rabbi Lebowitz looked up to meet Yacov's gaze. He drew a deep breath. "Only God—blessed be He—knows, Yacov."

Then he stretched out his arms to the boy and held him close as he told as much of the news as he had heard on the radio. Yacov simply frowned and stared vacantly out the window to where a sparrow chirped happily on the branch of a sapling.

When the rabbi finished, Yacov said quietly, "I want to go home, Grandfather. Home to our little apartment in the Old City. I want to go back to the way it was before—"

The old man stroked Yacov's head and patted his shoulders. "We can go home, Yacov, to the holy places behind the walls. But we can never go back. It will never be as it was."

"We were happy," the boy wailed, burying his face in his grandfather's shoulder. "We did not know she was alive! We had buried them all—all of them—years ago! And now we have been given hope, only to have it taken from us! Better she had not come back than to find out what *they* did to her! Better we never knew. Never loved or hoped!"

The mongrel, Shaul, sat silently beside the old rabbi and the boy. He laid his big head against Yacov's thigh. Rabbi Lebowitz saw the grief in the dog's eyes as he studied his young master.

The rabbi shook his head. "We can go back," he said again, "but it will not be the same for us, Yacov." He winced. "You are learning too young about loving. Too young you are learning."

"Take me home, Grandfather! Home to my own bed and Torah school and—I want to go home again!"

For a long time they clung to one another until at last the rabbi replied softly, "Yes. Yes, Yacov. Home to the Old City. If we are all to die, young and old alike, then it is better to die facing the Holy City than to die away from it." He nodded as determination strengthened his own heart. "Yes. We will go home."

At that, the boy raised his head and wiped his tearstained face with the back of his hand. "Perhaps Rachel lives. Perhaps she and the professor survived—"

"We can hope." The rabbi closed his eyes and turned toward the window. "Today we will wait. Today we will wait for word from her. She will send word if she lives. She would not leave us to grieve and wonder. So for today we will wait."

"And then?"

"Tonight we will enter the gates of Jerusalem once again." Rabbi Lebowitz took Yacov's hands in his own. "Tonight, before they lock the Gate of Zion, we shall go home without fail."

"Grandfather," Yacov asked quietly, "will they shoot us?"

The old man stuck out his lower lip thoughtfully. "A very good possibility, Yacov."

"If Rachel is dead, like Mama and Papa and my brothers, then I shall not mind so much the dying." He stroked Shaul, who whined unhappily. "I would not like to go on living all alone."

Again the rabbi embraced his grandson. "They will think hard before they shoot an old man and a boy, I think. So we will stay very close to one another, and in the darkness they will not be able to tell which is which." He smiled. "Perhaps an angel will walk with us, *nu*?"

In the far distance, dawn glistened on the Old City walls and the sounds of the ancient holy places called across the hills and valleys.

"Home," Yacov said to Shaul. "After so many months, we are going home, Shaul!"

Then the old man began an ancient prayer, the prayer of pilgrims and exiles for two thousand years:

"How shall we sing the Lord's song in a strange land?
If I forget thee, O Jerusalem, let my right hand forget her cunning.
If I do not remember thee, let my tongue cleave to the roof of my mouth;
If I prefer not Jerusalem above my chief joy!"

On this morning in the Old City of Jerusalem, it was as though nothing had changed in a thousand years. It was as if there were no war, no barricades or barbed wire, no soldiers waiting tensely on the rooftops.

Yehudit Akiva stood at the narrow window of her bedroom and watched the first rays of morning bathe the Holy City in soft light. She tucked her shawl closer around her. The voice of the muezzin called out the hour of prayer to those in the Muslim Quarter, only a few streets from her home. Seconds later a flock of pigeons rose as the bells of the Church of the Holy Sepulchre rang out to announce the beginning of the Christian Holy Week. Yehudit followed the flight of the birds that spiraled upward, then scattered like messengers carrying the resonant sound of the bells.

A few housetops to the west, in the Armenian Quarter, the red-tiled roof of St. James Cathedral caught her eye. The hint of a smile appeared on her lips as she waited for the call to worship that was so familiar to her. Thirty seconds passed until the hollow sound of a hammer beating out a rhythm against a wooden plank was clearly heard. Centuries before, the Muslims had forbidden the use of bells to announce Christian services, and long after the ban had been lifted, the Armenians continued to beat out the message on the plank.

Traditions die hard in the Holy City, Yehudit thought. *Even those born of persecution and humiliation.*

Soon the bells of a dozen other churches joined in to welcome the morning. Christian, Armenian, and Muslim quarters all announced business as usual within the one square mile that marked the center of the universe. The labyrinth of ancient bazaars came alive with the cries of merchants and shoppers. The smells of fresh bread and the bleating of sheep blended in to complete the picture.

Yehudit opened the window slightly and inhaled. She closed her eyes and remembered that every morning of her young life had been much like this one. Things had not changed. Not so very much. Then she opened her eyes and looked into the empty streets of her own quarter, the Jewish Quarter. On the rooftops, Dov Avram's Haganah volunteers gazed across sandbagged barricades to the bustle of their neighbors' streets. Beyond them were British outposts, where armed soldiers watched and waited for the next riot or the next sniper to fire upon the old rabbis on their way to the synagogue. The high wall of rose-colored stone wrapped around them—keeping them in while food and provisions were easily blocked out. Though the Christian and Arab quarters had plenty to eat, the spectre of hunger hovered over the fifteen hundred Jews who remained within the Old City.

For weeks the path to the Wailing Wall had been closed to Jews. This morning the only silence found in this City of the Soul was within the boundaries of the Jewish Quarter.

High atop the dome of the Great Hurva Synagogue, the flag made from Moshe Sachar's tallith still waved. For days it had remained where Dov placed it. It had become a symbol for the Jews who wished to remain in their Old City homes, and it had become a target for every Jihad Moquade with a bullet to spare. The once-smooth fabric was now tattered and riddled with bullet holes. Yehudit had heard it whispered that both Dov and Rabbi Vultch rejoiced. Every cartridge spent to shoot down the Star of David was one less to take a Jewish life. And so it remained a banner of defiance over the Quarter.

Yehudit wished that one of those Arab bullets would somehow find its way into her heart. She stood in the fresh light of the morning, longing for death to strike her down and end her imprisonment. Since she had been returned to her father's house by the English captain Stewart, she had not been allowed out of her room. She had not seen the face of her father in all that time. Scant meals had been handed in to her by the dour old woman who now served as her father's housekeeper and cook. For three days no words had been spoken to her. Bits of conversation and news wafted up from the street, and many times, the angry voice of her father rose through the wood planks of the floor.

"Deir Yassin . . . Kastel . . . Bab el Wad . . ." All these names had risen to her in her father's furious voice as he talked to British headquarters. This morning, when the phone rang insistently in the room below hers, she knelt and placed her ear against the floor.

"So what did the Zionists expect the Arabs would do after Deir Yassin?" the voice of Rabbi Akiva boomed. "Of course they would avenge their dead! How many Jews killed? . . . *Oy!* So many."

A long silence followed as news of some other disaster was evidently related to Akiva.

A series of incredulous protests assaulted whomever he was speaking to. "They cannot pull you back! . . . No! Not after what has happened! . . . You think the mobs will stop after the murder of seventy-five Jewish doctors? . . . And now you say the Zionist gangsters have butchered another village in the pass? . . . You cannot pull back today! . . . You cannot leave our protection to a handful of foolish young Yeshiva students! . . . We will be overrun. If it is as you say and the soldiers of Haj Amin are coming here, we will be overrun. Stewart, you must speak to the authorities! We are lovers of peace here in the Old City! We wish only to—"

Rabbi Akiva's voice rose to a new height of desperation. "Stewart! The whole world will hold your government responsible if we are massacred because you have withdrawn! . . . Only for today? But why on this day? Why?"

Yehudit pressed herself against the floor in hopes of hearing an answer. There was none. One last, outraged bellow echoed up, followed by the sound of the telephone crashing to the floor. The heavy footsteps of Akiva stomped from the room, and then came the familiar sound of doors slamming in the distance.

Yehudit sighed and sat up. She leaned her back against the bed and stared thoughtfully at her hands. *The British are pulling out of the Old City today. Just for today. Why?* She sat for another moment, then scrambled to her feet and rushed to the window once again. She squinted against the morning light and shielded her eyes as, in the distance, the British soldiers who manned the forward outposts gathered their weapons and slipped quietly away. Haganah soldiers then moved across the rooftops to take up their positions. For the first time, these Jewish soldiers carried their rifles openly.

"The English are afraid," Yehudit said aloud. "Something is coming here today, and they are afraid to be caught in the middle."

The tops of English berets disappeared over the sides of buildings. The men seemed to be in a hurry. Yehudit put a hand to her forehead and tried to reconstruct the bits of news that she had gathered in her confinement. All of it led to one conclusion: Kastel and Bab el Wad had fallen to Jewish forces. Now the soldiers of Muhammad Said Haj Amin el Husseini, the Mufti of Jerusalem, were coming here—here to the Old City, where they would finish off the Jewish Quarter. And the soldiers of Captain Stewart would not stay to stop it.

A key rattled in the lock, and Yehudit spun as the door to her room swung open. The lined face of Goldie Levy appeared. She carried a tray in her gnarled, arthritic hands. She looked toward Yehudit, then quickly lowered her eyes.

"What is happening?" Yehudit rushed to take the tray.

The old woman put a crooked finger to her lips. "Shhh," she warned. Looking back over her shoulder, she whispered, "Your father is angry. Zionists have opened the road to Jerusalem—"

"That is cause to rejoice."

"They have killed a great leader of the Arabs. The Muslims will mourn first; then they will burn. The English have been told to stay away from the Old City today." She inclined her head toward the Yeshiva students who now darted across the rooftops. "They are leaving us—God forbid— in the hands of a few students and even fewer men of the Haganah. It is an affront to your father, Rebbe Akiva. He is angry." She turned on her heel and slipped out of the room, locking the door behind her.

Yehudit carried the tray of meager rations to the ledge of the window. She sat and sipped weak tea as she watched the effects of the news ripple and spread through the Old City. The bells of the Christian Quarter fell silent. Angry shouts and wails of grief resounded from the souks. The shutters of shops closed against the fury that was sure to follow. More young Haganah men poured from the little houses of the Jewish Quarter and crowded behind the barricades to watch the all-too-familiar rage simmer and build.

Then silence engulfed the City of the Soul, the center of the universe.

Yehudit Akiva sat on the window ledge and prayed again that some stray bullet would find her heart and end her short, unhappy seventeen years of life.

THE MESSAGE

The message about the sinking of the arms ship *Trina* was sent from Zionist headquarters on the top of the orphanage in Rome, then relayed from one station to another until it reached headquarters in Tel Aviv. The sun was already up by the time the code was deciphered.

Four men and two women—members of the Mossad, the Jewish Intelligence Service—debated the issue over cups of coffee. They knew the fate of the Arab arms ship in Italy before the news had even reached the Teletypes of the European Press Corps in Rome. What they were uncertain of was the future of the three men and one woman who had put the ship on the bottom of Bari Harbor.

"Four of them? *Four?* Bernie Greene, David and Ellie Meyer, we know. But who is the fourth?" The dark, swarthy captain took a long drag on his cigarette and waited for an answer.

"Word from Avriel was that they picked up this fellow in Cyprus."

"In Cyprus?" the captain questioned, incredulous. "The place is crawling with British."

"And DP camps. This fellow was supposed to have escaped from a camp. Avriel simply said he was an explosives expert."

"Well, if he had anything to do with the sinking of the *Trina*, that is proof enough."

"Proof of what? You think the British mind if another arms ship bound for the Middle East is sunk? This fellow might well be a plant. A British plant. Ready to worm his way into our intelligence organization."

A heavy silence fell on the group. They sipped their coffee and contemplated the words of their leader. Finally, brushing sleep from her eyes, one of the women asked the captain, "They have requested passports—help from Rome. What are we to do?"

"If they are apprehended," came the thoughtful reply, "certainly they will be linked to us."

"An awkward situation. Very awkward indeed," sighed a small, balding, middle-aged man.

"Well then, perhaps we should do something to help them escape." The captain smoothed his thin mustache and studied the message once again.

"Of course, without jeopardizing our Rome operation," added the second woman.

"We might sacrifice this fourth fellow," offered the youngest man in the group. "If he is indeed a plant, then this will reflect badly on the British."

"And if he is not?" asked the captain.

More silence followed. "If he is not, then at least he will have only as much knowledge of the Mossad as we give him."

"Bernie Greene is the only one in the group who knows anything about it. He would not tell anyone anything. Not without the usual approval. Not even David Meyer will be told the location of the Rome headquarters."

"Yes. Greene knows the rules. He plays the game well."

"So?" The captain tapped his pencil impatiently on the side of his cup. "What are we suggesting here?"

"Passports for the three. Something less for the chap from Cyprus," volunteered the little man.

"Passports." The first woman nodded. "Enough money to get them to Paris. Then Bernie will know what to do."

"And we keep our distance," said the little man. "No contact whatsoever, eh? All Italy will be looking for the team that blew up Bari Harbor. By midmorning it will not be safe to be within ten miles of them."

"I will say a sacrifice is the safest order," said the young man. "In the Resistance, when we weren't sure, rather than risk exposure of the whole organization—"

"That is not the way we operate." The captain's eyes were hard.

"What about the priest?" protested the young man. "Surely he is an even greater risk. He will still be in Bari and will certainly become suspect." He slammed his palm on the table. "I say that a sacrifice is in order. To save many, we eliminate a few."

The second woman leaned in closer. Her face was intense. "And if you were among those eliminated?"

The young man did not flinch. "If it would preserve our dream of freedom—"

"—any means is acceptable?" The discussion had become more philosophical than practical.

"If that is the way we are to be," said the second woman with disgust, "then that is all our freedom will be—a dream!"

"Enough!" The captain raised his voice as tempers flared. "They are waiting, and we have settled nothing!"

"We should watch. And wait," said the little man. "Passports, clothing, some money . . . yes. But nothing further until we know for certain."

A murmur of assent passed around the circle. The young man, his eyes burning with the rightness of his cause, did not reply.

"So then," said the captain, his gaze remaining on the young man, "it is settled. We all agree. All but you, Ari. But you will consent because you are overruled, yes?"

Ari nodded grudgingly. "If I must."

"Good. Then pass our decision on to Rome. Leave the finer details to them as to destination and pickup," the captain instructed as the young man rose. "And, Ari," he added, "we were all in the Resistance, remember. For now there are better ways to play it safe than sacrifice."

The streets of Washington, D.C., were slick with the rain that had fallen constantly for the last two days. Only a few drops sprayed the windshield of Tom Kane's new 1948 Ford sedan. The wiper blade groaned and scraped across the glass with a noise that made Kane grimace and grope along the dark dashboard in search of the switch.

It was 1:00 AM, and the broad boulevards of the city were nearly deserted. Kane's headlights reflected on the shiny black asphalt of Washington Parkway. To the right, several DC-4 passenger planes were parked wingtip to wingtip along the quiet tarmac of Washington National Airport. The runway glowed with a row of blue lights that bordered the Potomac River, and ahead, Tom could see the Fourteenth Street Bridge reflected in the water.

The rain-washed air made everything seem brighter and more distinct. Even though Tom had been roused from a sound sleep for this midnight run to the State Department, he felt clearheaded and wide-awake. A dozen times in the last three weeks, he had made similar trips and had come to enjoy the stillness of the sleeping capital. A daytime trip took three times as long for the same miles. Rush-hour Washington was crammed with honking taxis bearing men with strained faces to meetings designed to raise the blood pressure of even the calmest of lawmakers.

Lately Washington had been the focal point of every reporter in America as the 1948 hearings on un-American activities hunted

Communists with a fervor that often destroyed the innocent along with the guilty.

The Russian takeover of Czechoslovakia and Communist threats to cut off Berlin from the Allied Occupied Territory in West Germany had raised anti-Communist fever to a new high. And now legitimate concerns had become a witch hunt. All of that was beginning to affect opinions about the small corner of the world that was the specialty of Tom Kane.

As special adviser on Middle Eastern affairs, Kane had been called out into this peaceful Washington night to review news that was anything but peaceful. He yawned as he circled the Lincoln Memorial. Honest Abe watched pensively on one side while the great marble obelisk of the Washington Monument pointed toward heaven like an accusing finger. *Didn't Americans just fight the bloodiest war of all time? Why, then, is the whole world still churning with hatred and revolution?* Those thoughts had come more easily to Tom as the conflict in Palestine escalated. He had concluded that there were no answers—none at all. There were only questions.

He slowed and turned right onto Twenty-third Street. Two blocks ahead was the imposing stone structure that housed the State Department. Even at this late hour, the face of the building was a checkerboard of lighted windows. For every crisis now being enacted around the globe there was a small staff of junior members of the State Department who monitored the events throughout the night.

Tonight, as it had so often, news had come from Palestine that had rattled not only the Teletype but also the aide who had decoded the message. A stammering young voice had jarred Kane awake with the ominous warning, "This one involves a prominent American citizen, I'm afraid, sir. It might deserve an immediate evaluation."

Of course, it seemed that lately there was nothing happening in Palestine that did not need a high-priority examination in the middle of the night. That was the trouble with living half the world away from the place that was his field of expertise. He had often cursed the time difference between Washington and Palestine and wished his Georgetown University degree was in American history. The most devastating events in Palestine had happened right at the moment when Kane had settled down for a long night of sleep. The final decision to call—or not to call—the peacefully resting secretary of state, George C. Marshall, could be made only after Kane had reviewed the information.

Tom showed his pass to an unsmiling security guard, then hurried toward the staircase to climb to the second floor of the building. At the top of the stairs, he ducked into the men's room to splash water on his face and straighten the bow tie that was his trademark.

Tom studied his reflection in the glare of the bathroom light. He looked older than his thirty-eight years. His eyes were puffy, and the lines in his high forehead seemed deeper than usual. He ran his hand over his thick black thatch of hair, then wet his fingers with cold water and pressed them gently against his eyelids. The treatment did not help. The green eyes were still bloodshot, and the eyelids drooped more than usual.

"Look like a Christmas wreath," Tom muttered. "You're lookin' old, Pappy." He used the nickname his comrades had given him when he'd served in the Office of Strategic Services during the war. Even then he had appeared older than he was. He had always looked, somehow, more confident than his peers. The illusion had served him well, even if the truth was that Tom Kane was, as his ex-wife had said, "about 90 percent bluff."

It had become Kane's secret belief that anyone successful was 90 percent bluff. That left 10 percent inside a man that was the genuine article. It was that remaining mix of courage, brains, know-how, and common sense that got a man through, even when he was scared to death. And the bluff only served to make him seem older and wiser than the next guy. It was a philosophy that had moved Kane along rapidly in the State Department. He had never allowed himself to submit to fear, so the fearful rallied around him. Tonight, he knew, would be no different, even though his insides resounded with the hollow clang of uncertainty.

No one in the entire department was certain anymore about the partition of Palestine. And those who seemed to be sure were convinced that it had been a horribly bad idea from its conception. Time and again the United States had wavered on the issue of a homeland for the Jewish people. The shattering events of the last weeks and months had left a bad taste in the mouths of diplomats and politicians alike. Cries had arisen from all quarters that Partition must be revoked. That Palestine must come under the government of the United Nations itself. Kane had seen evidence of wavering even among the American Jews. The bluff and resolve of everyone were being worn down by the horror of everyday reality in Palestine.

A pale, scholarly young man sat at the typewriter in the decoding room. A cold cup of coffee remained untouched where he had placed it an hour ago.

"The three messages came in one after another," he said, handing three folders to Kane. "The wire service had the stuff. It will be in the

Times' early edition." He jerked a thumb to where the Teletypes hummed and rattled, spilling information onto the floor by the yard.

Tom flipped open the top folder, scanning the contents. Wordlessly he tossed it onto the desk as he opened the second. Halfway through the first page he grimaced and exhaled loudly. "Get the secretary on the phone for me," he said in a monotone. "Now."

AT HADASSAH

The bright morning sun was a stark contrast to the dark, brooding mood that enveloped Jerusalem. Rachel Sachar stood in numb silence at the window of the small, drab room on the third floor of Hadassah Hospital. Closing her eyes, she leaned her cheek against the glass as behind her, Dr. Rimsky touched his stethoscope against the tiny rib cage of the infant Tikvah.

He clucked his tongue in sympathy as the baby struggled against the cold, insistent instrument. "A good healthy squawk, Tikvah," he admonished gently. "You are enough better to be angry with me, eh?"

The baby replied with clenched fists and an indignant wail that filled Rachel with relief. "She is doing well, is she not, Doctor?" Rachel asked, not turning away from the window.

"Yes. Quite. Perhaps better than her mother now, eh?"

Rachel did not reply or turn to face him.

At the foot of Mount Scopus, a thin plume of black smoke marked what remained of the Hadassah Hospital convoy where so many had perished the night before. Only a handful had survived. Rachel was among those few, yet she could not find it in herself to rejoice. She was grateful for the sake of the child she carried within her and for the sake of little Tikvah, who needed her so desperately, but joy had not come to her with the morning.

Below her and to the south, the Dome of the Rock towered over the crooked alleyways of the Old City. It was there that the Muslim mobs were now gathered from every corner of Jerusalem. Light reflected against the irregular stone walls, then shimmered up in waves of heat that distorted the ancient scene. Rounded rooftops, crisscrossed with lines of tar, seemed to sway and bob like a thousand skullcaps crowding toward the sacred Muslim mosque.

In the shadows of those houses and shops, fresh Arab rage and anguish were building to a passion that would once again rip the fabric of the City of Peace as it had done a hundred times since Partition had been voted five months earlier.

Perhaps, Rachel thought as she watched, *the trembling air is their anger rising to choke us like a poison. . . .* She closed her eyes again as if to shut out the images of the convoy that pushed into her thoughts against her will. *Smoke and machine-gun bullets slamming against the metal of the ambulance. The cries of the dying. Howard Moniger pulling me to safety and then the pale white of his face as his life drained away.* And then the memories of another time came to her. *Angry voices.* "Schnell Juden!" *Bayonets and the thunder of Nazi jackboots on the cobblestones of Warsaw . . .*

"He told me not to hate them," Rachel whispered, forgetting for a moment the presence of Dr. Rimsky.

"Who told you this?" The doctor's voice was only a step behind her. He, too, had come to the window.

"Professor Moniger. Before he died." Her words were a monotone of exhaustion as she continued to gaze in disbelief at the sight at the foot of the hill.

"Not hate the Arabs," the doctor repeated bitterly. "An impossible request."

Rachel studied the smoking skeletons of the vehicles below the hospital. Tiny figures of British soldiers prowled cautiously through the rubble. "The doctors and nurses who died were your friends," she said simply, understanding Dr. Rimsky's rage.

He drew a deep breath. "Friends of the very world. The finest minds and hearts. It is senseless. Senseless and without reason . . ." His voice was thick with emotion. "And now there is not enough left of them to bury."

The floor beneath Rachel seemed to heave with his words. A wave of nausea crashed over her, and she gripped the windowsill as the air became a pale yellow before her eyes. She sagged slightly. "Help me," she whispered. "Help me, God."

Dr. Rimsky's strong hands grasped her arms and guided her to a chair. "I am so thoughtless, Mrs. Sachar. I forgot myself," he said in genuine remorse.

Rachel let her head sink into her hands as the room whirled around her. In her helplessness, she wanted only to lean against Moshe. *If only he were here. If only . . .* "Moshe," she murmured as tears dropped onto her lap.

"Take a few deep breaths, Mrs. Sachar," Dr. Rimsky instructed. "You have had a difficult time. Good food is what you need . . . and rest. For the sake of your baby, if not for yourself, eh?" He had again assumed the role of a doctor.

"I . . . I cannot eat," she replied in a quavering voice.

He answered with a pat on her back. "Of course. This is usual in the first stages of pregnancy. But you must try. If not in the morning, then perhaps small amounts in the afternoon."

She waited to open her eyes until the world began to right itself.

The doctor was still standing beside her.

"A bit better now," she said, distantly aware of the hoarseness in her own voice.

"Give yourself another moment. You will be right again soon enough."

"Thank you." She glanced up at him, surprised that he looked so much older than when she had first seen him only a week before. The patience of his tone skillfully concealed deep weariness and sorrow evident in his eyes. His once-starched white coat was wrinkled and flecked with tiny drops of blood. His large brown eyes behind thick spectacles were red-rimmed, and the flesh on his face sagged with exhaustion.

She had not noticed his person or his features when he had first come into the room to check the baby. She had not seen anything but the inferno that burned in her own mind. Now she studied him with compassion. The grief she felt for the death of Howard Moniger must have been a hundred times deeper in Dr. Rimsky as the names of his dead colleagues were whispered through the halls of Hadassah. *How very lonely he must feel!*

"Perhaps you should also rest, Doctor," she said, surprised at her boldness.

The corner of his mouth turned up for an instant. "I was saying that very thing myself . . . yesterday. But we are as short on sleep here as we are on medicine. Unfortunately, there is no queue we can stand in for a ration of rest." He frowned and faltered.

She could see in his eyes that his thoughts had fled again to the men and women who had died last night. He glanced at the small box on the bed table. In it were the personal effects of Howard Moniger.

Rachel followed his gaze and answered the question he was afraid to ask. "My husband has an office at Hebrew University. He asked Professor Moniger to retrieve some things from there; that is why the professor came along. Or so he said. But I am thinking that he came to look after me. And he did that. At the cost of his own life. He was a good man. . . ." She gazed toward the blue square of sky that shone through the window.

"I still cannot believe this thing has happened." The facade of Dr. Rimsky's professionalism dropped away again. "I had hoped . . . hoped the world would be finished with barbarism. And now even our own fellows have behaved like Nazis. It is little wonder that the Arabs murder a convoy of doctors after what the Jews have done to the village of Deir Yassin,"

Rachel thought of Moshe and longed for news. "Does anyone know . . . is there any word yet from the battle for Kastel?"

He looked curiously at her. "Your husband is there?"

"Yes."

He smiled slightly. "Then I can at least offer you some hope on this black day, Mrs. Sachar. A Star of David flies over Kastel."

She leaned forward eagerly. "We have won the battle?"

"In a manner of speaking. In the same way the Hebrews defeated the Egyptian chariots at the Red Sea—by a miracle. News is meager at best. No one is quite sure how or why, but the armies of Haj Amin deserted in hordes. They are all gathered in the Old City now. Thousands. And civilians as well." He opened the window slightly and stepped aside. "Listen."

A high, thin wail spiraled upward from the Old City. Ten thousand voices twisted together as one moan of grief and despair.

"What is it?" Rachel asked as Dr. Rimsky slid the window shut again.

"No one knows what it means yet. A few minutes ago the Jewish Agency notified us that this might be an opportunity to evacuate some of the less critical cases from the hospital." He looked at Tikvah, who lay happily watching her own hands. Her breathing was easy now and without the fearsome rattle that had nearly claimed her life.

"May I take her home?" Rachel asked.

"If indeed the way is open. If the Arabs are preoccupied in the Old City, I see no reason why she cannot be released, eh? And with my blessing. At any rate, we should know shortly if the Arabs have left the road through Sheikh Jarrah unguarded or if it is just another rumor."

"Are you leaving also, Dr. Rimsky?"

His smile faded and he pressed his lips together. "No. No. I think not. Some of us have to stay. This is certainly only the eye of the hurricane. A calm passage before the next storm hits, if you take my meaning. No, Mrs. Sachar. I will not be leaving. There is sure to be fighting over this hilltop. Doctors will be needed. I won't leave. Not of my own free will, at any rate."

He raised his eyebrows slightly and glanced at his watch in the habit of a man in a hurry. "I must be going. There are rounds to finish." He blinked as though his own brusqueness startled him. "Business as usual, I suppose." He was no longer speaking to Rachel. "Even with all of it, there is still life to get on with, isn't there?"

Before she could reply, he slipped out the door, leaving Rachel alone with Tikvah and thoughts of release.

4

CASUALTIES

The road into Jerusalem was littered with debris that had been dropped in the wake of the living Arab tide that had flooded the city from the surrounding villages.

Moshe lifted the canvas flap on the back of the transport truck. He blinked against the sunlight and glanced down at the roadside, where a child's small sandal lay abandoned in the new grass. He imagined tiny brown legs churning to keep up as the whispered horrors of Deir Yassin pursued the innocent and the demon of fear chased them from their homes.

At this moment, the suffering of the women and children of Palestine, both Jews and Arabs, seemed as grim and terrible as that of all the millions who had died in the death camps of Europe. The lost shoe of a homeless, terrified child painted a portrait of suffering much clearer than a list of numbers in mass graves. And this was what Palestine and the City of Peace had come to. Massacre and torture. Hunger, fear, and ten thousand people fleeing to an unknown destination.

Moshe clasped his hands around his knees and rested his head for a moment. A hundred smiling, friendly faces passed before his mind. They were not the faces of Jewish comrades fighting to hold Kastel but faces of Arabs who had worked with him at various archaeological digs around the countryside throughout the years. Christians, Muslims, and Jews had worked shoulder to shoulder in the dust of Palestine to uncover a common past. In the heat of the sun they had shared a common cup of water and rejoiced when something new and exciting was found. They had been his friends, his brothers. Now they were his enemies.

The thought stung Moshe as he wondered how many of those same men he had fought against last night. How many had he killed? How many of those Arabs who had so cheerfully wielded a shovel now carried a rifle and repeated the evil rhetoric of Haj Amin Husseini?

"And so Palestine has come to this," Moshe muttered. "All for the sake of one man's political ambition. For the glory of Haj Amin we all suffer."

It was, he was sure, no different than Germany under the iron boot of Adolf Hitler. For the glory of the Fatherland, children were taught to hate, and young men died to conquer the world. But in the end, it was the innocent who suffered. Six million Jews died in the camps, it was true, but the Allies were not innocent by any means. In one night the city of Dresden was reduced to rubble. One hundred thousand old men, women, and children were sucked into the heat of the city's inferno to perish as Allied bombs dropped their answer to Hitler.

All over Europe it had been the same. The cities were left in charred heaps of rubble, and only the children were left to fight. *We have learned nothing*, Moshe thought grimly. *War makes barbarians of us all. That little Palestinian child will come back someday, but not to search for a lost shoe. No. He will come with a gun and a mind full of memories of what our men did at Deir Yassin. He will come back to find his home again. And his heart will be full of hatred for us. We have sown the seeds that will bring us a bitter harvest.*

Moshe searched the faces of those who were with him in the back of the truck—faces covered with grime. Some stared blankly ahead, while others, like Ehud Schiff, slept and, most likely, dreamed again the nightmare of Kastel. The drone of the engine was the only sound as they rode the final mile to Jerusalem.

These few had survived the ordeal at Kastel unscathed except for memories of dying comrades who now seemed to share the dim twilight beneath the canvas tarp that covered the back of the truck. It was as if they were all locked into some dreadful, living purgatory between the horrors of battle and a return to life. Each man hoped to wake and find that Kastel had not really happened. Each sought to deny that their friends would not return with them to schoolbooks and political discussions over endless cups of coffee and Mrs. Bett's pastry. The politics of Palestine had gone far beyond discussion now, and issues were settled in blood and lives.

The gears of the truck groaned and jerked as they crossed the first barricade into the Jewish Quarter of the city. Moshe listened as a fresh-faced, eager Haganah recruit filled the driver in on the events of the past few hours.

"They say the way is open through Sheikh Jarrah to Hadassah Hospital now . . . a horrible mess . . . Arabs have paid us back for Deir Yassin in kind . . . seventy-five dead. . . ."

The driver of the truck answered with more questions. Now the men who shared the cargo area with Moshe stirred with curiosity and listened to the news.

"Looks like you fellows killed someone very important to the Arabs last night. All the Arabs have gone to the Old City. To the Dome of the Rock. Perhaps a riot is coming, but for now they are quiet. Waiting. Waiting for the funeral."

Ehud opened his eyes and turned to Moshe. "What was it he said about the hospital? What has happened there?"

The truck lurched into gear as Moshe shrugged, then shouted to the guard at the barricade, "What about Hadassah Hospital?"

The guard cupped his hands around his mouth and shouted as the truck slid by, "Seventy-five dead in Sheikh Jarrah!"

"Jews or Arabs?" Moshe called.

"Us. Doctors. Nurses. Lost in a convoy ambush."

Moshe felt ill at the words of the young man. There were not many people who worked at Hadassah that he did not know personally and well. "How many?" he shouted in disbelief.

"Seventy-five!"

The number was staggering—too horrible to be true.

"Did he say doctors?" Ehud asked. "Our doctors? And nurses? Seventy-five dead? How can this be? Why would they kill doctors?"

Moshe sat back and leaned against the hard steel stays of the truck. More horrible than the reality of the battle he had just fought was the thought that seventy-five lives had been lost for the sake of revenge. "We will pay for Deir Yassin a thousand times," he murmured at last. "Ten thousand lives will be spent for this one terrible act, and the world will say it is just."

The men sat in stunned silence until the truck slowed and stopped at the rear of a long line of vehicles—the second convoy delivering food to Jerusalem. The tailgate of their truck clanged down and a distracted middle-aged man pulled back the tarp. "Zion Square. Everybody out."

Moshe and Ehud slipped to the ground and gazed around at the spectacle of men and women bustling about the stacks of cargo that had come up the pass unmolested. As others in his group dispersed to find their way home, Moshe stood in uneasy confusion. He put his hand to his forehead as a sickening thought assailed him. *Tikvah is at Hadassah! Rachel may have gone there—and Howard. I asked Howard to get the things from my office at the university!*

Moshe swayed, struck by the possibility that they might be numbered among the dead. He grabbed the arm of the driver and forced himself to speak. "Please!" He swallowed hard. "Is there a truck going to Hadassah? I must get there!"

The driver jerked his thumb across the square. "They are running supplies up there. Under guaranteed escort, this time. But you wouldn't catch me going through Sheikh Jarrah, my friend. Not after what happened last night. I don't care if every Arab in Jerusalem is at the mosque! I wouldn't go up there if I were you."

Moshe was already walking toward the cargo truck. He stepped across piles of food and supplies. "Is there a list of the dead from the Hadassah convoy?" he asked, repeating the question a dozen times. "Do they know yet who was on the convoy to Hadassah last night?"

He was answered by desparing shrugs. "Some they know for certain. Dr. Liebermann. His wife."

"Liebermann?"

"But some they do not know. British soldiers were down there, trying to find something in the wreckage."

Moshe's mouth went dry with fear. "My wife and I have a child at Hadassah. She might have been on her way there."

A stevedore, his face flushed from the exertion of unloading cargo, stopped and stared at Moshe. "You have a child there?"

"Yes. Our baby. I . . . I need to go to Hadassah."

"Of course you do, friend." The man's voice was gentle with concern. "A terrible thing, what has happened. Terrible. Such a night. Such a dark time for us all."

"Is there anyone who might have a list of passengers?"

"It has not been released yet. The English have an incomplete list, it is said. But they have not released the names of the dead and wounded."

"I must go to Hadassah," Moshe begged.

The stevedore pushed his cap back and wiped sweat from his brow. He called to a tiny man in thick spectacles who was prowling through the crates, checking off numbers on a clipboard. "Harry! This fellow just came in from Kastel! He has a child sick at Hadassah. Is there any way he can—?"

The little man's face sparked with recognition at the sight of Moshe. "Professor Sachar, is it?"

Moshe nodded. "My wife may have been a part of that convoy. I must get up Mount Scopus—"

The little man frowned. "I am sorry, Professor. So sorry that you fight such a battle and come home to this, eh? We should all be celebrating this morning, but instead—" He frowned and looked away. "You were an associate of the American archaeologist Professor Howard Moniger, were you not?"

Moshe nodded, feeling his heart beat harder and hearing the rush of his own blood in his ears. "I am. Yes. What are you trying to say?"

"He was an American."

"What do you mean *was*?" Moshe grabbed him forcefully.

"Since he was American, of course his name was released first. He was not Jewish, you see, so his death with the convoy is news." The man's words seemed far away.

Moshe groped for a place to sit down and couldn't find one. "Howard!" he moaned, cradling his head in his hands. "Howard! He wouldn't have left her. He wouldn't have left Rachel."

The tumult in the square receded to the background. Moshe stood helplessly by as a stevedore shoved past him and cursed impatiently at the delay. Moshe raised his eyes, speechless at the thoughts that assailed him.

The booming voice of Ehud called to him, pulling him back to reality. "*Oy!* Moshe!" Ehud raised his thick arms to wave. "There you are!" He shouldered his way through the crowd of workers.

Ehud's pockets were crammed full of oranges and thin pieces of matzo bread. He extended a meaty hand and pulled Moshe to him in an embrace.

"Howard Moniger was killed last—," Moshe began.

"Yes. I was looking for you to tell you this very thing," Ehud said grimly.

"Rachel must have been with him."

"Yes," Ehud agreed. "She was."

Moshe eyed him sharply. "How do you know this?"

"They have not yet released a list of the dead, but they have told the names of the six who survived." He pulled a mimeographed sheet from his pocket and thrust it into Moshe's hands. "There. You see—" he pointed—"Rachel Sachar. There is her name."

Moshe stared down at the blue ink, hardly daring to believe what he saw. "Where—?" he began. "Are you sure?"

"You think I printed the list myself? To make you feel better?" Ehud peeled an orange as he watched Moshe. "And that fellow over there—" he gestured toward a truck—"he says he saw her at Hadassah. But maybe she has gone home now. He is not sure. They were evacuating some patients from Hadassah, and he thinks perhaps she was among them."

Moshe was already walking toward the truck. He clutched the paper in his hands and called out. "Which of you saw Rachel Sachar?"

Ehud followed him. "There. The one on the tailgate."

A harried young man stood on the tailgate of the cargo truck and shouted directions to the men loading the crates. His jaw was set with determined urgency, and he glanced up as Moshe neared the truck.

Moshe recognized him instantly as a former student at the university.

"Uri Korsikov!" Moshe hailed him. "You have seen my wife?" He knew there was a desperate edge to his voice, but he couldn't help it.

The young man nodded curtly as he shoved a crate of sardines into the cargo area. "At Hadassah, Professor. They said the woman was your wife. Black hair. Very pretty."

Moshe clutched the cold metal of the tailgate. "She was—she seemed well?"

Uri looked him full in the face. "As well as anyone could be after such a calamity." His tone was flat and without comfort. "She seemed uninjured." His eyes were dull with exhaustion and shock. "They said she was your wife, and you see her name is on the list." He caught another box as it was tossed to him.

Moshe closed his eyes and breathed in hope for the first time since the long ordeal had begun. "Rachel," he whispered inaudibly. "Alive. God. God, thank You." Then he called up to the young man, "You are going to Hadassah?"

Uri shook his head. "Old City."

Ehud stepped forward. "What are you saying, boy? Eh? Are you a meshuggener? No one can get to the Jewish Quarter of the Old City."

"The British High Command has ordered a withdrawal," Uri said gruffly. "Until the funeral is finished."

"Funeral?"

"Whoever you killed up there last night was someone very important. The Arabs have pulled back everywhere. They are over there." He jerked his head toward the Dome of the Rock. "They are waiting. Thousands. And so we are going to try to break through Zion Gate with food. Supplies. Many old rabbis are evacuating. The people inside the walls are in a state of panic. We must get through to them."

Moshe stared at the list as Ehud pumped Uri for more information. "The English will allow this? A food convoy?"

"They will not dare to stop us," Uri said. "Not after last night. Not after . . . and so, for now the way is open. And the decision is made that we must try." He paused. A large sack of powdered milk was slung over his shoulder. "Will you come? The English soldiers will not arrest us unless they wish to die." His eyes burned with anger. "Not after last night."

Ehud shouldered a huge barrel of beans. "You think I would miss such a chance to return to my little soldiers? When are we leaving?"

Moshe saw the determination in Ehud's chin and knew he was thinking of Hannah Cohen, Dov Avram, young Joseph Rabinowitz, and the Krepske brothers—all still in the Old City.

"Ehud"—Moshe put a hand on the hard muscled arm of the captain— "what of Stewart?"

"What of him? Better I should die with a rifle in my hand shooting that English momzer than I should die at the end of a British rope." He narrowed his eyes and stared at Moshe. "And you? Are you coming? *Nu?*"

Moshe folded the paper and shook his head. "I must find Rachel."

Ehud grunted. "You have lost your heart for the cause?"

"She is alive, Ehud." Moshe needed to know that Rachel was safe. Yet he was also overwhelmed with a sense that he, too, should climb aboard the convoy truck to break through Zion Gate.

"There will not be any more chances, Professor Sachar." Uri's words seemed almost accusing. "The defense has fallen apart since you were arrested. The only leadership is Akiva. And you know how he feels. Dov and Rebbe Vultch do not command the authority that you—"

"You saw my wife!" Moshe snapped, unwilling to hear more. "You say she is at Hadassah?" He turned away.

Without a break in the rhythm, Uri continued to stack the precious cargo. "When I saw her," he said dryly, as though such things did not matter. "Like I said, they were taking some out when I—"

"You are going through Rehavia," Moshe interrupted, "on your way to Zion Gate?"

The young man shrugged as if to ask, *"What of it?"*

Ehud looked hard at Moshe. His large brown eyes were filled with sympathy. He tapped Moshe gently on the shoulder. "I will stop there," he said quietly. "If she is there, I will tell her you are coming."

"Stop where?" shouted Uri angrily. "What is in Rehavia?"

Ehud spat on the ground. "Shut up!"

"Who are you to come in here and—?" sputtered the young man.

"I am Captain Ehud Schiff!" Ehud boomed as he leaped onto the tailgate and drew himself up to his full height. "Blockade runner. Joint commander of the Old City. Fighter at Kastel. Arrested and tried and sentenced to die by the British!" He moved within inches of the young man. "And who are you?"

THE WISH
TO DIE

Ahkmed el Husseini rose slowly from the prayer rug in his drab one-room flat. He shared the room with his three older brothers, but they had gone ahead to wait in the streets for the coffin of Ram Kadar to pass by. They had taken their rifles and carried them openly now in defiance of the British, as did every man who fought against the Jews of Palestine. Ahkmed, at eighteen, had been left with the oldest of the weapons: an aged revolver that had served his father in the war against the Turks.

This day, Ahkmed was called upon to put the revolver to use in the service of his family once again. With it he would make an end of tragedy and disgrace and would prove his ultimate loyalty to the clan of Husseini.

With infinite care, Ahkmed cleaned and oiled the gun until the cylinder spun easily and the heavy barrel glistened. He muttered one last prayer from the Koran, then bowed low, cursing the enemies who had brought him to this moment.

His hands were sweaty when he pocketed the weapon and pulled his keffiyeh across his mouth like a veil. His black eyes shone with tears of emotion as he contemplated his duty. Touching the hard steel of the weapon once again, he prayed for courage and descended the steps that led to the crowded streets of Sheikh Jarrah. There were tears on the cheeks of every man who watched and waited for the body of Ram Kadar.

The young man passed through the throngs, his mind set on a different purpose. The air of the Arab Quarter was still heavy with the scent of charred flesh and burning tires. There was some satisfaction in the fact that so many Jews had died as retribution for the massacre of the innocent of Deir Yassin. Moving quickly through the mourning throngs, Ahkmed cast his eyes upward to the slopes of Mount Scopus and Hadassah Hospital. He hoped the Jews there mourned for their dead with the same anguish that he felt now in his heart.

The throng pushed against him as the shout arose that soon the funeral of Ram Kadar would begin. Ahkmed caught his reflection in the glass of a shopwindow and was startled that he looked so young when he felt aged and weary in his rage. As the crowd thinned out, he turned a corner onto a nearly deserted street.

He stopped to contemplate the shuttered house of his cousins. He had spent many happy hours playing in the sunny courtyard of the Tafara family. Memories of a young girl with glistening black eyes and bright brocade dresses caused him to reel at the thought of what he must now accomplish. The duty had fallen on him by lot. Allah had willed that he alone put to rest the misery of his childhood playmate and destroy the disgrace of the Husseini clan.

He touched the revolver again, knowing that he would find the girl alone in the house. His instructions were simply to make her vanish so that her father's heart would no more be torn by the sight of her anguish.

A collective moan rose from the mourners and swelled over the housetops. It was as if the whole world grieved for what he had to do.

Drawing a deep breath, Ahkmed steadied himself and set his gaze on the bars of the upper-story window where he knew Sarai waited. "Allah," he muttered, "give me strength." He stepped from the curb and strode across the deserted side street to the back entrance of the house.

There was a strong scent of incense inside the darkened house. It was a reminder that Ramadan was upon them, a time of fasting and prayer. Thick Persian carpets spoke of the wealth of this household, but Ahkmed did not stop to gawk at the expensive furnishings or the ornate lamps on furniture of finely carved and inlaid wood. He knew the way to the stairs. The silence of the rooms was broken only by the loud ticking of the clock. Ahkmed hoped that when he reached the room of Sarai, it would be empty.

Reaching for the latch of her door, again he prayed, "Allah, give me courage." His hand held tightly to the revolver, and sweat poured from his brow, soaking his checkered keffiyeh as he nudged the door open.

The room was shuttered and dark. Only a few rays of light filtered in to form pools on the deep red of the carpet. Ahkmed stood blinking in the doorway while his eyes adjusted to the darkness. A tall chest of drawers was against one wall, and a narrow bed was opposite.

A small cry of fear sounded—so much like a wounded animal. It came from the corner of the room. It was too dark for Ahkmed to see who was there, but he heard breathing.

It could only be the young woman, Sarai. He shuddered and said her name softly. "Sarai."

Again a whimper answered. Then a childlike voice begged, "Do not turn on the light."

"Sarai—"

"They will find me. . . . Do not . . ."

Ahkmed's eyes probed the shadows, finding her clutching her knees to herself as she huddled in fear. She was dressed in the black dress of mourning. She wore no veil, and her shorn head was uncovered. Against his will he gasped as the memory of her glistening black hair and flashing teeth came to him. "Allah! They have done this thing to you!" He stepped toward her.

Sarai drew back against the wall. "Do not turn on the light!" she pleaded. "They will come for me!"

He extended his hand to her, his heart racked with pity. "Sarai, it is your cousin Ahkmed! Sarai! It is Ahkmed el Husseini!"

"Ahkmed!" she whispered hoarsely. "Please. Help me." She stretched out her arms, and in one swift movement, he knelt to gather her to himself. He buried his face in her neck and touched the stubble of her hair as she wept against him. The reality and certainty of what he had come to do weighed heavily on him. The hard bulge of the revolver pressed against his ribs in their embrace.

"Yes, Sarai," he murmured. "I will help you." Fury rushed through him as he thought of the Jewish soldiers who had so savagely abused the young woman he now held. Her disgrace was now the disgrace of the family. The agony of her shame must be put to a quiet rest forever. "I will help," he finished, lifting her in his arms and carrying her toward the door.

She clutched wildly at his neck. "Do not take me into the light. They will see me! They are out there!"

He held her tighter and groped for her veil and shawl on the top of the chest. "You must wear your veil, Sarai," he told her gently. "Then the Jews shall not find you. They will not see you again." He laid her on the bed and helped her cover her head and attach the veil until only her eyes showed fearfully from the slit.

Her breath pulled the cloth against her face and then pushed it away as she gasped with terror at the thought of daylight. "They killed Basil. They killed everyone. Oh, how I wish they had killed me as well! If only I could have . . . do not let them find me again, Ahkmed! I must vanish. You must help me."

His duty seemed reinforced by her words. He frowned and found courage in her wish for death. "I will help you, dear cousin. I have come to help you."

Captain Stewart was the last of his men to leave the Old City. This temporary withdrawal from the confines of the walls was unceremonious, to say the least. Dressed in crisp fatigues and jaunty berets, the men of the Highland Light Infantry stood in clusters beneath the shadow of Zion Gate and smoked and talked as they waited for the trucks to carry them back to Allenby Barracks.

As the hush settled over the city, they, too, spoke in whispers as they wondered aloud what actions the Arab mobs would take against the Jewish Quarter today. There was among the soldiers a universal relief that they would not be there to be caught in the middle should the rage of the Arabs spill over the barricades.

Stewart stared back through the Armenian Quarter, where a ragged band of Jews held their positions behind a stack of sandbags and an overturned vegetable cart. Among them, Stewart spotted the slight figure of their leader, a fragile-looking man known only as Dov. Stewart tapped the long iron key to Zion Gate against his thigh.

"What about *them*, sir?" asked a young, ruddy-cheeked corporal.

Stewart shook his head in disgust and narrowed his eyes as the barrel of a gun poked over the top of the Jewish-held barricade. "They are fools. The whole lot of them." He turned his eyes away to where a column of British transports moved up the hill in a cloud of dust.

"The Arabs will attack today, you think?" asked the soldier.

Stewart grunted in reply. "The Jews can't say they weren't given every opportunity to get out. I spoke with Akiva myself this morning. Offered escort to every civilian wishing to evacuate—"

"I thought he was the only reasonable Jew in the lot."

"He owns half the real estate in the Jewish Quarter." Stewart smiled sardonically. "He will negotiate with the Arabs all right, and he blames all his troubles on the Zionists, but he'll not give up his Old City holdings. I suppose he would rather ride out the typhoon and trust the Haganah to defend his property—for today, anyway."

"Seems like they would know to get out. Can't they see what's brewing over there?"

"They can see. They can see well enough to know that if they leave now, they won't be coming back." Stewart held up the key, then scrutinized the huge, steel-plated doors that marked the only exit for those Jews still in the Old City.

"Shall we close the gates, sir?" asked the corporal. "Lock them up now?"

Stewart toyed with the key, considering the possibilities of Jewish survival if the Arabs did attack as expected. Zion Gate offered the only chance of retreat to the civilians and defenders. If it was locked, they would be trapped and doomed to almost certain annihilation. He looked back through the long twisting alleyway of the nearly deserted Armenian Quarter. There was also the possibility that those Armenian civilians who remained—mostly priests at St. James Cathedral and their seminary students—could also be trapped.

"No, I think not. We'll leave the gate open. A way of retreat for them should they survive."

"Won't the Jews in the New City try to break through once we leave?"

In answer, Stewart raised the key and pointed to the distant ramparts of the city wall. Every few feet an armed Arab stood gazing down toward the New City. "Let the Jews try." Stewart half smiled. "Old Saladin built these walls with that very thing in mind, Corporal. If we can see The Citadel and Jaffa Gate from here—well, let's just say that the Arabs have a clear view of everything. They'll not turn their eyes away long enough for anyone to roll up the open road through this gate."

He leveled his gaze at the young man. "They are fools and gangsters, these Zionists, but I cannot imagine that they will brave that." Again he pointed the rusty iron key toward the Arab watchmen. "There are enough Old City Jews who will want to leave that Akiva and the Haganah chaps may find themselves alone together in their precious quarter." He grinned. "Strange bedfellows, eh, Corporal?"

The gears of the British transports groaned as they wound up the exposed road to where the British soldiers waited. Half a dozen empty vehicles had come, expecting to haul a load of frightened Jews from their homes. "If they won't leave with us now, Cap'n Stewart," asked the soldier, "when will they come?"

"When it is too late," Stewart replied with certainty. "When it will do them no good at all."

A flock of crows rose awkwardly into the air from a newly tilled field. Sunlight caught their blue-black wings as they circled above a row of rain-washed cypress trees. The clouds had rolled back, trimming the blue sky like a hedgerow. This morning Italy seemed clean and unchanged, untouched by anything but the rain.

Lawrence C. Crabtree yawned and pulled his rumpled brown fedora low over his eyes. He doubted that he would sleep as the bus bounced and roared its way over the painfully rutted Italian roads toward Bari Harbor, but he was less likely to be bothered if it looked like the shades were down and he was dozing. What he most wanted was time to think, and while the rest of the reporters laughed and joked, he was already composing his lead paragraph for the front page of the European edition of the *New York Times.*

"Hey, Tree," someone shouted from the back of the bus, "how about a hand of poker?"

Crabtree did not respond as another American voice cursed loudly. "Leave him alone. You know how he is when you wake him up. A real Crab!" A burst of laughter replied to the very old, very overdone joke about his name.

For those who knew Crabtree and liked him—or at least respected him—he was called Tree. Only five feet five inches tall, he was a very short and gnarled tree, at best. His thick-muscled arms and jutting lower jaw gave him the appearance of a bulldog. Behind his back, colleagues called him Crab, which was fitting to his short temper and surly air.

Only his mother called him Lawrence, and occasionally a few fools had ventured to call him by his initials, L.C., which sounded too much like *Elsie* for Crabtree's liking. It was a favorite joke of the European Press Corps to send a big, strapping newcomer over to meet little Crabtree with the words, "Be sure and call him by his initials, pal." Seconds later, the newcomer would find himself blinking up at the ceiling of some bar as Crabtree returned to his beer.

Crabtree had mellowed some in the years since he'd covered the war from the angle of General George Patton. The latest victim of the L.C. joke had received only a scathing stream of epithets, after which Crabtree had thoroughly beaten the fellow who had instigated the joke.

After the war, Crabtree had returned to New York to cover dock strikes and city hall. An ongoing argument with his second wife had convinced him that Europe was tamer than New York, so he had packed his bags and caught a steamer back across the Atlantic.

Two days ago he had received a cable from New York instructing him to catch a flight to Palestine and try to unscramble the news that even the United Nations couldn't seem to decipher. *Who are the good guys and who are the bad guys in this little Middle Eastern drama?*

The ticket to Tel Aviv was still in Crabtree's carpetbag when the news arrived over the Teletype that the Palestine conflict had come to Italy— in a big way.

Last night, a tramp steamer from Yugoslavia had been sunk in Bari Harbor right under the noses of Italian port authorities. Rumors had been pitched back and forth as to the reason for the incident. Finally the news had leaked that the hold of the ship had been crammed with weapons bound for Palestine.

But the question still remained as to whether the ship was full of illegal weapons for the Jews or if the arms and ammunition were, in fact, legal and on their way to the Arabs. A garbled message from the Italian authorities seemed to indicate that the cargo was being sent to Italian Communists bent on capturing the Vatican, but this was largely doubted by the majority of the European Press Corps. After all, why should the Communists take the Vatican by force when they might well take Italy by popular vote next month?

Tree yawned again as whoops and curses arose from the poker game behind him. Personally, Tree was convinced that the only hand to bet on was that the Jews in Palestine were playing for keeps. He had little doubt, even though the details were unconfirmed, that the weapons at the bottom of the harbor had been bound for an Arab port and that the Jews were laughing up their sleeves this morning.

Tree also had no doubt as to his ability to get to the bottom of the story, whatever it was. He was the right man for an assignment that had left nearly every other reporter fumbling for words—and sweating in their beds as they wondered where the next terrorist bomb would explode.

Crabtree had seldom sweated in his life. He had calmly covered the war against Rommel in North Africa, then gone on to Italy—and ultimately the Battle of the Bulge. He had followed Patton to Berlin and viewed Hitler's bunker while German snipers still fired from the bombed shells of buildings. When Patton had stopped outside the gates of Dachau concentration camp, unwilling to set foot in the chamber of horrors, Crabtree had walked past him and revealed it all to the world with unflinching accuracy. He had felt little emotion, even though he had written with a compassion that made the folks back home weep with the news that what had been suspected was true—true and then some.

Crabtree had come away from his experience with the sickening realization that, at heart, mankind was somewhat less human than the wildest animal in the deepest jungle. He had also acquired an extreme disgust for the Jews of Europe who had gone like sheep into the exter-mination camps. Why had they not fought back? Why had they offered themselves as victims to a nation gone mad with hatred? These were questions he hoped to answer—for himself, if not for the American populace and the *New York Times*.

It was immaterial to Tree who won the argument over Palestine. He felt more like a sports reporter covering a good fight in Madison Square Garden. He would report each punch with accuracy and drama. He would describe the drops of blood on the canvas, the broken noses and swollen eyes. And then he would give the name of the winner and attempt to explain where the loser went wrong. What lack of courage or foresight, what fatal error, led to the final outcome? These were matters that Crabtree felt qualified to judge and wire home.

Palestine was a poker game. The whole world was betting, cheering, and cursing. The Jews were playing for keeps—betting their existence. For the Arabs, the stakes were not so high. It was this fact that made Crabtree bet on the Jews. But then again, it was not usually the most desperate men who played their hands the wisest.

Crabtree raised his head and peered out the grimy window of the shuddering bus. The sunny countryside crawled by slowly, little changed since Tree had last driven this road during the war. He pursed his lips in thought. The fact was, hardly anything had changed since the war. Except that Europe was a little safer than New York City.

THE CONTACT

Whole flocks of priests and coveys of nuns were descending on Rome in an annual migration for the Easter season. Capes and robes and long black dresses billowed in the wind. Silver crucifixes glistened in the sun, and new rosaries dangled from hooks in the carts of street vendors.

Photographer Ellie Meyer gaped at the spectacle from the back of Father John Antonell's cramped sedan. Her husband, David, and Bernie Greene of the Jewish Mossad flanked her. Mikhail Gregovsky, who had been a Resistance fighter against the Nazis, occupied the front passenger seat, and Father Antonell drove.

Each of them had donned the borrowed clothes of Catholic clergy for their journey into Rome. It would be unlikely, the priest had explained, that anyone would look for members of the Haganah behind white-starched clerical collars, and Ellie's bright copper hair was easily concealed beneath the habit of a nun. Even the stiff plaster casts on Mikhail's arms were hidden under the thick folds of a medieval-looking cape.

There was very little else that they could do this morning. A hastily coded message sent to Haganah headquarters in Rome had produced a result promising little hope as to their predicament. Decoded, it read like a warning against the black plague:

DO NOT COME TO HEADQUARTERS STOP UNDER CONSTANT
SURVEILLANCE, DOUBLED THIS MORNING STOP YOUR PRESENCE
COULD JEOPARDIZE OPERATION STOP THIRD STALL MEN'S WC
RIGHT OFF MAIN ENTRANCE CENTRAL RAIL STATION ROME STOP
TANK STOP

No further explanation had been offered. Their salvation, it seemed, waited in the tank of a toilet in the railroad station in Rome. How they were to get to it was their own concern—and the concern of Father John

Antonell, who had told Ellie that his main goal in life had become the desire to return to the quiet existence of a priest in one of the worst slum districts in Italy.

Now, in pursuit of that goal, Father Antonell maneuvered through the frantic traffic of Rome, bearing his cargo of counterfeit Catholics. He winced as the gears groaned and complained when he turned onto the boulevard that led to the grand railway terminal. Ahead, pillars of smoke rose into the sky to mark the massive locomotives that emptied their pilgrims onto the platforms of the huge building.

No one paid any attention to the complaining automobile as the American Armed Forces radio station blared out the news about the sinking of the *Trina* for the hundredth time this morning. Bernie translated for Mikhail, who nodded with grim satisfaction when the newscaster speculated on the method of detonating the homemade bomb that had sent the ship to the bottom of Bari Harbor.

"Demolition experts dispatched to the scene believe that the device used to sink the Trina *was of the simplest construction. . . ."*

Father Antonell jerked his head toward the radio. "How can they know such things?" His face revealed a sense of amazement mixed with dread.

"Quite easily, Father." Bernie grinned. "No crystal ball involved in their conclusion. Mikhail says that every detonator worth its salt is simple, you see. Why make it complicated when it can be easy, eh?"

Father Antonell raised his hand to silence Bernie's jovial explanation. "No, no! Say no more! I don't want to know. I already know enough. Too much already. I'll simply drop you off here to use the men's room, and then I'm on my way."

Ellie sympathized with the plight of the little priest, who had unwittingly become a party to the most sensational news event of the year. The war in Palestine had spread. It had plopped down right in his own little Bari Harbor and exploded.

"Don't worry." Ellie leaned forward to put a hand on his shoulder. "If we're arrested, we won't tell them about you. We won't mention your name."

"You won't have to, young lady." He inched the car into a long line of taxis moving toward the main entrance of the station. "No doubt someone will remember that it was my hot tip that got the crew detained long enough for you to do your work." He chuckled, but without amusement. "I will return the favor, however, and if I am arrested, I will not mention your names. As far as I know, you are three brother priests and a nun that I gave a lift to the railroad terminal. We should keep our story simple. Like the detonator."

The car rolled to a stop and Father Antonell set the hand brake, then swung around to catch the eyes of his passengers. "We shall not meet again, I think. Not in this life, at any rate. I will pray that if we chance to meet in the afterlife, it shall be in a place less warm than your little Palestine!" He extended a hand in farewell as horns began to honk impatiently behind them.

"God bless you," David said quietly.

"And God go with you," the priest returned warmly. "Wherever you are going."

"*L'Chaim*, Father," Bernie said hesitantly. "And if you think of it, you might offer a little prayer for us Jews, eh?"

"I have already planned an entire Mass," Father Antonell replied seriously. "And now, if you don't mind, get going, will you? And remember—" he looked at Ellie—"it is not proper for a nun to hold hands with a priest!"

With that, he reached across Mikhail and flung the passenger door open for him as the others climbed out onto the crowded, bustling sidewalk that led to the great arch of the terminal building itself.

Ellie did not glance back as the automobile horns blared and the little priest pulled away. Fighting the urge to grasp David's hand, she studied the facade of the building. She had never been here before, but she recognized it instantly from newsreel footage of Hitler and Mussolini emerging from this very place. Instead of crowds of nuns and priests and pilgrims, the lobby had been packed with SS guards and Italian Fascists raising their arms in salute to the two leaders. How frightening that image had been to her as a girl! Somehow the building itself still retained the echoes of that terrible time. She hung back as the others pressed ahead through the throngs of porters and people.

David turned and frowned at her, jerking his head toward the door. "Come along, Sister." He raised an eyebrow slightly.

Instantly relieved by the sound of his voice, Ellie tucked her hands into the enormous pockets of her ankle-length habit and lowered her gaze as she followed a few paces behind the trio.

Above them towered a huge vaulted ceiling of steel beams and glass. The terminal echoed with the roar of locomotives, loudspeakers announcing destinations, and the rumble of a thousand passengers who waited on long polished benches for their trains. Here and there American servicemen sat among the local populace. Ellie felt a twinge of anxiety at the sight of their uniforms. Perhaps they had seen her photograph in *LIFE* magazine, as Father Antonell had.

For three terrible, stormy days in Italy, trains had been rerouted and delayed. Only now had the backlog of stranded passengers seeking passage out of Rome begun to move. Many in the cavernous building still sat where they had put their luggage three days before. Their faces were haggard with bored exhaustion. Babies cried fitfully as Italian mamas scolded and reprimanded. Vendors hawked their wares in every corner.

David nudged Bernie and Mikhail and pointed to the sign that marked the men's room in three languages. He turned to Ellie, who shrugged and waved briefly as the three headed toward the restroom door. Then she walked to the newsstand across the corridor.

Books and magazines were piled high in the unadorned cubicle that served as Tom Kane's office. Maps of the Middle East were tacked unceremoniously to his walls, nearly concealing the plaques declaring that Thomas James Kane was a Rhodes scholar and had been decorated countless times in clandestine service of "Wild Bill" Donovan's OSS during the war. His actions in Egypt and Algeria had been invaluable to the Allies fighting the Axis.

Kane's ability to observe and interpret the political climate of the Arab nations in that conflict had earned him the reputation of being a diplomatic Lawrence of Arabia, who was able to bridge the cultural barriers and get to the heart of Middle Eastern thought and action. While others had fought the war with rifles and artillery, Kane had fought with his mind.

He knew, for instance, which sheikhs had made alliances with one another and which carried on ancient blood feuds. That information, relayed to the proper Allied commanders, prevented a multitude of errors that might have sent one sheikh or the other scurrying off to join the Germans against a hated rival who had allied himself with the Americans and British.

The miracle of the First World War had been that an Englishman named T. E. Lawrence had united the Arab tribes long enough to battle the Turks and win. Now a new generation of soldiers had arisen, and the army of Lawrence of Arabia was under the command of another Englishman. John Glubb, in the service of King Abdullah of Transjordan, had led his Arab Legion to fight the Germans. In doing that, he had fought against Haj Amin Husseini as well. King Abdullah and the Mufti of Jerusalem were mortal enemies, and yet it seemed that, for one fight at least, they would unite—to fight against the Jews in Palestine. It was this unlikely partnership that seemed to be the weakest link in the unity of the Arab League.

Kane reviewed the files before him. He scanned each page again and again, searching for clues to what might be happening behind the scenes.

"Item one," he muttered. "Jews hold position of Kastel against Arab Irregulars under the command of Ram Kadar." Kane furrowed his brow in thought. "Kadar. Yes. Military officer of Haj Amin. So . . . this was a Palestinian action against Jews." He made a quick notation in the margin: *Mufti's Irregular Army defeated by Jews in Bab el Wad. Road to Jerusalem open to Jewish convoys.* In spite of his need to evaluate the facts coolly, Kane found himself pleased that the Mufti's henchmen had been beaten back by the Jews. Such a defeat on the field of battle would also serve to defeat Haj Amin as he sought support among the leaders of the other members of the Arab League.

Kane scribbled additional notes, then set the folder to one side. He opened the second file and reread the scanty information dealing with the explosion of an arms ship in a small port in Italy. There was considerable confusion about the purpose and destination of the cargo. There was a possibility that the entire cargo had been meant for Italian Communists, but a second opinion existed that the weapons had been bound for Palestine . . . for the Mufti's forces, to be exact. For this reason, the information had been passed along for Kane's evaluation.

"SS *Trina*. Sunk Bari Harbor. Possible action by Jewish agents." More notes were made in the margin. *Zionists becoming more bold. Placing their own arms embargo on the Arabs. Buying time until they can equip their own forces before British leave Palestine.* Once again, Kane was fairly certain that such a catastrophe would have an effect on Arab morale and diminish the stature of the Mufti as he vied for power.

It was the third file that offset any Jewish victory in Palestine. In sickening detail, the American envoy in Jerusalem spelled out the tragic ambush of the Hadassah Hospital convoy. Names of the dead and their occupations were listed. *Doctor, nurse, nurse. Doctor. Doctor. Professor.* And near the end of the lengthy dispatch that told of British complacency during the horrifying incident, the name of Professor Howard Moniger of the American School for Oriental Research was listed.

Died. Hadassah Hospital. The Arabs who attacked convoy were heard to chant the name Deir Yassin *throughout the attack. From Damascus, Haj Amin proclaimed a great victory of revenge on behalf of those martyred in the village of Deir Yassin. City in turmoil. Arabs and Jews alike. We are expecting riots at any moment. Please stand by for further details. Will relay more as events develop.*

If Haj Amin Husseini could not exact a victory on the field of battle, he would have the blood of his enemies as he had always done—through ambush and terror.

Kane remembered Professor Moniger. Only two weeks earlier he had received a lengthy letter from him. He had met him during the war and had been impressed with the hardheaded American's determination to remain in Jerusalem in spite of an advancing tide of German troops. It had been on that same occasion that he had been introduced to Moshe Sachar, whom he later recruited into the Office of Strategic Services before the Battle of El Alamein. Sachar's impeccable mastery of Arab dialect and his understanding of the customs had made him invaluable as a source of information behind German lines.

Now, Kane knew, Moshe Sachar fought on a different front, even though the enemy seemed always to be the same. Strangely, the Zionist battle against Haj Amin Husseini in some ways made them allies of Jordan's King Abdullah.

Kane printed this thought in all capital letters, then underlined the words with a red pen. Perhaps there was something more in this that might be explored later. At that instant, the red light on his intercom flashed and a thick Southern drawl cracked over the receiver, "Sec'tary Marshall's waitin' in his office, Mistuh Kane."

Kane gathered his papers and prepared to lay out the whole scenario of one day's events in the Middle East before a very tired secretary of state. The decision to call or not to call President Harry Truman would then be up to him.

The bow of the dilapidated freighter protruded from the water like an ancient tortoise surfacing for air. The faded lettering of her name was scorched by the explosion but was still plainly visible for the cameras of the international press corps that swarmed the waterfront of Bari Harbor. The *Trina* was now the object of discussion over every morning cup of coffee in Italy. Italian police and government officials mingled with reporters, all searching for some clue to the identity of those men who had blown the gaping hole in the hull of the unfortunate vessel. The air rang with questions concerning the sinister cargo and destination of the ship. Word of the event had invaded the wire services of Europe and America. Stories of the massacre of seventy-five Jewish civilians in Jerusalem were placed side by side with the dramatic photos of the half-submerged hulk that had exploded right at the dockside of Bari Harbor.

Crabtree watched with interest as the harbor police pushed back onlookers and cordoned off the dock within three blocks of the ship.

The carnival atmosphere that followed nearly every catastrophe was something that Tree had learned to expect and recognize in his twenty-two years as a reporter. People everywhere, it seemed, were ambulance chasers. His first week as a reporter for the *Times*, Tree had made the observation that more people had come to watch the burning of a three-story tenement than had come to the Ziegfeld Follies in a week. The following years in his profession had convinced him even further that most people enjoyed disaster . . . as long as it was not their own.

This morning at the dockside of Bari Harbor offered no surprises to Lawrence C. Crabtree. He buried his wallet deep in his inside coat pocket as a protection against thieves. Then he munched on a sausage as he scribbled in his notebook, which he held against the rusty hull of the half-submerged freighter. It was, he thought, a wonder and a miracle that the tub hadn't simply sunk on its voyage from Yugoslavia to Bari Harbor. He was convinced that a good stiff kick with a hobnailed boot could have penetrated the barnacle-encrusted hull and sent the *Trina* to the bottom of the harbor.

The harbor police strutted importantly and played to the drama like bad actors in a poor play. "Yes! *Si!* We had just released the crew when the ship, she blow up!"

While other reporters asked probing, irrelevant questions about the politics and passion of this event, Crabtree simply strolled from group to group, watching and absorbing the moment that others created.

The distraught captain of the vessel wrung his hands and wept as he described the loss of his livelihood. Personally, Tree believed the man was lucky the *Trina* had not sunk at sea and taken all hands down with her. The following tale of the belligerent Arab who had come on board in Ragusa and insisted that they sail in the face of the storm sent a deeper message to Crabtree, however. He stood with his back to the captain and listened as the man related his story again and again to a stream of eager reporters. Each time the story was told, it offered one more detail than the last time.

"And he tells me he will kill me if we don't sail! An' that we goin' to Palestine, not Lebanon no more!"

"Yeah? Where is this guy?"

"Gone! Back to Damascus! Gone! An' he don't pay me, neither!"

Tree scribbled his notes as the other reporters moved on to a fresh interrogation of the harbor police chief. *Why*, he wondered, *was this Arab agent so anxious to sail—even with gale-force winds predicted? Why was the destination suddenly changed from Lebanon to Palestine? Especially when the*

British were intercepting all arms shipments along the coast of Palestine, even Arab shipments?

Piece by piece the picture began to fall into place. Perhaps the Jews of Palestine were not the only ones who were desperate. Perhaps the Arabs were growing panicky in the face of a few minor Jewish victories. As the sovereign Arab nations surrounding Palestine simply spouted rhetoric condemning the Jews and vowing to drive them into the sea, it was in reality the Arabs of Palestine who were taking the brunt of the fighting. And according to this morning's wire-service reports, the men of Haj Amin were taking it in the teeth. Could this Arab agent have been a representative of Haj Amin?

Nonchalantly, Tree wandered over toward a large woman who spoke in exaggerated Italian through a small boy who interpreted for her in English. The woman's eyes were bright and her face flushed beneath her rouge.

The little boy seemed ragged but intelligent and well-versed in the use of English. ". . . an' madame say that Arab man ist very angry! Very angry when he come in the hotel! He don't say nothin', but ist much upset about massacre in Palestine, yes? Girls he don't want in his room. He break some glass. This is true!" the boy said. "When I go to get the English for Father Antonell an' the American lady, I myself see this Arab man. He has a paper in his hand an' it tell all about the killings in Palestine."

Angry that the boy was obviously telling more than she had told, the madame raised her hand as if to strike him. A stream of Italian curses humbled the child, who lowered his eyes and seemed to shrink even smaller in the midst of the teeming crowd.

"Who was this American lady?" shouted a gruff reporter.

"Like you she ist. She from American newspaper."

Bored with the information that yet another American reporter was in Bari Harbor, the ring of newsmen dismissed this answer with a dozen other questions in rapid succession. None of them seemed quite as interesting to Crabtree as the one they had just passed over.

The bathroom attendant in Rome's railway terminal was a wrinkled, toothless old man who stood as close to attention as his crooked back would allow. He wore a faded green porter's uniform that looked as though it had seen many years of use. He smiled and bowed slightly as the three priests entered. His eyes widened when the tall, fair-haired one dropped a handful of change into the saucer that held his tips. This in itself was strange, because he was not to receive a tip until the patron had dried his hands on a clean, fresh towel that the porter was to provide. It was also peculiar for a priest to tip so well. Usually the old porter got little more than a blessing from men of the church.

And now, in no uncertain terms, the tall one closed the door of the bathroom and turned the key as the old porter stood by and blinked in confusion. The tall one put a finger to his lips for silence and positioned the old man in front of the door as though he were a guard. Then the three priests crowded into a stall and managed with difficulty to close the door.

"Communistas," muttered the old man, pulling up his chair and plopping down. Oh yes, since the war he had seen everything. Some conspiracy was being hatched in the stall, but it did not matter to the porter. He had outlived all the conspiracies of the young men, and he would outlive yet another small one, he was certain. As long as they tipped him well, he would close his eyes and sleep awhile.

Standing on top of the toilet, David handed his jacket down to Bernie and then removed the lid of the high water tank. "You think the old guy will tell?"

"Tell what to whom?" Bernie whispered back. "We paid him to keep the door locked. He will do that and never mind what goes on in here. WC attendants are very discreet fellows, I tell you."

"Well, a guy in the john handing out towels beats everything I've ever seen." David reached into the tank. "Makes me nervous."

"Have you found anything?" Bernie hissed.

David ran his fingers over the slime-lined tank, searching for some unknown treasure. He peered into the tank. "I need to get a look in here. A little more light. Think the old man's got a flashlight?"

"Doubtful," Bernie replied. "Let me have a go at it."

"Be my guest." David ran his fingers slowly across the bottom of the tank, grimacing at the muck. Then a small clean bit of metal pressed into his hand, gathered up in his fingers like a leaf in a rake. "Hold it!"

"Hullo!" Bernie whispered. "What have you got?"

With a low whistle, David pulled his hand out and opened his palm to the light. A small, shining key lay there, and the three men bent to study it. "Well, for sure it's not a car key. No fool would lose it in there anyway."

Bernie turned it over, and David whistled again. The number 359 was clearly engraved on it. "Of course. A locker key, old man. They've left us the key to a locker full of—"

"Of what?"

"Well . . . something useful, I'm sure."

David pushed past them and went to the basin to wash the key and his hands and arms while the attendant snoozed peacefully at his post. Pocketing the key, he dried his hands on a neatly folded towel, then tossed it into the large towel bin. "We'll know soon enough. You guys wait here. It'll only take a minute." He snatched his jacket from where it hung on Mikhail's stiff arm, gently shook the porter awake, tipped him again, and slipped into the lobby, where a nervous young nun was reading the headlines of the London *Times*.

Briefly, David flashed the key for Ellie to see. Her brow furrowed with confusion. "That's all?"

"All. But not everything. Sit tight. I'll be back in a minute with the goods." David resisted the temptation to kiss her on the cheek. Instead he winked broadly before starting off across the terminal lobby at a brisk pace in search of the lockers.

7

WOUNDED
HEALER

"Is there any word yet about the men who fought at Kastel last night?" Rachel anxiously asked the nurse who checked the baby's vital signs.

Stethoscope in her ears, the nurse frowned irritably and held up her hand for silence. Rachel quickly lowered her head and stepped back, ashamed that she had been so thoughtless. The square-featured woman scribbled on Tikvah's chart without acknowledging Rachel. It all seemed very mysterious and official—without the kindness that had been displayed by Dr. Rimsky.

"Is she all right?" Rachel asked timidly as the woman turned to leave.

"The doctor will have to tell you that!" snapped the nurse.

Rachel stepped forward. "And have you heard anything about Kastel? about Jewish survivors?" Her voice trembled with anxiety.

The woman grunted as she shoved the door open. "What few there are may be coming here. Or maybe they will be going to another clinic. They aren't telling us anything," she said bitterly as she disappeared into the busy hallway.

"Oh . . ." Rachel faltered, feeling lost and very alone in the vast hospital. "Yes, I see." But she did not understand the hostility of the woman who had just left the room.

As if sensing the unfriendly attitude of the nurse who had just checked her, Tikvah responded with an unhappy wail of protest. Her face grew red, and she shook her fists as tiny tears dampened her eyelids. The instant the door swung shut, Rachel gathered the child into her arms. Rocking her, Rachel clucked her tongue in sympathy, all the while feeling the same indignant hurt. "*Oy!* Tikvah!" she crooned. "*Yihiyeh tov!* Everything will be all right. *Yihiyeh tov!*" But even as she spoke the words, she was not certain that, indeed, everything would be all right.

At last the child rested peacefully in Rachel's arms. Rachel returned her to the crib and stood over her, wishing she could hear the voice of

Moshe say to her, "Yihiyeh tov, *my darling. . . .*" She closed her eyes and pictured his face on the last night they had been together.

I fell asleep in his arms. I felt so safe. So loved. And when I awoke, the moonlight was streaming in through the window and the room was silver. Moshe sat looking at me, loving me with his eyes, and I thought I was dreaming. Then he spoke—"Yihiyeh tov, Rachel." And he reached out to touch me. Later Moshe was gone, and I was left with the dream of his lips on mine . . . one last time.

She touched a finger to her lips, holding the sweet memory. "Moshe," she said aloud, "I am afraid . . . afraid that it will never be all right for us anywhere." The tenderness of her memory was replaced with a longing so deep and profound that she nearly cried out at the pain of it. She gripped the rails of the crib and fought off tears of worry and exhaustion. "Lord," she said through gritted teeth, "help me now, or I will break! Some word from him. Some word of his safety . . ."

Only silence answered her. She drew a deep breath and shook her head as though to clear it of her desperate fears. Not knowing what to do, she turned to find even some small task to take her mind off Kastel. A half dozen diapers were stacked on the night table. Rachel refolded them until the edges were perfectly even. Tiny gowns were smoothed and straightened, then refolded and stacked beside the diapers. All the while, Rachel paced to the window to stare down at the road through Sheikh Jarrah, but there was no sign of Haganah trucks. The English who had prowled the wreckage of last night's ambush had disappeared. The street was totally deserted. Beyond that, a last few Arabs moved toward The Citadel and Jaffa Gate.

The whiteness of the city was almost blinding as the sun climbed higher. Ancient terraces, overgrown with olive groves and vineyards, clung to the Judean hills. White stones seemed like scattered flocks of sheep on the slopes, descending into green ravines and small meadows that were strewn with wildflowers.

In the center of all of it, Jerusalem had sprouted like a bouquet of white marble that had sprung full grown from the surrounding countryside. *How beautiful and peaceful it seems,* thought Rachel—and yet it was that very beauty that filled her with grief. The blue of the sky reflected in her cobalt blue eyes: the mirror of her sadness. Her pale, flawless skin seemed paler now, as though she herself had been carved from the stones that were Jerusalem.

"My home," she said at last. Then she thought of the grayness that was Poland. Slate sky and smoky stone had blended together into one colorless landscape. The black coats of the Hasidic Jews had been pursued by the shadows of brown-shirted Nazi storm troopers. In Poland, war and death had seemed to complement the landscape.

"But here," she said aloud as her thoughts groped for expression, "it is too beautiful, Lord. The city glistens in Your light. Should not also men find their hearts clean and bright with Your love?"

She thought again of Moshe, fighting on the slopes of Kastel. And then of Howard, a man of peace whose last words had been his hope for the City of Peace:*"Hate no man!"*

Rachel frowned as she felt again the grasp of Howard's hand in hers. *And yet he was a Zionist. A man who prayed for a homeland for the Jewish people. Did he imagine that we Jews could live beside those who wish us dead? Should I love those who have killed Howard and perhaps even my husband?*

Rachel pondered Howard's words, wondering where he had found the peace to utter such words in his last breath. *Isn't it right for me to hate those who nearly destroyed my life? who now seek to destroy this tiny remnant of Israel? You will have to teach me such a hard thing, Lord. I cannot find such love in my heart for the Arabs who have done this. My own heart is not at peace. How can I expect Jerusalem to be at peace? They hate us. We hate them. And so, beneath the surface, this place is as gray and gloomy as Poland.*

With a heavy sigh, Rachel turned from the window. Her eyes fell on the small white box the nurse had brought to her earlier. There, on the lid, Howard's name had been hastily scrawled in blue ink. The nurse had tossed the box onto the bed table—angrily, it seemed. "This is a Jewish hospital," she had said gruffly.

Now Rachel took the box to the light of the window and slowly opened it.

She examined the contents. A ring of keys. A wallet. A wristwatch. Loose change. A small, frayed pocket Bible. It was a pitiful little pile to represent the personal effects of a man.

Picking up the watch, she turned it over in her hand and ran her fingers along the curve of the leather band that had fit Howard's wrist. The face of the watch was smashed. The time read 11:34—probably the exact moment he had pulled her from the flaming ambulance and shielded her with his own body as they rolled into the ditch beside the road.

The back of the watch was engraved with words that surprised Rachel. *Howard, Love Marie 12–25–27.* Rachel touched her finger to the letters and tried to imagine the professor twenty years younger and in love with a woman. Suddenly she wished that she had known more about his life. Over the months she had known this kind and gentle man, she had wondered why he was not married, but she had never asked Moshe about him.

A wave of longing returned. *Will I ever see Moshe to ask him all my questions? Perhaps the professor was married once . . . perhaps he loved as deeply as we do. Yet he spent so many years alone.* She tried to imagine her life without Moshe, but even the thought was too painful. She put her hand over the place where their child grew. "You are in my thoughts and in my heart," she murmured.

Rachel replaced the watch and picked up the little Bible. A dog-eared picture fell from its pages and tumbled to the floor. Rachel bent to pick it up, startled at the handsome couple who gazed out from the photograph. The professor smiled proudly. Howard was a young man, younger even than Moshe was now, it seemed. He stood with his arm around a beautiful young woman with shining eyes and fair hair tied back in a ribbon. She was slim and athletic, and Rachel guessed that she could not have been older than twenty-five when the photograph was taken. The professor was lean and suntanned and handsome. The back of the photo was inscribed *Howard and I. Commencement dance, 1924.*

Rachel spoke to the smiling woman in the picture. "It must have been a happy day for you both. I am glad that you had that day together to be in love. I am glad you could not see the future, or you would never have smiled again."

Grief stole her breath. She bowed her head and let tears flow freely. "I have also been happy." Again she wondered if she would ever feel Moshe's strong arms around her. She had no photograph of him to carry, but the picture of his face was etched in her memory. "Some word of hope, God, or I will break!" She thumbed through the Bible, searching the black print for some familiar word, but every phrase was written in a language she could only barely comprehend. "English," she said, sitting down mournfully. "Every word in English!"

Then, as she turned the pages, she came upon a small piece of paper. Moshe's familiar handwriting was scrawled on the outside. Rachel blinked, feeling almost as though God had heard her prayer for some word from her beloved Moshe and had sent a special message through this little book.

Her fingers trembled as she opened the note. A smaller slip of paper fell from the first. This time her name was written on it. She glanced at the first sheet. It contained the number of Moshe's office in Hebrew University and a scant list of books. At the bottom Moshe had hastily written, "Watch over her for me. If I do not return, see that she gets this. Moshe."

Rachel smiled and held the paper to her heart. "Thank You," she said aloud. "Oh, thank You!"

The note was carefully penned in Polish, but still Rachel blushed at the thought that such words might have been found and read by anyone but her. Howard, she knew, did not speak or read Polish, so Moshe had felt comfortable entrusting such a private message to him. It was dated on the night of Passover. Beneath that, Moshe had written, *As you sleep in the moonlight.*

My dearest ishti, my wife,

> *Have you ever had a blazing light*
> *burn so brightly that you still see*
> *it when you close your eyes?*
> *Until tonight I would never have believed*
> *that moonlight could produce such an effect. . . .*
> *And yet, moonlight must be stronger*
> *than the most brilliant flame,*
> *at least when reflected by your*
> *glowing skin . . . because when*
> *I close my eyes, I still see*
> *you lying there . . . and will*
> *see you so, forever.*
> *You are magic. . . .*
> *Soon I must leave you again, but*
> *the thought of you is a fire*
> *that warms my very soul.*
> *Some may pity us that we have had such*
> *a short time of happiness together, but*
> *I say God has blessed us with the happiness*
> *of a thousand lifetimes in every mingled*
> *breath and sigh that we have shared.*
> *Think of what has been and what will be,*
> *and in that, find happiness for even*
> *such brief moments as these.*

Your loving husband, Moshe

Rachel pressed her cheek against the paper. She wept openly as she read the words again and again, careful not to let her tears stain the ink. "Thank you. I *am* happy. You have given me that one moment in my life."

A few minutes passed as Rachel shed tears of joy and grief. And when she was finished, she felt somehow cleaner and lighter. She wiped her tears away and splashed a handful of cold water on her face.

A voice behind her startled her. "That water is for washing the baby!" barked the gruff and angry nurse. "It is not for you!"

Rachel turned with a soft smile to face the embittered woman. "Never mind. *Yihiyeh tov!* Everything will be all right, I think, Nurse."

The nurse scowled and turned on her heel at Rachel's reply. "Everything will be all right," she said, mimicking Rachel cruelly.

Rachel simply shrugged and whispered to the sleeping baby, "Poor lady. She has not been happy. Or maybe she just cannot remember, *nu?*" Rachel sat down and studied the note Moshe had left with Howard concerning the books that remained in his office. "These are things important to your papa, Tikvah," she said at last. "So I will leave you here just for a while to fetch them. . . ."

8

ESCAPE

The loudspeaker competed with the human din, bellowing out the arrival of a passenger train from Vienna.

David looked up at the large face of a clock surrounded by brass cherubs that suspended it from the high archway. A whistle blew as a locomotive chugged slowly toward the long loading platform. In that instant, David's eyes met those of a tall, balding man who seemed to study him with peculiar curiosity.

Suddenly self-conscious, David tugged at the brim of his hat and turned away from the man. He moved rapidly toward a cadre of priests who chatted excitedly in the center of the aisle. Involuntarily, he glanced back over his shoulder. The stranger still had not averted his eyes, and now his expression was grim, almost angry, as he pulled a briar pipe from his coat pocket.

David moved into the center of the priests as though he belonged with them. He shook hands and patted backs as they responded with confusion and tentative cordiality. He felt the gaze of the man hot on his back.

One more sideways glance told him that the man had gone. But questions remained. Where had he gone, and why had he stared at David with such disapproval? Did he know? Did he recognize him?

With one final slap on someone's back, David moved away from the priests. He quickened his pace through the long rows of wooden benches. Stepping around luggage and over the outstretched legs of sleeping soldiers, he hurried to distance himself from the fresh apprehensions that had come to him.

Trying to appear calm and deliberate, he stepped into a phone booth and closed the door behind him for privacy. He needed a moment to think, to calm himself. Flipping through the Italian phone directory, he looked toward the teeming throngs of people, hoping to catch even one more glimpse of the man who had been staring at him. He was nowhere in sight.

David wiped sweat from his brow and picked up the receiver, pretending to dial. After a short pause, he slammed the phone down and stepped out of the booth. Across the lobby were two dimly lit corridors filled with metal lockers. Fingering the key in his coat pocket, David walked toward a newsstand near the lockers.

A tired-looking man of about fifty handed him a newspaper and made change. He raised his eyebrows in surprise at the American bill David passed him.

"I speaka English, Father," said the man, with no hint of a smile. "You come to Rome for Easter, eh? To hear the papa?"

David put his hand to his clerical collar, remembering his appearance. "Right. To hear the pope." He smiled and took the change, noticing for the first time that the man had only one arm. "Thanks."

"You come to Rome at such a time, Father!" The man seemed eager to talk. "You hear the news? Communistas bring in a boat fulla guns. Gonna take over the government, *si*? Justa what Italy need. Another war." He pointed to his empty sleeve.

David nodded absently without hearing the man's bitter words. Sitting directly across from where he stood was the tall man. This time he smoked his pipe and alternately glanced at David and a recent issue of *LIFE* magazine. David's heart hung in his throat. He was being watched. And quite openly, at that.

David stared frankly at the tall man, sizing him up. Brown herringbone jacket and slacks. Brown loafers, run-down a bit at the heels. His face was long and lean; his mouth turned down slightly at the corners. He had the look of a Scotland Yard inspector of the caliber David had seen in old Sherlock Holmes movies. When the man looked up again, their eyes locked. David offered a tight-lipped smile and tipped his hat. The watcher looked almost insulted and stood suddenly, snatching up a hat from the empty bench beside him. He hurriedly checked around the terminal, consulted his wristwatch, and strode back toward the main terminal entrance.

David's smile melted away as the one-armed vendor asked, "You know disa fellow, Father? He looka like to me he need to go to confession."

David stared after the retreating form of the man for another minute before tucking his paper under his arm and walking directly toward the lockers. No doubt if this one man was watching him, there were others roaming about the terminal as well. David turned the key over and over again in his pocket. He hoped there was a gun in the locker.

With every step, a sense of desperation filled him. He had known this same feeling when he had been alone and outgunned in the skies above Germany. *Fly into the sun,* he thought. *Outsmart them. Face them head-on if they're after a fight. And steer them clear of Ellie.*

As he searched the long, cold corridor for the right number, he abandoned hope of all subtlety. He imagined the form of a man who waited in a shadowed corner for him to plunge the key into the lock. He scanned the sequence of numbers until, at the very end of the third row, he came to 359. He hesitated, then inserted the key and turned it, pulling the metal door open. In one swift move, he yanked a small brocade carpetbag out, then ran his hand across the bottom of the cubicle to check for anything else that might have been left for them. There was nothing. Nothing but the bulging bag that looked no different than a hundred others in the station.

His breath came faster as the clang of another locker was heard down the row. He started, then gathered up the bag and jogged out toward the mobs of people again. He worked his way back to the main entrance in a nerve-racking route that took him completely around the massive hall.

Ellie still waited for him near the main newsstand. She rocked on her toes and stared toward the distant lockers. She did not look toward him and appeared unaware that he now stood opposite her.

Holding tightly to the carpetbag, he walked briskly toward the men's room. A small sign hung on the door, announcing that it was out of order. He sighed with relief. Maybe it would all be this simple. Get the key, get the goods, and go. Maybe the man in the herringbone suit was nothing more than a people watcher, caught and embarrassed in his game. That is what David wanted to believe, and it seemed almost possible. Twenty paces away, he thought, Bernie and Mikhail were waiting for his return. Waiting to see what tickets and money and instructions had been left for them so they could conveniently melt away into the maze of a thousand trains, each leaving for somewhere outside Italy.

The illusion lasted only as long as it took to run through David's mind. Behind a thick marble pillar, the tall, balding man in the herringbone suit waited for him. David smelled the man's tobacco even before he saw him. Like the acrid scent of gun smoke and aviation fuel and flames, it filled him with dread.

The man stepped directly into David's path. He glanced at him only briefly, his cool eyes full of a slow, simmering anger.

David's body tensed. He prepared to swing and prayed that Ellie would simply disappear into the crowd and find her way to safety when she saw what happened to him.

"Not real subtle, are you, fella?" David's voice was menacing.

"Don't be a fool," the tall man said. "Don't go in there." He inclined his head toward the men's room.

"Are you the man to stop me?" David allowed a slow smile to cross his face.

His attempt at humor was met with disdain. "Get your wife and go, Captain Meyer," the man said, his voice quite tired. "They are dead, you know."

"What?" David said, looking first toward Ellie and then at the closed door of the men's room.

"Get out while you can," the tall man said urgently as he brushed past David. "Go now, I tell you."

David stood dumbfounded as the man disappeared into the crush of waiting passengers. Just above him the PA system roared:

"Express Français now boarding. . . . Track 3 for Paris . . . last call . . . . now boarding."

David licked his lips and tried to swallow as the realization of the man's words sank in. He moved numbly toward the scratched walnut door.

"All passengers with tickets on Express Français now boarding at Track 3 please report."

David stopped three feet from the door and stared at the small *Out of Order* sign. He reached out his hand and gently pushed, feeling the door yield to his touch. Then he entered the tiled room. Only one step was enough. In an instant of horror, he backed away, fighting to suppress the panic that made him want to shout their names. *Bernie! Mikhail!*

"Last call for the Express Français now boarding. . . ."

Ellie glanced nervously at the paper, then back to where David had disappeared down a tiled corridor that led to the rows of metal lockers. Her heart felt stuck in her throat as she waited what seemed like forever for his return.

Suddenly a horrified shout echoed from the men's room behind her. A barrel-chested man, his face ashen, emerged from the swinging door. In his hand he held a white towel soaked in blood. He clutched his chest and shouted for the police. The terminal fell silent, then resounded with the screams of women as they caught sight of the apparition who leaned heavily against the entry to the men's room and shouted the same words over and over.

A hundred police officers appeared at once. Their slapping boots echoed like an army as they rushed to the aid of the distraught man. He wept and pointed toward the horrors from which he had just emerged. The newspaper vendor circled around and stood next to Ellie as the crowd swelled and police began pushing people back.

Ellie was sick with fear and panic. *Where is David? What happened to Mikhail and Bernie? Are they still in there? Whose blood is on the towel? What happened?*

"Please, can you tell me?" she begged the vendor, who spoke a little English.

The vendor wiped sweat from his brow and crossed himself. "Someone hasa kill da priest! Two priest, Sister! Angelo also—da old man—isa dead!"

Ellie grew dizzy at the man's words. She groped for a place to sit down but, finding none, sank to the tiled floor of the terminal and listened to the faraway wail of the sirens.

"Who hasa done sucha thing, Sister?" the vendor wailed.

"David," Ellie whispered in a voice that was drowned by the din of grief and confusion. "God, send me David."

An instant later David's strong hand lifted her to her feet. "Come on." His voice was tense and urgent. "We've got to get out of here. *Now!*"

Tears streamed silently down Ellie's cheeks. David did not pause for an explanation. Almost lifting her feet off the ground, he propelled her against the surge of the curious crowd that moved toward the ghastly scene.

Moments later, as they stood at the edge of a train platform, David stared blankly toward the hub of activity across the terminal. "They're dead," he said simply. "Dead. Both of 'em. And an old man, the washroom attendant, too. I wasn't gone more than a few minutes. Fifteen minutes. I went back and . . . someone had got 'em."

Ellie covered her face with her hands. "What can we do, David? What should we do now?"

He continued to talk over her questions. "Mikhail and the old man didn't have a chance. Bernie must have gotten it first. He tore the place up in the fight. Mikhail's arms. The casts . . . he didn't have a chance," he finished helplessly. "One look. I knew. Got out of there and waited for someone to find them. Then I came back around for you." Beads of sweat stood out on his brow, and he was panting.

"What should we do?" Ellie asked again.

A train slowly began to edge away from the platform. Carpetbag under his arm, David pulled her toward the door of a car. He tried the door handle, and it opened easily. With one swift motion, he lifted Ellie into the compartment and swung in after her. Right now it did not seem to matter where the train was going . . . as long as it was far away from Rome.

9

A PLAN
FOR PEACE

A blue halo of cigarette smoke circled Harry Truman's desk in the Oval Office of the White House. Tom Kane sat among four other grim, irritated officials of the State Department while Secretary of State George Marshall nervously paced the length of the carpet and back.

On the cluttered desk of the wiry president from Missouri, a placard proclaimed *The Buck Stops Here*. Tonight, as he pored over the latest intelligence reports from Palestine, Truman felt the burden of that sentiment. In silence he scanned the pages of each document and looked for some sign of hope among them. There was none.

"Well, George, you've got me out of bed at three in the morning for this—" He tapped a forefinger noisily on the stack of manila folders. "Just what exactly did you have in mind?"

"We'll have to back away on our stand for Partition, of course," volunteered Undersecretary Lovett.

Truman narrowed his eyes. "Hold it, Junior. It was George who got me out of bed for this. I want to hear from him."

Lovett squirmed under the sharp reprimand.

George Marshall cleared his throat loudly as a warning against further interruption. "Mr. President," he began in a slow, sad drawl, "in this instance I agree entirely with the opinion just stated. These latest episodes are unspeakably barbaric. Arabs against Jews. Jews against Arabs. *Revenge* has become the watchword of Palestine."

"Huh!" Truman snorted. "What time is it over there right now, Mr. Kane?"

"Nine o'clock in the morning, sir."

Truman leaned forward against the desk. "By the time we hear about it here, it's always the middle of the night on our side of the ocean and they've gone on to something more terrible over there." He frowned. "God have mercy; I wouldn't wish this job on any man," he mumbled.

"This morning the American people are going to get up with headlines designed to give a man indigestion for life. Not only are seventy-five prominent Jewish scholars and doctors dead in a massacre in Jerusalem, now we've lost an American archaeologist. With connections to Johns Hopkins and Georgetown and . . . well, it just doesn't seem to let up."

"This is entirely out of control, Mr. President," Marshall said.

"And in an election year, too," Truman added. "You are recommending we propose a trusteeship of Palestine to the United Nations?"

That was the dominant opinion of the State Department, Tom Kane knew.

"Exactly," Marshall replied firmly.

"Well—" Truman cast a glance around the room—"I know we have a few different opinions floating around in here. Let's hear them." His eyes lingered on the strained face of Kane. "Mr. Kane, state your case. Or bust."

Kane managed a slight smile. "Mr. President, the actions in Palestine are motivated by revenge. That is true." He coughed nervously, then continued. "Giving the government of Palestine to the United Nations will not stop the bloodshed. The Palestinian Arabs are not only determined that there will be an annihilation of a Jewish state if such a state is declared. They are determined that there will be no Jews at all in Palestine."

"Perhaps," Marshall said in a patronizing voice, "they realize that these Zionist Jews will open the way for Russia to completely take over the Middle East in twenty years. What would stop the immigration of Communist Jews from Russia into Jewish-occupied Palestine?"

"A good point." Truman leaned back and glared at Kane. "What do you say to that?"

"That the United States must be the first to recognize Israel, Mr. President. If the state is declared on May fourteenth, then we must be the first to offer our congratulations and our *help*."

"You are suggesting that we back the establishment of a potentially Communistic state in Palestine?" Marshall appeared appalled.

Truman raised his hand for silence. "Hold it now, George. The young fella might have something worth thinking about here."

Encouraged, Kane drew a deep breath. "They say Golda Meir arrived here a few months ago with ten dollars in her pocket. When she went back to Palestine, she took fifty million dollars for the cause of a Jewish homeland. Raised by private donations of American citizens—"

"Jews," said Lovett. "American Jews."

Truman slammed his palm on the stack of briefs with a resounding crack. "*Americans*, Lovett. American citizens."

"What I'm saying, sir," Kane continued, "well, Mr. President, it doesn't seem like we even need to take this one to the polls." He turned to Lovett. "And you're wrong about the contributions being all from Jews. People in little churches everywhere gave to help out. There are, I understand, as many Gentile Americans as Jews who have volunteered for service over there."

"And they'll lose their passports for it," Marshall said angrily. "Lose their American citizenship."

Truman flinched at the thought. "Then they sure must think they've got something worth fighting for."

"They believe, as I do, that we're still fighting Hitler," Kane said. "That the Jews have no place else to go. How many years can they continue to rot in the refugee camps across Europe and in Cyprus? They have lost everything. This is their final hope."

"We all saw the newsreels, too," said a disgusted junior official. "There was a war. The Jews got caught in the middle. It happens. Now are we going to make the Arab countries in the Middle East pay for what happened?"

Truman's eyes moved back and forth, as if he were watching a tennis match.

Kane drew himself up. "The Jews have been in Palestine since the turn of the century. They have purchased land for settlement, not stolen it. If the British had followed some rule of decency in the war . . . if they had allowed European Jews to immigrate to Palestine, then there would be six million fewer dead!"

He continued with controlled anger. "*That* is the only point left to discuss in this room tonight. If we deny them a homeland now as the British did in the White Paper of '39, aren't we doing exactly what we all deplored? This is a question of survival. The Jews of Europe are still homeless after three years of waiting behind wire. There are children who don't know what it means to walk free in the streets. And there is not one survivor who does not have memories of loved ones who are never coming back. They are a mere remnant . . . a small piece of what they were before Hitler. Argue with that if you like."

"And what of the Arab nation of Palestine?"

"Come on! There has never been an Arab nation in Palestine!" Kane's emotions boiled to the surface. "The British have ruled there since 1917. Before that, the Ottoman Turks ruled for how many hundred years? And the Arabs, Jews, and Christians alike suffered under that rule. Thirty years before Hitler built Auschwitz, the Turks were murdering one and a half million Armenians at the same time they were administrating the government of Palestine. And the world was silent then, too." Kane paused for effect. "Undoubtedly that is why the Armenians who now live in Jerusalem are so sympathetic to the Jewish cause."

Lovett sighed impatiently. "That certainly has no bearing on what we are discussing."

Kane smiled slightly. "On the contrary. The history of the Middle East is filled with examples of genocide. Haj Amin Husseini will begin a new record against the Jews if they don't have a homeland."

"Haj Amin Husseini himself fought against the Turks. On the side of the English," offered Lovett. "His dream has always been for an independent Arab nation in Palestine."

"One without Jews," Kane finished. "And with himself as king and absolute monarch. He has been offered a nation with the Arab High Committee as provisional government, and he rejects that—simply because there would be a Jewish state beside an Arab Palestine."

Kane looked around the room at the stony faces of the men who listened to his argument with irritated disinterest. They had made up their minds.

"Gentlemen—" Kane spread his hands—"it is the Arabs of Palestine who are saying no. Haj Amin Husseini's military coalition, to be exact. And it looks to me like the Jews are making a stand against the Arab Irregulars."

Truman thumped the folder. "Well, if making a stand means seventy-five innocent civilians are killed, including an American citizen, then I would hate to see what would happen if the Jews were losing."

"My judgment"—Kane picked his words carefully—"is that the opening of the Pass of Bab el Wad by the Jewish Haganah is a major factor in the conflict. They have broken the siege of Jerusalem. The cost has been high, yes, but we are seeing a turning point in the fortunes of Haj Amin."

"You're saying that the Jews can hold out against the Arab Alliance?" Truman gazed intently at Kane.

"No," Kane said flatly.

"Well then"—Marshall drew himself up in challenge—"what is the point?"

"The point is quite simple, gentlemen." Kane's pause was dramatic. "I believe that we can save Partition and prevent a large-scale war in Palestine as well."

Truman flipped the switch on his intercom. "Send up plenty of hot coffee, Harmon. We're going to need it." He narrowed his eyes to appraise Kane carefully. "If you think you can stop a war, young man, I'm willing to listen."

Again Lovett protested. "Only God can stop a war unless we *revoke* Partition."

"I always said God was a diplomat." Truman raised a hand to silence Lovett. "So, what's the plan?"

Kane cleared his throat and tugged nervously at his bow tie. "There is one man in the Arab League who may well be open to negotiation. His nation has the most sophisticated army of any of the Arab nations."

"You are speaking of King Abdullah of Transjordan?" Marshall asked. "He is as eager to drive the Jews into the sea as the rest."

Kane shook his head. "I cannot believe that. He is a reasonable man."

"Reasonable! He is a Bedouin chieftain who came to power through Lawrence of Arabia! He is still a warrior, not a peacemaker," Lovett said sarcastically.

"Admittedly," Kane said, "his rhetoric is as hot as the other Arab leaders', but there is a marked difference in King Abdullah."

"How do you know this?" Lovett challenged, while Truman leaned back in his chair and prepared to watch the junior staff members argue it out.

"I know him," Kane replied simply, meeting Truman's gaze with confidence. "And I know the British general who commands his forces. John Glubb. Glubb Pasha, as he is known to his Arab Legion troops, is not a man who will happily march off to war. Not if a peaceful compromise can be negotiated."

"And what is the compromise?" Marshall asked.

"King Abdullah and Haj Amin are mortal enemies. Of course we all know how Haj Amin attempted to unite the Germans and the Arabs in the war. King Abdullah and Glubb Pasha brought their Arab Legion to the aid of the Allies. The Arab Legion fought fearlessly against the Germans, and it has always been the opinion of King Abdullah that he should have been more justly rewarded by the British."

"Rewarded? How?" Truman glowered at Harmon as the tray of coffee was brought into the room. A heavy silence lasted through the pouring of the coffee, and Kane thought through his reply again and again until Harmon slipped out the door.

Kane took a sip of his coffee. "King Abdullah was—still is—hoping to annex Palestine into his kingdom of Transjordan. I believe there is room here for negotiation."

"What about the other nations of the Arab League?" someone asked quietly.

"The most powerful force in the Middle East right now is the Arab Legion of King Abdullah. There is a chance, gentlemen." Kane looked at each face and saw that his arguments at last were making some impression.

"There is a slight chance that if King Abdullah were allowed to take over the Arab sector of Palestine, the rest of the Arab League would back away. Transjordan controlling the Arab half of Palestine and the Jews holding their own homeland—you must admit that the idea has some merit."

A thoughtful silence filled the room.

At last Secretary of State Marshall cleared his throat. "A stirring speech, Mr. Kane. But I still say we're looking at a hotbed of Communism . . . a Russian takeover in Jewish-held Palestine."

"The American people do not seem to agree with you. Nor do I," Kane said dryly. "The Russians are enjoying our current rift with Britain over the Palestine question, but if we are first to recognize a new Jewish nation, the Russians will not have a chance."

"And now you are an expert on the Russians as well?" Lovett said sarcastically.

"No," Kane objected, his voice confident. "Just on the Middle East. And I had enough experience in the OSS, seeing the way Arab alliances work, to know that this is a possibility." He held up one finger at a time, as though instructing a classroom of small boys. "Haj Amin wants all of Palestine. King Abdullah wants as much of Palestine as he can get. The Jews want a homeland. Why not promise part of Palestine to Abdullah and then let him and Haj Amin slug it out?"

"And how do you propose getting the Jews and King Abdullah to sit down at the negotiating table?" Marshall pointedly asked Kane.

"The Jewish Brigade and the Arab Legion served together during the war. I am under the impression that King Abdullah feels friendlier toward certain members of the Jewish Agency than he does toward Haj Amin Husseini and Palestine's Jihad Moquades."

"Maybe you would like to set up such a meeting." Truman was now staring intently at the door of a small closet in his office. "God and diplomacy," he muttered.

"Mr. President," Marshall protested, "if news of this leaks to the press—"

"What? That we're trying to stop a massacre? That we might have a small part in establishing peace in Palestine? Seems to me the American people feel the same way about it as Kane here does. Fifty million dollars given to the cause is quite a statement." Truman flipped through a report. "And of course there are the material goods that have been shipped to Palestine. Seventy thousand flares from Ohio. Fifty thousand helmets from Illinois. Farm tools from Missouri. The Jewish people will be able to farm in the dark and keep their heads warm all at the same time if the American voter has his say in this, gentlemen."

Truman grinned. "It's worth a try, at any rate." He swiveled his chair to face Tom Kane. "At ten o'clock this morning I'm going to hold a press conference to denounce all the violence in Palestine. I'm going to tell the press—and the American voter—that we are still pursuing a peaceful solution to the Partition problem and that someone is already on his way as a representative of this government to aid in our purpose." He nodded, agreeing with the statement he had just made. "Yes, I like the sound of that. I like the thought of it as well. Mr. Kane? How long will it take you to pack your bags?"

Yehudit looked up as a key rattled in the lock of her door. Since her morning meal had already been brought to the room, she had not expected to see the housekeeper again until midafternoon. The heavy wooden door swung open, and Yehudit gasped as the face of her father emerged from the shadows. His thick eyebrows were knit together in a frown. He did not raise his eyes to meet hers, nor did he step into her room. In the dim light of the hallway, his black coat and hat blended into the darkness, leaving only his grim and brooding face visible to her.

"Father . . . ," she said faintly.

"Captain Stewart has called," he blurted out. "The English are pulling back." His voice was tight with rage that simmered just below the surface.

Yehudit longed to explain to him why she had left the Old City, why she had disobeyed him for the first time in her life. "Father, they have saved the child!" she began hopefully. "At Hadassah Hospital they have a new medicine, and the child is—"

He raised his fleshy hand to the side of his face, a familiar gesture that demanded immediate silence. Yehudit bowed her head. He would not hear her, even if she spoke. And never would she regret her role in helping to save the life of Tikvah.

Her father had not come for reconciliation or explanation. That much was immediately obvious to Yehudit. And so he had come because he wanted something from her.

There was no softness in his voice as he spoke. "Hadassah Hospital?" The words were as sharp as a drawn knife. "Well then, the child will most likely be dead soon enough, anyway. The Jihad Moquades have attacked and murdered a convoy full of Jewish civilians . . . and the American professor was among them."

Yehudit drew in her breath.

Rabbi Akiva plunged on. "Soon the British expect that our quarter will be under attack in the same way. They cannot—or will not—attempt to control the mobs your Zionist friends have stirred up!"

"Why? Why has this happened?" Yehudit asked, still attempting to absorb the news of the death of the professor.

Again Akiva changed the subject. "The British are offering safe escort for complete evacuation. I was counting on the English to protect rights and property here in the Quarter. They will not. At least, not for today . . . If our people evacuate, as many shall wish to do, then I will lose everything." For the first time there was a hint of regret in his voice.

Yehudit nodded in understanding. As the largest property holder in the Jewish Quarter, her father would indeed lose everything if the Quarter was now to be deserted. "Yes, Father."

"So, the English will not defend. Therefore I am forced . . ." He stalled as if the words came with difficulty. "You . . . you . . . go see these Zionist hoodlum friends of yours. Tell them . . . that I will not resist them if they encourage the people to stay . . . and fight." He blinked and shook his head slightly as though he could not believe what he had just said. "This man Dov. Rebbe Vultch. The others. You know them. It is they who have caused this calamity, and now I am swept away in it against my will. We could have negotiated with the Arabs. . . . We could have. . . ." He stood mute and bitter before her.

For the first time he raised his eyes. His face was filled with revulsion and resentment when he stared at her. "So?" His eyebrows moved upward almost impercepibly as if to ask if she understood everything. "Go. . . . I will not speak with you again." He turned and was gone, his footsteps receding down the long stairway.

Yehudit gathered her shawl closely around her as she climbed the familiar steps of the community kitchen, Tipat Chalev. Its name meant "Drop of Milk," but Yehudit knew that lately the children of the Quarter were lucky if they had so much as a drop of milk in a day.

Inside there was a clamor as the youngsters stood in line to await their morning ration of watery borscht. Stale crusts of bread were being handed out with the tin cups of soup. The smaller children received theirs first.

Yehudit opened the door and stepped in quickly, as though it might slam in her face and keep her from her errand. No one noticed her at first, but her heart swelled with joy as she spotted Hannah and Shoshanna, wrinkled and bent, dishing out rations to the quarreling Krepske brothers.

"He got more than me!" shouted one.

"No! His bread is more than mine!" blurted the other.

At the threat of a fight, Shoshanna reached forward and grasped the earlocks of each boy. As they squealed with unhappiness, Hannah took their portions from them and exchanged them. "There! So! Now you have *his*! And you have *his*!" shouted Hannah over the din. "And if there is one more word from you, Shoshanna will hang you from the ceiling by your earlocks, *nu*?"

The other children roared with approval. If they enjoyed anything better than a fight between the brothers, it was witnessing their reprimand by the two old ladies. Tall and lanky, red-haired Joseph Rabinowitz banged a spoon against his empty cup, and soon the rest of the children joined him in a symphony of delighted laughter as the Krepske brothers pouted and slunk off to find an empty table where they could argue without interference.

Yehudit laughed out loud as she stepped into the center of the room.

Instantly her name was whispered down the line of children. As each child turned to stare, the room grew quiet.

"It is Yehudit!" Shoshanna cried, passing her ladle to Joseph, who took up her task. The old woman shuffled toward her with outstretched arms. "Come! Come, child! What news have you for us?"

Yehudit had not expected such a friendly greeting from those who had looked upon her with such mistrust only a week before. "Rachel . . . and the baby . . . are well," she said haltingly, a faint smile of pride on her lips.

"Yes!" Shoshanna grasped her arm. "We heard. All of it. How Stewart brought you back here in the night. . . . How you were locked in your room these many days. . . . *Oy!* Such a time you have had!" The old woman lowered her voice as she led Yehudit to the basement door. "Come now. You must tell us all! Tell us what you have seen! There is something brewing among the Muslims. . . . Come now, you must tell Dov how you escaped your father's house!"

A minute later Yehudit sat across a small wooden table from Dov and Rabbi Vultch in the basement of Tipat Chalev.

Dov's intense black eyes searched her face, lingering on her bruised cheek. "Joseph spotted the English soldiers when they brought you back the night of Passover. He said your wrists were tied behind you." Dov took her hand in his and pulled up her sleeve to see the rough, red line of a rope burn on her wrist.

"I am all right." She blushed at the attention and pulled her hand away. "I had to go with them, you see. Or they would have searched the house and found Ehud."

"Ehud!" The exclamation from Dov and Rabbi Vultch was simultaneous.

Yehudit nodded eagerly. "Yes. Ehud and Moshe. Although Moshe did not come for Passover. I did not see him at all, but Ehud said he was well. They opened the Pass of Bab el Wad and came to Jerusalem."

They gazed at her in blank astonishment. "We heard they were hanged," Dov said at last.

"No. But then Captain Stewart came. He was looking only for me, so I returned here with him to prevent my father from being shamed."

Dov reached out a finger to touch the bruise on her cheek. "And you have been a prisoner ever since."

"Y-yes," Yehudit stammered, uncertain how to respond to Dov's gentle concern. "And for my father's purpose he has let me come here," she said, suddenly serious. "Or I would spend my life in the locked room for what I have done to him." For the next several minutes she related the angry words of her father to Captain Stewart. Dov and the rabbi listened intently as she explained the reason her father had sent her here.

Finally Dov spoke. "The British expect that we will not be able to withstand any all-out attack by our neighbors, eh? We should pack up and run like old women?"

At his words, Shoshanna blustered in resentment. "*What* old women? *Oy!*" she protested.

"I meant *Turkish* women, Shoshanna." Dov peered at her over crooked spectacles that had been wired together in several places.

The old woman pulled herself up with dignity. "Turks, eh? . . . Yes. They did run when the English general came into Jerusalem! *Oy!* Such a panic! They ran away from Palestine with tablecloths full of loot slung over their backs. And along came their men schlepping behind! Such a day that was! That I should live to see such a day again!"

Dov waited patiently for Shoshanna to run down. Then he waved a hand in the air as though he could make the Arabs disappear as the Turks had done in 1917. "Patience, Shoshanna, patience, *nu?* We Old City Jews will keep our Shabbat tables covered and our good china in the cupboards."

"Even if we have no food to put on them!" the old woman said dryly.

Dov stroked his beard and frowned at the tabletop. "We still have provisions of grain from the Armenian baker. A meager amount, but perhaps we are not forgotten outside these walls. If Ehud and Moshe still live, they will remember our need."

"We must convince the people of this whether it is true or not, Dov," the rabbi said quietly. "If they leave now, the Old City is lost. Even Rebbe Akiva sees the reason of this. Even he is now willing to endorse Haganah presence in the Old City."

"For *today* he is willing." Dov clasped his hands together. "And so *today* we are suddenly allies. For different reasons, but allies nonetheless." He pulled his fingers apart. "*Tomorrow* when the English return—"

"If there is a tomorrow." Rabbi Vultch smiled wryly.

"True. True. If there is a Jewish Quarter tomorrow . . . if we are still here and the English return . . . perhaps it will not matter if Akiva is an ally any longer. If we could hold the Arabs for one day . . . if our brothers could slip through Zion Gate with one truckload of supplies, then we have justified our presence here. And it will not matter who approves of us. True? Of course true."

"You think the Britishers will come back?" asked Shoshanna.

"Most certainly," Dov said. "After the trouble is over. After we have proved that we can survive."

The old woman put a hand to her head. "*Oy!* Such a thought." She frowned. "What if the English are right and we cannot hold the Arabs?"

"Then we will not have to worry about it any longer, *nu*?" A hint of a smile was on Dov's lips. He turned his eyes back to Yehudit. "And what about you? Eh? What do you do now?"

"My father said he will not speak to me again when I go home. I believe him." Yehudit bowed her head.

"And will he beat you again? Without comment, of course. And then lock you in your room?" Dov sounded angry.

Yehudit shrugged, her eyes still downcast. "I . . . I . . . do not know what he will do. I have delivered his message. Perhaps he will have more. . . . I should go back." She lifted her head with fresh determination. At last, it seemed, her life had some purpose. An aching to belong stirred within her once again. It seemed that these people—Dov, Rabbi Vultch, and Shoshanna—really did care . . . about her, Yehudit Akiva.

Dov studied her. He shook his head slowly. "You should not go back, Yehudit," he said firmly. "If he has a message, let him bring it here to us himself. We stand between the Arabs and his property. We are the only thing that stands between him and ruin. You go with Shoshanna, eh? Stay in Rachel's flat. It is empty."

Yehudit couldn't help but feel excitement at the thought of freedom. "I . . . I would like to . . . help."

"Right. You wish to be a member of the Haganah, *nu*?"

She nodded quickly in response. "I will . . . do anything required."

Dov glanced at Rabbi Vultch, who had listened thoughtfully to Dov's suggestion. "What do you think, Rebbe Vultch?"

"She has already felt the burn of an English rope," the rabbi said. "And she has saved the life of a Jewish child. Already she has been Haganah. Only she did not know it. True?"

"Of course true," Shoshanna finished, wrapping a protective arm around the young woman. "Today we are all soldiers."

MOURNING

Freshly washed and dressed in a military uniform, the body of Ram Kadar was laid in a simple pine coffin and draped with the flag of Arab Palestine. Candles flickered in the dining room of the Sheikh Jarrah house where he lay in state.

The scent of flowers hung heavy in the air from the thousand bouquets that had been gathered from the hillsides around Jerusalem and brought as final offerings to the great commander of Palestine's Jihad Moquade forces. Bright blue lupines mingled with the red and yellow of poppies that even now seemed to wilt and shrivel like the hopes of those whom Ram Kadar had led into battle. The blush of hope had faded into the pale gray of their dead commander's face.

A special guard ringed the coffin. Rifles were held before them as they stood at rigid attention. Eyes were straight forward, but tears streamed freely down their cheeks. Outside the room, men spoke in hushed tones, each one asking who could ever take the place of Ram Kadar. The questions spilled from the somber house into the packed souks of Arab Jerusalem. *"Who is like him? Who will lead us now to victory? What must we do next?"*

For the thousands who flocked to pay Kadar homage, those questions remained unanswered. There was nothing left to do. In the end, the Jews had taken possession of Kastel, and even now fresh Jewish convoys rumbled up the undefended pass from Tel Aviv to Jerusalem. Arab warriors had left their posts to come to the city and mourn for Kadar with their comrades. To lay a flower beside his coffin. To weep with anguish at the loss of one so trusted and respected.

On every street corner and in every coffeehouse, radios boomed out the voice of the Grand Mufti, Muhammed Said Haj Amin el Husseini, from Damascus.

"My fellow Arabs of Palestine! Today we have lost a kinsman! A leader of men! A friend! We grieve together for the Jihad martyr, Ram Kadar!"

Murmurs rippled through the crowds that gathered to hear the words of the exiled leader of the Arab High Committee of Palestine. Sobs and wails of anguish stilled. The thin, reedy voice echoed and resounded in the alleyways of Jerusalem. Haj Amin transitioned from grief to passion and rage, taking the Arab population with him.

"Yes! Palestine has this day lost a brother in martyrdom to the cause of our nation! Killed at the hands of our enemies! At the hands of those who butchered our kinsmen in Deir Yassin! At the hands of those who defiled our women and butchered our children!"

Anger rumbled now. When the voice of Haj Amin floated into the room where Kadar lay, one of the guardsmen collapsed to the floor in grief. *"Ya Allah!"* he cried. *"All is lost for us! All!"* Shadows played on the cold face of Kadar. Coins closed his eyes, and his face seemed frozen in a soft smile. *"Ya Allah! Oh, god! Where shall we now turn?"*

"Remember the acts of the infidel Jews against these sons and daughters of the prophet! Remember, and steel yourself to revenge! Take no pity! Give no mercy! We must forever end this blight upon the face of the earth! The Jews must be silenced eternally!"

A roar of approval exploded from the crowds, all but drowning out the promises that followed.

"Soon we shall return to Palestine and to Jerusalem in final victory! The nations of all Islam unite with us in our fight! We shall live in freedom! Jihad!"

The masses replied with raised fists and a fierce chant: *"Jihad! Jihad! Jihad!"* Sobs returned as men tore their clothes and shouted out against the Zionists who had come to steal Arab land and murder the innocent women and children who had remained behind while brave Moquades went to do battle.

Haj Amin's words rose to a crescendo:

"Remember Deir Yassin! Remember the fallen martyr, Ram Kadar! Fight for the sake of Allah and his prophet! For the sake of Palestine!"

In the corridor of the hospital, doctors and nurses gathered tensely around a radio someone had brought in. The familiar voice of Haj Amin Husseini echoed through the hall. A stoop-shouldered physician interpreted the fury of the Arab leader for those who could not understand.

Rachel stood in the doorway of Tikvah's room and watched from a distance as the faces of the listeners reflected anger, grief . . . and fear. Although she could not hear the quiet words of the interpreter, she could feel the inflection of the Mufti's dark hatred. She did not need to understand the words to know their meaning.

A twinge of anxiety knotted her stomach as another voice raged in her memory . . . *Mama and Papa sent us to bed early, but I sat on the stairs and listened. Mama held baby Samuel very close. Papa paced back and forth in front of the radio. And then the voices. Twenty thousand in the Sportpalast of Berlin. "Heil Hitler! Heil! Heil! Heil!" It was like the sound of hell opened up. Mama held the baby closer and Papa looked at her. There was fear on his face, and even in the dim light he grew pale. And then came the voice of hate. . . .*

"He was speaking about us, wasn't he?" Rachel murmured to herself, remembering.

"What difference does it make? What business is it of anybody else if we are cleaning our house?" Then there was applause and cheers. "Nobody should trouble himself if we in Germany lead the defilers of our race through the streets to deter others." Again the mob cheered, louder this time. "The Jewish question has not, as many people assume, been solved with the assumption of power by those of the Nazi Party. On the contrary, the hardest work is only beginning!" And then they began to chant again. "Heil Hitler! Heil Hitler!" Papa put his arm around Mama's shoulder. Then he looked up and saw me. And he told me softly to go back to bed. . . .

Rachel put a hand to her head as the voice of Haj Amin raged old threats over the airways. *I was such a little girl then, Papa. Was I even ten years old? That was 1935. Why did we not run away then before it was too late, Papa? Why did we not leave Poland when we heard his threats and the way the multitudes cheered him?*

"Listen to this," said a doctor gruffly as Haj Amin continued his broadcast.

Rachel stepped closer so she could hear the interpreter.

" . . . and so, the Zionists have asked for war! They have murdered and raped! It is they who will pay the full penalty for their deeds! Once they were neighbors, you say? They came among us as rodents invade the marketplace. Seek out their nests! Destroy their young! Stamp out the

old among them! Let it be said that we who work to liberate Palestine
have finished the work that others began! They have killed our women
and children! Tortured our old ones! Do likewise to them! For the sake of
your families! Remember the fallen martyr of the Jihad! Remember Ram
Kadar, whom we bury in honor today!"

Those gathered before the crackling radio gazed at one another with
the same pale look Rachel had seen on her father's face so many years
before. "We did not leave," she whispered, "because we had no place to
go. No country that would take us in. I remember; I remember."

Rachel held Moshe's letter close to her heart and at that moment
knew what her father must have been feeling when he had looked into
the wide blue eyes of his child. A chill went through her. She wanted to
take Tikvah in her arms and find a place to hide.

The voice of Haj Amin continued to rage:

"Show them no mercy! For the glory of Allah! For the liberation of
Palestine! End the threat of the Jews forever. . . ."

Rachel glanced over her shoulder toward the sleeping child. *Where*
can we hide now, Papa? It is thirteen years since you saw me on the stairs,
and still I hear that voice. Where shall I hide? Her father had not found an
answer to that question then, and he had perished with everyone but
Rachel and Yacov.

Rachel smiled at the irony that Yacov had not even been born when
Hitler first came to power. She remembered how Papa had struggled
to find them all some place of refuge as month after month the world
grew darker. Palestine, of course, had been closed to all but a trickle of
refugees, thanks to the political power of Haj Amin. Papa had applied to
nearly every other nation that seemed outside the threat of Hitler's reach.
Then, in July of 1938, Papa's hopes had risen as the nations gathered
for the Evian Conference to debate the fate of millions of threatened
European Jews. But one after another, the representatives expressed their
unwillingness to accept refugees.

Australia, whose expanse was vast and unpopulated, declared, "As
we have no real racial problem, we are not desirous of importing one."
New Zealand would not lift its restrictions. Canada needed only workers
for agriculture, for which the Jews were obviously not suited. Colombia,
Uruguay, and Venezuela followed the same line. The worldwide empire
of England reported that in all its holdings, there was no territory suit-
able for the large-scale settlement of Jews. France had already taken
in two hundred thousand refugees and three million aliens and had

reached its saturation point. Nicaragua, Costa Rica, and Panama issued a joint statement that they could not accept "traders or intellectuals." Argentina, although it had a population of less than one-tenth of the United States, announced that it could not be counted on for large-scale immigration.

The Netherlands and Denmark followed their traditional policy of humanitarianism. Holland had already accepted twenty-five thousand refugees and continued to offer itself as a country of temporary residence for sojourners. Denmark, which was densely populated, had already taken in a large share of refugees. And the United States? Even with vast tracts of unsettled land and unlimited resources, it merely agreed to take in its legal quota of 27,370 immigrants from Germany and Austria.

Rachel remembered her father's face as he studied the news of the Evian Conference. "They have shut the doors," he had said bitterly. "Shut them." He had let the letter fall to the floor. Rachel had picked it up and read it over, finally asking her mother, "Might not we be among the lucky ones to go?"

Mama had nodded and stroked Rachel's cheek, but the worry remained in her eyes. *"Yes, perhaps we will."*

It was years before Rachel realized that those who were chosen for immigration were people with money or family in the United States. Those nations that opened their doors the widest had eventually been overrun by the Nazi war machine, and many hundreds of thousands of Jews, who dreamed that they were safe, suddenly found that the nightmare had followed them, pursuing them to mass graves that yawned open on the soil of France, Denmark, Norway, and Holland.

Look, Papa, Rachel thought. *Now I am grown. God has given me a child, and I carry a little one within me. And still the hounds are chasing us. Still I hear them baying as they circle and nip at our heels. There is no place. Still there is no place to go. Don't feel bad, Papa—you did not fail us. The world failed us. And you see, still they are doing the same. Even though you died to show them, they have forgotten already. So where can I take my little ones now, Papa? Where shall we hide?*

She lowered her eyes as the tirade of Haj Amin continued.

"The people in the Arab souks will go wild today," said a nurse.

"It reminds me of Hitler in 1938," said another.

So the broadcast had also reminded someone else of the prewar days in Germany. Without looking up, Rachel walked past the listeners, made her way down the stairs, and drew a breath of relief as she emerged in the sunlight outside the hospital. Moshe's office, in the great stone buildings of Hebrew University, was a short walk from there. She bit her lip in apprehension as she looked out over the city. It was easy to imagine groups of angry Arabs gathered before radios in coffeehouses and in the open bazaars of the Old City. The silence that hung in the air was more frightening than the sound of the Mufti's voice had been. Rachel quickened her pace and turned her eyes away from the walled enclave, where she knew hatred now simmered and grew toward an inevitable end.

Everywhere she looked, the perimeter that surrounded Mount Scopus was being reinforced. Men were digging sand and stuffing it into pillowcases gleaned from the hospital laundry. No one looked at her as she passed. They continued with their work, convinced that soon the firestorm would roll from the gates of the Old City and roar toward this one Jewish outpost in the center of the Arab districts of Jerusalem.

Rachel turned back to peer along the road through Sheikh Jarrah. Still the hulks of the burned Jewish vehicles smoked. She shuddered and held Moshe's letter tighter. Finally she broke into a trot, hurrying toward his office as though she hoped to find him waiting there.

Haj Amin Husseini dabbed sweat from his brow as he spoke to the Faithful of Palestine. The tiny cubicle inside the radio station was stifling. It seemed too small for the force of his words.

He was accustomed to the answering swell of emotion that followed his speeches. Now, as he was about to finish his broadcast, only silence returned to him. It was a silence like death. He had no way of judging the reaction of his followers in Jerusalem—or even if, indeed, they had heard him.

A swarthy man dressed in a Western business suit held up ten fingers, indicating that only ten seconds remained in airtime. The sheaf of papers in Haj Amin's hands trembled slightly as he shouted, "*Allah Akhbar!* For the sake of your homes and our nation, we must stand and fight together! *Jihad!*"

At that, the red light blinked off, leaving the voice of Haj Amin ringing in his own ears. There was no reassuring roar of approval from his audience, no rattle of rifles firing into the air.

The soundman opposite the thick glass window removed his earphones and laid them beside the panel of switches and lights before him. The distant sound of martial music crackled over the speaker. Haj Amin placed his speech in a leather carpetbag and looked up as the man in the suit opened the door to the cubicle.

"A very stirring speech, Haj Amin." The Syrian smiled, revealing a row of gold-capped teeth.

Haj Amin did not respond. Instead he eyed this minor official of the government of Syria with disregard. He raised his chin slightly and swept past the still-smiling man to where his bodyguards waited outside the cramped quarters of the radio station. Haj Amin's own words had fallen flat, echoing desperation and defeat inside his heart. At this moment, his true frustration and rage were not directed at the Zionists of Palestine, but rather at the nations of the Arab League who had filled the press with threatening rhetoric. Who had shouted against Partition and promised the Arabs of Haj Amin's forces assistance, but who had, in reality, delivered nothing.

Haj Amin tugged at the bulletproof vest under his brocade robes as his men crowded around him in a protective circle. Never before had Haj Amin felt such an intense need for protection as here and now, in the center of the political intrigue that tore through Damascus like a riptide beneath seemingly calm waters. The leaders of the Arab nations considered him a liability now. Of this Haj Amin was certain. The nations who hoped to carve up Palestine among themselves when the British withdrew cared little for the Arabs of Palestine. And with the death of Ram Kadar, Haj Amin's hope of an independent Arab Palestine finally dimmed in the cold light of reality.

As the Syrian official followed the entourage, blinking against the bright sunlight, Haj Amin swept toward the black, armor-plated Mercedes that awaited him. Two of his own men acted as chauffeur and bodyguard, assisting him as he stepped into the backseat. On the fragrant leather upholstery, the morning paper lay neatly folded in half. Already news of the fiasco of Kastel was splashed across the front page. Below that was a photograph of mangled Arab civilians of Deir Yassin. The story told how their bodies had been doused with gasoline and burned just outside the village by the Jews.

Haj Amin skimmed the paper silently as the automobile bumped back toward his hotel in Damascus. His cool blue eyes seemed without emotion as he read accounts of the survivors. He smiled slightly at the story of the Hadassah Hospital massacre. Reports were still incomplete, but sources indicated that members of the Jewish terrorist group that had attacked Deir Yassin had died in the ambush of the Jewish hospital convoy. It seemed to be a just and satisfying retribution. There was no mention of the sinking of the *Trina* in Bari Harbor, but Haj Amin had received word of the disaster before dawn.

He reached into his pocket and pulled out the crumpled telegram he had gotten from Yassar Tafara only a few hours before. He smoothed the paper and studied the words carefully.

TRINA SUNK BARI HARBOR STOP WEAPONS LOST AT HANDS OF
ZIONISTS STOP RETURNING DAMASCUS STOP TAFARA

With these words, Haj Amin had gathered his men around him. The
Arab League had promised him the contents of the *Trina,* yet their words
had come to nothing. Not only had they not come to his aid, but one
had shot at the plane of his trusted servant Montgomery. Now she was
dead. It was clear the League wanted to carve up Palestine for themselves once the Jews were exterminated. What else could they be planning against Haj Amin himself?

A taster had tested his coffee for poison as Haj Amin slipped a loaded
revolver into the folds of his robe. But no assassin had come to his suite.
Only the news of Kadar's death had entered the chamber to put an end
to Haj Amin's hope of leading Palestine. Now he contemplated a place
of safe exile.

The desolate countryside around Damascus rolled by the thick windows of the Mercedes. *I will live someplace green and verdant,* Haj Amin
thought as he calculated his personal assets.

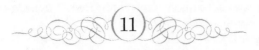

11

AMONG
THE ASHES

Ehud rode as a passenger in the lead truck of a convoy of six cargo vehicles. He carried his rifle openly, as did the other twenty-one Haganah who accompanied the cargo. The weapons were of American, British, Czech, and Russian make, with a few German guns thrown in for good measure. Along with sacks of beans and rice, crates of ammunition were included on the manifest. Clenched jaws marked the determination of the men—this was one cargo that would not be inspected without a fight . . . not after what had happened last night.

As they pulled into the Rehavia district of the city, Ehud directed the vehicles to the home of Howard Moniger. He banged his palm against the side of the truck and shouted as the Moniger house came into view, "Stop there! That house there!"

"We cannot wait more than a minute!" The driver was surly as the brakes whined and the convoy slowed to a rumbling halt.

Ehud jumped from the cab and sprinted up the steps. He slammed his massive fists against the door and shouted, "Rebbe Lebowitz! Yacov! Open the door! *Oy!* Open up, I say! It is Ehud Schiff! Open the door!"

He could hear the angry barking of Shaul. It was a sound like home, and for a moment Ehud did not want to leave. Someone fumbled at the latch, and then with a great cry of joy, Yacov flung the door wide and buried his face against the big captain.

"Ehud! Ehud! Is it you?" The boy was crying. "Rachel and the professor left and their convoy was—"

"I know." Ehud picked him up and shut the door behind him. "Your sister is well," he soothed. "She is well."

The worried face of Rabbi Lebowitz appeared at the top of the stairs. He raised his gnarled hand in silent greeting, as if words were too difficult.

"Grandfather!" Yacov cried. "It is Ehud. He says Rachel is alive!"

The old man raised his eyes toward heaven. "Then God is merciful."
He walked carefully down the stairs.

"They say she is at Hadassah," Ehud explained breathlessly. "Moshe
has gone to look for her. He sent me here in case she came ahead. But
she is not here, so she is there—" Words tumbled out almost too fast to
be understood.

"Then Moshe lives?" The old man clutched at the handrail. "God is
merciful," he said again.

The rumble of truck engines penetrated the door. "I cannot stay."
Ehud set Yacov down and tousled the boy's hair fondly. "I have only a
moment to tell you—"

"Please—" the rabbi's voice was shaking—"we have had no news
except of the murder of the doctors. We thought that Rachel and the
professor had been—" The lines on his face were deep with exhaustion
and grief.

Ehud's fists clenched involuntarily as he delivered the news. "The
good professor is dead."

The old rabbi caught his eye and nodded in understanding.

Yacov covered his face with his hands and cried out. Shaul whined
and nudged his young master.

Rabbi Lebowitz inclined his head toward Ehud, then toward the
sound of the engines. "And you . . . you are not finished yet?"

Ehud stuck out his lower lip. "I am going back. Back to the Old
City."

The old rabbi gasped. "How can this be? We hear only that the
English let our people come out from the holy places. How can you
then go back in?"

"Because of . . . last night . . . the English have pulled back. Only for
this moment it seems is the way open. The Arabs mourn the death of
their leader. No one stands guard at Zion Gate. No one."

The rabbi leaned forward slightly. "Who can go in?" His voice was
full of hope.

Ehud frowned and sucked his teeth thoughtfully. "No, Rebbe." He
answered the unspoken question. "Only soldiers. Only Haganah, I fear.
The risk is too great."

"Risk!" Rabbi Lebowitz scoffed as a horn blew impatiently outside.
"The Old City is my home. You think God is only interested in guns for
the defense of Zion? So, *nu*? You leave the prayers of the Holy City to
the likes of Akiva?" He nudged Yacov. "Get up the stairs, boy. Gather our
clothes. Quickly."

"But what of Rachel, Grandfather?"

"You did not hear? She lives. She has a husband to care for her."

Ehud backed up a step. "Rebbe Lebowitz," he stammered, "there is no time. We cannot bring you and the boy—"

The old man narrowed his eyes. "Then we shall return home on foot." He raised his voice as Yacov clambered up the stairs. "There is a note to your sister! Bring it to me! It is on the night table." He turned back to Ehud. "I had determined that Yacov and I were going home tonight, you see, Captain." He leveled his stern gaze on Ehud. "If you had not come here—blessed be the Eternal—I was taking the boy home tonight regardless, *nu*? Better to die walking toward the Holy City than to live away from it. For seventy-two years those walls have been my home—"

"Rebbe Lebowitz, you cannot come. I cannot bring you." A horn blared again. "You see. I must go now."

Yacov ran down the stairs. A white slip of paper was in his hand. "I found it. Here it is!"

"Then we shall walk through Zion Gate. And the British or the Arabs—may their brains be turned to steam—they may shoot us, but we shall die within the walls. This I had already decided." He snatched the paper from Yacov and quickly added a line at the bottom of the paper. "It is the will of the Eternal that you have come now."

"Moshe asked me to come." Ehud had his hand on the doorknob. "I am sorry, Rebbe Lebowitz. *Oy!* I am sorry. But you cannot come. It is too dangerous." He lowered his gaze. "You can pray just as well outside the walls." He opened the door and stepped out. Raising his hand in reluctant farewell, he gave a quick salute. "*Shalom—*" Then he turned and raced off toward the lead truck, which was already slowly under way.

"Captain Schiff!" The old man had stepped onto the porch and spread his hands out as if to stop the convoy. "Please! Wait!"

Ehud heard the rabbi but did not look back as the trucks roared down the deserted street. He felt the eyes of the old man and the boy burning hot on his back. It was unreasoning, ridiculous, for the old rabbi to demand to be taken along. Ehud clenched his teeth and set his eyes forward toward the shining walls of the Old City. It was, he reasoned, not his business to cart an old man and a boy over dangerous territory into a besieged area. And this small window of time might possibly be the only moment that a Jewish convoy could break through. There could be no waiting. It was sufficient that he had stopped long enough to bring the news that Rachel had survived the ordeal of Hadassah. It was more than sufficient.

Ehud rubbed a hand across the stubble of his beard as a twinge of guilt assailed him. He shook his head. No, there were other things to think of. More important things than the hopes and prayers of an old rabbi. He cleared his throat loudly, and the driver of the truck glared at him sideways as they rounded a curve that led toward Zion Gate.

"What was that all about?" asked the man.

"The old rabbi came from the Old City some months ago," Ehud explained gruffly. "He expected us to wait for him to come along with us. *Oy.* Such nonsense." He spread his hands in exasperation. "As if we don't have better things to do than to look after an old man and a boy." But the guilt returned.

"Some of those old ones have never before been outside the walls." The driver shifted into low as they moved up the rocky slope. "Some of them say this is the center of the universe." He drove in silence for several minutes. Then he asked quietly, "How many people have died for the sake of that superstition? I wonder."

Yes? How many? Ehud wondered. So many wars had been fought through the centuries to breach the walls of Jerusalem. And more and more Jews had died . . . until only a remnant was left. Ehud brooded as he searched the top of the wall for the ominous figures of British or Arab sentries. The ragged stones appeared to be empty. "There are no watchmen. Where have they all gone? Where are they?"

The domes of Al Aksa and the great Dome of the Rock towered above the Old City. Somewhere from the depths of the stone courtyard a low moan began in reply. It rose on the wind like the spiraling shriek of a deadly whirlwind until even the loud drone of the truck engines was drowned out.

Heavy mallet blows marked the sealing of the coffin of Ram Kadar in the house in Sheikh Jarrah. A high wail of grief was matched by another . . . and another . . . until the sound rolled like a flood from the windows and door into the streets and coursed up each alleyway. And then, borne on the shoulders of the Jihad Moquades, the wooden coffin was carried out into the sunlight.

Bursts of gunfire ripped the sky as men emptied their rifles. Their voices were not loud enough to express the anguish they felt at the loss of so great a leader.

"Kill the Jews!"

"Remember the martyrs of Deir Yassin!"

"Revenge for the martyrs of the Jihad!"

Thousands of rounds of precious ammunition punctuated the slogans as the din of hysteria drowned out the shattering glass and splintering wood of buildings around them.

Then, draped in the colors of a Palestinian banner, the casket was wrested from the hands of the honor guard. Men and women alike struggled for the chance to touch it briefly as it bobbed over their heads like a little boat on a stormy sea.

"Allah Akhbar! *Remember the fallen martyr! Avenge Ram Kadar!*"

Past the walls of the American Colony the remains of Ram Kadar floated on the human tide. The crowds that it had first passed over followed more slowly behind its course. It twisted upward through Musrara toward Damascus Gate and the old Muslim Quarter. A fresh burst of rifle fire erupted from the walls of the Old City as the coffin came into view.

Wild bullets felled a dozen participants in the funeral procession. The wounded scrambled to escape the unheeding feet of the crowds, or else they lay where they fell and slowly bled to death as only Ram Kadar was mourned.

There was no funeral dirge, no dignified officials to carry their leader's body through the gate. There was only the mob and the coffin and the resounding crash of guns that fired in unending succession until the very air itself seemed to explode with the sound.

No Muslim remained indoors. They hung from windows and tossed bouquets of flowers from the rooftops. The minarets were crammed with mourners who had climbed up to watch as the casket moved through the narrow streets and souks of the Muslim Quarter where Ram Kadar had been so revered. Never before had Jerusalem witnessed such an outpouring of grief . . . or such a waste of Arab ammunition.

The coffin's course was true as it twisted and turned through the alleyways; some unseen navigator had set the final destination of Ram Kadar. Over the Via Dolorosa, where legend said that Christ had carried the cross; past the Arab headquarters, where once Roman soldiers had gambled on the stones in the courtyard; through vaulted streets and past ancient Muslim tombs and landmarks—always toward the Dome of the Rock. As the coffin passed through the double gate of Bab el Silsileh and onto the ground where once the Hebrew Temple had stood, the sky above Jerusalem became dark with the acrid gunpowder that rose to heaven like a new kind of incense.

The great auditorium of Nissan Bek Synagogue was packed with frightened citizens of the Old City Quarter. The walls surrounding them were painted with murals that told the story of the destruction of the Temple two thousand years before. Now each man and woman contemplated the reenactment of the ancient legend in the Jewish Quarter. The packed gallery pitched like a restless, stormy sea while above the crowd, a Haganah soldier kept watch on the narrow scaffolding suspended from the high dome of the cupola.

Rabbi Vultch raised his hands to silence the group as Dov, acting commander of the defense, stepped forward. Small and fragile looking, Dov had the appearance of one who had spent too many years in Yeshiva school to know how to organize a defense. His trousers were baggy and ill fitting, nearly worn through at the knees. The knee-length black coat of the Hasidim was tattered and hung loosely on his slim frame. Dark eyes gazed somberly from behind wire-rimmed glasses that continually slipped down the bridge of his ample nose. Every few seconds Dov shoved them back into place whether they needed it or not, which gave the impression that he was constantly putting a hand to his forehead in deep thought. Now as Rabbi Vultch called for silence, Dov pulled his broken spectacles off and carefully cleaned them on the hem of his coat.

"Brothers!" Vultch called. "If you will listen . . . if you will only listen, *nu*? Dov has for us good news!"

"Dov!" someone scoffed from the back of the dim hall. "His name means 'Bear,' but look at him!"

Dov squinted, then put on his glasses and smiled benignly in the direction of the jibe. "It is not the size of the bear in the fight, *nu*? It is the size of the fight in the bear!" A roar of approval greeted his reply, and he pulled back his coat to reveal a bandolier of bullets and a pistol tucked into his waistband.

Rabbi Vultch raised his hands again for silence. "Dov fought the Wehrmacht in Warsaw! We should listen now!"

Dov pushed his glasses up, then stood with his finger on his forehead as a hush fell over the assembly. He cleared his throat and looked out into the sea of black coats. "Yes. I fought in the Ghetto," he said at last, "with much less than this." He tapped the pistol. "We held the German panzer at bay, and we were then a very small bear indeed!"

"And the Warsaw Ghetto was destroyed!" shouted someone from the audience. "As we will be!"

Another voice called, "Did you not see? The Britishers have left our quarter! From my window I can see the Arab mobs in the souks!"

"We will be overrun!"

Dov frowned and shook his head. "No, brothers! One of the Englishmen has told me. The Arabs have come into the Al-Harem and the Old City for a funeral! To bury their commander, Ram Kadar, who died last night in the Pass of Bab el Wad!"

The news caused another rumble of astonishment. "And what if, God forbid, the Arabs should decide to attend one funeral, then make a few more on this side of the barricade?" shouted an elderly rabbi.

"Uri," chided another octogenarian, "we are too old to worry about funerals, eh?"

"Well, I am not!" A young, black-bearded rabbi stood up. "I for one can study Torah in the New City in safety until this matter is settled!"

Dov recognized the man as a member of the anti-Zionist faction allied with Rabbi Akiva. A dozen others raised their voices in agreement.

Dov removed his pistol and placed it in plain sight on the bema. "I tell you, we held the Germans at bay with stones and homemade bombs! We can keep this Arab rabble from entering the Old City!"

"Our blood alone will not stop them! How many have left from among us already?" asked the young rabbi.

Ancient and frail, his beard in white wisps against his coat, the oldest of the rabbis stood to challenge his young counterpart. "You—" he began in a soft voice that caused all to fall silent—"you were not born here, young Levy. But I . . . I have lived some ninety-one years within these walls. Once I went beyond Zion Gate . . . only once . . . when I was a boy of ten." He raised a trembling hand toward the billowing smoke of the mural. "Is it not written, 'Out of blood and fire Judea will fall'?" All eyes followed his to the lurid image of the burning Temple. " 'And out of blood and fire it will be reborn!' "

The old man nodded at the silence that answered him. "Yes. You all have heard this. So," he challenged, "whose blood shall give birth to Zion?" He thumped his chest. "The blood of Jews! Your blood and the blood of this old man, if the Eternal so blesses me with such privilege!"

Dov raised his voice. "Do you not understand? The Pass of Bab el Wad from Tel Aviv to Jerusalem has been opened! Food convoys are pouring into the New City by now! The soldiers of Haj Amin have pulled back—"

"Yes!" challenged yet another young rabbi. "And now they are at our very gates! The British have had the good sense to leave."

"And this is our opportunity!" Dov held the pistol aloft. "The pass was opened by Jewish blood, not English! The Old City will be held by Jewish blood, not English! Our nation shall be reborn by fire and blood—our own blood. Perhaps in the flames of what we most love." He lifted his chin to gaze into the dome of the cupola. "But we will remain. Even in the ashes, brothers, we will be reborn, as it is written."

Rabbi Vultch added, "Now it is our own watchmen on the walls! You shall see! Our brothers beyond the gates will not forget the holy places. We must stand firm and trust!"

The very old rabbi stood and carefully picked his way through the crowded room toward the front of the bema. "Only once I left the Old City. I will not do so again." He smiled a toothless smile. "Where shall my post be?" he questioned Dov. Then he turned to the men. "And who shall remain to serve with me?"

The oldest men stood first. Shopkeepers and scholars, they shuffled forward. Some leaned heavily on their canes; others helped their comrades. As they formed a proud line of stooped soldiers with trembling limbs, the younger men, shamed by their elders, came forward one at a time until only a few remained on the hard benches.

Just then a crash of Arab rifle fire raked the sky above the Muslim Quarter.

Dov raised his head and smiled, knowing that every bullet spent in this demonstration for the fallen Arab leader was one less threat to the blood of the tiny Jewish Quarter.

12

IN THE SHADOW OF DEIR YASSIN

The headquarters of the British High Command was high atop the Hill of Evil Counsel, to the southeast of Jerusalem. From this vantage point, those who served in the office of the British high commissioner were near enough to see the smoke of a riot but far enough removed that the cries of the people had faded away in the wind. It was, in this way, much like the policies that governed Palestine in these last weeks . . . very distant from the human element of suffering.

Colonel Robert Halloway watched from the window of his office as a thin column of darkness rose into the sky just beyond the Dome of the Rock. "The Arabs are at it again," he muttered, standing with his hands in his pockets for a full minute as the smoke darkened and spread. A rattle like popcorn sounded from far away. Gunfire. He shook his head in disgust at the ridiculous habit the Arabs had of wasting enormous amounts of ammunition.

With a sigh, he sat down at his impeccably neat desk and flipped open a file to review it before he flipped the switch of his intercom. "Captain Stewart, please, Miss Hibbs."

"Right, sir."

A moment later the door swung open and Stewart strode in with his hat tucked under his arm. He stood erect and saluted, waiting until Halloway returned a halfhearted salute and pointed to a heavy, red-leather, wingback chair. Halloway continued to review the details of the report in front of him while Stewart stared out the window.

At last Halloway closed the file and laid it to one side. "Well, Stewart," he said, leaning back in his chair and rubbing a hand over his receding hairline, "you were the officer on duty last night. What is your explanation?"

Stewart spun his hat slowly around in his lap. He raised his eyebrows as though he did not understand the question. "Your pardon, sir?"

"Come off it, man," Halloway spat. "The Jewish Agency is raving mad at this! And little wonder! Seventy-five civilians massacred under our very noses! They claim headquarters was called for help a dozen times! For an armored vehicle!"

"They got help." Stewart was cool and unruffled. "As soon as it was available."

"How many Jews escaped? Six? And an American professor killed to boot."

"Corporal Chandler did his duty." Stewart's voice was level. He tapped at the shiny brim of his hat. "He lost the machine gunner. There is a British fatality in that report, you may well note, sir."

Halloway slammed his hand solidly on the desk. "After how many hours, Stewart?" He swore softly. "You were in charge."

"And following orders. Orders are to send as many British soldiers home alive from this place as is possible."

Halloway swallowed another oath and gritted his teeth. "Why weren't we contacted here sooner?" he hissed menacingly.

Stewart smiled slightly and looked out the window again. "I thought you had been."

Halloway considered the man who sat before him. Stewart had always seemed the model of the perfect soldier. A row of ribbons on his chest spoke of valor and accomplishment. He commanded the respect of his men and had volunteered for this despicable duty when other men were clamoring for a boat ticket home to England.

But there was one aspect of Stewart's personality that Halloway had seen only since the young man's arrival in Palestine. He was a racist, an anti-Semite in the truest sense of the word. And it was little wonder, considering the death of his brother at the hands of Jewish terrorists two years before. It had been Halloway's recommendation that placed Stewart in his present command. Now the colonel was ready to admit that he might have made a mistake. "All right, Stewart, you hate the Jews. But a convoy full of doctors, for heaven's sake . . ."

A muscle in Stewart's jaw twitched. "I did not pull the trigger. This is a nasty business between the Arabs and the Jews. The latest order from London was to remain uninvolved, if possible."

"Yes. Quite. But the murder of civilians—"

"Like the Arab villagers of Deir Yassin?" The corner of Stewart's mouth turned up slightly. He had won his argument. "The rule of Palestine is an eye for an eye, Colonel Halloway. And I, for one, wish to retain my vision for the trip back to Trafalgar Square."

"A question of judgment, I suppose," Halloway conceded. "I might have called it differently. Called for intervention sooner."

"And there undoubtedly would have been more English names on today's death rolls. I did what I felt was my duty. British lives first. British lives at all costs. Wasn't that the order?"

"Yes. That was the order. It remains so. And we have come under sharp criticism from the nations of the world because of it."

"Soon the world will be the policemen of this state. Then let them criticize."

Halloway let his breath out slowly as he stared over the top of Stewart's head. He shook his head. "Quite. They'll find it out soon enough. Today the Jews are carrying their weapons openly. As are the Arabs. Two more Jewish convoys have arrived from Tel Aviv while this"—he jerked a thumb toward the site of Kadar's funeral—"is going on. When we leave, Stewart, the only hope of any sort of disciplined army will come from the troops of the Arab Legion of Transjordan. Led by an Englishman. Equipped by our surplus supplies. The rest of the Arabs are a rabble. Peasants led by uneducated hoodlums controlled by Haj Amin."

He dropped the barrier of authority and leveled his gaze confidentially at Stewart. "If you ask me, the United Nations may have it all, and welcome. I'm for a nice easy post training recruits back home."

Captain Stewart smiled appreciatively, but he felt no empathy for Colonel Halloway's words. He was angry at the United Nations. Angry at the world that sat back in judgment against the policies of Great Britain. The same attitudes that had lost India to the likes of Gandhi were now about to open up the Middle East to an invasion by Russia.

"Well, I'm just a soldier," Stewart said. "What do I know about foreign policy? Until we leave, I'll do my best to keep the peace. Arrest those I see with weapons—"

"By the way—" Halloway leaned forward in a burst of energy—"it was you who captured Moshe Sachar and Ehud Schiff, was it not?"

Stewart nodded curtly. "Yes. They headed the Haganah within the Old City. Of course, now that they are gone—"

"Well, they have been sighted. Several times."

"Good. Then we'll have them back behind bars where they belong." There was satisfaction in the thought.

Halloway stuck out his lower lip and laughed abruptly. "Not according to General Staff."

"What are you talking about?" Stewart's voice was low and hoarse.

Halloway nodded and held a piece of paper out to Stewart. "New information, it seems. The chaps are innocent. Pure as the driven snow.

It is a blessing that they were not hanged—" He was smiling sarcastically now.

"This can't be!" Stewart angrily snatched the paper from Halloway's hand.

> *Captured Jewish terrorists interrogated after the Deir Yassin raid have yielded further information as to the innocence of Professor Moshe Sachar and Ehud Schiff in the Jaffa Gate bombing. . . . Charges to be dropped . . .*

The memo went on, but Stewart read the words *charges to be dropped* again and again. He felt the blood rise to his cheeks in outrage. "All well and good, but Sachar was the one organizing the entire defense of the Old City! What of that?"

Halloway shrugged. "What of it? Everyone in Palestine, it seems, is carrying a weapon. After what happened last night to the hospital convoy personnel, the decision has been made that perhaps they are justified in doing so. We are to stay clear of it."

Stewart raised his chin defiantly. "If I see Moshe Sachar, I can guarantee he will be in jail again."

"Sorry to disappoint you, but you will guarantee nothing of the sort. The fellow is internationally known. Unless he breaks the law—"

"He has done so—"

"He has been exonerated of the Jaffa Gate bombing, I tell you. The papers will have it this afternoon."

"But the other charges!"

"Self-defense. The high commissioner has offered him a pardon. If he is harassed while he is obeying the law, you will be dismissed. Of course, if you should find him actively involved in breaking the law—"

"This is a travesty!" Stewart said as he flipped the paper back toward the colonel.

"His innocence has certainly cast doubts on our judicial system here in Palestine. Of course, the Jewish Agency is pushing this for every mile of publicity it can." Halloway lowered his chin and studied Stewart. "Whatever you have in mind, Stewart, forget it. You are on the edge anyway with this fiasco last night. We can dismiss that as a question of judgment. But if you pursue any course of harassment against this chap, you are finished. The Arabs have reserved a bullet for him, at any rate. Remember, it is not your concern."

Stewart swallowed hard and changed the subject. "Are you saying that we may no longer enforce the no-weapons rule against the Jews in the Old City? And in all of Jerusalem?"

"Let's be quite clear, Captain Stewart. Our main concern is for the welfare of British subjects. That includes our forces here. If their lives are threatened as they perform their duty, then do what you must. Otherwise, confiscate weapons; then stand clear of the Jews. Stand down from the middle of this. The Arabs will take care of the situation soon enough, and we would not like to appear the villain in this melodrama."

"According to American newspapers we already are," Stewart said sourly as he mulled over the thought of Moshe Sachar and his buffoon of a friend walking free on the streets.

"The United Nations will inherit something quite beyond them, I'm afraid. Then they will see they've judged us too harshly. In the meantime, let's not give them anything else to criticize, shall we?" He leveled a finger at Stewart. "It is no secret how you feel, old fellow, and no one blames you, considering what happened. But it is important that we maintain our image of fairness in all this. Justice is the thing, isn't it? We'll let the Jews and the Arabs take one another's eyes, and we'll be the only ones left who still can see."

Ahkmed gripped Sarai's small hand tightly in his as they walked together. She shielded her eyes against the sunlight. A warm breeze blew, causing her black robe to billow up. Their footsteps and the rustle of her garments were the only sound in the now-deserted streets. In the far distance the roar of those who followed the coffin of Ram Kadar was clearly audible.

Ahkmed felt suddenly alone. It seemed as though his whole world had died, leaving houses vacant and litter on the cobblestones. "They have all gone to the Al-Harem," he murmured to himself. "Everyone has gone to see Ram Kadar laid to rest in the walls of the Dome of the Rock."

Sarai did not respond. She did not seem to hear him, and he heard her mutter softly, "*Ya Allah.* Oh, god."

Vacant windows gazed down on the two as they walked in the center of the street. Ahkmed raised his voice a little louder and pulled the revolver from his pocket. "Everyone grieves for Ram Kadar." His eyes darted across the silent stones of the buildings that towered over them. "We have made even the Jews to weep for what they have done." Sarai still did not answer, and he continued, "I will show you, little cousin. I will take you so that you might see. Your disgrace has been avenged. Those who cause your death shall also know that they go down into the dust of the earth."

A great wail swept across the sky from the direction of the mosque.

"You shall see how we repaid them in kind for their murder and abuse. You are avenged, Sarai." A canvas awning flapped, and then a roar of gunfire cracked the air above the Old City as thousands of bullets rose from Arab guns.

Sarai followed his guiding hand with a reluctant shuffle. He led her to a knoll overlooking the smoking hulks of Jewish vehicles that lay in the center of the road to Sheikh Jarrah. She did not raise her eyes to look at the gruesome spectacle until Ahkmed spoke. "You must see." He pulled her around in front of him. "You are avenged." He pointed to the smoldering ashes of what had been a bus.

She raised her eyes slowly, blinking hard at the sight. "Are these the bones of those who raped me and mocked me?" she asked in a barely audible voice.

"These are the ashes of Jews, and soon all who still live will also be ashes. None shall live who injured you, my cousin." His voice trembled, and his eyes were fierce. "And for your life I shall take the lives of a thousand Jews myself!" He raised his revolver and fired into the air, the sound of his bullet merging with the distant rage of the others.

"And when they are all dead—" Sarai turned her gaze to the rigid features of Ahkmed—"will that then return to me my husband? my village? my life?"

Ahkmed lowered his outstretched arm. The look of triumph faded. "I will do this for you," he said, his voice trembling with grief.

"But first you must help me." She was crying again. She sank to her knees and lifted her hands to him. "You must end my shame. You must give me rest as they would not, though I begged them. . . ."

He nodded once. "Then fix your eyes on the fate of the wicked. Their deaths were more terrible than the ending of your life." He cocked the revolver and pointed the barrel of the gun at her right temple.

She closed her eyes and whispered, "There is no god but Allah. . . ."

The silent gun shook violently in Ahkmed's frantic grip. "*Ya Allah!* Cousin! May you live in Paradise." Tears streamed down his cheeks as yet another volley of gunfire erupted from the Muslim Quarter of the Old City.

Sarai wrapped her arms around his knees and cried softly, "*Allah Akhbar. Allah Akhbar . . .*" as she waited for the bullet to end her misery.

Haganah trucks bearing supplies to Hadassah Hospital tore through the deserted quarter of Sheikh Jarrah, taking advantage of the fact that now no Muslim remained outside the walls of the Old City.

Moshe and two other men sat in the cab of the lead truck as they topped the rise that led down to the scene of the small holocaust at the foot of Mount Scopus. The stench of the burning was almost overwhelming as the charred remains of the vehicles came into view. His hands became clammy, and he was instantly drenched in a cold sweat. *Howard perished here.* The continuation of that thought led him into the terror of those who died—and the six who had survived—last night. He could only see Rachel among them and hear her voice as he pictured the flames surrounding them.

The driver first slowed at the sight of the spectacle. Then he shoved the accelerator to the floor until the man beside him pointed to a knoll at the side of the road. "Look! *Oy vey!* What's that?"

In spite of the horror that filled him, Moshe's gaze followed the direction of the second man's outstretched arm. There, beyond the charred earth, an Arab woman dressed in black was clutching at the knees of a man who held a gun to her head. At the sound of their approach, the Arab man looked up, startled. Then he crouched, hesitated, and fired his gun at the Jewish trucks.

"He's going to kill that woman!" shouted the driver, swerving as a bullet pelted the iron skin of the truck.

"Or us!" shouted the second man. "Get him!"

The driver slammed on the brakes, and Moshe leaped from the truck, taking shelter behind the massive steel plate as another bullet clanged against the vehicle. Moshe had no gun. He ducked low as half a dozen Haganah men rolled out onto the road and took aim at the young Arab.

As the veiled woman screamed and covered her head, the man fired three more shots before a Jewish bullet slammed into his body. He seemed to hang, suspended in agony for a moment, before his empty revolver tumbled to the ground. Then he crumpled to the earth on top of it.

A cheer arose from the Haganah men as the Arab lay twitching in a final contortion of death. The woman screamed and tore her veil from her face, throwing herself against the body of the Arab. The roar from the Old City now drowned out her cries as the Jews ran toward her and circled her with hands outstretched to aid the woman they had just saved from death.

CLUES

As the train left the station, David pulled Ellie down a corridor lined with private compartments. One after another, he jerked open the doors of the berths, then slammed them shut as startled passengers turned to glare at him for the unannounced interruption. Quickly checking the right of the aisle, then the left, he finally found one door ajar and the tiny cubicle empty.

Pulling Ellie after him, he flung the carpetbag onto a narrow bench, closed the door behind them, and locked it.

Ellie was trembling with the certain fear that whoever had murdered Mikhail and Bernie was now in pursuit of them. "What should we do?"

David did not answer simply because he had no answer to give. "Pray there's a gun in here," he said as he opened the carpetbag and peered in at the jumble of contents. Men's shirts and trousers were on top. He dropped the bag, pulling out a manila envelope, which he tossed onto the seat. "Take a look," he instructed Ellie as he continued to rummage.

Her hands shook so badly that it was difficult to open the envelope. She drew a sharp breath when a .38 revolver emerged from the bag and David held it aloft.

"Here's our ticket," he said, his words reflecting the anger and desperation he felt. "What have you got?"

Ellie upended the envelope and gave a little cry of relief as an American passport with her own picture on it tumbled to the floor. "That's *me*!" she said in wonder. "*My* picture. *My* passport!" David retrieved the document from her feet as she dumped three other passports onto her lap.

"That's you, but not your name." He looked at it closely. "These guys are good. I mean, they are really good."

The pages contained stamps of a dozen different countries. Each one looked authentic. "Here is one for you." She lowered her voice. "And

Bernie. British. A special visa here for someone named Helgam Gregof. No photo."

"That would have been for Mikhail." David flipped through the pages of his passport. "I'm still American, I see. Hope someone tells the State Department. The passport has my occupation listed as aeronautics specialist."

"I'm in public relations for Service Airways."

"Good cover. Looks like we're traveling together, even though they've given us different last names."

"Zelda Sue Conner! Someone's idea of a bad joke."

"It's just bad enough to be believable. I'm James Clement Madison."

David took the two extra passports and opened the window slightly to drop them out. Then he pulled the shade and sat down beside Ellie to examine the other contents of the bag. A well-worn wallet contained a thick stack of bills—French, Italian, and British notes. There were photos of people whom he had never seen before: a slim girl in a swimsuit and an elderly couple holding a small shaggy terrier.

"The usual bits of flotsam and jetsam from a wallet," he said absently. "No instructions. Nothing at all." He looked stricken as he examined each piece of paper in the wallet. "Okay. We've got passports. About six hundred bucks American, give or take, but they've cast us adrift. All we have here is a stack of junk from some guy's wallet. Laundry receipts and stuff. No instruction. No numbers. I don't even know how to get in touch with the guys in Rome now that Bernie is dead." He sat in stunned silence as Ellie laid out the contents of a man's shaving kit in front of her.

The items were sparse, limited only to the necessities of one man. "Razor. Toothbrush and powder. Hairbrush. Soap. Fountain pen. Pipe and matches." She drew a deep breath, her trembling finally subsiding into weak exhaustion.

"What do they want us to do? What do they expect?" David was angry at the abandonment by the very people they had risked their lives to help. "We can't go back to the States. Palestine is out. We'd be arrested the minute we set foot on the tarmac of the airport at Rome. Those two guys at the hangar are the only ones I know—"

"Just a minute, David," Ellie said impatiently. "They wouldn't do this to us. There has got to be something. Something we're overlooking. If Bernie were here, he would know."

David ran his hand through his hair in frustration. "Well, some-body should have let us civilians in on the secret. So what's your idea, anyway?"

"There was this guy. In the press corps in Jerusalem. He was British, but had worked in France in the underground during the war. One night he was drinking. Gin and tonic—"

"What's the point?"

"Well, he got to talking . . . you know, tricks of the trade. He talked about the ways they used to hide stuff from Nazis—secret messages and stuff. I told him he ought to write a novel someday—"

David's impatience surfaced. "The point, Els, the point! Get to it! So where did they hide these messages?"

"Everywhere. In razors and bars of soap and tooth powder and pens and . . ."

David picked up the briar pipe and tapped it gently on his palm. "And pipes?"

"Wasn't the man at the station smoking a pipe?"

David had already begun unscrewing the stem from the bowl. His eyes were filled with anticipation. "Right. The pipe. I smelled the tobacco before I even saw him. And he was the one who warned me to get you out. Quick."

Ellie nodded.

Just then someone rapped on the door of the compartment. An angry voice called in Italian, then French, and finally heavily accented English.

"Porter. Open upa da door!" the repeated as Ellie scooped the contents of the bag back into the carpetbag.

David replied in a loud and sleepy-sounding voice as he slowly unlocked the door. "Coming!"

The shocked round face of the porter greeted him. Eyes went instantly to David's collar. "Apologies, Father." The little man bowed. "This isa empty compartment, no? Your ticket, Father."

David flung the door wide so the porter could see Ellie still in her habit with the bag on her lap. "My assistant, uh, the sister and I were just looking for our tickets, you see. . . . It seems they have been misplaced. . . ."

The porter gaped at the pretty young nun sitting demurely on the seat. Ellie nodded slightly at him. "Well, Father ana Sister—" he tipped his cap—"this your compartment isa not. It ist empty."

"No, it is not," David gently corrected. "We are in it."

"But tickets you musta have."

David pursed his lips. "We have lost ours, it seems."

"Then ina this compartment you cannot ride."

David cleared his throat. "We would like to buy two tickets, then."

"*Si*, but—"

David pulled out the wallet and ran his thumb over the bills. "Two tickets."

"*Si,* Father!" The porter's eyes lit up.

"Where is the train going?"

For an instant, the little man looked confused. "Where you are going you do nota know?"

"I know where I am going. I just want to know where this train is going."

The porter clicked the destinations off on his fingers. "Florence. Bologna. Placenza. Milano. Turin. Susa—"

"But where is it ultimately going? I mean in the end."

"Paris, Father."

"That is where *we* are going."

A few minutes of negotiations took place. David paid the porter, promised him a good tip when he returned, then shut the door and locked it as the man scurried off to make up two tickets to Paris.

Ellie was already digging out the contents of the carpetbag. With one tug she pulled the stem from the bowl of the pipe and held it to the light. With a moan of disappointment, she handed the pieces to David. "Nothing. Just a pipe."

David examined the briar bowl, then tossed it onto the seat next to Ellie. For a moment, both of them contemplated the other items that were laid out beside her.

"So what next?" David ran his fingers over his cheek.

"You could use a shave." Ellie picked up the safety razor and held it to the light.

"We don't even know what we're looking for!"

Ellie was already dissecting the razor with tight-lipped intensity. Carefully she opened the head and turned the blade over to examine it for a message. There was none. "Harrel said they used to hide stuff in razors all the time—"

"Who's Harrel?"

"The guy I told you about. From the underground." As the pieces of the razor fell into Ellie's lap, David took them one by one and conducted his own search.

Five minutes later, the razor was a small heap of useless metal between them. Ellie had just attacked the fountain pen with the same determination when the porter rapped softly on the door.

"*Mi scusi*—you tickets, Father," he called.

David cracked the door slightly and took them from the man, then slipped him another bill and scanned the tickets. "What if we want to change destinations?"

"You cash ina da ticket, Father. Isa nota problem, *si*? I can do some-thinga more for you?" he asked as he examined the cash with amazement. It was unusual that a priest would tip at all. This was more than generous by any standards.

David tucked the tickets safely away and glanced to where Ellie had just broken the pen. "I could use a razor," he said dryly.

"Of course, Father."

"And a pen."

"*Si*."

Ellie was unscrewing the lid to the tooth powder. "And tooth powder, if you have it," David added.

"*Si*. A simple request, no?"

David nodded and shut the door. Sliding the bolt into place, he watched Ellie as she tapped the can and white powder spilled onto the black nun's habit she wore. "Tooth powder in the tooth powder, huh?" he asked, still feeling abandoned. "I'll bet we're going to find soap in the soap, matches in the matchbox, and a hairbrush in the hairbrush."

Ellie did not reply. Instead she demolished the contents of the shaving kit one after another in search of a message that was not to be found.

David crossed his arms and stared skeptically as Ellie smashed the bar of soap with the heel of her shoe. When the search proved fruitless, she shoved the pieces back into the leather case and crossed her arms in angry frustration.

"Well, I guess that's that," she said at last. "They've paid us off and left us to fend for ourselves."

"Let's face it, Els. We're poison. They aren't going to have anything to do with us until the flak over the *Trina* dies down. We really *are* on our own."

"But why—?"

"If one of our guys gets near us, he could be nabbed too. I'd say they're hoping we get away. After all, we got these phony identification papers . . . but they aren't going to get within a thousand miles of us."

"But, David . . ."

"It doesn't really matter where we go. They're through with us." He was still angry. "Six hundred bucks isn't going to last long."

"Looks like the Old Man is finally giving us a vacation," she quipped.

"I wouldn't mind so much if we hadn't left Bernie and Mikhail in a puddle of blood in Rome." He put his head in his hands. "Or if I knew who did it. Or why. And whether they're looking for us, too." He stared at the floor for a long time. "You want to go any place besides Paris? Like I said, it doesn't matter."

"Paris is fine," she whispered in a barely audible voice. "Paris in springtime . . . and I don't even have a camera."

David checked the contents of the wallet once again and decided that he would not tip anyone else. "The place is jammed with little hotels," he offered. "We can make it on a few francs a day if we're careful and lie low. Paris is a big city. Big enough that we can disappear for a while. That's what they want us to do."

"Maybe we could get in touch with Uncle Howard," Ellie said hopefully. "He could tell them where we are. . . ."

"Nothing doing." David's voice was stern. "Every letter and wire into Palestine is subject to investigation. Howard Moniger is probably being tailed by everyone from the British Foreign Service to the American Embassy. Let's give it a week. Or two weeks. Or until the money runs out. If these are the rules they want to play by . . ."

"I'm scared, David," Ellie said as she moved into his embrace. "For the first time it hit me that we *can't* go home! And all of a sudden, nothing means more to me!"

He held her against his chest and hoped she could not hear his fear in his heartbeat. "Remember the sparrow," he said finally. "Remember . . ." He tried to encourage her, but his words sounded hollow, even to him.

Crabtree leaned heavily on the worn counter in the lobby of the Bari Harbor Hotel. His feet hurt and he was tired, but four hours mingling with the local population at dockside had yielded him a wealth of information. He patted his coat pocket, checking for his precious notepad out of habit. Right now it was even more important than his wallet.

The rest of the European reporters were still milling around the *Trina*, gathering information and rehashing bits of news that Tree had long ago gleaned from snatches of conversation. And while they made their way to middle-class lodgings in the heart of Bari, Tree had chosen this location as his headquarters. He gazed around the seedy interior of the lobby. It reeked of old garlic and mildew. Paint chips flaked from the high, water-stained ceiling, and the worn-out sofas and chairs spilled stuffing from their cushions.

The metal cage of the elevator groaned and squeaked as it rose slowly beside the stairway. It moved even more slowly than the broad-hipped redhead who walked languidly up the stairs. Tree eyed her appreciatively until she disappeared into the hallway at the same moment the elevator clanged to a stop. He turned to pound the bell once again and was met by the large, smiling face of Madame Hortencia, who blinked at him with an air of innocent curiosity.

"I see you are a man who appreciates a beautiful girl. No, signore?" she asked in Italian.

Tree replied in nearly flawless Italian, with only a slight trace of American accent. "In Italy they seem to drop from the trees. Like good fruit."

She threw her head back in laughter, her double chin wagging with delight. "You have been in Italy long enough to know," she said at last, blotting her brow with a lace handkerchief. "Still, I can tell you are American! Oh yes! I recognize the accent!"

"That is correct. *Si.* I am American, but I have made Italy my adopted home. And now I would like a room. Perhaps with a view of the harbor?"

"And you would also enjoy a companion?" She nodded in the direction of the redhead.

Tree pretended to be tempted. For an instant he entertained the thought, then shook his head. "No. *Grazie,* madame, but no. I am, alas, here on business."

"You cannot enjoy a little pleasure with your business?"

"No, madame. My wife lies dying at this very moment in Rome. And out of respect for her . . ."

Madame Hortencia crossed herself and gazed at him with sympathy. "I am sorry, signore. Of course, yes. For your poor wife . . ."

"But perhaps I would like conversation. Yes. I am a very lonely man. Perhaps if you have a girl who is very good at conversation—"

"Oh yes! *Si!* Of course I have such girl! Several, in fact!"

"And it might be helpful also if she spoke English well."

"Of course! Of course!" She shoved the registration book across the counter. "A view of the harbor and a girl who speaks English! Yes! A simple request."

Tree stuck out his lower lip thoughtfully and took the pen. "My business is quite confidential."

Madame Hortencia's thick lips formed an *O,* and she nodded rapidly. "You need not sign your real name, signore."

"Good." He appeared relieved and signed with a sense of satisfaction at the woman's obvious curiosity.

"Is it about the *Trina?* the ship?"

Tree put a finger to this lips and glanced furtively around the lobby. "A very nasty business. All the reporters roaming about Bari. I would not want any of it to get to the reporters. There has been a very large reward fund set up, you see, and . . ."

Madame's penciled eyebrows rose in an arch of excited surprise. "A reward!"

"Shhhh!" Tree was satisfied that the bait was being nibbled before the eyes of the hunter. "I am hoping no newspaper people will be staying here. They must not know of my investigation."

Again the madame crossed herself. "By all the saints, there is no one—and if they come, I shall tell them there are no rooms." She narrowed her eyes. "A reward, you say. How much? And for what is it to be given?" Her voice was low and thick with calculating greed.

"I have said too much already. I should not say more. A very complicated case of international intrigue. The United Nations is quite eager to get to the bottom of it."

The madame paled at the mention of the United Nations. She thumped her chest and drew back, her eyes wide. "Of course! *Si!* It is no wonder you must remain secretive! And I shall not breathe a word of your presence!"

"That is best. . . . Just a bit of diversion would be helpful. A young woman who can talk, as I said. To take my mind from my troubles and these troubled times."

Madame Hortencia stood rooted to the floor in a sense of awe that her poor establishment had been so honored by an investigator for the United Nations. In salute, she crossed herself again, then turned about-face to fumble for the key to the room that best overlooked the wreckage of the *Trina.*

Mentally checking off her list of girls, she settled on the broad-hipped redhead who had ascended the stairs a few minutes before. The truth was, none of her girls spoke more than a few words of English, but this American investigator spoke Italian well enough. Perhaps Sophia would stir his interest so it would not matter that the only English she spoke was the word *yes.* As a matter of fact, that was a word that Sophia knew in a dozen different languages.

Madame Hortencia smiled and handed the man the key as she rang the bell and shouted for a porter.

A ragged, tousled-haired boy emerged from the back office. "*Si,* Mama," he said in a drowsy voice.

"Help this important gentleman with his bag." She snapped her sausage fingers and pointed at the man's scuffed suitcase. "Room 18."

"*Si,* Mama." The boy looked curiously at the investigator. "He is a foreigner?"

"An American. But that is none of your business." She raised her hand threateningly. He was to ask no more questions.

With an air of indifference, the boy picked up the bag and struggled toward the elevator.

Tree recognized the boy from dockside. He spoke English quite well and had been in the thick of the reporters interviewing every dockhand and lackey who had been within a mile of the explosion.

After a moment, Tree cleared his throat. "I would like a good lunch, madame. In my room. With a bottle of wine. You will send the boy up with it in an hour."

"You would like your companion to sup with you?"

"No. I will eat alone." He glanced at his watch. It read eleven-thirty. "Send the girl after."

"As you wish." She bowed slightly and batted her eyes at him. "Such an important official. I am certain you have work to do, no?"

Again he put his finger to his lips to feign confidentiality. "Not a word," he whispered, certain that the woman would spread information about him like warm butter on hot bread. Soon informants would be lined up around the block to offer him bits and pieces of the puzzle. Most would be of no value, but perhaps one might come forward with one bit of unexplored information. With what he had already gathered, he had enough to at least make the late edition of the European *New York Times*. Whether his story was made up of mostly fact or fiction at this point seemed immaterial to Tree.

He smiled, inwardly certain that by two-thirty this afternoon he would have enough to stop the presses and sell out the newsstands.

14

WAITING

Dov crouched behind the sandbagged barricade that marked the farthest boundary of the Jewish Quarter and the Armenian Quarter. A dozen others were with him. Their fingers were poised and ready at the triggers of their weapons as they waited for the inevitable Arab onslaught.

Every rooftop and crooked street in the Old City was likewise held by the few defenders who had finally pulled their rusty weapons out of hiding. Ammunition was precious, and as Dov left the meeting at Nissan Bek, he had passed the word to every defender that each Jewish bullet must find its mark.

Most of the men now under Dov's command had never fired a real cartridge. They had practiced with empty rifles aimed at silhouette targets placed against the basement walls of the Old City synagogues. As Dov looked down the line, he saw the faces of frightened but determined men, and for an instant he remembered his fallen comrades of Warsaw as they had hurled homemade firebombs and rocks at advancing Nazi Panzer units. The Germans had called their action an *Einkesselung*, "encirclement." But the Jews had called the German work a *kesl*, a "cauldron." Smoke and fire, anguish and terror had seethed and whirled in a living hell that called to mind Dante's *Inferno*.

The roar of the fire, the noise of falling walls, and the screams of the dying returned to Dov as once again he waited to die. It had been spring then, too, when he fought against the Nazis in Warsaw. Outside the Ghetto walls the world had been green, but where he fought a holocaust had raged.

Is this day not an anniversary? He gazed at his brave little band of fighters. *Yes. Early April, Passover. The reading of the Haggadah shattered by gunfire and shell bursts. How we wept as the rabbi read, "Pour out thy wrath upon the heathen that have not known Thee, and upon the kingdoms that have not called upon Thy name. For they have devoured Jacob, and laid waste his dwelling place."* And *we were the living torches who fell from burning buildings that day. Fell into the cauldron . . .*

A month later, Warsaw had fallen while seventy-five Jews escaped through the sewers and slime beneath the city. Dov had been among those few, and now he listened and remembered the hundreds of thousands who perished in the Ghetto.

"Will they attack this way?" asked one of Dov's men—a nervous, bookish-looking Hasid.

"If they do," Dov said calmly, pointing to the narrow corridor before them, "then they are bigger fools than we are for staying here!"

Nervous laughter replied, but beads of sweat stood out on every forehead.

The sound of the funeral drowned out the low moan of truck engines as the six Jewish trucks crept up the exposed face of Mount Zion toward Zion Gate.

Unknown to Ehud, Rabbi Lebowitz and Yacov had climbed aboard the last truck in the line. Now they crouched together beneath the canvas while Shaul pressed himself against the body of his small master. A young man who had once attended school in the Old City shared the cargo area with them. He had instantly recognized the old rabbi and Yacov and had extended his hand to help them aboard as the trucks began to pull away from the big house in Rehavia.

"Rebbe Lebowitz!" the young, smooth-shaven man shouted above the din. "Keep your head covered!"

"A good Jew," the rabbi replied, "always has his head covered! *Nu?*"

"Ha! A good one, Rebbe Lebowitz! That is why I always enjoyed your class!" His words were lighthearted, but his face was pale as he searched the high walkway of the Old City walls for the Arab snipers who had terrorized Mount Zion for months.

The rabbi's face was pale as well as he cupped his hands to call to the man, "So! You know my name! But I never had a student in Yeshiva dressed like you!" Another louder volley of Arab bullets nearly drowned out his words.

"I am . . ." The name was lost in the cacophony that shook the earth beneath them.

"Who?"

"Nahum! Nahum Kowalsi!"

The truck lurched violently around a curve, and a flour barrel turned over and cracked, revealing a load of ammunition. Yacov scrambled to right it, but the young soldier pulled him flat against the rough planks of the truck bed.

"Nahum!" The old man continued as though nothing really important had happened. "You shaved! Tell me . . . have you forgotten how to pray since you left Yeshiva school?"

"Why do you think I helped you aboard, Rebbe?" The jarring ride knocked another crate to the floor, narrowly missing Nahum's head.

"You want I should say mourner's kaddish over you?"

"In about another sixty years, Rebbe Lebowitz! Keep your head down, if you please. I don't want to say kaddish for *you!*" The young man lifted the canvas flap and peered cautiously toward the Tomb of David. There were no Arabs there, and all the smoke and noise seemed centered over the Dome of the Rock. He scanned the walls that were normally crowded with armed Jihad Moquades. "They are gone—" Again, his words were lost on the old man.

Rabbi Lebowitz cupped a hand around his ear and raised his head slightly as the firing of Arab weapons merged into a constant roar above the Old City. "Wha—?"

"The watchmen! . . . They are . . ."

Yacov read his lips and shouted in unison as he scrambled to the young guard's side. *"Gone!"* He gazed with disbelief at the smoke-filled sky and the empty ramparts of the wall. "Gone! Gone! Grandfather, they are gone!" He pointed broadly as the old man crawled cautiously to his side.

At first choking dust obscured the old man's view as he squinted into the daylight. Then he saw that five trucks snaked ahead of them. Haganah soldiers with guns looked like shotgun riders on a wagon train. The green cypress trees beside the towers of Dormition Abbey seemed to sway in the terrible noise that emanated from the Muslim Quarter. To the right, only a hundred yards away, was the Arab village of Silwan. Its streets were deserted, its rooftops left unguarded.

The rabbi strained his eyes to see Zion Gate far ahead. "The English guards! Can you see the Britishers?"

Nahum shook his head, no longer attempting to reply over the din.

"No British guards at the gate!" Yacov cried hopefully. "Look! Look, Grandfather!"

Where the road made a final turn toward Zion Gate, a black shadow appeared beneath the arch. "Have they locked the gate?" The old man tried to focus on the black iron of the gate to see if it was closed and locked or if the way was somehow miraculously open.

Nahum's finger played nervously on the trigger of his rifle. Rabbi Lebowitz caught the young man's eye. He looked genuinely worried.

How could it be this easy? the old rabbi wondered. Zion Gate was wide open and unguarded. What, then, awaited them on the other side of the walls of the Armenian Quarter?

"Get down, Rebbe Lebowitz! Stay down, boy! No matter what happens! Stay down! We are not safe until we are safe! Stay down!"

Rabbi Lebowitz frowned, filled with foreboding. He wrapped an arm around Yacov and crooked his finger to call Shaul to come lie across the boy. Even the yellow eyes of the big dog displayed fear as they neared the yawning opening of the gate.

Better to die inside the walls than out, eh, God? the old rabbi thought. *Yes. Oy. So we decided this morning. . . . But, God, do not kill us in the Armenian Quarter,* nu? *They do not know how to say kaddish there.*

The trucks themselves would only barely pass through the gate. Of this the old man was certain. Beyond the gate, a narrow corridor followed the angle of the wall and led the final one hundred yards into the Jewish Quarter. Before he had left, there were only a few pitiful attempts at barricades along this slim alleyway. The old man could only hope and pray that there were Jewish men near enough to see their entry into the Old City and come to aid in the unloading of the precious cargo.

"They are stopping!" shouted Nahum. "Why are they stopping?"

Again Rabbi Lebowitz rose to peer around the canvas that protected them from sight but not from bullets. The lead truck had stopped just before entering the gate. The rabbi recognized Ehud as he leaped from the truck and rushed forward to press himself against the stones of the wall. He held a Sten gun in his hand. Two other men followed him as he cautiously slid along the stones toward the metal of the huge gates. They slipped beneath the arch and disappeared inside the gate itself.

Rabbi Lebowitz knew the way by heart. To the left lay the main body of the Armenian Quarter. To the right was home.

So, God, are You watching us here, eh? Have You struck the Arabs blind in their grief and tears? Not such a big miracle for You, is it?

Yet another volley of thunder rose from the Dome. The old man stared and ducked at the sound. Then he shrugged and rose again to stare hopefully at the vacant opening where Ehud and the others had slipped in.

"They are turning around!" shouted Nahum as the lead trucks began a slow, awkward turn. "Something must have happened! We are turning around!" At that, their vehicle backed and began maneuvering a laborious turn on the narrow, unpaved road.

A sense of dread weighed the old rabbi's soul—a certainty that indeed something terrible had happened to the three men who had vanished into the shadows of the Old City.

"I am the wife of Professor Moshe Sachar," Rachel explained to the serious young man who stood guard before the locked door of the Hebrew University Department of Archaeology.

At her words, his face broke into a broad grin, displaying a gap where his two front teeth were missing. "Professor Moshe's ishti, eh? *Tov!* Yes! Very good! Come ahead! I had him for two classes!" He held up two fingers, and Rachel noticed that his index finger was amputated from the first knuckle. He tapped the stub of his finger. "I keep forgetting." He grinned. "This looks like only half a class when I hold it up, *nu*?"

Rachel smiled slightly and nodded in response, uncertain what to say. "He . . . my husband . . . wishes that I get some important books from his office, please?"

"Of course." He had already pulled a large ring of keys from his pocket and was trying several in the lock of the huge bronze door. "A good teacher, your husband! You tell him you saw Edward standing guard at the archaeology building. Maybe he will give me a better mark when we have classes again! Tell him Edward Sharon." He held up the hand with the missing finger again. "And tell him I got this in a fight at the Damascus Gate, will you?"

Rachel nodded again and glanced back toward the hospital. "Edward Sharon," she repeated the name. "I shall remember you to him."

"Why did he send you here? Don't you know how dangerous it is?" He grinned again.

Rachel guessed that he had lost his teeth in the same fight. "He is in Kastel," she replied evenly.

Edward swung the massive door open with a clang. "Then we shall hope he comes home with eyes to read his books and all his fingers for digging," the youth said as Rachel passed him and entered the vast, empty corridors of the building.

Rachel did not reply to the student's thoughtless remark. She swallowed hard and stared at the slip of paper with the number of Moshe's office written on it—Room 223A. She had already determined that she would not ask this talkative young guard for help. It would be faster to find the room herself than to endure his conversation. She looked up a wide stairway toward the landing.

"Not that way," called the guard. "It is quicker to go to the stairway at the end of the corridor."

Without acknowledging him, Rachel started down the hallway. A thin film of dust coated the once-glistening mosaic tiles of the floor. Her footsteps echoed noisily in the emptiness. Light shone from a high window at the far end of the corridor, illuminating the stairway. For an instant, Rachel almost smiled. She imagined the halls crowded with busy students rushing to class . . . to Moshe's class. A glimmer of pride rose in her as she thought of how Moshe must have walked this way every morning. Students must have greeted him: *"Professor Sachar!"*

She climbed the stairs to the second floor and stood grasping the banister for a moment as she peered down the vacant hallway. The doors of classrooms were still ajar, as though classes were in session. Rachel looked again at the number written on the paper, then squinted to see the numbers above the doors. *Moshe's class is just there. The third door on the right.* Still touching the banister, she imagined his hand on it as he had climbed these steps a thousand times. She thought of the words in his note and felt a renewed sense of hope. She was seeing his life as it had been . . . and perhaps what their life together would be in the future.

Someday I may come here, Moshe, when you are finished teaching. Or I will come to stand at the back of your class and listen to you. And the students will whisper that I am your wife. She smiled at the thought. *When it is all over, you will teach again and come home to us at the end of the day, and there will be nothing ever so sweet in my life as the sight of you in the doorway.*

Then, as quickly as she imagined it, the dream was crowded out by a fresh wave of fear and doubt. In the distance, the sound of a rifle report shattered the stillness of the corridor, and she shuddered with the realization that there was no one else in the building. No students in the classrooms. No Moshe standing at the podium. Rachel glanced down at the slip of paper once again and then moved into the void of reality.

The green frosted glass of the door had been stenciled with Moshe's name.

Professor Sachar
Department Chairman
Archaeology

Rachel waited with her hand on the doorknob. She swallowed hard, pushing back the disappointment she felt. *He will not be here,* she told herself. *It is only an empty room. He cannot be here as you imagine. Walk in. Find the books he wrote down and leave! Someday he will be here and then you can remember how your heart filled with longing at the nearness. . . .*

She was angry with herself for letting dreams cloud her task. Turning her eyes away from the stenciled letters on the glass, she pulled the door open.

Books and binders lay open on empty desks, mute testimony to the urgency with which the students had evacuated the university some months before. On the blackboard was the familiar scrawl of Moshe's handwriting.

Assyrians attack—King Hezekiah diverts Spring of Gihon 1800 feet into the city. Jerusalem withstands siege!!!

She shook her head at the enthusiasm with which Moshe had written these words. He had underlined *withstands siege* three times. "Did you write these notes for your students, Moshe? Or for me?"

There was no reply. Her eyes caressed the words he had written and the place where he had stood. She felt as though he were with her now. *Think of what will be. . . .*

The door into his cramped, book-cluttered office was to the left, behind the podium. She moved through the rows of desks, unable to shake the feeling that Moshe was waiting for her. She paused, certain that she heard the rustle of papers from inside the cubicle. The din outside the windows became louder as the fervor of grief increased in the Old City.

Rachel's mouth was dry, and she was suddenly afraid as she walked slowly toward the office door. "Moshe? Is someone there?"

A chill crept through her as the high distant wail swept over the Jewish barricades. Suddenly it seemed as though a thousand demons gaped at her through the window and waited for her on the other side of the wall. "Moshe?" she called again. And again she heard the distinct rattle of papers from his office.

For an instant she thought of running from the room, clattering down the stairs to where the guard waited outside the building. But she did not turn away. She seemed almost irresistibly drawn toward the half-open door. A cold knot of fear formed in her stomach, yet there was the irrational hope that when she passed the threshold, Moshe would be sitting at his desk.

Ten feet from the office, she stopped. A whole wall of bookcases was visible to her. A file cabinet, heaped high with papers, stood beneath a slightly open window. A breeze blew through the crack, flipping the pages of an open three-ring binder. Rachel watched the paper and listened to its rustle. Feeling foolish, she put a hand to her forehead, then stepped forward. But there was another sound that pursued her. It was unmistakable, no product of imagination or fantasy—the clatter of footsteps in the corridor!

Rachel glanced at the clock at the back of the room. It had long since stopped. She flipped the wall switch up and down. No lights. *Deserted! There is no one in this building but me!* The footsteps came nearer. She seemed planted where she stood, staring apprehensively at the door. A shadow moved behind the green frosted glass. The large shadow of a man. Then the door swung wide, and Rachel cried out at the face she saw.

Dirty and unshaven, clothes covered with filth from the trenches of Kastel, Moshe stood framed in the doorway. His eyes grew wide at the sight of her. Dark hair fell across his forehead, and his face filled with joyous relief. Suddenly he was shaking his head as tears streamed freely down his cheeks.

"Rachel!" he cried. "I couldn't find you at the hospital!"

She rushed to him, still wondering if this was a dream. And then she felt his arms around her. "Is it you, Moshe?" she asked in a small voice. "Is it really you?"

15

THE GAUNTLET

Haj Amin sat silently before the fifteen men who had gathered in the ornate suite of the Oriental Palace Hotel in Damascus. The high vaulted ceiling gathered their angry words, then threw them back again and again as they argued their strategy for the ultimate conquering of Palestine.

Although the representatives of King Farouk of Egypt wore double-breasted suits and ties like the British, the other representatives were dressed in the traditional keffiyehs and long white shoubs of Bedouin chieftains.

"I cannot trust this Englishman Glubb Pasha!" shouted a young Iraqi general.

An old, weather-beaten Arab drew himself up and glared at the young man. "He may be English, but he leads the Arab Legion of Abdullah. He is like unto Lawrence, who led us in victory against the Turks! It is he who should lead us against the Jews!"

"Yes," agreed another. "John Glubb is a strong fighter!"

"These are not Turks we fight against!" the young Iraqi mocked. "These are Jews! My army alone could defeat them! Do we want it said that it took an Englishman to lead us in a battle against Jews? Are we not also strong fighters?"

Nods of agreement passed among the men. Each imagined leading an army to a quick victory in Palestine. No one wanted to share such glory with anyone else—least of all with the British general who led the Arab Legion of Transjordan.

"My army will take Galilee."

"The Negev will be quite simple for us. The Jewish settlements there are weak and isolated."

"Jerusalem is mine."

"Golan."

"We shall push down through Gaza."

Like vultures contemplating a dying animal, they had already carved up Palestine. Their mouths watered at the prospect of supping on such an easy prey. After the British left, it would be only a matter of days until the Jewish Yishuv fell to them.

Haj Amin did not speak. He fingered the revolver in his pocket. His bulletproof vest chafed his pale skin, but he dared not take it off in this company. He knew that he had been the one roadblock preventing these men and nations from taking the action in Palestine that they had desired from the beginning. In their words and arguments, hope for a United Arab Palestine was finally and irrevocably being put to death in the mind of Haj Amin. Although his features appeared calm and serene, he seethed inside to hear their true intentions aired at last. No mention was made of the Arab Irregulars of Palestine. The name of Ram Kadar was never mentioned. It was as if they had cause now to celebrate the defeat of Haj Amin in Palestine. It gave them the excuse they needed.

"Glubb Pasha could defeat Jerusalem in three days!" shouted the old Arab.

"It is said that the king of Transjordan, whom he serves, does not wish to fight against the Jews of Palestine!" retorted the Iraqi.

For an instant it looked as though the two might come to blows. They stood with their fists clenched until their friends urged them to sit in peace. They sat down reluctantly, muttering oaths against one another.

Haj Amin cleared his throat. Startled that he wished to speak after so long a silence, the men looked at him. He pressed his fingertips together and furrowed his brow in thought. "General Hamed is correct," Haj Amin said as though he had been made judge of the issue. "The king of Transjordan does not wish to fight the Jews. King Abdullah, even now, looks for a way to divide Palestine between himself and the Jewish Agency. With Jerusalem remaining neutral."

The old Arab jumped to his feet again. "This is not true!"

Haj Amin smiled patronizingly as the old man shook with anger at the statement. At last, when the furor died, he spoke again. "It is true. And there is more also. The Arab Legion of King Abdullah and Transjordan would have Jerusalem also. And there will be nothing left for you." He hesitated, choosing his words carefully. "Just as you plan to leave nothing for me."

"Why should we leave anything for you?" shouted a tall, dark-skinned Syrian. "What have you done but lose ground and lose men and lose—"

"Because I am Palestine," Haj Amin said slowly. "It is I the people will follow."

"They followed Ram Kadar to his tomb! They left the fortress of Kastel to follow the body of Ram Kadar! Now how many Jewish convoys have gone up the pass to Jerusalem? How many?"

"If you had provided us with the weapons you promised . . ." The voice of Haj Amin was calm and quiet, even though he was shaking inside.

Azzam Pasha of Egypt stood slowly and shook his head in derision at the words of Haj Amin. "Your so-called army of Jihad Moquades is nothing more than a collection of untrained peasants. A mob that you have aroused to passion. A passionate mob is still a mob, nonetheless. You cannot make them otherwise."

Haj Amin studied him. Azzam Pasha carried himself like an Englishman. He had risen through the British ranks and had been schooled in England. He smelled of lime water and talc. He seemed little like an Arab.

Haj Amin hated him as he hated all the colonialists. "We have had only the weapons we used to fight against the Turks thirty years ago," Haj Amin insisted. "We were a mob then yet we ended the rule of the Turks. Those weapons were adequate then. Now they are next to worthless. If this committee had delivered our weapons to us, Bab el Wad would not be in Jewish hands. Perhaps Ram Kadar would still be alive."

"You are finished." The words of Azzam Pasha to Haj Amin were measured and deliberate. "The death of Ram Kadar is the death of your hopes and folly in Palestine."

"Who is this to speak of my country as though it is his own?" Haj Amin's burning eyes touched each face in the room. "You are not Palestinian. It is not for you to decide—"

Azzam interrupted angrily. "Palestine crouches on your doorstep! Hungry and ragged, Palestinians come to us by the hundreds and thousands! Shall we feed and clothe and house all of Palestine while the Jews defeat the fools under your command? Starve Jerusalem, you say! Defeat the Jews with hunger! Yet you cannot hold the Pass of Bab el Wad against them. How many convoys came through while your men mourned the death of Ram Kadar?" His voice rose to a crescendo. "I tell you, the ambitious Haj Amin and the House of Husseini are finished forever in Palestine!"

"They are loyal only to me!" Haj Amin's voice rose in fury, matching the fervor of Azzam.

"Of course." Azzam's tone was mocking. "Perhaps that is why your peasants now flock to Damascus? Perhaps they come here to bask in your presence?"

Silence fell on the room. Those representatives of the nations of the

Arab League who had gathered in Damascus now looked upon the plans of Haj Amin with disdain and anger. Haj Amin gazed back with rage and mistrust. "You have planned my defeat from the beginning," he said menacingly. "From the beginning you have obstructed my rightful path to victory in Palestine. All your promises have been empty—"

"And so your agent pirated an Arab League arms ship!" Azzam retorted. "Forced it into a storm that drove it off course and into the hands of the enemy! Now its cargo—*our* cargo—lies at the bottom of an Italian harbor!"

"It was the will of Allah," mumbled an elderly sheikh. "Only the hand of Allah can cause such calamity."

Haj Amin glanced sharply at the old man. "Yes. The will of Allah himself. And it is not his will that Palestine be torn in two by the infidel Jews! Or that it be carved up among the Arab nations! No! It is the will of Allah that Palestine remain in the hands of those who have tilled its soil for two thousand years! It is—"

"It is finished for you, Haj Amin!" Azzam sneered defiantly. "*That* is the will of Allah."

"Then it is you who are the fools." Haj Amin smiled coolly. "Allah has little to do with this matter of holy war. My ambition pales by comparison to your own." His eyes brushed every face in the crowded room. "Yes, my people—"

"*Your* people!" Azzam scoffed.

Haj Amin continued as though he had heard nothing. "My people will flee perhaps to your borders. Perhaps you may encourage them to do so. Then you will take Palestine for yourselves. Is that not the plan? Uproot the Arabs of Palestine and take over the moment the English are gone?"

His words were met with silence. Then he continued. "Yes. I am certain of this. But here is something you should think about in the darkness of the night. *We* are Palestinians, not you. And if you should rule the land, it will make little difference to us. I am Palestine, and so it shall always be. My people will not forget—"

"Your people!" Azzam said again. "They follow you only because you have murdered anyone in Palestine who questioned you. And who then is left? The ignorant peasants who have risen to leadership only by blind obedience to you."

Haj Amin contemplated his words. "This may be so," he admitted. "But they are still followers of the House of Husseini. And they are Palestine. Crouched on your doorsteps, hungry and ragged. Camped in your fields because you let them be driven from their home. They will always be Palestine."

"And it is our strong hand that will bring them back into peace in their own land again." Azzam raised his hands to the light.

"Then who shall rule over them?" Haj Amin regained his composure. His voice was thick with amusement. "Shall Egypt? Or perhaps Syria? Iraq? Transjordan? Maybe all of you." He glanced around the room. "Each of you shall have his own little kingdom, eh?"

His words had been meant to humiliate. Instead they moved these men to new anger against him.

"You are finished," Azzam repeated, his voice shaking. "You are finished in Palestine."

Haj Amin tucked his hands into the pockets of his brocade robe. He fingered the revolver, then stood to face the men of the Arab League. "If you think you will rule even a small part of Palestine without me, you are mistaken."

He snapped his fingers, and the guard at the entrance opened the walnut doors wide to let him pass. Instantly his bodyguards surrounded him, and he glided down the corridor to his room.

"They are coming!" shouted the young Hasid who crouched at Dov's elbow. Without thinking, the boy fired off a precious round at the three shadows who dodged and zigzagged from one doorway to another. His panicked reaction jarred eight other Haganah soldiers to follow suit. Bullets ricocheted dangerously off the stones of the narrow corridor.

Dov shoved the young man hard and shouted to the others as the wasted ammunition screamed off into a hail of stone chips. The three intruders had jumped back into the archways and pressed themselves against the stones of the buildings.

"Do not fire!" Dov's voice was angry, easily heard above the echo of Arab weapons. "You fools! Fools! Wait until they are upon us! Wait until you cannot miss!" He did not look at the shamed young men who sweated and huddled with him behind the sandbags. "I will tell you when you must shoot!"

"What if you die? Who'll tell us then?" called a voice down the line.

Dov did not have a chance to reply. At those words, a thick, heavily muscled arm extended from a doorway. A Sten gun was held aloft.

"I can shoot him!" cried one of the men. "I can shoot his arm off!"

"Wait!" Dov demanded.

"But, Dov—"

"I said wait!"

"He is in my sights!"

"If you shoot, then I will shoot you! Wait!"

Dov watched as the big arm slowly lowered the Sten gun to place it gently on the cobbled street.

"He is surrendering!" called the Hasid with joyous disbelief. "We have frightened them! You see! They are surrendering!"

Dov shoved the man again, then stood and shouted out, trying to make his voice carry beyond the noisy grief of the Arab funeral. "Come ahead!"

There was no reply, only the deafening echo of Arab rifles. Dov climbed over the barricade as his men gasped in astonishment.

"Come ahead!" he cried again. There was no movement from the doorway as Dov walked slowly forward. Then Dov raised his voice in an old song that had been sung in Warsaw. The Polish words were interspersed with the rattle of rifle fire.

"Hitler won't be able to cope
With the English fleet
And the Russian sleet,
With American dollars
And Jewish smugglers. . . ."

A larger, booming voice joined in from the shelter of the doorway; then the massive figure of Ehud stepped out and rushed forward to embrace Dov.

Ehud grimaced at the twelve inexperienced soldiers and pointed at a bullet mark made by a strike on a stone too near his head. Then, with a wave of his arm, he signaled them forward to run the gauntlet from Zion Gate into the Jewish Quarter with the priceless supplies of six cargo trucks.

THE
HUNTER

Were it not for the sake of the story, Crabtree would have described the Jewish terrorists who blew the *Trina* as "bumbling and amateurish." But there was very little glory in that. So, even though they had left a trail as wide as General Sherman's march through Georgia, he flattered them for their stealth and deadly determination.

Stealth was a word he hesitated to use at first, but it had a ring to it, and it gave the copy an air of mystery and deep intrigue. The prostitutes of Madame Hortencia's hotel had spoken cheerfully of their midnight sortie onto the doomed ship. They had described in detail the young woman who had gone on board with them for the sake of the story. Tree was certain—or at least almost certain—that this "reporter" was somehow linked to the explosion.

He flipped through the notebook that lay open on the sagging bed. After talking with the prostitutes, he had gone to the hospital and interviewed the nuns there. The story of the broken young man, injured in a plane crash on the coast, had told Tree everything else he wanted to know.

A beautiful young redhead—a reporter—in the company of three men— one of whom was injured in a plane crash, his notes read. *While the woman and a man went to stay with the village priest, one of the fellows remained behind in the Bari Harbor Hotel.* Crabtree smiled. They had told him the man had stayed in this very room . . . the room with the view of the *Trina.* It seemed ironic.

Crabtree grinned as he checked a small file containing information on Americans in Palestine. He alone had guessed the identity of at least two of the fugitives, even though, it seemed to him, they might as well have scrawled their names on the side of the ship they had sunk.

For a moment he toyed with the idea of publishing his conclusions, but instead measured the impact of a story built on several days of small revelations. Tomorrow, he decided, he would interview the priest, if the man could be found. Then he would take photographs of the plane wreck.

Like the plot of a ten-cent novel, his stories would reveal the details, one at a time, leading to an exciting conclusion. As for the Italian authorities, they, too, were bungling and amateurish, and Tree was determined that even they would have to buy a copy of the newspaper to read what he already knew. Tree would tell them nothing.

He glanced at his watch and wondered how far the foursome had gotten in their escape. It was nearly two o'clock in the afternoon. Surely by now they would be tucked away in some seedy hotel in Rome or well on their way out of Italy. Of course, there was nowhere they could go in Europe that was far enough to escape the European edition of the *Times*. A few days from now they would wake up and find their faces splashed across the front page of the newspaper . . . that is, if the Rome office had their photographs on file. In the meantime, Tree would keep that much of the story to himself.

Rocked by the gentle clacking of train wheels against the track, David slept with his head on Ellie's lap. The precious carpetbag was tucked under his arm, and the pistol was within easy reach.

Ellie sat very still with her fingers tangled in his hair. Outside, the towns and villages of Italy passed by the windows like pages from a guidebook. Houses painted in pale pastels were festooned with flags of laundry hung out to dry. Ragged children stopped their play to wave as the train slid by. Everywhere the heaps of rubble served as reminders of the recent war, but anything of value had long since been salvaged.

Cathedral spires pointed skyward and marked the town squares that had been named Hitler Platz or Mussolini Plaza until the Britons and Americans had come through to rename them Churchill Square and Roosevelt Place. The resilient Italians had waved the flags of every conqueror, then torn down the signs and banners and returned to their old ways the minute the last jeep had disappeared down the road.

Now, three hours out of Rome, the track made a wide arc to the east and followed the deep blue swath of the Arno River toward the Gothic domes of Florence. They crossed the river on a newly rebuilt bridge, and in the distance Ellie caught her first glimpse of the city as it glistened in the late-afternoon sunlight.

The train whistle shrieked their approach to the city. David stirred slightly but did not awaken. Ellie stroked his hair and gazed with tenderness at his profile. "Someday we will come back," she whispered. "In better times."

She smiled at the irony that their desperate passage now took them so near all the places she had dreamed of seeing. In Florence, she knew, Michelangelo had carved the majestic sculpture of David. For four long years the artist had toiled over the huge block of Carrara marble until the youthful form of David had been set free. Now David stood with stones in hand as he had done the moment before he faced Goliath, his only armor his confidence in the strength of God.

The whistle wailed again, and Ellie studied the outline of the city. *You see us, Lord,* she prayed silently. *Trapped here, just as Michelangelo saw David trapped in the marble. Bit by bit he chiseled him free. One chip of stone at a time. I have to believe that You are doing the same for us. Still, I am afraid . . . afraid to face Goliath. Afraid I'll drop the stones or miss the target. Afraid that maybe this Goliath really is too big for us.*

She tried not to think of Mikhail and Bernie. Tried not to wonder whether the same hand that had killed them was near. She shuddered at the violence of their end. Her reflection gazed back at her, mirrored in the window of the train. Strain and worry were etched on her face. The whole world seemed hostile. Every stranger was to be suspected, every dark corner feared. Again and again she replayed the short quarter of an hour when David had gone to the locker and their two companions had been murdered. Every detail was studied like a frame of a motion picture. No, she had seen no one enter the men's room. She had not noticed anyone leave. All her attention had been focused on David's safe return.

The train crossed another arched bridge spanning the Arno River. The cathedral dome and the medieval tower of Palazzo Vecchio rose above a sea of red-tiled roofs. A solid wall of shops and hotels reflected in the river—a picture postcard scene—but Ellie found no pleasure in the sight. As the train slowed, she shook David awake and pulled down the shade over the window. There was no use inviting even a glance from anyone who might recognize them. Right now it seemed to Ellie as though they were surrounded by enemies.

David ran his hand over his eyes and sat up. "Where are we?" he asked groggily.

"Florence," she answered, feeling yet another wave of anxiety as the train hissed and finally stopped. Outside the compartment, a porter roamed the corridor announcing their arrival.

"Do we change trains here or what?" David patted his pocket and pulled the hastily scrawled ticket out.

"No. A fifteen-minute stop, then Bologna."

He stuffed the ticket back in his pocket without looking at it and stood up. "You want to stretch your legs? send a postcard from Florence?"

Ellie grabbed his hand. "Please, David," she said, letting her worry rise to the surface. "Please. Don't go out there. Don't leave the train. . . . I . . . I'm scared."

His brow furrowed as he gazed down at her, searching her eyes. "Yeah," he said at last. "I am, too. I dreamed about all of them just now. . . . I kept seeing the guy with the pipe. Hearing him tell me to get you out of there. I don't know, Els." He sat down beside her. "I don't know who he was or who he was working for, but he sure knew us. It gives me the feeling that the walls have ears, you know?"

She nodded. "You think *he* could have killed them?"

"And let us go? It doesn't make any sense."

"Does anything make sense anymore?"

David reached into the carpetbag and pulled out the revolver. "Until we get some answers from the Mossad, I guess *this* is the most sensible solution if anyone gets rough." He tapped his finger on the butt of the gun and pressed his lips together in thought. "You know how to use a gun?"

Ellie drew back and shook her head slowly. "I . . . I don't want to touch it."

"You've got to know how to fire it, Ellie. If anything should happen to me—"

"Then I would want to die, too."

"Stop it!" he snapped, grabbing her by the arm. His voice was fierce and angry. "I lost a hundred buddies in the war, and it never made me want to die. Stop talking like that, Ellie. It's too much for me to carry. You've got to tell me that you'll be okay. No matter what happens, *you've* got to be all right!"

"I can't tell you that," she said slowly. "Without you, David . . ." Her voice trailed off in unfinished anguish.

David took her into his arms, kissing her long and hard. She yielded to him, savoring his lips on hers and his breath against her cheek. Still he held the revolver in one hand as he stroked her back with the other. The warmth of his touch coursed through her, and she smiled through his kisses. "Put . . . the gun . . . away, David. Someone could get hurt."

He leaned down to kiss her throat, then slipped the revolver back into the open carpetbag.

They loved each other gently, David holding her as though she were fragile and might break at his touch. Later, as she lay content in his arms, Ellie thought she saw tears in his eyes, but he turned his face away from her and fell into a deep sleep. Then Ellie dressed in the long white undershift of her nun's garb and drew up the window shade.

The train had climbed the foothills of the Apennines along the same route where a hundred armies had marched to battle. Freshly cultivated fields still bore the scars of conquest. Stone barns and farmhouses were pocked with bullet holes, and walls tumbled in on themselves where artillery had found its mark. Yet with all of that, the fields were rich with the green of spring, and the mountains still glistened with white caps of snow.

Tiny villages seemed carved out of the slopes themselves. The train whistled and slowed for brief stops at picturesque stations in the high mountains. Far below, in deep gorges, a twisting ribbon of blue water flowed toward Bologna and the rich checkerboard of farmland in the Po River Valley.

For a while, Ellie rested as she watched the landscape slide by the window. Any other time she knew she would have seen it all through the viewfinder of her camera. Now she had to be content to mentally photograph each scene.

As the afternoon sun began its descent, the world took on a golden glow. Light reflected on the windows of the houses and illuminated the lakes like sheets of silver. For a while, Ellie almost forgot the fearful uncertainty of their future. The past seemed very far away.

She sat curled up on the seat, her bare feet tucked beneath the long white shift she wore. Her hair tumbled down to her shoulders in thick auburn curls. For nearly three hours David had slept peacefully beside her. She did not know he had awakened until he spoke.

"Beautiful," he said quietly.

She turned to find that he was not looking at the scenery but at her. His eyes were soft and filled with her reflection. His shirt was untucked and his hair tousled.

"How long have you been awake?" she asked, turning back to the window.

"Long enough." He reached out and took her hand in his. "Long enough to see you. And know I'll never forget the way you look right now."

For an instant she was tempted to tease him about being out of character for a nun and a priest, but again she looked at his face and savored the tenderness of his words. She brushed his cheek with her fingertips. There was a question in her eyes, but she did not speak as he moved close to her.

"Your hair . . . ," he said haltingly. "The way you shine sitting there like that . . . I think I never saw anything more beautiful."

"David!" she said, feeling embarrassed.

"Shhhh." He put his finger to her lips. "Let me say this, will you? Let me say all the stuff I've been thinking but haven't said to you."

She frowned briefly, touched by the intensity in his voice. "What, David? What is it?"

He appeared to grope for words. "I was dreaming," he said hoarsely. "About everything that has happened the last few weeks. About Michael Cohen. Mikhail and Bernie. The ship. Palestine . . . all of it. And through the whole thing I saw you far away in the distance. You were . . . dressed like this. Your hair loose on your shoulders. Shining . . . sort of." He shrugged. "And I thought you were . . . too far away to hear me, but I kept trying to tell you—" He stopped and closed his eyes.

"Tell me what?"

"That I love you."

"I know that, David."

He took her face in his hands and held her with his eyes. "No, you *don't* know! Not how much. And it will take a lifetime for me to tell you . . . to show you . . . how much. I kept trying to tell you in my dream, but you never heard, and I thought I would never reach you . . . that I would die without you knowing." His words came in a rush. "Then I woke up and found you here. Like that. Shining. And . . . and . . ."

He pulled her to him and nestled her in his arms. His heartbeat thumped loudly in her ears.

"I'm here, David. And I know, darling."

"If anything ever happened, I just want to be sure you know. Life is so fragile . . . short. It's over too soon, and I don't want to waste even a minute of it. And since this all started, we haven't had time to talk."

"It's okay," she soothed, stroking his face. "I know. I know how you feel." She kissed his chin, then leaned against his chest again, reveling in the warmth of his nearness.

"I want to take care of you. Protect you. And I'm not doing a real good job at it."

"I haven't given you much chance."

"And now I'm not sure if there is any place left in the whole world that is safe for us."

She clung to him. "There isn't, David. No place to go. Nothing to do but remember the sparrow. Remember the guys in the boat with Jesus. He is the only safe place. All the rest is wind and waves and rocky shore. But we're in the boat with Him. Me and you. And Palestine. He has that under control, too, doesn't He?"

David nodded and pressed his lips against her hair. "I just want you to be safe. I don't ever want to be farther away from you than this."

For a long time he held her, and she rested against him. Finally she slept.

17

THE
HUNTED

The nurse who stood before Moshe and Rachel in the corridor was angry. A sharp edge of impatience hung on every word as she spoke to Moshe. "And what are we supposed to do with the Arab girl you brought here? We barely have beds enough for our own people, and after what they did last night—"

"The girl seemed injured"—Moshe's tone matched hers—"so we brought her here. To the hospital."

"There are no medical supplies to spare for one of *them*," spat the nurse. "She will speak to no one. She should be in a mental ward."

Rachel glanced at Moshe. His eyes smoldered as he held her hand tightly and faced off with the nurse. "What are you saying?"

"I'm saying I don't want one of *them* in my ward. Isn't it enough that nineteen members of my nursing staff were murdered last night by them?" There were tears of rage in the nurse's eyes now. Rachel studied her set jaw and the dark circles of exhaustion under her eyes. The nurse's uniform had lost its crisp white contours and hung on her stocky frame like a sack. The woman's eyes were red-rimmed and swollen. "I don't want a filthy, crazy Arab woman in my ward!"

Moshe absorbed the venom in the woman's voice. "I would like to speak to the doctor in charge," he said evenly.

The nurse turned her back and stalked away from the desk. "Fine. He will tell you the same thing. You shouldn't have brought that creature here."

Moshe did not look up or speak to Rachel as they waited in the dim light of the corridor. Rachel stood silently by him, stroking his hand and gazing down the hallway to where the angry woman gestured broadly as she spoke with a small, very tired-looking man with a stethoscope dangling around his neck. The doctor looked toward them, catching Rachel's eye. He motioned for them to come to him as the nurse tossed her head in triumph and strode away.

"He wants to speak with us." Rachel tugged Moshe's arm.

He looked up defensively. "Good."

The doctor stared grimly at a lined sheet of paper on his clipboard. His spectacles were low on the bridge of his nose. Graying hair stood out on one side of his head as though he had slept against a wall. His mouth was a hard line that barely moved when he talked. "Nurse Epstein is correct," he said matter-of-factly. "We have no room. No medicine for such a case as this—"

"But this is a hospital!" Moshe protested.

"We are not being cruel," the doctor explained abruptly as he flipped the sheets on the clipboard. "All of these are *our* people. She is not our responsibility. We cannot deal with—"

"Where else were we supposed to take her?" Moshe's disgust was evident in his voice.

"Come with me, Professor Sachar." The doctor turned on his heel and walked stiffly toward a room at the far end of the corridor.

Rachel noticed how frail the man seemed. His white coat hung well below his knees, and his shoulders were stooped. His head appeared too heavy to carry. He pushed open the door to the semidark room and stepped aside to let them enter.

Only a small night-light burned. The window shade was pulled down, allowing only a few rays from the late-afternoon sun to penetrate the cubicle. A white screen surrounded a bed, and Rachel could see only the delicate feet of the young Arab woman. At the sound of the doctor's voice, the feet drew suddenly back from sight.

"She cannot be more than fifteen or sixteen years old at most," the doctor said, his words now tinged with an edge of pity. "She has been severely sexually abused. I examined her myself."

Rachel's breath caught at his words, and she stared hard at the empty space on the bed where the girl's feet had been.

Moshe jerked his head in a quick nod of understanding. "That explains why the young man was going to kill her. There are some in that culture who still hold to ancient ways. When a woman is raped—"

"She would have been better off, poor creature," the doctor said.

Moshe stared at him. "This is 1948, Doctor!"

"We cannot help her here." He cleared his throat. "She is frightened to the point of being catatonic. She wants only the dark. There is . . ." He faltered. "On her forearm . . ."

Rachel stepped toward an opening in the screen that surrounded the girl. She felt somehow irresistibly drawn toward the one who cowered in the darkness.

The doctor continued. "Whoever did this to her carved a Nazi swastika in her forearm." He lowered his voice. "It could only have been done by the men who took Deir Yassin, I am afraid."

Rachel could wait no longer. She stepped into the privacy of the enclosure. Draped in a hospital gown, the young girl huddled on her bed. She clutched her knees tightly to her and stared straight ahead. She did not look up or seem to hear the hushed words being spoken by the men beyond her vision. A wave of pity surged through Rachel. She stepped closer still, until she stood beside the bed. The girl's skin seemed as pale as the gown she wore. Her scalp was gashed where a bayonet had cut away her hair. Her right cheek was bruised from the terrible assault.

"Deir Yassin." Moshe's voice was heavy with a mixture of rage and disgust.

The girl on the bed blinked at the mention of the village.

"The animals," Moshe continued. "They branded young women as our own people were branded. . . ."

Rachel reached out hesitantly to touch the girl's head.

"She cannot stay among Jews," the doctor said. "You can see why."

"And her own people will kill her," Moshe answered helplessly.

"She will speak to no one."

The girl did not respond to Rachel's touch. There seemed to be no fear, no anger, left inside her. A great void filled her black eyes, as though she had died already.

Like my eyes once, Rachel thought, not taking her hand away from the wounded head. *How often I have seen this! Oh, God, too many times! Too many! The very young ones who lost their minds first, and then when they offered no more pleasure to the officers . . . when they served only as reminders of brutality . . . they were killed.*

The anger and despair of the next thought nearly choked her. *And this was done by those who knew such grief themselves, by those who know what this means just as I do. Have we then become animals as well?*

Feeling the wounds herself, Rachel sat on the edge of the bed. Moshe's words swirled around her, and reality seemed very far away as the room filled with memories and emotions of Rachel's own past. She wanted to cry out that this could not have happened, that no Jew would do this to another human being. She wanted to cover her face and shout against the very thought of it.

They did this to me! To me! They did this to me! And all the while they shouted, 'NEVER AGAIN!'

"I can only think that you take her back to where she was found."

"It is a certainty that she will be killed."

"That is their business."

Rachel took the small and fragile hand in her own. She opened the girl's slim fingers and pressed her palm against that of the girl. *Our hands are nearly the same size.* She took the hem of the left sleeve of the gown and slowly pulled it up over the girl's forearm to reveal an ugly wound in the shape of Hitler's crooked cross.

"It is Jews who have done this thing." Moshe's voice was strong. "Surely it must be our responsibility, then, to—"

"To do what? Her mind is gone. She is full of fear."

Rachel laid the limp arm across the girl's lap, then unbuttoned her own sleeve. Her eyes did not leave the face of the young Arab as she rolled the cuff up until her own scar was revealed. The skin was still red where the hot blade of a knife had obliterated the words *NUR FÜR OFFIZERE* . . . "For Officers Only."

"Look," she said quietly. "Look . . ." Rachel extended her arm before the unseeing victim. She held it there, feeling as though her heart would break with grief. "I was fourteen when they took me," she whispered. She took the girl's hand and placed it on her scar. "Please." Her voice was small and helpless. "Please look. . . ."

"Perhaps we could find a place more neutral—"

"There is no neutrality in Jerusalem. If the British took her off our hands and contacted her people, she would be turned over to . . ."

"We are sisters, you and I." Rachel's voice cracked with emotion, and silently she prayed that this frightened little bird would somehow see into Rachel's own heart.

For a long time there was no response. Then, almost imperceptibly, those delicate fingers moved against Rachel's skin. The girl's eyes blinked with faraway consciousness. A frown furrowed her brow, and her mouth opened slightly and closed again as she gently stroked Rachel's forearm.

Rachel simply nodded, her breath coming in little sighs as she breathed the word "*Sister. Sister. Sister. . . .*"

Black empty eyes filled with sudden awareness. The girl clasped Rachel's arm to her and stared down at the ugly wound. She did not look at Rachel's face, but she laid her cheek against Rachel's scar and made sounds of grief until at last a flood of tears was let loose. "*Ya Allah!*" she wept.

Now Rachel was crying, too. She wrapped her arms around the girl and pulled her close, stroking her head and rocking her gently back and forth. "Yes. I know. I *know*. . . ."

"*Ya Allah*," the girl cried, holding tightly to Rachel. "Basil. *Basil!* Mama. Papa."

"Yes. I lost them, too. I know, little sister. I was there. . . ."

And the tears of the two women silenced the men who waited in the darkness on the other side of the screen.

Ellie did not know how much time had passed, but the blackness was thick when the porter rapped on their door with the announcement that the train was arriving in Turin.

"*Mi scusi*, signore," he said as David switched on the light and opened the door slightly. Ellie could see that this was a different, much younger porter than the first man. He glanced to where Ellie sat in her shift and then said more elaborately, "*Mi scusi!* Torino, signore!"

"You mean Turin?" David asked.

"*Si*, Torino!"

"The other porter. He was supposed to get me a few things. A razor—"

"*Per favore*." The man held up empty hands. "*Non capisco*."

"You don't understand English?" David asked.

"*Non capisco*." The porter grinned at Ellie and winked.

"At least this one doesn't know I'm supposed to be a nun," Ellie said under her breath. "This would make the scandal sheets, I'm sure."

The porter was still smiling broadly. "Torino," he said again.

"Thank you. *Grazie*." David began to shut the door, but the porter blocked it with his foot.

"*Per favore*, signore." He held out his hand. "Passaportos. *Si?*"

"Get the passports," David instructed Ellie, but she had lifted a corner of the shade to stare out at the scene on the platform of the Turin station.

The tiled platform was crowded with Italian policemen who swarmed among boarding passengers, checking identity papers and tickets. Ellie did not move or speak as anxiety dried her mouth.

"Ellie?" David questioned, then paused, as if immediately aware of his careless use of her name.

She managed a slight smile. "Something going on out there, I guess. They must be looking for someone."

David's voice was steady. "Hand me our passports, will you?"

She fumbled in the carpetbag, trying to control her shaking hands as she passed him the documents along with the tickets.

Still smiling, the porter checked their tickets. "Roma," he said punching the corner. "Paris. *Si.*" He handed the tickets back to David, then waved the passports briefly. "*Bene.*" He bowed slightly and slipped a stack of passports out of his deep pocket. In pencil he marked their compartment number on the corner of their documents, then tucked them all back into his pocket. "*Grazie,* signore." Then he moved to the next door.

David peered cautiously out at the Turin station.

Ellie's thoughts tumbled out in a jumble of rapid questions. "Why did you use my name? Do you think he is really a porter? What happened to the other guy?"

"Look at them out there. Questioning everyone. Who are they looking for? This is no routine passport check."

David let the shade fall back over the window. He sat down heavily beside Ellie. "I almost blew it. From now on I'm James and you're Sue. Easy enough."

"They're looking for us, aren't they, David?" Ellie's voice sounded hollow.

"I don't think they know who—or what—they're looking for. But probably all this has something to do with the *Trina.* Maybe even with what happened to Bernie and Mikhail. They're looking for terrorists. For murderers. Not American citizens."

"They're not looking for a priest and a nun." Ellie tugged at the shift.

David sat in silent thought. "You might be wrong about that." He frowned. "Somebody might have seen us—seen you, waiting by the men's room."

Ellie paled. "Italy is packed with priests and nuns."

"Did you talk to anybody?"

"The vendor at the newsstand. But I don't think he knew I was waiting for anyone. I didn't walk into the station with you, remember?"

"Did he see *me*?"

"I don't know. I wasn't looking at him. I was looking the other direction . . . for you."

"That leaves the guy with the pipe. And I think he's the one who killed Bernie and Mikhail. It makes sense he'd set the authorities on our trail." He glanced at the long black dress that was draped over the seat. "No one on the train saw you in that . . . or me in the collar, except for the first porter. Apparently he got off somewhere between here and Rome."

"If they're looking for a priest and a nun, they'll have a million candidates."

"We'll have to get rid of this stuff, pronto," David said, tossing the habit to Ellie.

"And what do I wear in the meantime?"

"Your luggage is lost. Get it? There are a couple of shirts and trousers in the carpetbag." David peered around the shade once again as a large, beefy man in a dark suit flashed his open wallet to two policemen who stood at the entrance of the train car. With quick nods, they stepped aside. David got a good look at the face of the man as he swung up the step. He wore thick round glasses that gave his eyes the appearance of a fish. His cheeks were flushed and his jowls hung on his collar. "Get dressed," David whispered. "Get *DRESSED!*"

The urgency of his voice pressed Ellie into action. She tore through the carpetbag, pulling out a pair of dark brown, pin-striped trousers and a white shirt. Within moments she had exchanged the shift for the man's clothing that seemed to engulf her in folds of fabric. Quickly she rolled up cuffs and sleeves and tied the shirttail at her waist. Then she jammed the nun's garb beneath pillows and blankets in the luggage rack above their heads. Moments later, as the train lurched to a start, a solid knock sounded on the door of the compartment.

David took a deep breath, then opened the door. The porter stood before him with their passports extended in his hand. He was not smiling and he looked away nervously as David took the papers. *"Grazie!"* David said. *"Bene?* Okay?"

"Bene," said the porter.

David touched his hand to his stomach to indicate hunger. *"Pasta asciutta?* Spaghetti?"

The porter pointed back down the corridor. *"Si,* signore," he said, still not meeting David's eyes. *"Il ristorante."*

David slipped him a tip—American dollars—at which the porter brightened once again. He then made his way up the corridor, cheerfully whistling.

David closed the door with a sigh of relief and tucked the revolver into the waistband of his trousers. He left his collar button undone and chose a navy blue jacket to wear. "Time to make an appearance, babe." The train clacked as the wheels picked up speed. "We're going to hide in plain sight."

"Look at me," Ellie protested, braiding her hair and piling it on top of her head.

"Your luggage was stolen. It will give you something to talk about if we are stopped by the police."

"David?" Ellie stepped back. "I don't want to go out there."

"Look"—he rubbed a hand across his cheek—"I know a couple of guys . . . fliers . . . who got shot down over occupied France. They didn't speak the language except for a few words. They were surrounded by Germans. But they got out. They stole clothes. Food. Money. And then they walked out right through the middle of a bunch of Wehrmacht soldiers like they were going for a Sunday stroll. Not once did they hide. They stayed right out in the open, see?"

The train rocked slightly, and Ellie stood swaying before the door. "What if someone recognizes me? My face was flashed all over the papers a few weeks ago."

"Yeah. Ellie Warne died in Palestine. Now you're the PR representative for the biggest new airline in Europe. That's what your passport says. Zelda Sue Conner." He smiled and raised his eyebrows slightly. "They don't know who they're looking for. But I can tell you they'll be looking behind every closed door. Not in the dining car in plain sight. Okay?" His hand rested lightly on the door handle.

Ellie glanced in the mirror, then ran a hand over her hair. "Right. Sue Conner. Out for a stroll." She shrugged. "And my luggage was stolen in Rome."

David pulled the door open and stepped aside as Ellie squared her shoulders and marched boldly into the corridor, where a half dozen other passengers were making their way to the dining car.

The dining car of the train was crowded with travelers. They were mostly couples, like David and Ellie, who had made the journey across the Alps for the sake of this one romantic meal.

The moon shone down on the snowcapped peaks, and misty clouds floated through the steep valleys. The tables were set with gleaming silver and china on crisp linen tablecloths.

Sympathetic and amused glances were directed at Ellie as they made their way up the narrow aisle. Nearly every traveler knew what it was to have lost baggage. The headwaiter clucked his tongue and spoke of the shops that waited for Ellie in Paris. He seated them with a flourish and gave their attendant special orders to see to their every need.

David winked and smiled at Ellie over the menu; then he caught the eye of a man who sat across from them. Tall and thin, the man slouched moodily at his table. He was alone; the seat opposite him was vacant and the plate cleared away. In its place, a copy of the European edition of the *New York Times* lay open.

"It really is just like you said." Ellie spoke with quiet relief.

But David only faintly heard her words. His smile faded as he stared at the newspaper and read the bold headlines: "American Archaeologist Killed in Ambush!" And then the subhead: "H. Moniger Dies with 75 Jews—Truman Vows Investigation!"

David felt himself pale as the face of the solitary diner became openly curious. Quickly David looked back at the menu.

"James?" Ellie asked. "Are you all right?"

"Excuse me," said the man opposite them in a distinct British accent. "Americans, aren't you?"

Ellie nodded, not looking at the man. She pressed her hand against David's knee under the table. "Are you okay?" she whispered urgently.

Without looking at her, David shook his head. "No." His voice was hoarse. "We've got to get back to the compartment."

With no more explanation than that, he rose and took her by the arm, careful to stand between her and the terrible headlines that proclaimed the death of her uncle. His only thought was to get her back to their compartment, away from prying eyes, where he could tell her the news.

Ellie sat erect, rigid and silent in the dark compartment, as the words of her uncle's demise struck her heart.

"I didn't want you to see the headlines and react in the dining car. There's no telling who might be looking for us on this train." David reached out to touch her knee, but she drew back from him.

"Please don't," she said. "Don't. I don't want to cry, and if you touch me, if you . . ."

No tears came to her. She simply stared, unseeing, out the window.

David followed her gaze. Clouds and moonlight mingled on the craggy peaks in an unearthly panorama. Perhaps another time the beauty of the journey would have struck them both with a sense of awe. But tonight the mountains seemed cold, adding to the image of a nightmare from which there was no awakening.

David looked back to Ellie. He felt helpless. What could he say? There was no comfort for her in this terrible moment. "Can I get you something?" he asked at last.

"I would run away," she said, her voice small, "but there's no place far enough to get away from it, is there?"

"No." He wanted to touch her, to pull her into his arms and hold her like a child.

"And now I can't even go home," she said. "Not to Jerusalem. Or Santa Monica." The clack of train wheels punctuated the silence. She turned to face David. "What is to become of us? *What?*"

"We just keep on, I guess. Until we can't." His face was strained with grief—for her and for Howard.

She clasped her hands in her lap and rocked back and forth. David reached out to touch her again, but she gritted her teeth and resisted him. "Please *don't*!"

He drew back as though she had struck him.

"I don't . . . I *don't* want to cry! Not anymore." She sounded angry.

David let his breath out slowly. He did not take his eyes away from her face, although she would not meet his gaze. "Maybe we should—" he swallowed hard—"go to the American Embassy in Paris. Tell them who we are. At least then we might have some protection."

"There is no place far enough to run to," she said hollowly. "No matter where we go, this war will still be there when we get back." She was not speaking to him. "Rachel. Moshe. Yacov. Rabbi Lebowitz. All of them. Uncle Howard knew that." She leaned her head against the cool glass of the window. "There is no place to go that we can get away from it."

At last little sobs came, shaking her shoulders. Her breath fogged the window.

David moved closer. Gingerly he reached out and touched her shoulder, and she turned to bury her face in his chest.

"I'm so sorry," he said, relieved that she yielded to him. He stroked her hair and her back. "I don't know what we can do now. I don't know. . . ."

"He was such a good man," Ellie said softly through the tears. "He believed so strongly that this was the only thing . . . the right thing."

David simply held her and made little shushing noises as he would have if she were a child. He kissed her hair.

"I'm so afraid," she cried. "But where can we go?"

He grimaced, almost choking on the grief he felt for her. "Being brave," he said slowly, "is not always being unafraid. Maybe it's more like doing what you know is right even when you're too tired. Or scared. It's going on and doing it anyway . . . even when you think you can't take one more step."

She clung more tightly to him as he spoke.

"You're right," he said. "We can't run far enough to get away from this. So we might as well find a way to keep going. Face whatever we have to face."

"I just don't want to lose you," she sobbed. "That's all . . . all I care about right now. People falling all around . . . people I love . . . and I keep thinking it could be you . . . maybe the next one will be you. . . ."

David nodded. His jaw was set. A thousand times he had imagined and feared the loss of Ellie. "Yeah. And I worry about you, too. But then I figure the Lord is watching us. He knows everything from beginning to end; He even knows how scared we are."

"I am." She looked up at him, her eyes shining with tears.

"That's the time to keep going, then. Keep putting one foot in front of the other. Fly one more mission over enemy territory." He stroked her cheek. "That's what being brave is all about. And if we do that, Els, no matter what happens, we'll win, because the other side is just as scared as we are."

"My mom," she said, her face a mask of pain. "She'll be so worried. She must know about Uncle Howard by now. David, she'll be so worried about me, too."

"We'll send her a wire," he said firmly. "From Paris. We can do that much at least. They can't track us from that."

She seemed to relax with his words. Leaning heavily against him, she once again drifted off to sleep in his arms.

In the lobby of the Washington airport, Tom Kane read over the letter of Howard Moniger one last time before he slipped it into the manila envelope.

"Pan American Flight 135 now boarding. . . ."

The voice over the loudspeaker jarred him as he hurried to scrawl the address of the *Washington Post* on the outside. Moniger had written a dozen letters to senators and congressmen of his acquaintance. But in this matter, the final judge of the issues would have to be the American people. The final words of a man who had died in such a senseless way would surely get some attention in the press.

Tom had written a brief note of explanation to the editor of the *Post* but had not offered his own opinion of the situation in Palestine. By the time the letter arrived at the newspaper, the full details of Howard's death would be public knowledge. And these words would be a plea from beyond the grave, a prophecy of things yet to come.

"Final boarding call . . . Flight 135 . . ."

For a moment Kane stood beside the mailbox. He stared at the envelope as though it contained the essence of life itself. *I guess it does,* he thought, his hands trembling as he dropped it into the slot and rushed to catch his plane.

Sarai Tafara stood beside Rachel and gazed out into the blackness of the city. A final trail of taillights thinned and then vanished down the road that led out of Jerusalem.

"My people have left," the young woman said in halting English.

"Where have they gone?" Rachel asked.

"Away. I heard them talking today. Everyone is leaving except the soldiers. The soldiers are coming and coming and coming now." Her expression was blank, like that of a sleepwalker. "The people will all come back when Jerusalem has fallen. But now they get out of the way of the battle that is to come."

"Your family left without you?" Rachel's question was gentle. She put a hand on the arm of Sarai.

"I am dead to them now." Her voice was distant and hollow. "They will think of me and weep. But they will not look for me again. I am dead to them," she repeated.

Rachel did not speak for a long time. From early evening until now, the mass exodus of Arab civilians from Jerusalem had created a spectacle of panic that reminded her of the cold winter flight of thousands of Polish Jews from Warsaw. Carts and wagons carrying the sick and the old. Children perched atop mounds of household goods . . . *How frightened we were. Only we knew there would be no coming home for us.*

"Where are they going? Do you know? Perhaps we could get word to them that you are—"

Sarai shook her head slowly. "No. It is best. I died at Deir Yassin, you see. Ahkmed was meant to simply finish it."

The streets of the neighborhood of Sheikh Jarrah were now totally deserted.

"They flee from Deir Yassin," Sarai continued. "They are afraid that what has happened to me will happen to them. So only the soldiers will stay here. And more will come. So many, many more soldiers will come. They have promised to avenge. So many soldiers will come here to fight. . . ."

"Then you will come home with me," Rachel said tenderly. "You have no place else to go?"

"No," Sarai replied. "There will be soldiers in the home of my parents. It is no place for me to be. I have no right to return there, anyway. I am dead to them." She frowned as she repeated the phrase, as though the realization of her words pierced her soul.

Moshe knocked softly on the door of Tikvah's hospital room, then nudged it open. "We must hurry, Rachel. The road is open now. *For now.* The Arabs have evacuated Sheikh Jarrah. Gather the baby's things. We must go home now."

18

UNTIL WE
ARE SAFE

Far below the train, the Arc River cut a course through the Alps. Some hours before, Ellie had fallen asleep nestled against David. Though he remained awake, he did not move for fear of awakening her. They were in France now—he was almost certain of that—and the knowledge that they were out of Italian jurisdiction relieved him tremendously.

It was midnight when he finally slipped his arm out from under her and lifted her onto the narrow upper berth. He stood and tried to stretch, but the ceiling was too low. So, with a backward glance, he slipped out the door and into the dim corridor of the car.

Inhaling deeply, he stood in the center of the aisle. The roar of the train was louder outside the compartment, and a rush of cold air told him someone had opened the door and entered their car. He turned, half expecting to see the porter. Instead, the scowl of the fat Italian official greeted his. David nodded briefly, but the man did not respond. He crossed his arms and stood as if to block the corridor.

At the same moment, the door of the far end of the car also opened, and the tall, thin Englishman who had sat across from them in the dining car entered. Even in the dim light David could see a copy of the European *New York Times* tucked under his arm.

As the train swayed and lurched, the Englishman made his way slowly up the passageway toward where David stood. His face was set and grim as well, but he seemed to stare past David to where the fat man blocked the corridor ahead.

In one swift motion, David flipped the handle of their door and stepped back into their compartment. He shut the door and slipped the bolt into place. Pressing his ear against the panel, he heard the muffled sound of a conversation in French between the two men. There was a slight bump as someone passed by outside, then silence.

David scarcely breathed as he strained to hear. Minutes ticked by until at last he relaxed and wiped a hand across his face. Only then did he notice that he had been sweating. A thousand questions ran through his mind. And like the white-water rapids of the Arc River, they all spiraled downward to the same conclusion . . . or at least to the same possibilities.

Perhaps the man in the dining car had left his newspaper open on the table for a purpose. Perhaps he had hoped for a reaction from the American passengers. If this was the case, was he also an ally of the Italian official who still patrolled the train?

Drawing a deep breath, David opened the door once again and stepped out of the compartment. His heart sank as he noticed that the bulky Italian was still blocking the aisle at one end. David yawned and stretched, then nodded cordially to his unresponsive companion. Then, not wishing to appear intimidated by the large man's presence, he turned to stagger down the rocking aisle toward the toilet. The room was occupied, so David stepped back to wait nonchalantly while the Italian official eyed him from a distance.

David yawned again and tapped his foot in apparent impatience, not daring to look toward the glowering man. He was certain that the Italian was not displaying a merely casual interest in him. He was watching—openly and with apparent hostility. Yet why, if he was on to something, had he not arrested them before the train had crossed the border into France?

The door to the small cubicle containing the toilet finally popped open, and the Englishman emerged.

"I say!" the Englishman chirped. "The American from dinner, aren't you? Feeling better I hope!"

"Not really," David said, holding his stomach.

"Well, the WC is frightful!" He jerked his thumb back toward the lavatory. "Wouldn't find these conditions on an English train, I daresay!" He glanced toward the fat Italian, then back at David. There was a knowing in the Englishman's eyes that David did not like.

As the Englishman stepped aside to let David pass, he half smiled and thrust his newspaper into David's hand. "Got this in Turin this evening. I've already read it clear through. If you'd like—"

"Yeah. Thanks," David said brusquely, taking the newspaper and shutting the door behind him. He clutched the paper and leaned against the small metal basin. His reflection in the dim mirror was ashen. No doubt the color of his complexion helped convince the Englishman he was sick. At this moment he did, indeed, feel ill.

The tiny cubicle was windy from the open hole in the train that served as the toilet. The room smelled of urine and vomit. David twisted the spigot of a large stainless-steel canister to wash his face. He glanced at the front page of the paper. The massacre of seventy-five civilians took all of the top half, but a large photo of the *Trina* and a corresponding article were splashed across the bottom half of the paper.

He held the print close to the quavering lightbulb and scanned the stories.

> . . . *the work of Jewish terrorists. Two men escaped over the side of the boat only moments before the explosion rocked all of Bari Harbor.*
>
> *It has been rumored that an American newswoman was also on board the ship last night. She may have been linked to the terrorists.*

In frustration, David slapped the front page. "I *hate* reporters!" he exclaimed quietly. "How do they find out this stuff?"

He quickly read through the rest of the story, amazed at the detail it offered. He stayed in the cramped, unpleasant room until a sharp rap sounded on the door.

Without answering, David jerked the door open and pushed out past a very weary-looking man wearing a robe and slippers. David glanced up. The fat Italian was still guarding the door at the far end of the corridor.

Behind the large man, the door opened and the conductor muttered and inched around him. "St. Michel," the conductor said as he moved up the aisle toward David. He rapped on two doors and announced again, "St. Michel. St. Michel."

David slipped into their compartment. His heart was beating rapidly now as he switched on the light in the lower berth and glanced over the paper once again.

The byline on the story read *Lawrence C. Crabtree, European Correspondent, NY Times.*

"Ellie," David said urgently. "Ellie, hon, wake up."

Ellie moaned and rolled over. "Wha—?"

"What do you know about a reporter for the *New York Times* named Lawrence Crabtree?'

It took her a moment to reply. "Crabtree?" she asked through a yawn. "Why?"

"Do you know him or what?"

"Everybody knows Crabtree. Or knows *of* him. He's practically famous, he's so mean."

"And does he know you?" David tried to control the anxiety in his voice.

"I don't know. I wish he did." She leaned over the bed and looked down at David. "Why?"

"Because he's been to Bari Harbor. That's why. And he must be one incredible reporter."

Ellie moaned as David held the story up to her. "That," she continued, "plus the fact that the first place he would go would be to talk to Madame Hortencia. He goes places they never tell you about in journalism classes, David. The guy is . . ."

". . . about to get us arrested," David finished. "Get up, Els. Get dressed. I think someone is on to us."

As the train wound down the gorge toward the little village of St. Michel, Ellie opened the window and dropped out the nun's habit and David's clerical collar. There was no use leaving behind any additional evidence that they had been aided by Father Antonell. According to Crabtree's story, the good priest would be held for questioning as it was.

"Isn't there some other way to get off the train, David? Like maybe through the window?"

David shook his head and jammed the revolver into the waistband of his trousers. "No. Too obvious. He'll be expecting that. Watching for it. A few minutes ago in the hall, he started to come for me. Then that Englishman came out of the bathroom, and he stopped. All I can figure is that this Italian is hoping we'll meet up with the other two of the foursome mentioned in the newspaper article. If he thinks we're going to make a break, he'll arrest us on the spot."

Ellie put her hand to her forehead. She felt dizzy at the thought of an Italian jail. For an instant she pictured herself running through the night with barking hounds in pursuit. "That means they don't know about Bernie and Mikhail yet. I mean, who they are."

David handed her the wallet and the passports. He searched through the contents of the shaving kit, finally pocketing the safety razor and the bowl of the broken pipe. "Just do what I told you and we'll be all right," he said firmly. "Remember, five minutes, while the other passengers are getting off. Then knock."

She nodded, feeling her heart in ther throat as David opened the door and stepped aside for her. She did not look at the huge man who watched them intently from the end of the corridor. What was he waiting for if he knew? Was he hoping to catch others besides them?

Ellie stretched out her arms to David, who clutched his stomach and feigned illness. He put his arm around her shoulders and leaned heavily against her as she escorted him toward the lavatory under the watchful eye of the Italian.

"St. Michel!" the porter announced through the corridor as David stepped into the lavatory and closed the door behind him.

The train hissed and slowed to a stop as Ellie stared at her shoes. Two couples emerged from their compartments and toted their luggage past her rather than going toward the unmoving giant.

Ellie tossed her hair and carefully counted five minutes before she knocked on the door. "You all right in there, darling?" she asked loudly. "Honey, do you need help?"

The big man narrowed his eyes and leaned slightly forward as the door to the lavatory opened slightly and Ellie slipped in.

David crouched on the floor, the head of the safety razor clamped securely around the last bolt that held the wooden stool over the open hole that led to the tracks. Three other bolts lay in the planks beside him. "Almost got it," he said breathlessly as he strained to loosen the bolt.

"David, hurry!" Ellie's heart was pounding. She could hear the announcement of the train's imminent departure. "He was looking at me, David! Waiting! You were right. If it hadn't been for the other people getting off—"

"Shhh!" he warned, shoving hard against the final stubborn bolt. Again and again he slammed the palm of his hand hard against the makeshift wrench until at last the bolt began to give just a fraction at a time.

"Express Français now boarding. . . ."

With a strength born of fear, David loosened the last bolt and squirmed to his feet. As Ellie squeezed to one side, David lifted the stool, plopped it on the sink, then removed the plate that covered the opening in the floor of the train.

"Come on!" he whispered hoarsely. "Get going!"

Ellie hesitated, staring at the opening that was big enough for her to slip through. For an instant a fresh wave of fear paralyzed her. The whistle of the train echoed in her ears. "David—"

A second time the whistle sounded. "Get out there!" David hissed. "We'll be run over."

David did not reply. Instead he grabbed her and shoved her down through the opening. "Lie down between the wheels," he instructed as the whistle blew the third and final time. Then he squeezed feetfirst through the hole, working his broad shoulders through the tight space with difficulty.

The gravel beneath the train was damp with diesel fuel. David lay on his back and groped for Ellie. He found her pressed against the rough wooden ties as the train hissed and roared. Above them, metal clanked against metal and sparks cracked as the wheels slipped to find traction against the rails.

David gripped Ellie hard against him and, with one mighty effort, rolled them both from beneath the groaning train.

The train was twenty miles from St. Michel before the fat man moved toward the lavatory. He stood before it, hesitated, then raised his meaty fist to pound against the door.

"*Scusa,*" he implored. Then, looking from side to side furtively, he said, "Signore, are you all right in there?"

There was no reply. Again he rapped. "I said, are you all right in there?" He cleared his throat and tried again. "Open up! Come on!"

When there was no answer and the darkened train rumbled through a tunnel, the man put his massive shoulder to the hinges with the force of a sumo wrestler. The fragile door gave in easily to his weight and popped open to swing crazily with the rocking motion of the train.

The man moaned and shook his head at the sight of the displaced stool and the gaping hole in the floor of the train. Mountain wind whistled up to ruffle his hair, and the sparks on the tracks were clearly visible, illuminating the strange mix of disgust and admiration on the man's face.

For a full minute he stood in the doorway. Then he stooped and picked up the safety razor that was still attached to a bolt. He wriggled into the cubicle and closed the door behind him. Not knowing what else to do, he replaced the plank, put the stool over the opening, and rebolted it to the floor with the care of a patient nanny cleaning up after naughty children.

The windows of the house in Rehavia were dark. Somehow Rachel knew that Grandfather and Yacov were gone, even before Moshe took the note from the door.

Rachel cuddled Tikvah in her arms. Sarai, her head bowed, followed as Moshe opened the house and groped in the foyer for a light switch.

"No electricity," he said with resignation. "I know where there are candles." He felt his way down the hall toward the kitchen as Rachel and

Sarai waited in the darkness. Rachel reached for the hand of the young Arab woman. It was ice-cold with fear.

"You will be safe here," Rachel said gently. "Would you hold Tikvah, please?"

She passed the sleeping infant into the outstretched arms of Sarai and felt her relax instantly at the touch of the child.

Moshe appeared a moment later with the glow of a candle illuminating his exhausted face. He handed the note to Rachel, then stood at her side as she read the words of her grandfather:

> *My dearest Rachel,*
>
> *No word yet as to your safety. How I pray that you are alive and well! If you find this note, then know that Yacov and I have done what we must. I have determined that these old bones will not rest until I again stand in the Holy City—*

"They have gone back to the Old City," Rachel said with an edge of dread to her voice. She continued to read:

> *I could not do otherwise. For that is my home. The place of my heart and my hope. If you also have died in the flames of the Hadassah convoy, then perhaps we shall meet tonight in Paradise, and there will be no need for this letter. If you live, then pray for us, and look for us. For if God wills it should be so, we shall meet again in this life.*
>
> *Shalom.*
> *Grandfather*

At the bottom of the note, in handwriting that was nearly illegible in its excitement, the old man had added this postscript: *Praise be to the Eternal! You live! Ehud Schiff is taking us home now! Do not fear for our safety! Psalm 139:9-10.*

Three hours later, as Moshe slept soundly and the even breath of Tikvah filled her heart with peace, Rachel crept from bed and lit the candle stub. Carefully she lifted the lid of the small white box she had carried from the hospital. In the flickering light, she searched the pages of Howard's little Bible until she found the passage Grandfather had given to her. She read the English words with difficulty.

The faces of David and Ellie, Grandfather and Yacov appeared in her thoughts as she contemplated the meaning of the promise before her. *If I rise on the wings of the dawn, if I settle on the far side of the sea, even there Your hand will guide me, Your right hand will hold me fast.*

She remembered the fires of Warsaw—*even there*, the great cauldron of human misery—*even there*. She thought of the fearsome prophecy of the young Arab girl: *"The people will all come back when Jerusalem has fallen. So only the soldiers will stay here. And more will come. So many, many more soldiers will come."*

Rachel studied the sleeping face of Moshe and tried not to think of the future. "Even there," she whispered. "Even in the future, Your hand will guide us, Lord."

She blew out the candle and slipped back between the sheets. Moshe moved toward her, unconsciously wrapping his arm around her and pulling her close to him. She burrowed her face against his chest and stroked his back gently with her fingers. *How would I live without him?* she silently questioned.

As if he heard her thoughts, he moved to kiss her. "I thought I was dreaming." His voice was sleepy but full of contentment.

"No. This is no dream, my love," she whispered, eagerly returning his kiss. There was no room for thoughts of the future in their embrace. There was only the joy of this moment and the certainty that a hand stronger than their own had brought them safely this far.

It was after midnight in the Jewish Quarter of the Old City. The expected attack of the Arab mobs had not come. As if by a miracle, the hordes of Jihad Moquades had indeed been struck blind in their grief. They had wasted thousands of rounds of ammunition in their demonstration, and not one Jewish life had been taken. In contrast, fifteen Arabs, participants in the riots that followed the interment of Ram Kadar, had been killed by their own people.

The twenty-one Haganah reinforcements who had entered the Old City with Ehud were now spread throughout the Quarter. The midnight watch had come in to relieve Ehud, who now sat in the tiny apartment of Yacov and Grandfather. Shaul sat with his head across the big man's knee and blinked contentedly up at him with peaceful amber eyes.

"I was angry at you at first, Rebbe Lebowitz," Ehud boomed.

The rabbi put a finger to his lips and pointed to the sagging iron cot where Yacov slept peacefully. "So. You are not angry now?" the old man asked with a half smile.

"No," Ehud answered more quietly. "Because we are all alive, eh?"

"And if we had all been killed?"

"Then I would still be angry at you."

"No. Then you would be dead. True? Of course true."

Ehud pondered the rabbi's words and nodded grudgingly. "Then *Moshe* would have been angry!"

"What difference would that have made if we were all dead? How can Moshe's anger bother you if you are dead?"

Ehud frowned and rubbed a hand across his eyes. "I would not have liked having Moshe angry, even if I was dead," he insisted.

"One consolation—"Rabbi Lebowitz stroked his beard—"you wouldn't have known he was angry, *nu*?"

"Enough of this." Ehud's voice rose to its usual level again. "I cannot reason with a rabbi! I am only a seaman, not a Yeshiva scholar. I was simply trying to say that you should not have come with us! You might have been injured."

"But we were not." The rabbi sat back with contentment and gazed around his little home. "And we are here, eh?" He shrugged. "Two more soldiers for the Jewish Quarter. The boy knows these streets and alleyways better than any rat. He shall serve you well."

Ehud stuck out his lower lip. "And what will *you* do for our defense, Rebbe?" He glowered.

"I shall pray. Pray for miracles, as I prayed today for your six little trucks to break through. As I prayed that this old man might die on the soil of Zion instead of outside her gates."

Ehud ran a hand through his thick hair as he remembered the words of Dov while they had stood watch together tonight. "Dov expects that this place may become a *kesl, nu*? A cauldron . . . like it was in Warsaw, Rebbe Lebowitz. We are encircled. Today may well have been the last chance any of us had to escape."

"You have jumped into the cauldron. Do you expect me to do otherwise? Especially when the cauldron is my home?"

There was no dissuading the old man, but Ehud jerked his head toward Yacov. "What about the boy?"

"There are other children here. True? Of course true. Will you ask them to leave?"

Ehud considered the words of the old man. He thought of the boys who loved him and followed him like seagulls trailing a fishing vessel. He shook his head. "No. We shall all stay, I suppose. All of us." He sighed, resigned to the fate that would certainly befall some, if not all, of the innocent.

"Yes. For the sake of Zion, we will stay. Yacov would not have it otherwise. He knows well the saying, as we all do: 'Out of blood and fire Judea will fall. Out of blood and fire it will be reborn.' "

Rabbi Lebowitz gazed steadily at Ehud. "Today in the truck Nahum said that we will not be safe until we are safe. A wise saying, I think."

He smiled. "Perhaps we should write this in the Midrash, eh? And then, Ehud, we might add this. . . ." He stroked his beard. "For two thousand years we have said, 'Next year in Jerusalem,' true? Always we Jews have looked to the future . . . to Jerusalem. Now the future has waited long enough. If *we* do not grasp it, other hands, grasping hard and bloody, will."

The old rabbi held his leathery, gnarled, and crooked fingers up to the candlelight and turned them slowly. "Once these hands were young"— he looked toward the sleeping boy—"like his. Once they were strong with hope, Ehud. If I, being old, let go of Jerusalem and the hope for her future, what will be left for him? And when will our children say— forever—'This year in Jerusalem'?"

PART II

The Cauldron

The wise man in the storm prays to God, not for safety
from danger, but for deliverance from fear.
RALPH WALDO EMERSON

19

THE CHARITY OF JEWS

"You have given up too easily." Fredrich Ismael Gerhardt, servant of the Mufti, stretched his wounded leg out on the small stool.

Haj Amin considered his words carefully. "It is not the Jews who defeat us in Palestine. It is our brother Arabs. Palestine would be mine for the taking if they would but provide us with weapons."

"They think they do not need us." Gerhardt's face was hard. "They think they *will* not need us."

Haj Amin gazed out the high arch of the window and down into the streets of Damascus. Below him a camel driver passed, his beasts laden with heavy packs. "We are not so far from our beginnings," he said bitterly. "Still we Arabs are tribes of sheikhs and chieftains, ready to cut one another's throats."

He turned back to Gerhardt. "They need us. They need the Palestinians. We will provide for them the excuse they need to fight. The Arabs will for a time fight the Jews and not each other. And once the Jews are gone, they will turn their knives on their neighbors across the border. As they have turned their knives against me."

Gerhardt's massive jaw was set as he listened to the words of Haj Amin. "Yes. Our Arab brothers wish us to be weak and not strong. But we are still strong! With a little money I could—"

"Money!" Haj Amin laughed hollowly. "They have given us a fraction of what was promised. They say they fear that if they provide us with modern weapons, we will be defeated in battle anyway, and then the Jews will take all that they have provided. They will give us nothing more," he finished angrily.

"But you are a wealthy man, Haj Amin."

"I have enough to live out my days in comfort."

"In exile. When you could be ruler over Palestine."

"They have said it. The death of Ram Kadar is the end of hope."

"He was only one man. We have a martyr now. . . ." Gerhardt narrowed his ice blue eyes. "As you would have made me a martyr for the jihad."

Haj Amin did not respond. He raised his eyebrows slightly. "Perhaps we shall all be martyrs, and then there shall be no one left to carry a rifle."

Gerhardt lifted his chin. "You did not see my men and how they follow me. When they attacked the hospital convoy—"

"A foolish action. We seem to be barbarians before the eyes of the whole world."

"We *are* barbarians. Why pretend any longer? Jews and Arabs—we are all alike." There was a hint of a smile. "None of that matters anymore," Gerhardt continued. "So Kadar is dead. Our men are stirred to passion."

"Their wives and children flee to the borders, and our villages are empty."

"We have a month, Haj Amin! Let the civilians run! Then they will be out of our way!"

"The Jewish civilians do not flee."

"Then let them stay and die!"

Haj Amin pressed his fingertips together. He drew a deep breath. Perhaps there *was* hope in the words of the madman who sat before him. Perhaps there was still one chance of victory before the British left and the surrounding Arab nations invaded. "What is your plan?"

"With fifteen thousand pounds I can buy everything we need right here in Damascus. The souks are full. And with what we already have—"

"What we have already is old and—"

"We are a thousand times better equipped than the Zionists." Gerhardt's scarred face was flushed with excitement. "Our volunteers bring their own weapons and ammunition. We have a month to starve the Jews. To terrorize them. If we have firm control of Jerusalem when the British leave, who will dare to take it from us? Jerusalem is Palestine. In the Old City the holy places are near to collapse now. We must attack! And attack! And attack!"

"Our men will follow you?"

"They have proved that. And Egypt, Syria, and Transjordan would not dare to invade with their armies until the English are gone. By then the Zionists and the Jewish Agency will be begging for peace. The people are near panic now. Others may look upon the hospital ambush as barbaric. You and I both know what a stroke of good fortune it was for us."

Haj Amin nodded curtly. "Perhaps. Yes. Surely this must strike terror in the hearts of the Jews. As Deir Yassin has frightened our own people."

"Retaliation and revenge will unite the warriors of Palestine. With fifteen thousand pounds I can level the entire Jewish city of Jerusalem and then Tel Aviv. Here in the souks of Damascus I can hire mercenaries to fight with us. And when the British finally leave, our brother nations will find a strong and sovereign nation in Palestine. And you shall be at its head."

Haj Amin smiled slightly. "I can see, Gerhardt, that we need one another."

"Those who rallied to Kadar will rally to me as they did in Bab el Wad. And they will serve you as they serve me."

In the morning, Sarai, clothed in the same long black dress she had worn to the hospital, stood at the window of the kitchen and silently looked to the east.

"They are praying now, my people," she said at last. "The muezzin has called them to worship, and everywhere they are praying."

Rachel did not ask why Sarai did not also pray. She understood the anger and bitterness the young woman now felt. She poured herself a cup of weak coffee brewed from the grounds that had been reused for three days. "Sarai, you brought no clothes with you—"

The girl looked at her with amused disdain. "I had no need of clothes where I was bound."

Rachel stirred her coffee thoughtfully. "I have some things upstairs. I would like to share if you—"

Sarai drew herself up proudly. "I am of the House of Husseini, a daughter of the prophet and a Muslim descended from the first caliphs who conquered Jerusalem. I will not wear the clothes of those women of the West. I would not. Even in this living death, I would not wear such clothing!"

Moshe, who had been standing in the doorway, cleared his throat self-consciously. Then, with a clatter, he retrieved the coffeepot from the stove.

"I understand," Rachel told Sarai gently, without hint of resentment. "These new ways are strange for me also. The world is changing so fast."

"We do not change," said Sarai. "And so we endure, as the prophet foretold."

Moshe still had not spoken, but Rachel could sense the tension he felt at the girl's revelation. The House of Husseini! Of all the people to rescue . . .

"Moshe"—Rachel turned to him as though she had not heard the threat in Sarai's voice—"might we somehow find something fitting for Sarai to wear?"

"It is not so easy as all that." Moshe's voice was hard, tinged with an uncharacteristic edge of sarcasm, as if certain the stranger would throw any gift back into their faces. "The borders are closed between Arab and Jewish quarters."

"I was a Husseini," Sarai said proudly. "Husseinis do not take the charity of Jews!" She made her exit, leaving behind a heaviness, a sense of helplessness.

Moshe stared at the door angrily, then took a gulp of coffee and gasped. "We should not have brought her here," he sputtered, wiping his burned mouth with the back of his hand. "It was a mistake. She hates us."

"I pity her," Rachel said slowly. "She is so alone. Afraid. We must give her time."

"She may not allow us to help her. You heard the way your kindness was received. I do not like the way she spoke to you."

Rachel put a hand on his arm and blinked her eyes at him in amusement. "I have received much worse than that, Moshe—and from my own people. I think I will survive it."

"Well, no one will talk to you like that in my presence." His tone conveyed his anger.

"You must let me handle this, Moshe. You are a man and cannot understand what it is she is feeling."

"I suppose," he snapped. "But she is a Husseini! Even a *man* can understand what that means!"

"Moshe," Rachel corrected, "you did not hear what the poor girl said."

"I heard Husseini. That is enough." He crossed his arms and sat back in worried contemplation.

"She said she *was* a Husseini—before she was defiled. Now she is homeless and without a family."

"Still proud enough to reject your kindness."

"Moshe, what has happened to you? I have never seen you like this before! When you brought that poor young girl to Hadassah—"

"I did not know then what I know now. I did not know she would be coming to this house. And I did not know she was a—a Husseini! She is our enemy, Rachel!"

"She is a young girl who has been badly mistreated with no place else to go, no one to turn to!" Rachel's eyes flashed fire. "Let go of the affront, Moshe. She is afraid, striking back."

"And what is to say that she won't strike back in the way that Husseinis have become famous for? They might consider her dead, but she is still very much alive and full of hatred for us."

"And does our Messiah not teach that we are to love those who hate us, to care for our enemies as we would care for Him?"

Moshe gaped at Rachel, taken aback by a fighting spirit he had never seen in her before. He hesitated, knowing that Rachel was right but unwilling to acknowledge her point.

"Rachel, the girl is an Arab. We are fighting her people for the salvation of our homeland! Her people killed Howard, Rachel." He stopped, surprised at the force of his own words.

"Moshe, I know who she is. And not so long ago, I thought that I myself would never be able to forgive the Arabs for what they have done to us—to Howard, to the others in the Hadassah convoy. But Howard's last words to me were 'Hate no man.' I cannot love Howard—or God— and turn away from this poor girl who so desperately needs our help."

"Even if she rejects your offers of kindness?"

"It is nowhere written that she must love me in return, only that *I* must love."

Moshe stared at his wife, astonished at the sincerity and power in her words. "You have thought about this very seriously, haven't you, Rachel?"

"I cannot explain the change that has come into my heart, Moshe." Rachel paused and gazed deep into his eyes. "Perhaps Howard's last words found their mark. Perhaps I see one terrified Arab girl in a different light than I have seen our enemies. I only know that if I hate her because of what she is, I am no different than the men who tortured me."

She pulled up her sleeve, revealing the angry scar that remained on her forearm. "This is the mark of their hatred, Moshe. It is also the mark of my compassion. I am scarred, just as Messiah was scarred, by those who hate without reason. And just as He loves, I am bound to love."

A heated response rose to Moshe's lips, but he stopped, struck by the depth of love in Rachel's face. She, who had been so terribly wounded by the enemies of their people, was able to return good for evil, to lay aside her former bitterness and reach out to an enemy who despised her.

Tears filled Moshe's eyes, and he spoke with difficulty, choking back the lump in his throat. "Forgive me, Rachel. I, too, am bound by that love, but my hatred for the enemy has blinded me from seeing it."

"There is a greater enemy than the Arabs," Rachel murmured. "One who would keep us imprisoned in our hatred, one who delights in the bitterness that divides us."

"Yes. And he is the enemy we must defeat within ourselves."

"Perhaps," Rachel offered, "we defeat him by loving. And perhaps we can pray for the peace of Jerusalem by loving one tortured child of our enemy."

"My dear and loving wife, I cannot promise that it will be easy, but I will try. For you and for Howard and for Yeshua." He put his arms around Rachel and kissed her tenderly.

"Now, Moshe," Rachel resumed when he released her, "you can help me decide what to do. All she has to wear is that dreadful black dress. The Arab women wear such beautiful clothes. I have seen them at a distance—flowing robes with hand embroidery. I need to think of some way to find clothes she will be comfortable in."

"If your enemy is naked, clothe her?" Moshe smiled at Rachel's determination.

"It seems the logical place to begin."

"What about old Miriam's stuff?" He motioned toward the door that led to the room where Howard's housekeeper had stayed. "No one has touched it since she was killed in the bombing; I am almost certain."

"But she was an old woman." Rachel frowned.

"Well, she was . . . ordinary, I suppose." He sighed wistfully. "But when she managed Howard's parties—people were always coming in from the States, and there were wonderful parties. One minute I would poke my head in here and she would be sweating over the stove and shouting at the hired help. Then, five minutes later, she would be dressed in these really beautiful caftans—her own making and embroidery, I'm sure. Very nice. The women guests were always impressed, anyway."

"You think it would be all right?"

"Who is left to mind? Old Miriam was a Christian, staunch and fierce." He laughed. "I remember how she scolded Ellie for the clothes she had brought from America. They had just hung in the closet going to waste, you see. Miriam would be the first to offer her clothes for such a worthy cause. She would not imagine that even a beautiful caftan could win the heart of a Husseini, however."

"I wish I could have known her." There was regret in Rachel's eyes. "She sounds wonderful."

"And terrible. Depending on which side of her you were on. She always liked me, I think. Probably because I was a little bit afraid of her. She simply managed this house like a Jewish mama. Howard loved it, and Ellie gave back as much as she took. Those were good days." Sadness glimmered in his deep brown eyes. "I will miss them all."

Rachel had already opened the door to Miriam's room and was admiring the spartan neatness of the old woman. The olivewood cross still hung above the bed. The dresser was a bit dusty, but her hairbrush, comb, small mirror, and well-worn Bible were still all in a row.

Slowly Rachel opened the top drawer. Nightgowns and underclothes were precisely folded. In the second drawer, the drab fabric of clothes for market and work carried a cheerful scent of lilac. And finally, in the third drawer, a neat stack of caftans spoke of the joyful and vibrant spirit of the old woman who had sewn them and embroidered the brightly colored fabric in arabesque patterns that dated back centuries.

Rachel's heart felt somehow knit to that of the old woman as she touched the soft pastel blue of the top gown. "How beautiful!" she whispered. "A work of love, Miriam." Rachel prayed that these clothes would also become a work of God's love in the heart of the tortured young woman who now shared the house with them.

"Well?" called Moshe from the kitchen. "What do you think?"

"She has stitched a garden," Rachel returned with admiration. "Colors and flowers and happiness must have bloomed in her soul."

Miriam would have gladly offered her clothes as a gift to young Sarai, but a gift serves no purpose if it is refused.

"I will not take charity." Sarai turned on her heel.

"It is not charity." Rachel stood in the center of the room, her arms laden with dresses. "You need something to wear."

"I will wear what I came in. I wash it at night. It dries by morning. I will not take the charity of Jews!"

Rachel frowned in thought and stared at Sarai's back. "You have not looked," she said gently. "The handwork—it is done by the hand of an Arab. An old woman named Miriam."

"A Christian!" Sarai spat. "Miriam is a Christian name."

Rachel did not answer for a long time as disappointment filled her. "She wanted to share these with you, Sarai. She—"

"And did you tell her all about me?" Her tone was mocking.

"No." Rachel debated telling her about Miriam's death in the bombing of the Semiramis. "No, I didn't tell her. But she . . . lost everything when the Hotel Semiramis was destroyed. She knows something about the pain that has touched you—and I know, too."

Sarai did not turn to look as Rachel laid the stack of dresses on a chair and left the room.

20

CRABTREE AND THE PRIEST

Bari Harbor was bright and warm with sunlight, but the ancient cathedral was damp and chilly all the same. Crabtree pushed his collar up and crossed his arms to ward off the cold, much as he would have done sitting in the bleachers of a football stadium back home.

He looked toward the ceiling. The light from hundreds of glowing votive candles barely penetrated the gloom of the vaults above him. The thin, reedy soprano voices of the orphanage boys' choir circled up in an unearthly melody that told a story of things long past, or maybe things yet to come.

Latin, thought Tree, somewhat bored with the entire show. *Why don't they at least sing this stuff in Italian?*

It was Palm Sunday. The vast, cavernous hall was packed with people, many of whom Tree recognized from the Bari Harbor Hotel. Today the ladies were dressed a bit less elegantly, in cotton dresses covered by frayed wool coats instead of tight skirts and high heels. Without the abundance of rouge and lipstick, they seemed to be the most ordinary of Italian women.

Watching the women with their eyes turned piously downward or gazing wistfully at the Blessed Virgin, Tree could not help but think that they looked like hopeful candidates for a convent. Madame Hortencia presided over the coterie of silent women. She wore a lace-trimmed scarf over her head, and Tree noticed with amusement that each of the twenty-two others wore an identical head covering.

The little priest stepped up to the altar, and two young boys trailed after him in acolyte robes. Tree recognized the smaller of the two as the boy who called Madame Hortencia "Mama."

The boy had told Tree the day before that the madame never missed a Sunday Mass and that she was a great supporter of the church and the orphanage since Father Antonell had come to help the homeless children of Bari Harbor. Tree had little interest in religion, but this item of information had all the makings of a great story.

The complexity of this plotline had the great diversity of a novel: *"Arab supply ship blown up in Italian harbor. Jewish terrorists aided by Italian madame and Catholic priest!"* Tree could almost visualize the headlines in the cracked plaster of the cathedral walls.

To top it all off, he was convinced that these particular Jewish terrorists were, in fact, Americans. Not just any Americans, but a war ace and a photojournalist related to the American archaeologist murdered in Jerusalem! Now all he had to do was track down the last two people in this story line and he might win the Pulitzer . . . or at least a box of Cuban cigars from his editor.

Tree sighed with contentment and settled back against the hard pew. He clutched a dog-eared copy of *LIFE* magazine that had been sent from the Rome office by special courier the day before.

"Hail, Mary, full of grace . . . ," recited the crowd.

Tree flipped through the pages of the magazine as an astonished and indignant old woman clutched her rosary and tried to look at the irreverent stranger out of the corner of her eye. He grinned back at her and opened the pages wider for her to see the devastation of a bomb that had destroyed a street in Jerusalem. The old woman frowned, crossed herself, and closed her eyes to concentrate on the Mass. Tree resisted the urge to laugh out loud. Instead he studied each photograph, memorizing every caption beneath the work of the young American photographer.

The Mass was particularly long. Choir boys squirmed, and Tree caught himself nearly dozing off a few times. Only the continual kneeling kept him awake toward the end. He watched the back of Madame Hortencia and followed her every move until, at last, the Mass ended and the crowd filed out into the sunlight.

"Signore Crabtree!" Madame Hortencia was delighted as she passed where he sat. "You have come to Mass! *Ecce homo! Si?* Behold the man!" The girls giggled and waved as they walked by.

"Just business, I'm afraid, uh . . . Madame Hortencia."

The large woman shrugged with a broad and typical Italian gesture. "Always I say . . . it cannot hurt. *Si?*"

"Well, I'm a little surprised the place is still standing with me here."

"If it don't fall on *me*, signore . . ." She rolled her eyes and did not finish the sentiment. "Father Antonell . . . he speaks *good* English! He can tell you whatever you want to know." Then she was swept away in the crowd.

Crabtree remained in the pew until the last old man hobbled out, casting a puzzled glance his way. Only locals, it seemed, attended Mass here. After all, Rome and the Vatican were a scant few hours away. The pope would be offering Mass at St. Peter's.

Crabtree waited until the auditorium fell silent, then opened the *LIFE* magazine and glanced at the photos of David Meyer and Ellie Warne once more. *They were here!* he thought, sensing their presence like a bloodhound picking up a scent. The little priest reentered the auditorium. He had laid aside his robes and was now dressed in a simple black cassock. He did not look out at the pews but moved silently near the altar. He genuflected and knelt before the crucifix for a long time, evidently unaware that Crabtree watched him with undisguised fascination.

Then, as if to introduce himself, Crabtree coughed loudly. The priest did not turn from his prayers, so Crabtree coughed again.

The little man's head was still bowed. He crossed himself and rose slowly to scan the pews.

Crabtree stood and strode purposefully toward the priest. "Father Antonell?"

"Yes?"

"Enjoyed the service, Padre." Crabtree stuck out his hand.

"You are not a Catholic," the priest said suspiciously.

"How can you tell?"

"Trust me." The priest smiled. "*Experto credite* . . . I know a Catholic when I see one. This place is also not in the guidebooks. So, what may I do for you, Mister—?"

"Crabtree." Tree grinned broadly, putting on his most friendly manner. "And you're pretty good. I am a friend of Ellie Warne's."

Crabtree continued pumping the priest's hand as he smiled into the little man's face and hoped for some twinge of response.

There was none. Not so much as a flicker of recognition showed in the eyes of Father Antonell. "*Scusi?*" He lapsed into Italian.

"Aw, come on. Ellie Warne? She was here. With you." Tree would not accept the feigned ignorance of the priest.

Father Antonell shrugged. "No, I'm sorry. I am not familiar with—"

Crabtree was insistent. "Look." He flipped open the *LIFE* magazine and displayed her photograph. "I already know—"

"I can't say I recognize her." The priest's expression was unchanged, but now tiny beads of perspiration stood out on his brow.

"I already showed this to the girls at Madame Hortencia's place. Ellie Warne. American journalist—right, Father?" Crabtree pulled out his European press pass. "I am a friend of hers. David Meyer I could take or leave, if you know what I mean, but I've worked with Ellie, and—"

The priest held up his hand for silence. His face became suddenly angry. "I really don't care who you are—"

"Not real friendly of you, Padre. You know, you might have to go to confession for lying."

Father Antonell's eyes narrowed and a shade seemed to come down over his face. "You are not a member of my parish, and I am a busy man."

"I already know she was here." Crabtree spread his hands in protest. "Look, Padre, I've got her identified already from the girls down at Madame Hortencia's. You set it up for her to go on that ship. You think if I wanted to get you—or her—in trouble, I would be here like this? If I were some kind of bad guy, I'd be down at the police headquarters with this stuff right now."

Father Antonell studied him with a distant coolness. "What exactly is it you are after, Mr. Crabtree? I have nothing I can tell you except that an American reporter came to me and asked for my help with a small, shall we say, arrangement—for which a large offering was made to our orphanage."

Crabtree smiled. "She's a good kid. I've worked with her closely enough to know what she's all about."

"Mr. Crabtree"—the priest's tone was cool—"you must think I am a fool. Sophia told me you were here three days ago. You are a United Nations representative. When all the other reporters left, you remained behind. *Why?*"

Crabtree fished in his jacket pocket for the crumpled telegram that he had arranged to be sent to him from the Rome editorial offices.

"You want proof?" He handed the paper to the priest, who unfolded it slowly and held it to the light of the votive candles. It was dated three days before.

TREE STOP OPERATOR TOOK URGENT CALL FROM ELLIE W STOP
ASKED FOR YOU STOP SAID THERE WAS TROUBLE STOP LINE WENT
DEAD. . . .

The priest looked up at him now, concern evident on his face. He blinked and continued reading the telegram as Crabtree sighed and frowned.

CALL POSSIBLE LOCAL—ROME STOP COULD NOT LOCATE STOP
THOUGHT YOU SHOULD KNOW STOP JOHN

"Look," Crabtree said, confident that the wire had done the trick, "if you know where she is—she's a good kid, Padre, and I'd appreciate a little help."

Father Antonell's face was stricken as he read the wire again and again. He studied Crabtree, searching his face as if he could find some answer there. "Come with me," he said at last, leading the way out the side door of the church and through the tangled garden to the rectory.

Without speaking, he marched past the old housekeeper and into the sunlit dining room that overlooked the harbor. On the polished wood table, an English-language newspaper lay open. Father Antonell remained standing as he shoved the paper toward Crabtree and tapped a two-column article on the bottom of the page.

"Two priests found murdered," Crabtree read aloud, *"along with a washroom attendant in the Rome railway station. Priests unidentified . . . taller of the two shot through the head in execution-style slaying. Priest had both arms in plaster casts. . . ."* Crabtree glanced into the worried face of Father Antonell. *"Police speculate that the murders may have been executions carried out as revenge for some wartime activity by the men under Benito Mussolini. . . ."*

Father Antonell stood shaking his head. "I read it, and—"

"Ellie has something to do with this?" Crabtree asked, clearly having won the priest's confidence.

"I was afraid she might be in trouble."

"What has she got to do with this? Partisans have been executing ex-Fascists and Nazis since the end of the war."

"They aren't Fascists." Father Antonell gulped and sat down slowly. He put his face in his hands. "I don't know what they are exactly. I loaned them some clothes. The tall one broke his arms in a plane crash. David Meyer—"

"Slow down, Padre." Crabtree's face was flushed with excitement now.

"Mikhail—I don't know his last name—was treated at the hospital by the sisters. David and Ellie stayed here. She was the reporter, but you obviously know that already."

"Yes. A few days ago."

"I simply loaned them clothes. Dropped them off at the Rome station after the explosion of the ship. I don't know any more than that."

"So what about these two dead guys?"

"One of them must be Mikhail—the casts, you know. The other one could be David Meyer, for all I know. As for Ellie Meyer—Warne, you call her—I have been sick with worry for her safety since I saw this in the paper."

"Are they Zionists?" Crabtree asked, trying not to sound too eager. "I mean, with the Zionists?"

Father Antonell furrowed his brow and stared mutely at Crabtree. "You were in Palestine with Ellie. I would presume you would know that better than I." The facade of detached control returned. He had said much more than Crabtree had even suspected, and he knew it.

"We're all rooting for the Jews, Padre. That's not what I meant. I mean, were these two guys—this Mikhail—was he with the Zionist Underground?" Tree asked. Then, inwardly, he kicked himself. *Too eager. Too much a reporter.*

"*Si fecisti nega*, Mr. Crabtree. You know as much as I know now, eh?" The priest stood abruptly, almost angrily. As if he were sorry that he had let the man into his home and into his confidence. "And I do not see how what you know can help Ellie Meyer if she is in the difficulty the telegram suggests she is in. I will show you the way to the door now."

Crabtree feigned irritation and hurt as he followed the priest out. But in fact, he had all the information he needed. He could leave Bari Harbor now in the certainty that he would win his box of Havana cigars by the time he was finished.

21

THE CAULDRON BOILS

"What shall become of me?" Sarai asked as the radio blared the news into the tiny kitchen. Still she refused to wear Miriam's dresses, and her black mourning dress was a somber commentary on her state of mind.

"For the first time, Haganah forces have paraded openly in the city of Jerusalem. Dressed in a variety of salvaged uniforms, the Jewish army defied the British order. . . ."

Moshe's smile faded. He looked at the young Arab woman as though he could not comprehend her question for a moment. "You will stay here, of course."

Sarai did not respond.

Only Rachel caught the tone in Moshe's voice. He was still torn, she knew, but he was determined to try to accept Sarai and help her. He had promised Rachel.

"Of course, you must stay here, Sarai." Rachel reached her hand across the table and rested it on the girl's arm.

Sarai drew back. "I . . . I am not one of you. I am no one. . . . The Zionists who parade in Jerusalem. Those who now make you smile. They have taken my life from me."

"Shortly after dusk, the forces of the Haganah began their first offensive action in the New City of Jerusalem. In retaliation for the Hadassah massacre of a few days before, special units of the Palmach attacked the Arab Quarter of Sheikh Jarrah. Fighting is sporadic. The British have remained neutral. . . ."

Rachel saw Moshe's reaction. Clearly he wanted to shout for joy at the news. Instead he clasped his hands and stared at the saltshaker. "You will be safe here."

"Sheikh Jarrah was the home of my family," Sarai said with an edge of defiance. "Now the Jews attack my home."

"And only last week seventy-five Jewish physicians and scholars were murdered in Sheikh Jarrah. Including the dear man who owned this place." Moshe's voice was controlled, but Rachel heard his anger at the Arab girl's accusations.

"And that—" Sarai tore the scarf from her head, revealing her shorn hair—"was in retaliation for *this*!" Her teeth were clenched. Tears of rage sparkled in her black eyes. "Deir Yassin."

Moshe looked away.

"Meanwhile, the elite troops of Jordan's Arab Legion began flocking into the Muslim quarters of the Old City. Their leader, British-trained Fawzi Tell, has vowed that first the holy places will be protected and the Jews expelled, and then the Legion will strike west into the city against Jewish bastions of strength."

"Sarai," Moshe said, the uncharacteristic edge still in his voice, "you may hope for the Arab Legion to come, but if they come here, you may find yourself even more unhappy than you are with us."

"Moshe—" Rachel's eyes pleaded with him.

Moshe shrugged and fell silent.

Sarai sat rigid in her chair, her face full of confusion and pain. She clutched the scarf to her. "What is to become of me?" she whispered for the hundredth time since Moshe and Rachel had brought her home. She stood slowly and left the room.

"Sarai," Rachel called to her. Then she looked toward Moshe. "You should be more careful. She is still very tender."

"I am doing my best, Rachel. What do you expect of me?"

"Compassion!" Rachel was also feeling the stress.

"She told you herself that it was her husband who blew up the Jewish Agency."

"Her *husband*! She didn't even know him!"

Moshe drummed his fingers on the table. "It's hard," he admitted. "Hard to love when there's no response or when the only response we do get is hostility."

"For her, the hatred is hard to overcome. She does not know the love of Messiah as we do."

Moshe nodded and rose to clear the dishes. The discussion was finished; there was nothing more to say.

"Representatives from the UN Security Council have called for a truce. The Arab High Committee of Haj Amin Husseini has rejected this plea,

and fighting along the pass from Tel Aviv to Jerusalem broke out anew today. . . ."

Rachel left the room. The voice of the broadcaster followed her through the dark hallway and up the stairs to where Sarai sat alone in the small bedroom. Rachel did not light a candle, knowing that the young woman was more comfortable in the blackness. She knocked on the door, even though she had already entered. "May I come in?"

"You are in." Sarai's voice was shaking.

"May I sit with you, then? For a while?"

The girl did not reply to that question. But an instant later, a sob erupted. "Why did they not let me die? I belong to no one. I am not anything anymore. Your husband mistrusts me because I am an Arab. Because I have a heart for my people as you have a heart for yours. Why . . . why did they not let me die?" She covered her face with her hands.

Rachel sat on the edge of the bed in silence.

Minutes passed as the girl sobbed quietly. Rachel handed her a handkerchief. "I am sorry," she whispered, and her voice carried her heart with it. "Truly I am."

"Sorry does not give me back my family," the girl said bitterly. "Or my chastity."

Rachel nodded. She understood, and the knowledge of what Sarai felt cut deep into her own soul. "There is no answer, Sarai, for that. What was done cannot be undone. I know this too well."

The girl looked at her in the darkness, her eyes catching a glimmer of light. "Yes. The scar on your arm. I have not forgotten." There was an eagerness to know more.

"I was younger than you."

"It was not Muslim men who did this thing to you."

"Not Muslim—they were just men. Not anyone in particular . . . I know that now. Evil has no nationality. It simply exists and acts against the vulnerable and the innocent."

"It was Jews who did this to me," Sarai spat. *"Jews!"*

Rachel frowned and groped for words to begin again. She bit her lip and breathed a prayer for wisdom stronger than the bitterness that now confronted her. "I was thirteen when men broke in the door of my parents' home. They beat my father with the butts of their rifles."

"Deir Yassin."

"And a soldier broke my brother's arm when he tried to fight."

"Deir Yassin."

"They raped my mother before the eyes of my brothers and my father and me. I had never known a man. I was a child, and I . . ." Rachel faltered and fell silent until Sarai timidly reached out her hand to her. "We were assembled for the railcars. Separated. My brothers and my father taken away. Mama and me left together—for a while. Then at Auschwitz, after three days in the cattle cars, I was selected to live and she to die. I . . . they tricked me—offered me water—and when I turned, she was gone. . . ." Rachel's voice broke.

Sarai leaned forward and clasped Rachel's hands tightly to comfort her.

"And then I was branded and taken for use by the officers," Rachel continued.

"And you lived."

"I wanted to die. Every day I prayed to die."

"But still you lived. A prisoner among your enemies. As I am."

"We are not your enemies, and you are not a prisoner, Sarai. No one will hurt you here. You are free to go or stay as you choose."

"Why did you tell me this?"

"Because . . . I am a Jew. But not your enemy. Those who killed your heart and joy, they are men like the ones who nearly killed mine. I think they cannot be called Jew or Arab or German. They are the evil that labels us friend and foe and justifies wickedness by that label. Do not call them Jews."

Sarai bowed her head. "And now what am I? There is nothing left for me."

Rachel lifted the girl's chin. "You are most loved, Sarai."

"My family has denied me."

"But God, who is merciful, sees you and cares for you so very much."

Sarai laughed a short and bitter laugh. "Allah! Where was he when my enemies have done this thing to me? He cannot love me now. I am defiled. Fit only to live as a prostitute."

"If you will not let God love you in your anger, will you at least let *me* try? Will you let your enemy love you, Sarai? And then perhaps later we will speak again of God."

Sarai wiped her nose and lifted her chin defiantly again. "If you can do this thing, I will not stop you . . . my enemy."

Rachel smiled. It was a beginning. "Good. Then you may call me your enemy, but I will love you all the same. And Tikvah, who is also Jewish—she will be your enemy if you like, but she will love you, and you will see that you are not alone. It is agreed?"

"As you say it." Sarai turned her face away. "And now I am tired. Very tired."

The sound of the news broadcast still echoed through the house as

Rachel left the room. News of the Bari Harbor bombing and speculation about Jewish operations in Europe filled the airways.

Moshe glanced up guiltily when Rachel entered the kitchen. He sat with his arms on his knees and toyed with a spoon. "Well?" he questioned.

"She is . . . in such pain," Rachel replied. "I cannot blame her for hating."

"She will stay?"

"There is no place else for her."

"I do not feel good about it, Rachel." He shook his head. "God help me, I sense danger from her."

"Because she is an Arab?"

"Because she is of the House of Husseini, and she is—"

"What?"

"An enemy to everything we wish to accomplish. An enemy!"

Rachel smoothed back Moshe's hair. She sensed his torment, the seeming contradiction between the war they fought and the commands of God. "You are a soldier, my love," she whispered, "but a soldier whose life belongs to Yeshua. It will not be easy. But if Sarai is, as you say, an enemy, then we will love our enemy, even as Messiah loves her."

Tom Kane was greeted with enthusiasm by the Haganah men who had gathered in Tipat Chalev for the meeting. A few carried weapons openly, but most were unarmed, their weapons safely hidden for the moment when they would most need them. Dov and Ehud sat together at the front of the room. Twenty others were scattered around the long, low tables of the community dining room.

Kane cleared his throat and spoke loudly to the assembly. "I am here, of course, as a representative of the United States. We are a neutral party and not in a position to direct policy. However, our concern is great for the holy places of Jewish heritage—"

"Get to the point," someone called in Brooklyn-accented English from the back of the room. "So, who isn't worried?"

"The Arabs! That's who!" someone added.

A roar of laughter filled the room, and far from being insulted, Kane relaxed from his rhetoric. These were Americans he was talking to, so he would talk plainly.

"You guys are from the States?" he asked. Every one of the twenty, with the exception of Ehud and Dov, answered in the affirmative.

"We thought it was better you should talk to Americans since there are men from a dozen nations here and it would take all night to translate, *nu*?" said Dov.

"Hey, tell Truman I'm going to vote for him in November if I'm still alive and he helps us out!" More laughter followed.

"Nah! You can't vote no more, meshuggener! You ain't a citizen since you're here fighting!"

"So, who's going to know? You won't tell, will you, Kane?"

Kane was laughing, too. "Not if you are going to vote for my boss! And if you are still alive!" The laughter was nervous. "And that is just what I'm here to talk to you about. The Old City seems to be the main point of contention here—"

"You mean besides Tel Aviv, Haifa, Galilee, and Safed?"

"Don't forget the Negev!"

Dov held his hands up for silence. "Please! If I had known my Americans were going to talk so much, I would have brought the Polish!"

"And then they would have not understood what Mr. Kane was talking about!" The men laughed again.

"That's what makes politics, gentlemen," Kane retorted good-naturedly.

"So maybe in forty years the historians can translate this war for us, *nu*?" Dov said under his breath.

"We are hoping that we can avert a war," Kane said more seriously, and suddenly the room grew still. He searched the concerned faces of the men before him. They were mostly dressed in the garb of the Orthodox they now lived among. Most had, no doubt, been raised in neighborhoods around New York. They had come to the Holy City not to pray but to fight.

"How are you going to do that?'

"It's like trying to make an elephant fit into a phone booth!" This time no one laughed.

Kane frowned. To these in the heart of the siege and the center of the cauldron, peace seemed like an impossible dream. "It will take time," Kane said. "More time than you have, perhaps, here in the Old City."

A heavy silence hung in the room. Men stared at their hands as they contemplated the truth of Kane's words.

"We know what is beyond our barricades," Ehud said. "We know better than you."

"We are—" Kane spoke carefully—"the United Nations is hoping for a truce, and then perhaps that Jerusalem will be made into an international city."

"We will never give up the Holy City!" called a man from the back of the room.

"Not *give up*," Kane explained. *"Share."*

"We are already sharing with half the army of Jordan," someone said. "Or haven't you noticed?"

"And that is a problem that must be resolved—peacefully! Our State Department is actively seeking your relief here in the Old City. But you must be willing also if opportunity knocks."

"As long as opportunity isn't dressed like Haj Amin!"

Kane spread his arms in a gesture of innocence. "More likely opportunity will appear as a white flag of truce."

"Omaine!" bellowed Ehud.

"Preach on!" A bearded young man in the front said loudly.

Kane smiled broadly. "That is just what we wanted to know—if those of you who defend the Old City were willing—"

"Have you ever met a Jew who would not haggle?"

"As long as we can talk loud and use our hands, eh?" The laughter began again.

"Much better than dying! Can we talk Mamaloshen?"

"You want to talk Yiddish?" Kane surprised the men with his knowledge of the word for mother tongue. "Only in a minyan, I'm afraid."

"Well, while we're talking, how about arranging a regular meal ticket here in the Old City? They open the gate . . . they close the gate . . . they let a convoy in . . . they don't. I'm starting to look like a loksh." The tall man grinned at Kane. "So, you know what a loksh is?"

Kane shook his head. "I'm afraid that has gone past me."

"A *noodle!*" said the man. "And looking like a loksh is what everyone in the Old City is worried about! Not the Arabs—may their brains be turned to steam!"

"There are children here! Tell that to President Truman and the United Nations. We told the Arabs, but they don't seem to mind."

Kane nodded. "Yes. The children. The Arabs have offered to evacuate—"

Dov said to him, "The children will not go. They have made a vow."

Kane looked at him without comprehension. "But they are children!"

"They are Jews. All of us are soldiers. You must tell your president," Dov said quietly. "All of them know what happens to Jews. They were taught by the world not so long ago. They will not leave."

"I must know," Kane said, "what the general consensus is here in the heart of Jewish Jerusalem. What do the religious among you feel about this?"

"Come"—Dov took his arm as the meeting ended—"I will show

you." He led Kane down the steps into the basement of Tipat Chalev. By the dim light of candles, men and women, young and old, were stationed at tables. Before them was an interesting mix of items: gunpowder, cigarette tins, kerosene, empty bottles, and fuses.

A frail young woman with a sad face caught Dov's eyes and smiled shyly up at him. He waved and smiled back briefly. An old rabbi and a young boy worked together, laboring over Molotov cocktails.

"Rebbe Lebowitz," Dov called to the old man and motioned as Kane stood on the steps and watched the scene with wonder.

The rabbi rose stiffly and walked toward them. "Twelve we have made already tonight, young Dov," the old man said proudly.

"That is good, Rebbe Lebowitz." Dov clapped the old rabbi on the back. "Now I will introduce you to this American, Mr. Kane, who has come here from President Truman."

The two men shook hands. "You have not come to help us make bombs, I think, Mr. Kane. So why are you here?"

"To understand. Maybe to help in some way."

"Then tell your president what we are doing here. Tell him we are trapped and hungry and cut off." The rabbi smiled into Kane's compassionate face. "And tell him that an old rabbi said this message is for you to take to the people in Washington."

"Certainly," Kane said.

"Tell him we here in the Old City say to Americans, 'Remember the Alamo.' "

Kane must have registered shock, for the old man's eyes lit up, as if he had gotten his message through. "That's it?" Kane asked.

"That is all the American history I have heard." Rabbi Lebowitz nodded. "Is that not enough?"

The braying of donkeys and bawling of camels drifted through the open window of Haj Amin's hotel suite in Damascus. A tall, black, Sudanese bodyguard poured the delicate coffee cup full to the brim, then placed a hand to his forehead and bowed slightly to Haj Amin before he backed away from the broad desk.

Haj Amin did not notice the steaming cup or the massive hulk of a man in the room. Newspapers and magazines were spread out across the enormous flat surface of the mahogany desk, and with the intense concentration of a student studying for a final exam, the Palestinian leader scoured the pages containing the story of the *Trina*.

Already salvage operations were going on in Bari Harbor. Although

the ammunition was counted almost a complete loss, there was hope
that the rifles could be salvaged from the wreck. Story after story gave
details of the sinking of the *Trina*, but only one reporter seemed to have
complete information. Two of the Jewish terrorists had been elimi-
nated. Haj Amin had known that fact before any connection had been
made between the ship and the murder of two obscure priests in the
railway station in Rome. The news had given him some satisfaction,
of course, but now, beneath the name of an American reporter named
Crabtree, the saga of the Mossad continued to unfold daily.

What the Italian officials and Haj Amin's own European agents had
failed to uncover, this newspaper reporter seemed to know.

The call to prayer rang out from high atop the colorful minaret of
central Damascus. Outside, in the dusty streets, men bowed and spread
their prayer rugs to kneel and pray toward Mecca. The prayers of the
Faithful rose as one:

"Praise belongs to Allah, lord of the worlds—
The compassionate, the merciful.
King of the day of judgment.
Thee we worship and thee we ask for help.
Guide us in the straight path,
The path of those whom thou hast favored,
Not the path of those who incur thine anger nor of
those who go astray. . . ."

Haj Amin did not kneel today or turn his face toward the east, but
he heard the murmured words of the prostrate bodyguard who prayed
along with the crowds in the streets. And then, as if in answer to his question, thoughts came to him in a rush of excitement that caused him to
close his eyes and sigh in confident relief.

The Jews had made a fool of him in Bari Harbor. Two had paid the ultimate penalty . . . two had died. The leaders of the Arab states mocked him
for his defeat, and yet, if that defeat were turned to victory, would they then
not recognize that he had accomplished what others had failed to do?

"Guide us in the straight path," he murmured. *"The path of those whom
thou hast favored. . . ."* He turned his face and thoughts toward Rome,
where one still waited patiently for his command.

What glory there would be for the one who finally destroyed the
wheels of the Zionist machine!

"Not the path of those who incur thine anger nor those who go astray." Haj
Amin glanced again at the name of Crabtree. "Guide us," he whispered.
"Guide us."

❋

Crabtree stepped to one side as the huge, steel-plated door of the cold room rolled back. The cold room of the Rome morgue was, in fact, little more than an oversized walk-in freezer. Its dimensions were ten-by-ten at most, and open coolant coils rattled on the ceiling and the walls.

"This is where we keep the unidentified bodies, signore." The medical examiner switched on the single bare lightbulb that dangled from the ceiling in the center of the room. "There have been many since the war." He swept his hand over the metal slabs where a half-dozen bodies lay covered with white sheets. "We keep them ten days, and then they are given a Catholic burial. . . . We cannot do more. There have been so many."

Crabtree smiled. "I don't think you'll want to give these two a Catholic burial, Doctor."

"No?"

"No. Not if they are what I think they are." Tree turned a full circle, sweeping his eyes over the sterile white room.

The doctor had seemed relieved that Crabtree had come. It was a rarity that anyone came to the morgue in search of friends these days. Reprisals against Benito Mussolini's Fascists had been so common that thousands of executed Italians had passed through the morgue. This appeared to be just one more incident in a long list.

"Even Fascists deserve a descent burial, eh? The sacraments—"

Crabtree did not answer. The two men he had come to look at were neither Fascists nor Catholics. Of that he was certain. "No identifying marks, you say?"

The doctor moved down the row of bodies to the two on the end. He picked up a chart that dangled at the foot of a slab. "Here you are, signore. Read for yourself: height . . . weight . . . eye color . . . approximate age. There is little else. We assumed they were priests, but no one from the church—"

Crabtree lifted the sheet of the first man. He had seen death a thousand times before as a correspondent during the war. It had been a long time since he had felt squeamish about a body. His interest was purely clinical. Two bullet holes like small black dots in the chest. Hair dark brown. Thinning on top. The man died needing a shave. Maybe thirty years old. "You have photographs?" Tree asked.

"*Si*. We always keep such things on file for a long time after. In case some relative comes to look. But we cannot keep the bodies for long, you see." He frowned. "Do you know this fellow, signore?" The doctor seemed fascinated by the easy way Crabtree examined the face of the dead man.

Tree checked the left forearm carefully, then let the sheet fall back over the gray face. "And the man with the broken arms?"

"There, signore." The doctor gestured toward a slab with contours slightly different, as though something held the sheet aloft.

Crabtree lifted the drape and studied the features of the dead man before him: Large nose. High cheekbones. Fair skin. Tall. Fragile-looking. The casts were still on the slightly raised arms. "Why didn't you take off the casts?" Crabtree asked curiously.

"What use, eh?"

"Well, his bones aren't going to set now, Doctor." Crabtree could not resist the comment.

The examiner laughed out loud. "I see you do not know these men." He chuckled. "I shall remember your joke. Very funny, Signore Crabtree!"

Crabtree was not laughing. "No, I don't know them." He stared at the face of the young corpse. "But I have a hunch—" He tugged his earlobe and let the drape fall. "How much trouble would it be to get the cast off this stiff?"

The doctor shrugged and looked uncertain. "For a price, signore . . . perhaps—"

"How much?" Crabtree was used to the constant bribes and behind-the-scenes bartering that ran the wheels of postwar Italy. The black market was everywhere, whether one wanted to purchase a pack of American cigarettes or examine the forearm of a corpse.

"Times are hard in Rome since the war, signore. . . ."

Crabtree grinned and peeled off five one-dollar bills. "American cash, Doc."

"A pair of shoes costs sixty dollars."

"Well, I thought you got your shoes off these guys."

A flash of resentment appeared on the examiner's face. His voice became hard. "I have other business to attend to." He started to turn around.

"Ten bucks American. What do you say?"

The doctor hesitated, then shrugged. "Fifteen."

"Twelve. I could crack the thing off myself with a hammer."

There was a moment of silence, interrupted only by the rattle of the coolant coils. The doctor's rosy cheeks and bright blue eyes were the only colors in the stark white room. "Have you American cigarettes as well?"

Tree patted his breast pocket and pulled out half a pack of Lucky Strikes. "Twelve bucks and this . . . and I get a look at the stiff's arm."

Ten minutes later, the plaster crumbled and fell to the floor beside the slab. The arm of the dead man remained upright. Crabtree peered intently at the harsh blue of the tattoo on the inside of the left forearm. He took a notebook from his pocket and copied down the number. "You see, Doctor, you shouldn't leave any stone unturned, as it were."

The doctor was already inhaling the smoke of a cigarette. "So. They are not men of the church. Who are they, then? And who killed them?"

"In answer to your first question, I would call a rabbi to bury them . . . if there are any left in Italy. As for who they are and who killed them, I don't know . . . and I don't know . . . yet." He closed the little book and smiled with satisfaction. *B-B100786. This guy was in Bergen-Belsen and survived! Only to end up dead in a bathroom in Rome.* The irony of it seemed something like surviving a flood, then drowning in a bathtub.

"How else may I help you?" The doctor seemed pleased with his reward.

"A cup of hot coffee, for starters. Then a telephone."

The familiar clacking of multiple typewriters and Teletypes greeted Crabtree as he strode into the cluttered office of the *Times* European edition.

Desks were piled high with stacks of papers and clippings gleaned from two dozen foreign-language newspapers across Europe. The news of various nations was being translated and reinterpreted for transmission back to the States.

Of the twelve staff members in the European office, all were men. Most were seasoned by the conflict in Europe. One was a young, fresh-faced kid who had worked for the *Stars and Stripes*, a military publication during the war. All were misfits of one sort or another, who preferred the independence and autonomy of the European agency to the comparatively structured offices of American-based newspapers. And this was, after all, where the world's events changed and toppled and renewed on a daily basis. There was, as the saying went, never a dull moment for these reporters.

Even though Crabtree had been gone for four days, barely a head raised when he walked into the room. "Hey, Tree," the kid called. "Thought you had gone to Palestine."

"Not yet, Stripes. I'm on to something."

Jones, a dour, overweight reporter who had shared the bus to Bari and then returned to Rome completely bored with the story, raised a hand in halfhearted greeting. "Where y'been, Tree? You latch on to some cute dame down at that flophouse?"

"Sure," Tree returned, not willing to let out his secrets. "Got myself a real babe!"

Jones raised his eyebrows and shook his head as if to ridicule Tree's taste in women. "You musta been in some other town."

Tree plopped down at his desk and leaned far back in the chair to put his feet up. He shoved his fedora farther back on his head and just sat breathing the familiar scent of newsprint, wet ink, and cigar smoke for a few minutes. "Stripes?" he barked. He liked the kid. He had beat the living tar out of him the day he had met him, but that had been the fault of Jones. Jones had filled the kid full of stories about how much Tree liked to be called L.C., so the kid, of course, had tried it out right away. Crabtree had then given the kid a beating and the permanent nickname of Stripes.

"Yeah, Tree?" The kid was eager to help and eager to learn. He brought two warm bottles of Coke to Tree's desk.

"I got something for you to do for me, kid." Tree swigged the Coke, then reached into his pocket for the notebook. He tore off a page and handed the scribbled tattoo number to the kid. "I want you to trace this."

Stripes stared hard at the number. With his curly hair and smattering of freckles, he reminded Tree of Jimmy Olsen, the cub reporter in the *Superman* comic strip. It occurred to Tree that he really couldn't remember Stripes' name.

"What is it? A license plate?"

"No. A tattoo. Off a dead man's arm, kid." Tree lowered his voice as a signal that Stripes should keep his mouth shut about it.

"Yeah? Who's the dead guy?"

"A Jew." Tree looked furtively over his shoulder.

"Well, where do I find out—?"

"I figure he came from Palestine. Maybe out of the camps at Cyprus. One thing is for sure. He was in on the bombing of the Arab ship. Mikhail something . . . maybe that's his real name. Maybe not."

Stripes stared hard at the number. "What do you figure you're going to do with this?"

"Just get me his name." Tree smiled. The kind of smile that meant *"It's none of your business."* "If the guy was a fugitive, if he was registered at Cyprus or a refugee camp, the Brits will have this number. They'll have his name, most likely. It's worth twenty bucks to me if you follow it up."

Stripes bristled at the mention of money. "Naw. Just lemme do it. For the pleasure . . ."

Indeed, Tree liked the kid. He took another long swig of Coke.

"'Pleasure is the object, duty and the goal of all rational creatures,' " he quoted. "Voltaire said that. You know who he was?"

"Sure." Stripes appeared wounded. "Everybody knows who he was."

"He was a reporter. A reporter. Like us, huh? And you're learning to love the job more than money, aren't you? Like me. Just do it for the sport of the kill, as it were."

"Yeah, Tree, I guess so." The young man looked confused.

Crabtree laughed loudly and downed the rest of the Coke. "Okay. You get the guy's name for me and I'll buy you supper. What do you say? You can call me Supper-man!"

"Sure, Tree." Stripes stared at the number again and shrugged. "Then will you tell me what you're gonna do with it?"

Tree cocked his head sideways. "No. But I'll buy you a copy of the newspaper and you can read all about it!" He flipped his fingers upward as a signal that Stripes was dismissed. Then he pulled open his desk drawer and rummaged through the mess until at last he triumphantly retrieved a copy of the train schedules from the Rome Central Railway Station.

BELOVED ENEMY

Days passed slowly in Jerusalem, with the sun beating down hard on the backs of Jewish civilians who waited for the water trucks. As Moshe planned the defense of the city within the broken walls of the Jewish Agency, Rachel worked at food-distribution centers, rationing meager supplies of food as the convoys rolled up the pass from Tel Aviv. Whatever was not immediately handed out to the citizens was stored away in warehouses around the Jewish quarters of the New City.

Throughout the day, Sarai Tafara watched the baby and stayed behind the shuttered windows of the large, nearly empty Moniger home. She spoke little when Moshe and Rachel returned for a few hours' rest, but when she was alone with the child, she sang the gentle songs of her own childhood and wept with longing to see her mother and sisters again.

Yet she knew that dream was impossible. Now she lived in purgatory, an outcast. She was not able to fit with the people who sheltered her, yet she was banished from those of her own blood forever. The very building where Moshe Sachar worked each day had been destroyed by her husband. The father of the child she now held had been murdered by mobs of her people. And at Deir Yassin, she herself had received the punishment for those deeds. Innocence, it seemed, was of no consequence in the land of Palestine.

Sarai smiled sadly as Tikvah drooled a toothless grin and squealed in delight. "You do not even fear the world you live in," Sarai murmured. "And yet we are enemies, you and I. My brothers were there when your father died, but you cannot know what it is to hate. Not yet. You cannot know, but life will teach you, little one. I only wish I could be like you—how I wish I could be like you!" She closed her eyes and laid her cheek against the soft cheek of the baby. "We are enemies, you and I," she whispered. "Yet I cannot hate you. I have tried. And I cannot hate Rachel or fear her. She will not hurt me. She could not."

Sarai changed the baby and fed her milk so thin and watery that Sarai wondered how the infant could grow strong on it. Then she put Tikvah down for a nap as Rachel had showed her and went to the kitchen to stare out at the newly blossoming flowers in the small courtyard. Beyond that were the tall ramparts of the city walls, where soldiers of Jordan's Arab Legion now openly walked through the souks.

Even as her people had left their homes, the Legion had swarmed over the Jordan River to join the ragtag forces of her cousin Haj Amin. Now snipers fired from the city walls in an unrelenting barrage, halting convoys into the Jewish Quarter. Though food abounded in the Muslim quarters, milk here in the Jewish districts was more water than milk. Sarai fretted about the baby.

"I might pass through Jaffa Gate," Sarai said quietly. "Am I not a daughter of the prophet? I know where my mother purchased fresh goat's milk for little Alambra when my sister's own milk became dry. I might do this thing for Rachel—if I could walk through the Jewish barricades."

She considered the thought. Half in her mind was the hope that she would glimpse some member of her family, even though she knew they had left the city. The danger to a Muslim woman walking alone through a city populated mostly by soldiers was enough to bring a new rush of fear to her.

She let the thought die away and pulled down the window shade against the sunlight. Her mouth became dry, and her heart thumped wildly as she remembered the faces of her tormentors. Voices. Rough, clawing hands. Cruel laughter and her own screams. And then she heard the soft pleading voice of Rachel and remembered touching the scar on her forearm. "My enemy," Sarai said aloud as she recalled how Rachel had held her hands tightly and told her of her own sad life.

The window of her small bedroom faced east, and in the far distance, Sarai could see the barren hills of Moab lost in the haze of late afternoon.

Now the men of Jordan will cross those mountains and come here to Jerusalem. They will conquer this city as my ancient ancestors conquered it, and there will be rejoicing in Jordan beyond the mountains of Moab.

She imagined what it would be like in Jerusalem when the Arab Legion tasted victory. There would be revenge, a terrible judgment against the Jews of the city—of that Sarai was certain. The scenes of Deir Yassin would be replayed, only this time it would be Jewish women who begged for mercy for themselves and their children. The thought of such retribution brought Sarai no pleasure now.

She touched the black dress of mourning that she wore, then looked at the stack of brightly colored gowns that had remained untouched on the chair by the door. She remembered how she had rebuffed Rachel's kindness and the days that followed when every one of her unkind words had been met with gentleness.

Suddenly her own fear became fear for the life of this kind and beautiful young Jewish woman who had returned good for evil. Sarai buried her face in her hands. She cried out, angry that her hatred had been turned aside by love. "I want to hate them! Hate them *all*! It is so much easier to hate. . . . I do not want to care about them!"

After what seemed like a long time, she lowered her hands. The first thing she saw was the bouquet of bright dresses on the chair. It had not been pride that had kept Sarai from accepting the gift; she knew that now. It had been a desire to hurt Rachel, to refuse a love so freely given.

"My enemy." Sarai sighed in resignation as she picked up a deep blue dress embroidered with a profusion of flowers that intertwined around the hem and climbed the full sleeves. "My dear, beloved enemy."

American pilot Bobby Milkin chewed his cigar and glowered at the group of ten men who sat in a circle in the sparse office of the Jewish Agency. Within the hour he would be flying David Ben-Gurion, the leader of Zionism, back to Tel Aviv to meet with Tom Kane, the American official sent by the State Department.

Moshe Sachar sat across from the Old Man and stared at the yellow slip of paper. "Only David Meyer will do?"

Ben-Gurion nodded curtly. "Has there been any word at all? You have been staying at the Moniger house the last few days. We had hoped that—"

"No." Moshe shook his head. "We aren't even certain that Ellie knows about her uncle's death. No . . . no. There has been no word from them." He paused and looked up at the staff who shared the office with them. "Why don't we know where they are?"

Officers shifted uneasily in their seats as the Old Man glared at each one individually. "That is just what I have been asking." Ben-Gurion's face was red with anger.

Chaim Sharrett, one of the Haganah officers, pushed his spectacles up the bridge of his long nose and cleared his throat. "The last we saw of them was five days ago. Two of our agents in Rome were at the rail station when Bernie Greene and, uh . . . the other fellow . . . were murdered."

A second officer held up two copies of the European *Times*. "Mikhail Gregovsky was the second man. . . . Haven't you read this morning's newspaper?" His voice was tense and angry. "Have you noticed that this journalist—this Lawrence Crabtree fellow—seems to have better information than we have?" He held a paper up in front of his face and began to read:

> *"Although the two murdered men were dressed in the garb of Catholic priests, inside information reveals that they were in fact Jewish saboteurs connected with the recent bombing of the Arab arms ship the* Trina.
> *"One of the dead men has been positively identified as Mikhail Gregovsky, who served as an explosives expert with the Partisans in Bulgaria. His experience with explosives served him well after he was sent to a detention camp in Cyprus for attempting to enter Palestine illegally. He is suspected by the British to have masterminded an explosion that blew up a guard tower and . . ."*

He skipped down. "Now listen to this!" His voice rose. " 'According to inside sources—' "

"Inside sources again!"

" '—Mikhail Gregovsky was rescued from Cyprus by a pilot connected with the Jewish Haganah. . . .' " He looked up as the men sat in stunned silence.

"It is obvious we have a leak somewhere," Sharrett said, spreading his hands in disbelief.

"A leak!" spat another officer. "The dike has broken. This Crabtree chap knows more than we know! More than Rome knows! Did you see his article two days ago? All the world reads the inside workings of our operation with the *Trina* before we even know all the details!"

"So who killed Greene and Gregovsky?" a young, scholarly soldier asked.

"You're asking me?" exclaimed Sharrett. "So if you read it in the paper before I do, give me a call!" His cheeks were flushed. "Ask this Crabtree fellow. He knows everything!" he exploded. "Maybe he knows where David and Ellie Meyer are! We seem to have lost track of them completely, eh?"

"Arab agents must have killed Bernie and this Mikhail chap," volunteered yet another of the group.

"No kidding," mumbled Bobby Milkin.

"Quite beside the point," Sharrett interrupted. "David retrieved the satchel. Our man saw him do it. When the others were killed, our man warned David off at a risk to himself. Within the satchel, the usual method of information was employed. They were provided with enough money to get them to Paris and then to the rendezvous point. David immediately boarded the train with Ellie. Our man saw them. We wired ahead to Turin, and another of our chaps caught the train there."

Sharrett frowned and pursed his lips. "Our man would have made verbal contact, but they were obviously being watched. There was no opportunity. David must have had the same knowledge of the danger. Somewhere between Turin and St. Michel, they got off the train."

"Or were murdered and shoved off."

"Is there no way of checking?" Moshe swallowed hard. "If they are dead—"

"The wire we got from Rome said *David and Ellie Meyer down the toilet near St. Michel.*" Sharrett shrugged like a schoolboy as the others in the group stared at him and contemplated the cryptic message.

"Down the toilet?"

"Who decoded this? Are they dead? Does that mean *dead*?"

"Well, no. I do not think so," said Sharrett.

Moshe felt a wave of irritation at the confusion.

"Information indicates that, along with our man, there was a possible enemy agent on the train. As I said, this prevented contact. The Arab agent lost them at the same time our fellow did." Sharrett smiled. "As a matter of fact, they rode back to Rome together on the same train . . . each pretending not to notice the other." He rolled his eyes. "*Oy.* Such a war!"

No one spoke for a minute.

"Well," Milkin broke in, "if Tinman is dead, we ain't gonna get them ME-109s off the ground."

"We've checked the morgues in Turin. Also the police headquarters of a few small villages. No bodies have turned up."

Milkin snatched the cigar from his mouth. "Turned up! What? You think a couple of stiffs are gonna walk up and say, 'Here we are, boys'? If they was murdered and dumped in the Alps, ain't nobody ever gonna find 'em."

"Good point." Sharrett sniffed and nodded bleakly.

Ben-Gurion slammed his fist on the desktop. "It is not a good point! In a few weeks—God willing—we are going to have cargo planes flying into Tel Aviv every day and night. Without fighter cover they won't last long. The Egyptians have British-made Spitfires—"

"Gimme one of them and I could do a thing or two," mumbled Milkin.

"The best Avriel could do was German ME-109s."

"Yeah," Milkin said thoughtfully. "And that ain't the best. Those things is temperamental as a woman. If the guys don't get some training—like a few weeks—in the 109 cockpit, the Spitfires are gonna knock us out of the sky like sittin' ducks!"

He cleared his throat. "Tinman's the only one that's got any air time in them things. Shoot, he fixed one up all by himself when we was all in Italy. Him and Michael Cohen patched this Luftwaffe 109 up after Tinman chased a German back to our airfield and plugged his plane full of holes. The German had to land on our own field! Tinman was a legend after that, I can tell you. After him and Scarecrow patched the thing up, they took it for joyrides."

He puffed his cigar and sighed with resignation. "The big brass took it away from 'em, though. Said it didn't look good for an American pilot to be buzzin' the enemy in one of their own planes, even though Tinman painted Mickey Mouse givin' Hitler a kick in the pants on the wings. We all thought it was class . . . real class."

Ben-Gurion's eyes were bloodshot with weariness. "When are the pilots scheduled to rendezvous?"

Milkin chewed the cigar. "Most of 'em are already on their way from the States. But that ain't gonna do no good, Boss. Not if we don't have Tinman around to teach 'em. We're gonna have a bunch of dead pilots. I'm tellin' you, 109s are tricky. Tinman and Scarecrow picked these guys out themselves back in the States. They'll be a good bunch. But Scarecrow is dead and maybe Tinman, so that leaves me. And I ain't no 109 flight instructor, Boss."

The Old Man's eyes burned with impatience. "We have purchased aircraft—almost-new fighter planes. Certainly someone will know how to operate them. David Meyer must be considered expendable in this case."

"He's the one what bought the planes, Boss." Milkin shrugged helplessly. "And he hired the guys to fly 'em. Now, if you take a good look at the situation, it ain't promisin'. You got American pilots gonna fly German-made coffins . . . that is, unless you hire yourself an ex-Luftwaffe pilot to teach 'em. . . ."

The Old Man turned on Sharrett. "You lost him! Now find him!"

"But, Boss!" Sharrett protested. "He'll have to find us. We gave him an address. Gave him everything he needed."

Moshe frowned at the words of Sharrett. "Meyer is a pilot. No one gave him clearance for Mossad code." He looked around at the men. "Did they?"

The men who ringed the desk eyed one another for an answer. "We were thinking of Bernie Greene, naturally, when we packed the carpetbag."

"And Greene is dead. We are certain of that."

Quick nods. "Yes. Quite dead."

Moshe clucked his tongue and chewed his lip at the irony of the situation. "So David Meyer didn't even know what to look for?"

"The carpetbag was packed with Greene in mind," Sharrett repeated lamely. "Greene would have known exactly what to look for. Meyer hasn't got the information to contact us, even if he is alive."

Ben-Gurion spread his hands in a gesture that seemed to ask for suggestions. There were none. He glanced at Moshe. "So there you have it. A flock of German-made fighter planes that no one dares fly. And the man who bought them, the man who convinced us to purchase them, has disappeared—probably dead."

"I don't believe he is dead," Moshe offered hopefully. "He's too smart for that."

Someone held up a copy of the newspaper containing Crabtree's latest revelations. "Well, if he's dead, no doubt we'll be the last to know. And if he's alive, this Crabtree fellow is going to lead the authorities right to him—and then he might as well be dead, for all the good he'll do us in prison."

"If he is alive, Sharrett, *you* will find him!" the Old Man proclaimed. Then he stared at Moshe. "And what has being smart got to do with staying alive? Some of the smartest men I know are dead. True? Much smarter than the rest of us, I would say. They got out before things became so difficult!"

The men's room at Rome Central Railroad Station was clean and bright. A young attendant in a crisp new uniform stood beside a stack of fresh towels near the washbasin. Bloodstained tiles had been scrubbed and bleached, left without a trace of the violence that had taken place here only five days earlier. Tourists moved in and out the door, never suspecting that three men had been murdered within these very walls.

Crabtree glanced around the room. Four stalls. Doors with a fresh coat of paint. Urinal on the back wall. Chipped mosaic tiles on the floor. Three washbasins. Towel stand. Crabtree had been here a dozen times himself, and this was the first time he had seen it clean. *Everything smells of disinfectant. Wipe away death like a germ.* It made his eyes water.

Slowly he turned around, mentally placing the bodies and reconstructing the events as he had seen them in the police photos: Towel stand knocked over. The short Jew fought hard. Two bullets in the chest. The tall one with the broken arms died without much resistance. The old man had a bullet pass through an upraised hand as he had tried to protect himself.

When the scene was clear in his mind, Crabtree washed his hands and took a towel from the attendant. "New, are you not?" he asked in Italian.

"*Si.*" The young man smiled and bowed slightly.

"Does it bother you that there were three men murdered here?"

"With so many murders now ina Rome, signore—" he shrugged— "these men were no doubt ex-Nazis or Partisans or Communistas. They made somebody unhappy in the war. Me? I just mind my own business. I make no one unhappy."

Crabtree flipped a coin into the small saucer that held the young man's tips. "The only real way to do that is to be blind—" Crabtree fixed his gaze on the young man—"and deaf . . . or dead."

He pushed past the attendant and stepped into the teeming station. For a full minute, he stood just outside the door of the men's room and watched as men and women scrambled to catch trains. The entire vast hall seemed to be in motion, with one minor exception. Directly across from Crabtree, a news vendor stacked a pile of magazines in his booth. "Neither blind nor deaf," muttered Crabtree as he moved toward the man.

The vendor did not seem at all startled by the bluntness of Crabtree's question. "Ah, yes," he replied in broken English. "You reada it all ina papers, no? Well, I was here. *Si.* They killa the two priest an' they killa old Angelo as well. He see too much, eh?"

"What did you see?" Crabtree picked up a copy of his own publication.

"Me? I see nothing excepta the man who screams murder an' falls outta da door. He is an' Englishman. Gone back to England. Then the police come an' everybody is screaming an' running. After while they bring out da bodies. Two priest an' old Angelo."

"Did you see anything else? anybody else hanging around?"

"No, signore. The station is very busy thata day. But I don' see nobody . . . nobody strange, you know?"

In a deliberate gesture, Crabtree held out the photograph he had clipped from *LIFE* magazine. "You see this woman around anywhere?" he asked the vendor.

The man glanced at the picture, prepared to dismiss the question. Instead, at the clear recollection of Ellie's face, his eyes grew wide. *"Si!"* He snatched the photograph from Crabtree's outstretched hand. *"Si!* This isa da sister! She wasa nun! Standing where you stand now!"

Three hours later, armed with a fistful of notes, Crabtree left the train station for the office. With the help of Stripes, he had also located the porter on the Express Français who had made out the tickets for the young American priest and the nun who was his companion. "They did not seem at all like clergy," the porter had told him earnestly. "But then, what can one expect from Americans?"

Crabtree spent the rest of the afternoon writing a story that would certainly strike terror in the hearts of the two fugitives. Although Tree was careful not to mention their names, the details of their saga were an open book—worthy, at least, of two columns on the front page of the newspaper.

EL-KIAMA

As the world hung softly between twilight and dark, the birds sang the last few notes of the day and crickets began to chirp in the new grass of the rocky slopes around Jerusalem. Moshe walked Rachel home in the cool of the evening. They exchanged friendly words with the guards stationed at the barricades. He held her hand, and they did not speak as they passed the shady yards of Rehavia. Then Moshe quietly told her about David and Ellie.

"It is hard to believe, isn't it?" Rachel said after a long time. "I have been so worried about David and Ellie since Howard died—"

Moshe nodded. "They must be alive. I believe that. And now there is such hope." He changed the subject, unwilling to worry her further. "Our men have captured all of Sheikh Jarrah. Not much of a battle. The Arabs have pulled out in droves."

"I wish . . . ," Rachel began, but then she fell silent at the thought that it had been in Sheikh Jarrah that the hospital convoy had been attacked.

Moshe squeezed her hand in understanding. "Perhaps someday soon every place will be like another for us here in Jerusalem . . . and all of them safe for us."

"A pleasant dream." Rachel looked up at the dark wall, now a deep rose color in the dusk. The first light of a watchman glowed from the ramparts. Soon the shooting would begin anew. "We might hold Rehavia, but what of the Old City? What of my grandfather and my brother, Moshe? Today I heard the women talking in the line. They said that the Arab Legion has come across the Jordan now in force. That the Iraqis will join them. They hold all of the east from the Old City to the river, and they will begin in earnest soon."

"We have had discussions, Rachel—secret. I should not tell you."

She inclined her head toward him, amused by the thought that there was anything he could not tell her. "If you should not tell me, then . . ."

"The American, Tom Kane. I worked with him briefly in the OSS. He is now with the American State Department. President Truman has sent him here . . . and we have had discussions. He thinks perhaps we might settle this between Jews and Jordan. There is hope."

Rachel gazed at the darkening sky. A few stars glimmered faintly above them. "*Hope.* All the world lives and feeds on that one word. When there is no food, we hope. . . . When there is no love, we hope." She frowned. "And when there is no hope, we die. . . .

"Oh, Moshe, we must pray! We must ask God for a miracle for Jerusalem. Always we have prayed for the peace of Jerusalem. Now you mean it might be at hand?"

"A slim chance." He nodded reluctantly. "It will mean that Jerusalem is not a part of Israel . . . that it is an international city. . . . We in the Jewish Agency have conceded that this might be necessary to prevent war . . . to stop the war we are now in. Yes, we have a tenuous hold on the western half of Jerusalem, but Abdullah's legion will take the Old City and the holy places unless we can reach a compromise. It seems to be only a matter of time."

"Grandfather!" Rachel worried, turning her eyes back to the sidewalk. "Yacov! Dov and Ehud and Yehudit—what will become of them if we fail in this plan for the city?"

"We can only hope that they could hold out long enough—"

"Long enough for what?"

"We haven't thought that far ahead yet! We dare not think past our hope, Rachel. Tom Kane has left to meet with King Abdullah. Hopefully we will then meet with his representatives here in Jerusalem. I dare not talk about this in the house. Not with the girl there." He looked seriously into Rachel's eyes. "It is a98 danger for her even to be in the house with us."

Rachel pulled her hand away angrily. "Moshe! You should be ashamed! Even thinking such a thing! After what she has been through."

"Exactly! She must certainly hate us all—quite natural, after what she has been through."

Rachel walked a few steps in silence, then said softly, "Yes, Moshe. It is . . . quite natural." Her own pain was heavy in her words.

"I only meant that—"

She leveled her gaze on him. "I hated those who hurt me, but I learned, too, that not all Germans were evil . . . not all. Nor all Polish. Someone saved my brother. . . . Someone cared enough, Moshe. And now I will care enough also for this poor child. And maybe she will see that not all Jews are like Emile Dumas and those beasts in the Irgun."

"You are right." Moshe bowed his head. "I only meant that I should not speak of this secret at all."

"And we are one flesh." Rachel slipped her arm into his. "So I will not mention it either. I will hope and pray instead. And we will leave it to God, *nu*?"

Sarai was not at the house when Moshe and Rachel arrived home. Mrs. Konig, a gray-haired, grandmotherly woman from three houses down the street, was with the baby.

"Did she say where she was going?" Moshe lit the lamp in the front parlor.

Mrs. Konig looked worried and strained. "No. No. She simply came to my door saying you had told her to come to me if she needed help, and she asked if I would watch the child for a while until you got home, Dr. Sachar. I could only assume that perhaps she was one of old Miriam's relatives. . . ."

Moshe did not reply. Rachel had turned to the window to hide her concern. He put a hand on her shoulder to console her. "Thank you, Mrs. Konig," he said quietly.

"My goodness," said the longtime neighbor wistfully. "How sad this house seems without the professor and Miriam. Hard to believe—"

"It is almost curfew. I will walk you home," Moshe replied.

Rachel saw the pain on his face, as if even the reminder of Howard and Miriam and the laughter and good times that had once filled the house was too much.

Rachel quickly climbed the stairs to check Tikvah, who played happily in her bed with a ring of keys. The child squealed in delight at the first sight of Rachel. Rachel picked her up and held her close. "Why did she go away, Tikvah?" she whispered, bewildered.

It was Moshe who answered the question a few minutes later, after returning from walking Mrs. Konig home. "We are Jews, and she is a Muslim. There was too much hatred in her for her to remain in this house, Rachel."

"But where did she go?" Her words were slow with sadness and pity for the young Arab woman. "Where is there a corner for her?"

Moshe shook his head in resignation and took the baby from Rachel as though he, too, needed some comfort. "We have to let go of it, Rachel. It is not our problem any longer."

Rachel sparked at his comment. "And you sound relieved that she is gone." She was angry, and he was defensive. "You are relieved, aren't you?"

"I am glad to have her out of this house, yes. I hoped we could help her, but obviously this was not the place for her."

"Where is a place for women *like her* . . . and like *me*?"

He returned her anger. "You are nothing like her. You are—"

"No, Moshe!" Rachel put her hands up. "What is the difference between that girl and me? There is none, except that my pain lasted for years. Hers was only one night, and now she will live with the ghosts and fears for the rest of her life . . . as I did. At least she fought against the animals who hurt her. I submitted *willingly*!" She raised her chin in defiance.

"I took her to the hospital. We brought her here, didn't we? What else could we do?"

Tikvah began to cry, and Rachel took her from his arms. "She is a wounded child, Moshe. Alone in the world. I know of such things. I *know*!"

"My love, you can't save everyone. You will go mad if you try! I have seen it with my own eyes, and there is no justice here in Palestine. *There is no justice left!*"

Rachel couldn't speak. She only pleaded with Moshe with her eyes.

"Sarai only felt the reality of our lives here. Whether we like it or not, it is *us* against *them*. Our survival or the end of us forever. That is not just. It is simply war and the fact of war."

Rachel shushed the squalling infant as she studied Moshe. "What is happening to us?" she asked quietly. "Why does it have to be this way?"

"I was at Kastel, remember? When we counted the dead the next morning, I saw Arab faces that I recognized. Good men who had worked for me and Howard on the digs. Men I thought were friends. They shot at us. We shot at them. There is nothing about it that makes sense. We just have to get through this as best we can and . . . survive."

As Rachel stood in the center of the room, appraising him, Tikvah finally fell silent. "But it does not have to be so, no matter what is happening in the world. I have read the words of our Messiah. That we must love our enemy. That we must love them and pray for them, Moshe. That is the only hope."

"And you did your best to love Sarai. She could not accept it," Moshe responded. "I have thought much of Messiah's words as I stood in the Pass of Bab el Wad. And there is much I do not understand. How can you love someone you have to point a gun at? It is too much for a man to bear. I cannot think of them as men like me and then blow their brains out! I cannot think of that girl in the same way I think of you! It is not possible to remain sane and weep for all of them!" His face was lined with frustration and sorrow.

"But we can think of them one at a time!" Rachel answered. "*One* person! *One* life!"

It was clear by his expression that her words had struck him. "I do." His voice was quiet. "I . . . I think of you."

"Then remember what I was not so long ago. And see what miracles the love of God has done in my heart." Her words came with difficulty. "The world is always full of one more lonely person in need of hope. No. We cannot touch them all. But what about those whom God brings to us? If we do not try, Moshe, then there is nothing left. No hope at all."

He drew a deep breath. "She is gone now." His voice betrayed his regret. "What can we do now that she is gone?"

Rachel closed her eyes. "We can pray. Pray that God will protect her. That Yeshua will find her, wherever she is."

Evading the barricade guards had been easier than Sarai imagined. She had simply climbed the back wall of the Moniger home and crossed other yards and fences until, at last, she came to King George Street and then Mamillah Cemetery. Her black robes billowing, she had passed through the cemetery like a dozen other mourners who had come to lay flowers on the fresh graves of the Muslim dead. Once on Mamillah Road, it had been only a short walk to Jaffa Gate, its stones still scorched from the recent bombing by Jewish terrorists.

The soldiers of Jordan's Arab Legion were everywhere. Sarai was confident that they would not recognize her beneath her heavy veil, but even as she averted her eyes, she heard a call from the ramparts of The Citadel of David. She was a woman alone so would be thought to be a prostitute. Still, she had hopes that the soldiers would look at her mourning clothes and perhaps consider her as the recent widow she was rather than as a solitary woman on the street.

Just to the left of the pedestrian gateway, a cursive Arabic inscription proclaimed *In the name of Allah the Merciful, the Great Sultan, King of the Turks, Arabs, and Persians, Suleiman son of Selim Khan—may Allah make his kingdom eternal—gave the order to build this blessed wall.* A half-dozen guards stood beneath the inscription, their red-and-white keffiyehs marking them as part of the Arab Legion.

A tall, dark-skinned soldier stepped forward to stop Sarai at the gate. "What are you doing out alone, woman?" he asked gruffly.

"I am a widow. My husband is buried at Mamillah. It has been the prescribed seven days, and I went to pray for him."

"Allah is merciful to the widows," the man said as if by rote. He poked the paper-wrapped package beneath her arm. "And what do you bring into the city?"

"Handwork to sell. Allah is not merciful to the widows unless the widows work very hard. I have come to trade with the Christian merchants."

He smiled. "Well, there are a few of those brave souls left in the souks. May Allah bless you." He stepped aside.

She entered the gate. "And may he be merciful to you."

"Remember, we lock the gate at sundown, woman," he called.

She looked up into the shadows of the vault. This gate was called Bab el Halil—"Gate of the Friend"—by her people. The name had always seemed a strange paradox to her, and now was even more so. The road that led south to Hebron had its beginning here, and Hebron was the burial place of Abraham, the friend of God. How strange it seemed that he was the ancient father of both her people and the Jews!

There was no friendship in this gate. It was designed, in fact, for war. From the hollow turret above her head, hot oil and tar could be poured onto the head of the enemy below. *How many thousands*, she wondered, *died at these gates? And how many more will also soon lie at the Gate of the Friend?*

The heavy iron doors were already in use as they had been in days of old. At sunset they were shut and locked. In ancient times, when her ancestors rode with Suleiman, late travelers had to sleep outside the gate, and early risers inside had to be let over the wall with a rope. At noon on Friday, the Muslim holy day, the gates were also locked. Now these ancient traditions had returned, for all-too-practical reasons.

Sarai glanced back at the sun, set low in the sky. She would have to hurry in her errand, or perhaps she, too, would be locked in.

As she emerged from the gatehouse, a flight of steps ascended to the top of the wall. Soldiers stood every few yards, staring out at the New City streets. They had already identified the easy targets in the Jewish quarters, and Jewish civilians had learned to avoid these places, choosing safer routes home from work.

Sarai walked into the fortified Square of Omar, where shops had been turned into outposts for the soldiers. She stood for an instant, stricken by the change of the last few weeks. The only thing she recognized were the two great cypress trees that towered over the smaller fig tree and the graves of the ancient lovers who lay buried beneath them. From the time of her youth she had sat beneath these shade of the trees and dreamed of romance. . . . Now all of that was as dead for her as the lovers who were buried there.

She shook her head and hurried on, turning her eyes away from the countless stares of the soldiers who swarmed the area. There were few civilians among them. Some monks drifted through the panoply of armed men, but there were no women here at all—none, it seemed, but her.

Across the Latin Patriarch Road was the New Imperial Hotel, a three-story structure of dubious accommodations that had obviously been taken over by the Legion. Laundry flapped from the iron grillwork of the balcony, and here, at last, Sarai glimpsed women moving coyly through the crowds of men who clustered in the arcades. A chill rushed through her, and she wondered if perhaps it would be her fate to live her life among women such as these. She held tightly to the package and lowered her head as she passed. The shrill laughter of a woman echoed down from an open window.

Turning up the Street of David, she quickened her pace, noting with relief that some of the old sights and sounds of the markets remained the same. This was her first journey alone into the market. Her heart beat wildly as she moved among the differing merchants and shouting customers who bargained fiercely over the price of a small bag of oranges. Again there was a curious absence of women. There were some obviously Christian or Armenian women who walked arm in arm in a hurried rush to finish their marketing before the sun dipped lower, but there were no veiled women on the western end of the street. It was too near the armies.

Nearly faint with anxiety, she headed down the broad flight of stone stairs to where an arch spanned the street. She glanced at the arch with relief, knowing that this was the landmark that would take her to her destination. Here, amid a profusion of bustling Arab shops and restaurants, was the junction that led to the Street of the Christians. Only once, as a young girl, had she visited the street. Then she had held the hand of the old village woman who had been hired to watch over her. When Sarai had mentioned the journey to her mother in a rush of excitement, the old woman had been dismissed.

Now Sarai stood against the wall at the entry to the street. Shadows were long, and some shops were already closed. Sarai closed her eyes and gathered her courage. She had come so far.

She walked on, receiving blatant stares from the shopkeepers as she passed. There were a dozen shops in a row with shoes displayed on low tables outside. The soldiers of the Legion prowled from table to table looking for the best fit in a pair of new boots. Farther on were shops with displays of ceramics and one with watches.

But it was the displays of embroidered dresses that caught Sarai's eye. Most of the dresses on display were cheap hand-embroidered robes of thin cotton that hung like banners from racks in the street. She stopped to look at the price tags, swallowing hard when she saw the price that even a poorly embroidered dress brought in the Christian Quarter. *It is almost Easter,* she reasoned. *Such dresses are purchased by the Arab Christians and pilgrims. And now the soldiers of Jordan buy them for their wives and sweethearts.*

The thought gave her new resolve. Gripping the precious package, she moved through the crush of browsers and bargain hunters. *This will be no bargain,* she thought as she hurried by St. John's Convent. The huge dome that covered the Church of the Holy Sepulchre was clearly visible from where she walked. She remembered clutching the hand of the old woman as they came to its towering entrance on St. Helena Road. The old woman had explained that it was here that the Christians believed Jesus was crucified. Skull Hill, the place was called. It made Sarai shudder to think of it.

Six different Christian sects now argued over the holy sites beneath the great cupola. At night the doors were locked, and the keys were kept by two Muslim families, as they had been since the days of Saladin. The Arab word for the Resurrection was *el-Kiama,* but Sarai had grown up hearing the great church referred to as *el-Kamama,* 'the dunghill.' The mention of the place usually gave her a sick feeling.

But this time she aproached the entrance with a hope and a purpose in mind. Slowly she pushed open the massive door. Incense wafted instantly toward her nose. Lamps hung from the cavelike ceiling like so many planets in orbit. She stood just inside the doorway for a long moment until a bearded priest in a black cassock looked up and glided toward her.

He tilted his head as he questioned her. "What is it you wish, child?" he asked kindly.

Sarai licked her lips beneath her veil. She faltered, then whispered hoarsely, "I have something to sell."

"We do not buy and sell here, child," he explained. "You must go back to . . . What is it you are selling?"

"An embroidered dress."

"Ah. A dress. There are many shops along St. Helena Road and the Christian Quarter Road."

"But this is a special dress," Sarai blurted, almost tearfully. "When I was a child I came here with an old woman who sold a dress such as this. . . . She sold it here. . . . It was very special, and—"

He shook his head. "It could not have been here . . . and besides"— he stared at her with concern in his deep brown eyes—"what are you doing out alone? An Arab girl alone?"

"I must—" her voice broke—"please look at the dress."

"Well, I . . . this is unusual."

"But I know it was here." She looked through the haze of the huge grotto to the site of the crucifixion. "I remember."

"Let me see, then," said the priest, taking the package from her and slowly unwrapping it. He gasped appreciatively. The fabric was a deep blue. Thousands of beautiful stitches in reds and deeper blues joined with a dozen other shades, creating a garden of swirling arabesques. "Beautiful!" he said. "Truly, my dear, a rare quality of workmanship that one does not see anymore in the Old City, but . . . we do not buy and sell such garments here."

"But do you not see?" Sarai pleaded. "Can you not read?"

"What?"

"Look! Look at the stitches. Can you not read the words?"

The priest frowned and held the garment up to the light. There, among the swirling floral garden, were tiny words written with the thread in the flowing cursive script of Arabic. The priest gasped, and delight filled his face. "It is—" He could barely speak. "It is the story of our Lord's crucifixion! And here!" He pointed to a red rose surrounded by green leaves and tiny thorns. "My dear girl! Where did you find such a work of art?"

"It was given to me," she said defiantly, fearing she would be accused of theft. "And I have seen one other sold here at this church. One other like it. When I was a child. Read!"

The priest squinted down at the stitches, overwhelmed by the realization that everywhere he looked was a part of the great story. *"And the soldiers platted a crown of thorns"*—the words wove into a small row of thorns—*"and put it on His head, and they put on Him a purple robe"*—the color dipped into deep purple—*"and said, Hail, King of the Jews! and they smote Him with their hands. . . ."* He raised his eyes slowly from the passage.

"You see," said the girl.

"What is it you want for this?"

"I need money. To pay for my lodging and for food. I need to take food away from the Old City with me tonight."

He considered the young veiled Arab before him. "You would sell this?"

"It was given to me. I can do with it as I wish. There are others."

"Others?" He was amazed.

"This is the most beautiful."

"Yes . . . yes."

"The others are more plain. I did not read them. I did not read this except to see that it speaks of el-Kiama, the Resurrection. This is also the place where the legend is told of that event, is it not?"

He simply nodded. "But why are you alone?"

"I am not a prostitute." Her eyes flashed angrily. "I will not live by charity. So I sell this. I cannot wear it anyway." She felt defensive and angry. "I am no Christian."

"These days are difficult for all of us, young woman," he said kindly. "I will show this to the patriarch. You were right to bring it here. It would be unworthy to sell something like this to a shop to be hung in the streets. But this is highly unusual. I must speak to the patriarch, and we will decide what might be done. There might be a wealthy patron who would donate to the monastery for such a work as this. I cannot say. Highly unusual. Tomorrow—"

Sarai snatched the dress away from him. "I will not be here tomorrow. I need money and food tonight and then—" The loud clang of the church bells interrupted her words. "Why do the bells ring now?"

"It is sunset, child. Soon we will lock the doors of the church. You cannot stay here. That is the signal that all must leave, except those of us who—"

She blinked back tears of disappointment. She was indeed too late. All her hopes of getting real food and milk for Tikvah vanished. She had come all this way for nothing. "They will lock the city gates, then. I must hurry."

"You will not make it back to Jaffa," the priest protested. "Come," he said, taking her arm, "there is a place. But you must hurry, and you must hide until the gate is locked. Then come back in the morning." He led her out into the courtyard and pointed toward the Church of St. John. In hurried whispers, he instructed her where she must go to find safety and shelter for the night in the Old City. "But tell no one I told you this, girl." He slipped her a handful of change. "If you go now, you can buy bread and juice for your supper, too."

As the bells of the Old City churches began to ring dolefully, Captain Stewart stepped up to the great stone arch of Zion Gate. The last contingent of Highland Light Infantry had just entered the Jewish Quarter and would remain there throughout the night.

Now the heavy metal gates swung shut with a crash, and Stewart retrieved the foot-long iron key from his armored car. Without ceremony, he inserted the key and locked the metal bars into place. He and his small band were finished for the day. The Jews would certainly not brave the barrage of sniper fire from the Arabs atop the wall, and the British guards inside would see to it that no one got through the gate, at any rate.

This time of day never arrived in Jerusalem without being accompanied by bursts of rifle fire from the Arab Palestinians. The men of the Arab Legion who had arrived en masse over the last few weeks simply gambled and talked while the native Jerusalemites recited the speeches of Haj Amin and rioted in the souks.

Stewart could not help smiling at the mental image the ritual of the key brought to him each sundown. He remembered the musty warehouses of Liverpool where round arenas were built of salvaged packing crates. Gates had been built on each side of the arena, and sometimes benches and tiers of seats for the spectators who came to gamble. Rich and poor, the men came to mingle their money and their cheers as the gates slid up and two dogs rushed snarling into the center of the pen. In the glare of the lights, the blood seemed almost purple as it spouted and spattered against the boards. The eyes of the spectators grew wild, and their shouts and curses drowned out the agony of the bloody cauldron of snapping pit bulls. At times the dogs were mismatched—a larger dog set against a smaller, less capable animal. Then the end came soon. Still, it always seemed that there were fools who bet on the long shots. Usually they grumbled the loudest when their dog lay foaming and twitching under the lights.

This evening, as Stewart stood before Zion Gate with the key in his hand, he could not help but laugh at the fools who were hoping for a miracle for the Jews. The Old City was a cauldron of snarling flesh, and the Jews were, quite simply, underweight and mismatched against their enemy.

Stewart waved at a team of friendly Arab watchmen who walked along the top of the wall. It was only a matter of time before they would hold this key. There were no miracles in Stewart's book, and he never was a man to bet on the underdog.

Even as she ran from the courtyard of the church, the crash of the heavy metal doors sounded behind Sarai. *"Too late! Too late!"* her heart seemed to cry.

She stopped at a vendor and bought a small round loaf of bread, then quickly returned to the iron gate that led to the courtyard of St. John's Convent. Over the arch was the sign for *Taphos*, or "grave" in Greek. Sarai knew the sign well, as did every resident of Jerusalem. It marked the property of the Greek Orthodox Church and was a reminder that the burial place of Christ was nearby. Sarai shuddered involuntarily as she looked beyond the grillwork and into the shadows of massive, low stone vaults that covered a large water cistern. Around the corner, she knew, was an old crypt where she would hide until the gates of the courtyard were locked.

The streets were now nearly empty, and Sarai heard the footsteps of the night watchman as he hurried to lock the gate. She shrank back in the shadows, then stole around the rough stone corner and descended the steps that led to the large crypt twenty-five feet below the level of the street.

Sarai clutched the package containing the dress as the gloom thickened around her. Peering into the darkness of the crypt opening, she could not bring herself to enter. Instead she sat on the bottom step and listened to the faraway sounds of the Old City. The jangle of the watchman's keys rang like bells as he closed the gate to the street, locking her in for the night.

For a moment, sensing the presence of the dead inside the gloomy crypt, Sarai almost panicked and ran crying to be let out before the watchman went away. Then another sound rang out in the distant streets near the Jewish Quarter. Gunfire rattled a deadly rhythm as it had every night for months, and Sarai considered that she was safer tonight in the company of the dead of the Old City than she was with the living.

She leaned her head back against the cold stones and cradled the precious garment in her arms. Why was it a comfort to her tonight, of all nights? And why, she wondered, had she lied to the priest and told him she had not read the beautiful words of life and death that the woman Miriam had planted in this garden?

Sarai had seen the story there among the thorns and flowers: *Now in the place where he was crucified there was a garden; and in the garden a new sepulchre, wherein was never man yet laid. There they laid Jesus. . . .*

The bells of the great church began to toll the hour of darkness. Sarai looked up as the sky became frosted with stars far above where she huddled. How she longed for a small candle, a light by which she could read the rest of the story!

She frowned, ashamed of the thought. El-Kamama, *my people call the Resurrection—"the dunghill." Shall I then wish to read of such things?*

The pop of gunfire again reverberated in the streets, and Sarai trembled at the sound. She thought of the innocent of her people who had died like sheep, and then, for the first time, she thought of the innocent among her enemies who had also died. In anger, she flung the package across the stairway, and it bumped against the stone wall and lay at the opening to the crypt. "Where are You, God? That You let such terrible things happen? Why do You not stop this sickness in our hearts?"

She heard the sounds of shouts and footsteps running along the street. *Maybe more will die tonight. So near this place of el-Kiama, the Resurrection, within the shadow of the place where innocence was crucified, and still we shoot one another.*

"*Kill the Jews!*" came the cry from the souk as men encouraged one another for the night's raids. "*Kill the Jews!*" The sound was distant, almost like a ghost from the past.

Tears trickled down Sarai's cheeks. She groped for her precious package. Clutching it to her breast, she wept silently for the One who still seemed to linger in this place. Had He looked out from where He hung on the cross and seen Jerusalem this night?

. . . And He bearing His cross went forth into a place called the place of a skull, which is called in the Hebrew Golgotha: where they crucified Him. . . .

The wind carried ancient voices to her ears. *Crucify Him, crucify Him. Pilate saith unto them, Take ye Him, and crucify Him: for I find no fault in Him . . . no fault in Him . . . no fault in him.*

"*Ya Allah!*" Sarai cried aloud. "Then *why* must He die? *Why* do they murder the innocent?"

The new cry arose with a fresh surge of hatred: "*Kill the Jews! Death to the Jews!*" The words swirled around her, ever louder as the mobs found their passion.

"But Rachel is a Jew! And Tikvah!" Sarai said, but her voice was drowned in the clamor of marching feet. "And what am I? What am I? What am I?" She rocked herself back and forth as the tears fell freely. "Do You see me, God?"

She raised her hand toward the stars as a wisp of smoke obscured the sky. "You whom they also murdered! I call to You because You were not guilty, either! Do You see me? Can You see me from where You bleed and die on Golgotha? I am here in the darkness on the steps of the grave where they have laid me! Jesus! I have seen You in the garden. . . ." She laid her cheek against the package. "You were innocent . . . innocent, and we hated You."

"*For the glory of Allah!*" the shouts receded.

"*Death to the Jews!*"

"*For Allah the Merciful!*"

"*Death to the Jews!*"

"*For the Jihad martyrs!*"

"*Death to the . . .*"

"*Deir Yassin!*"

"*Death!*"

Sarai wiped her cheeks as the voices drifted away. Then she whispered to the Voice that remained, "The flowers said to me that You are el-Kiama. . . ."

24

KITZBÜHEL

Rabbi Shlomo Lebowitz stirred the pot of borscht on the open flame of his stove just as he had ten thousand times before. The shrieks and threats of the Arab mobs had begun again, but he chose to ignore them, instead concentrating on seasoning the soup. Shaul lay on the floor and licked his lips as Yacov studied Torah at the table.

"Supper is ready," the rabbi announced. "Clear the table."

"Grandfather?" Yacov asked as the old rabbi dished up the thin broth for their supper.

"Yes, Yacov?"

"What is the matter with Yehudit Akiva?" Yacov frowned and waited patiently while Rabbi Lebowitz washed his hands and said the grace before breaking the meager portion of bread.

"What do you mean?" he asked, sipping the hot soup gingerly. It tasted good, in spite of the fact that it was made with only two beets, one pitiful turnip, and a little garlic.

"She seems so strange since she has been back in the Old City." The boy winced and took a sip of cold water when the soup scalded his tongue.

The old man broke his crust and dipped a corner into the soup. "Strange? I had thought she seemed much more cheerful, *nu*? Singing around Tipat Chalev. Even smiling at the Krepske brothers. *Oy!*"

"That's what I mean. And on Tuesdays she has brought the phonograph records of Leah down to the center, and there she plays the symphonies . . . like it used to be."

"So? This is strange, Yacov?"

"Very." The boy slurped his soup noisily. "Her father has said she is dead. She is disowned by her own father! *Gevalt*, Grandfather!" Yacov exclaimed. "How can she be so cheerful?"

"Hmmm." Grandfather considered his words. "*Nu*, Yacov. It is spring, you see."

"Yes! And a terrible spring, I think! The Arab Legion is all around! Rebbe Akiva hates us and plots with the British captain to take our supplies so he can administer them—"

"*Tscha!* At least we are warm, boy! Have you forgotten this place in the winter? When we had no kerosene?"

"We still have no kerosene to cook with!" Yacov made a face. "Camel dung to burn! Yech. This is a terrible spring."

"Not so terrible. We have convoys sometimes."

"Never enough." The boy looked at his paper-thin slice of bread. "I can see through this . . . terrible spring."

"Not so terrible if you are young." Rabbi Lebowitz smiled with faraway memories.

"I am young! And I want to live to be old!" He frowned, as if suddenly aware that they had wandered far from the topic. "But as I was saying, I liked Yehudit better when I didn't like her. When she was sneaky and grouchy and we could make jokes about her. Now even the Krepske brothers like her!" He slapped his forehead. "But I don't like her this way. . . . She is . . . she is . . ."

The old rabbi lowered his gaze and peered down his nose at Yacov. "She is in love, Yacov."

Yacov drew back in indignation. He screwed up his face in revulsion at the thought. "You see! Yehudit Akiva in love! *Oy gevalt!* So the world has gone crazy, Grandfather!"

The tiny village of St. Michel was like a pastel jewel nestled in the mountain pass. The train station was a one-room building made of heavy, hand-hewn timbers and broad eaves that protected the platform from snow in the winter.

Crabtree stepped from the Express Français and drew a deep breath, inhaling the crisp mountain air. He nudged his fedora back on his head and studied the chalet-type buildings of the village just beyond the station. To one side of the platform, a bedraggled horse was hitched to a small, canvas-covered cart. Tree figured that this was the village taxi, since there did not appear to be any automobiles on the cobblestone street. As the train began to pull away, a thin man with a thick white beard and a blue-wool beret tottered around the corner and saluted the visitor casually.

Crabtree smiled at him and pulled his wallet from his back pocket. He slid the two photographs out and wrapped them carefully in a one-dollar bill.

"An American!" said the old man. "I speak good English; you need a ride?" He did not take his eyes from the bill.

"Maybe." Crabtree slipped the bill and the photos back into his jacket pocket. "I don't know yet. Mostly I need a little information." He squinted up at the sign announcing the population of St. Michel. *Four thousand. Not big enough for anyone to go unnoticed.* "Is that your horse and cart?" Crabtree asked the man, who had already picked up his scuffed suitcase.

"*Si.*" The old man nodded toward the horse. "Not many horses left in the village. Most of them were taken by the Germans. And the Italians. And anyone hungry toward the end of the war. But I hid her in the mountains. She is like my own little child." The old man smiled, revealing a mouth devoid of teeth.

"So you own the taxi concession," Tree said absently as he looked at the shaggy beast who slept peacefully at the hitching rail. "I bet you notice everyone who comes to St. Michel. Probably you haul them."

"Certainly! Certainly! There is only one hotel, you see. And that is owned by my daughter and her husband! Not many come to St. Michel. Not many . . ." He blinked into the sunlight that drenched the snow-capped mountains in warmth.

"I could have guessed that." Crabtree extended his hand to the old man, displaying the photographs of David and Ellie. "Last week"—he held the pictures up as the old man strained to see the images—"a man and a woman got off the Express Français. It was night."

The old man stuck out his lower lip in thought. "No," he said with certainty. "No. They did not get off the train."

"You are sure?" Crabtree was somehow angry at the reply.

The old man rubbed his head beneath the beret and nodded. "I am certain."

"You have never seen them?"

"I did not say that, sir. I said they did not get off the train."

"Have you seen them?" Crabtree's impatience was betrayed in his voice.

"It is difficult to remember." The old man looked toward the pocket where the American bill was stashed.

"Perhaps this . . ." Crabtree held the dollar up and waved it in front of the old man's eyes.

"Yes!" Aged fingers plucked the bill from Tree's hand. "A young couple. Oddly dressed. They came to my daughter's hotel many hours after the last train had passed through. They had their auto break down. In the pass. Anna, my daughter, said the woman seemed especially tired and dirty and all she cared about was a hot bath. Anna was paid extra to heat water for the tub, and—"

"Are they still at the hotel?"

The old man shook his head broadly as he gestured toward the still-dozing horse. "No. No. In the morning, Arabelle and I brought them here to the station, sir. They were also Americans. But they did not tip so well. The man seemed quite thoughtful and the young woman very sad. Yes. Very sad indeed. She said little. I supposed it was on account of the automobile. Or perhaps some lovers' quarrel."

Crabtree took his suitcase from the old man. "So they left St. Michel? On what train?"

The old man shrugged and pretended ignorance. "I cannot say. . . ."

Crabtree did not respond with another bill. Instead he tipped his hat to the old cabbie and walked past him into the little waiting room of the station. Only one clerk manned the ticket window. He, too, was an old man. His white hair poked out from a visor, and his bow tie was slightly crooked. White sleeves were stained with ink, and his face bore the irritated expression of a man who sat alone too long behind the bars of the ticket window.

"Good morning." Crabtree did not remove his hat. "Do you speak English?"

The man looked up with disinterest. "Of course. One cannot work along the rail lines without knowing languages." His accent sounded slightly British. "You have stepped off the train by mistake?"

"No." Crabtree laid the photographs of his quarry on the counter. "I am looking for these two."

A slight smile played at the corner of the clerk's mouth. Crabtree knew the man had seen them and remembered the encounter.

"Why are you seeking them? Eh?"

Crabtree watched a hundred theories run through the clerk's mind: *Perhaps this is a jealous husband? No. Too old for that. Perhaps a father. The two seemed preoccupied—sad and fearful.*

Crabtree judged his response by the look on the clerk's face. The reason for pursuit could not appear personal, or the clerk might refuse to answer. Nor could he tell the real reason for the chase. The sinking of the *Trina* and the murder of the priests was still too much an issue to reveal that the couple might be involved.

"We believe" —Crabtree lowered his voice—"the girl was kidnapped . . . forced to go with this fellow against her will."

The eyes of the clerk grew wide. "Yes? The girl a hostage?"

"Judge for yourself. How did she seem to you?"

"Very sad. Most unhappy! Yes! I remember *clearly*! She did not smile. She spoke only in a whisper to the man." The clerk had already pulled open a drawer and begun to rummage through a stack of papers.

"Here!" he said, triumphantly pulling out two dog-eared tickets. "They exchanged these tickets, you see!"

Crabtree studied the scrawled writing across the top of the tickets. He was aware of the old cabbie standing in the doorway behind him.

"Tell me." Crabtree leveled a stern look on the clerk.

"It was their automobile!" the old cabbie chimed in.

"No! No!" argued the clerk. "The young man wanted to trade in these tickets to Paris—"

"What tickets? They did not come on the train!"

"Shut up, Maurice! Go talk to your horse! You know nothing!"

Crabtree thumped a palm on the counter. "Enough of this! Where did they go? I don't care how they came here."

"You see, Maurice?" the clerk said loudly, and the old cabbie cursed quietly and turned away. "An old fool!" the clerk snapped. "What does he know? They came in on the express. These are their tickets, you see."

Crabtree took out a pad and pencil and wrote down the names on the tickets. "And where . . . ?"

"The young man did not seem to know where he wanted to go. Just not Paris. He said he had changed his mind. Some little place . . . any little place would do . . . perhaps in the Alps, yes? So I told him I could perhaps exchange his ticket for an exact fare if he wanted to go someplace besides Paris. I thought nothing of it. The young woman seemed distressed, and Paris is such a dirty and depressing place since the war."

"So—?"

"So I checked the rates and the map. For exactly the same fare they could go to Tyrol. A beautiful place in the mountains of Austria. Rail-roads and tunnels were damaged in the war, but the villages are still beautiful and the track is now mostly repaired."

The clerk scratched his thin face thoughtfully. "You see, the fare would take them beyond Innsbruck . . . a nice city . . . I have been there many times. A few miles beyond, in the mountains, is a little village called Kitzbühel. I said if they would like to ski there, if they knew how to ski, there is still snow and it is a very pretty place. I thought nothing more than perhaps they had had a lovers' quarrel, and the mountains around Kitzbühel make a pleasant spot for a young couple. . . ."

Crabtree had already retrieved his own Paris ticket and slid it toward the astonished clerk. "Kitzbühel," he said thoughtfully. "A small village?"

"Quite. Only a few thousand people."

"Hotels?"

"Yes. Of course. The young man asked me the same. I recommended one in Kitzbühel. It is a very old place called the Golden Griffin. And I told him of the place."

Crabtree smiled. "How long does it take to get there?"

"Two days. The tracks have many detours. They were so badly bombed in the war," he repeated. "A very slow but lovely trip through Switzerland first . . . where the tracks are good. It is when you come to Austria that the way grows slow. Still, it is better than the roads."

"The Golden Griffin." Crabtree wrote down the name of the hostelry next to the two names that appeared on the discarded tickets: *Zelda Sue Conner. James Clement Madison. So they have fake passports,* Tree thought with satisfaction. He frowned slightly at the possibility that his story might frighten them off. Even as the clerk filled out a substitute ticket for him, Crabtree carefully contemplated the wording of his next dispatch. If they were indeed following his progress in the paper, now, as he circled their camp and closed in for the kill, they must be led to believe that they were safe . . . safe and secure in Kitzbühel, Austria.

It was already six o'clock in the morning. Ellie smelled the aroma of frying sausage even before the bell in the tower above their bedroom clanged the call for breakfast. For nearly a week, Ellie and David had awakened each morning to the same ritual. This was the only moment in the day when Ellie regretted the fact that the Golden Griffin had been full to capacity and they had been referred instead to the house of the Wattenbarger family, who offered three rooms to rent to tourists.

Frau Wattenbarger had been up since four, Ellie knew. Already the sturdy, pleasant farmwife had made a fire, fed the chickens, cleaned the stable, and milked the two cows. She had separated the cream by hand with a centrifuge, then washed the centrifuge. Her next chores were to make breakfast, wash the dishes, and make the beds. However, she could not make the beds if the American Feriengaste, "holiday guests," were still beneath the quilts.

David pretended to ignore the bell. He merely snuggled deeper beneath the down quilts until only his tousled hair peeked out. Ellie opened her eyes and gazed around the room. A soft light illuminated the space. Walls were made of thick, hand-hewn logs that had been laid in place over three centuries before. The space between the logs was chinked with white mortar, kept bright through the years by an occasional coat of smooth plaster. The rough-hewn wood, by contrast, was darkened with the age of centuries.

The massive feather bed they slept in was nearly as old as the house. Huge posts were carved into spiraling grapevines with clusters of ripe grapes and tiny flowers in between. The date 1735 was carved into the footboard. It had been the wedding bed of Wilhelm and Olga Wattenbarger and was reserved now only for very special guests who were just married. Frau Wattenbarger had explained each detail to Ellie as she had led them up the narrow steps to their cozy room. ". . . Wilhelm and Olga had twelf children, my dear!"

Ellie smiled at the memory and snuggled next to David. For the first time in months she felt safe and at peace. She had loved the beautiful old house from the moment she had seen it at a distance—the bell tower to summon the men from the fields; a crucifix on the steep gable; the painted inscription above the door, which Frau Wattenbarger happily translated for her: "We appreciate the good that Jesus Christ has done for us." But there was something here that seemed stronger than what Ellie saw. The soft winds seemed to whisper that this house had never changed . . . it had not grown older . . . that if only she and David could stay here, they, too, would live on and on and never grow old.

Lifting the quilt slightly, Ellie studied David's sleeping face. His mouth was open and his hair stuck up comically on his head. Lines of worry had disappeared, and he looked like a little boy lying next to her.

She remembered how worried he had been at the sight of all the U.S. servicemen crowded at the registration desk of the Golden Griffin. Austria was, after all, a country occupied by the three Allied powers that had conquered the Reich. Since Britain and the United States shared the booty with the Soviet Union, it should not have been surprising to them that American GIs on leave would now be vacationing in one of the few places in Europe that seemed almost untouched by the devastation of the war. While David and Ellie had come here to hide from anyone who might recognize a former flying ace and his journalist wife, the GIs had come to see the chalets and the towering mountains fringed in dark firs and capped by ancient glistening glaciers.

Three miles above the village of Kitzbühel, David and Ellie had come to this refuge in a horse-drawn sleigh. It was April, but the snow was still thick, and a new flurry had kept them in the house for two days after they arrived. There were no other Fremde, as Herr Wattenbarger called strangers, and soon David and Ellie had been made to feel a part of the family. Ellie's grief had somehow been comforted.

Now Ellie moved closer to David, draping her arm across his chest and kissing his shoulder. "David, darling," she said in a drowsy voice. "Frau Wattenbarger ist cooking der breakfast! Ist six uhr!" She ran her fingers over his face, wincing at the sandpaper stubble on his cheeks. He had decided to grow his beard while they were here, explaining to

Herr Wattenbarger that it would protect him from the Alpine winds. But both David and Ellie knew that it was to shield him from the curious eyes of some GI who might also be directed to the hospitable farmhouse.

Ellie gingerly kissed him on the lips, careful not to scratch herself. "Hey, Tinman," she said when he returned her kiss with ethusiasm, "time to get up, huh?"

"Okay." He kissed her again.

She giggled and pushed him away. "Frau Wattenbarger will be knocking any minute."

"Remember old Wilhelm and Olga . . . twelve kids!" He reached for her and she dodged him, slipping out from the covers and onto the cold floor.

"Twelve!" She shuddered.

He rose onto his elbow and eyed her appreciatively. "Not all at once." He grinned and raised his eyebrows slightly. "One at a time, huh?"

"Twelve!" Ellie said again, reaching for the heavy, American-made robe they had purchased for her, along with skirts and sweaters, in the village. "I'll bet Olga died young."

"Young but happy." David winked, then lunged for her, grasping her wrist as she squealed and toppled into his arms.

"David!" she protested, conscious that the clatter downstairs in the kitchen had suddenly ceased. "David! They'll hear!" she whispered through his laughter.

"So what?" He kissed her throat and held her. "They're the ones who put us in this room. In old Wilhelm's magic feather bed."

She smiled and welcomed his kisses, perfectly content to yield to the warmth of his embrace. He covered her with the quilt and pulled her close, searching her face with tender eyes. "You're happy. Aren't you, Els?"

She closed her eyes, trying to hold the happiness in. "Uh-huh," she said dreamily.

"You have never looked more beautiful, you know. You make my heart hurt, you're so beautiful. Your eyes . . . green like the meadows down in the valley."

She looked up at him, seeing her own reflection in his shining eyes. She saw a radiantly happy woman looking back at her. "You're waxing poetic, Tinman," she said gently.

"No, I'm just saying . . . I've gotten to really look at you these last few days . . . and I haven't worried about anything. And if this is a foretaste of what our life together will be . . ."

He shook his head, as if he could not finish his thought. As if there was simply too much inside him for words. "Inside out, you're beautiful. . . ." His face was full of longing. "I wish I were a poet, Els. Then I could say it right."

"You're doing pretty good right now." She wrapped her arms around his neck to draw him nearer. Her lips parted in a slight smile. "How about some breakfast?" she whispered, touching her lips to his.

As David nodded and held her tightly, Ellie hoped that Frau Wattenbarger would not ring the breakfast bell again for a while.

The kitchen of the farmhouse was a tiny room, dominated by a great stone chimney charred by centuries of fires. A door to the right opened into the stable, where two sweet-faced cows and a fat Haflinger mare shared the warmth of stalls next to the chimney. These animals were all that remained of a large herd of milk cows and much-prized Haflinger broodmares.

"The others were taken," Frau Wattenbarger had explained simply. "In the war. Papa hid these, and we was blessed. Gott let not the Germans take them."

Indeed, the Wattenbargers were lucky. Most of their neighbors had been stripped of everything as the war progressed. Many had lost sons as well as cattle and horses. Young men had been forced into the German army and transported to Germany for forced labor. Karl and Marta Wattenbarger had lost all four of their sons in the war.

Photographs of all five of the children smiled down from the wall of the Stube, the great room. Over the days, Ellie had listened for hours as Frau Wattenbarger had worked and baked and spoken of the boys as though they were simply out in the fields and soon to come in for supper.

"I will teach you the making of roggenbrot," the plump, rosy-cheeked woman had told Ellie as she kneaded a lump of dough. "This is rye bread. The boys like especially roggenbrot," she said, showing Ellie how to mix the rye flour, salt, and caraway seeds with water, yeast, and a little beer. Then she slapped the dough, shaping it into round loaves and slipped it into the oven.

The aroma of baking bread seemed to swirl around the children's pictures, filling the house with warm, happy memories. After a week, Ellie had learned to bake bread and had come to expect Otto and Franz and Friedrich and young Helmut to burst through the front door and share a hearty meal.

Herr Wattenbarger had likewise taken David under his wing, showing him the fine art of milking a cow and choosing a good cow at market. His

English was not as good as his wife's, but the two men communicated well enough. ". . . And so the face of the cow must just sweet and gentle be. Like a pretty Fräulein. Long lashes . . . and horns not too long!"

Beneath the house in the basement, Herr Wattenbarger had a workshop. Here he made cupboards and repaired plows, and in the corner of the room a workbench was lined with fine-bladed carving knives. During the long winter months, he carved the delicate features of the Madonna and child, or perhaps tiny wooden angels to hover above a manger.

Just as Frau Wattenbarger had taught Ellie to bake bread, so Herr Wattenbarger sat for endless hours at the workbench, demonstrating the use of tiny knife strokes on the soft wood. "I taught all of my boys. Franz especially loved it and was good at it. Otto, my oldest boy, I taught from the time he was not so high as the bench," the old man confided in David. "A good boy he was, and kind. Then he went away from us and became a different person. This Hitler was a very bad man. From the beginning we in Austria know this, but there is no stopping the evil. It comes even here to these peaceful places. Even where it is not welcome."

David had watched the strong face of the kind Austrian man grow sad. The bushy gray eyebrows had knit together in the memory as he lit his long pipe and smoothed his curling mustache back.

During the week David had learned more than wood carving. He had seen that the men he had fought were not all monsters modeled after the supermen of Hitler's Reich. Some were simple farm boys who had their sickles torn from their hands to be replaced by rifles. They had died as fodder to feed the dreams of a madman.

Bit by bit the story had opened until David and Ellie saw the saga of an older couple who had helped streams of refugees across the steep mountain passes to freedom. Jewish men and women had come first. Later, only Jewish children. Then professors and intellectuals fleeing the persecution of the National Socialist state. Last came those who were fleeing Hitler's purges.

Otto, their eldest, had been a Gestapo agent but was really working secretly with the Jewish Underground. He had kept that secret even from his family until close to the end of his life, when he had allowed his harsh facade to crack on one visit home and show his tortured soul. Not long after, he had been arrested for harboring Jews in his apartment. He had died of cyanide poisoning in his cell before he could be interrogated. He had contributed greatly to the Underground's cause at the ultimate cost of himself.

Franz, the second oldest son, had guided the refugees over the mountain passes into Switzerland. It had been on one such run that he had been caught by the Gestapo and killed. Because he'd had no identification on him, he couldn't be linked to his family, but they had guessed what had happened when he didn't come home. His beautiful redheaded wife, Helene, had died a month later in childbirth, and so had their baby.

The next younger brother, Friedrich, had followed in Franz's footsteps. He had been killed by the Nazis on his most dangerous journey over the pass—guiding the man who had been a part of the assassination attempt on Hitler.

At last, as the Allies had bombed the railroads between here and Innsbruck, young Helmut had simply disappeared when he had gone into Innsbruck to market. Marta and Karl had hoped for years that he had escaped to Switzerland, but after so many years, hopes had died.

So now the older couple lived alone in the big house, comforted by the fact that their only daughter, who had married an American GI, now lived happily in the States and was expecting a child.

This morning it was past nine before David and Ellie tiptoed down the narrow steps to the Stube. The room was warmed by a fire built in a huge tiled stove with a dome that towered almost to the ceiling. The usual scent of fresh bread wafted through the house, and David's stomach rumbled loudly.

"Man does not live by kisses alone," Ellie said to him as he followed her into the kitchen.

Frau Wattenbarger stood at the washbasin, her hands in soapy water. "*Guten Morgen*, children," she said with a wry smile. "Or ist *Guten Abend*?"

"Sorry we overslept, Frau Wattenbarger—," Ellie began.

"We was wondering, Papa and me, why for a week you was getting so early up." Her round face was alight with some secret joke.

"The breakfast bell," David began. "We didn't want to miss breakfast."

Frau Wattenbarger stuck out her chin and smiled. "The bell we ring because we have always the bell ringed. That is not the bell for Feriengaste," she explained, "unless you wish to get early up. You was eating at the family breakfast all week. This morning you at last are more kind to yourselves. Go. Sit in the Herrgottseck, and I will your breakfast bring to you." She dried her hands on her apron.

The Herrgottseck was a large wooden table set in the corner of the great room under a slanting crucifix. Freely translated, the word meant "the corner of the Lord," where the family ate their meals under the watchful eye of the Lord. David was shaking his head at the thought that they had been rising early for a week when they needn't have bothered.

Ellie, however, told him she had no regrets. Somehow the family routine of the past week had comforted her grief over the death of Uncle Howard and calmed her fears about their own safety. Instinctively, it seemed, Frau Wattenbarger had included her as though she were a member of the family until the household chores had become second nature.

Now it was time to relax. As Frau Wattenbarger set out a platter of eggs and sausages and a plate of roggenbrot, David and Ellie bowed their heads for the customary prayer that had been spoken before every meal. Only silence answered them. David opened one eye to see the smiling face of the Frau looking down at him.

"It is now *your* turn. You have *Wattenbarger* prayers heard all week. Now you must for your *own* breakfast pray." She winked and disappeared into the kitchen.

Ellie looked at him and giggled. " 'You must for your own breakfast pray,' " she said, softly mimicking the awkward Germanic word order.

David took her hand. How many times had he heard his father ask the blessing over a meal? Yet it had never been more than words to David. Now he held the hand of his own wife, and his heart was full of things to be thankful for. He bowed his head and groped for words to say everything he felt. Words were too small, so he let them be small, finally whispering, "Thanks for everything. For taking care of us. For bringing us here. Bless this food and this house. Amen."

"Omaine!" Ellie said with the gusto of a native Jerusalemite.

David, still clasping her hand, gazed at her almost apologetically. "I never was very eloquent at praying. You mind?"

"Did you mean what you said?"

"Of course."

"When you said thanks for everything, did you mean thanks for our life together? for me and you? for this morning?" She touched his face.

He nodded. "Exactly."

"Well then?"

"Well, I just couldn't say out loud all the things I'm happy about," he whispered. "But you know—"

"Uh-huh . . . man shall not live by bread alone, right? David, I'll let you in on a little secret. . . . I think you are too eloquent for words. If God is listening to our hearts this morning, it has to sound something like a Mozart symphony or Glenn Miller's big band . . . or—" she gestured toward the small framed windows, to where a square of the majestic mountain was visible—"or like a thousand Alpine mountain climbers yodeling. So don't worry about the words. I feel the same way."

"Yeah," he said self-consciously. "*Yahoo* doesn't even say it."

"Nope. Not even close," she replied as she buttered her bread.

They ate their meal in silence in the corner of the Lord. Frau Wattenbarger did not disturb them except to pour refills of coffee. Thirty minutes passed until Ellie cleared the table, carrying the dishes into the kitchen.

"*Sehr gut!*" Ellie said and David mimicked her.

"*Gut!*" said Frau Wattenbarger. "Now today you must to Innsbruck go. You have a week been with us and must now buy more food coupons. You have forgotten?"

"Yes." David slid an arm around Ellie's shoulders. "A whole week already . . . only a week. I think we have lost track of time, Frau Wattenbarger."

The old woman nodded. "That is the magic of this place. But the real world says you must to Innsbruck go today for the coupons. Your own Secretary of State Marshall had himself this idea—"

"The Marshall Plan," David said, feeling disappointed that they would have to leave, even for a day.

"Yes. But you must yourselves show your passports at the tourist office in Innsbruck for the food coupons. Week for week that is how you pay for your meals and how we buy food, you see." She was very matter-of-fact. "You will the trip to Innsbruck enjoy, I think. Papa will take you to the village to catch the train at noon. You will be back by eight o'clock this evening, and Papa will pick you up at the station. There are old castles to see along the way and Solbad Hall. Innsbruck is a nice city also. Not bombed like Munich or burned like Dresden. I think your planes knew how we felt about Hitler in Austria."

Ellie frowned.

David caught her eye. He understood. Neither of them wanted to leave the seclusion of the farm, even though both understood the necessity of foreign visitors purchasing Marshall Plan food coupons. The tourist office sold coupons to foreign guests. They handed the coupons to waiters or hostel owners who then returned them to the office in exchange for precious food items. It seemed, to those living in nations devastated by war, an administrative miracle. "Could we give Herr Wattenbarger our passports?"

Frau Wattenbarger shook her finger sternly. "You must yourself show them. Of course many hours, but I will a lunch pack for you, and you will be glad for the trip. Papa must have the coupons, or tomorrow you eat only milk and eggs and bread all day." She rolled her eyes good-naturedly.

"Sure," David said, trying to conceal his apprehension. "It'll be fun. See the sights."

Frau Wittenbarger eyed them both approvingly. "And you look like one from us," she said, giving David's wool knickers a tug. "Americans will come and ask you for the way!" she said playfully. "Just act like you do not English speak, and they will think you are German."

This was advice that David took to heart and planned to follow.

Why is it so difficult to leave? Ellie asked herself as she slipped into the sleigh. *It is only for one day. Just a day in Innsbruck, and then we will be back.* But even as she spoke words of reassurance to her own heart, a weight of worry returned to her. All the old fears from a week earlier tumbled down from the lofty mountain peaks like an avalanche.

What if someone recognizes us? What if we have been traced this far? She looked back toward the farmhouse, unable to shake the sensation that she and David were once again jumping into a whirlpool that would carry them forever from this peaceful place.

Frau Wattenbarger stood in the doorway. Her cheeks were rosy, and her eyes radiated happiness and security. There was a peace about this kind Austrian farmwife that Ellie had felt in the presence of Uncle Howard and old Miriam—how long ago and far away that all seemed! Ellie smiled broadly in spite of what she was feeling and waved at Frau Wattenbarger. *Will I ever see her again?* Impulsively, she blew her a kiss and wished that there were a moment more to embrace her. *We will be back tonight, and everything will be fine again. Only a trip to Innsbruck!*

Herr Wattenbarger adjusted the harness on Edelweiss, the fat mare, then flipped a sleigh bell with his finger. He fixed his clear blue eyes on Ellie. "Mama will you today miss." He hesitated and tried again. "*Miss you today.*" He smiled, and gold-capped teeth glinted beneath his drooping mustache. "You children will today a fine day have. But the house will lonely be. . . ."

He dug into his pocket, pulled out a note, and extended it to Ellie. It was carefully penned, detailing the sights between here and Innsbruck that they must look for. A separate note contained directions to the tourist office in Innsbruck and the name of a small café that served real coffee and hot cocoa.

David slipped in beside Ellie. Herr Wattenbarger cracked a whip high above the back of the sure-footed little horse, and they were off. The sound of bells and the hiss of runners against the snow surrounded them with magic. Ellie imagined that it was not really April . . . that all the months before had been a bad dream.

It must be Christmas again, she thought, gazing up to where the sunlight and clouds played tag across the jagged peaks of the mountains. *And none of the tragedy ever happened. This is all there is. And if we stay here, this is all that will ever be for us.* She snuggled deep into the crook of David's arm and let the clean wind wash over her face. She felt the warmth of the sun on her hair.

"Magic! Magic! Magic! Magic!" the bells seemed to sing. *"Come back tonight! Come back tonight."* The hooves of Edelweiss tapped out the message.

Ellie closed her eyes to savor the sensation, then quickly opened them again, afraid to miss even one nuance of color on the face of the mountains. And then, all too soon, the ride was over. The tiny village of Kitzbühel came into view. Stone houses and the green copper dome of the church towered above them. Raucous laughter and American voices rang in the air as they passed the Golden Griffin hostelry on their way to the train station.

The smoke of the train appeared, black against the white backdrop of fresh snow. Ellie's spirits plummeted. She had hoped they would miss the train.

"On time we is." Herr Wattenbarger let the reins fall as Edelweiss stopped herself at the hitching rail. The little mare turned to look at them as if to say, *"Of course we are on time!"* As David sprang up the steps to get the tickets, Ellie lingered behind, scratching the mare's ears and feeling as if she simply wanted to climb back under the blanket and hide until the sleigh arrived back home at the farm. When two American GIs walked by, she leaned her forehead against the cheek of the horse.

Herr Wattenbarger stepped closer, his kind face worried. "Why are you frightened? Only you are to Innsbruck going, child."

"I . . . I just like it here," she answered softly, feeling silly. "I don't think I have ever been anywhere so beautiful . . . and I . . . I . . ."

"Edelweiss and me right here tonight when you are home coming . . . *coming* home." He frowned at his sentence and then smiled when Ellie laughed in spite of herself.

"Got the tickets," David said from the steps of the platform. His face also betrayed worry.

Ellie nodded and turned to go. Then, on impulse, she stretched her arms wide to embrace Herr Wattenbarger. "Thank you. *Danke,* Herr Wattenbarger."

"Bitte schön, little Fräulein." He kissed her on the top of her head.

He smelled of tobacco and wood shavings and smoke from the fire. Ellie held him a moment longer in farewell and for an instant thought of all those she had never had a chance to embrace. Howard. Miriam. Rachel. Moshe. How she hated good-byes now, even short ones! "Tonight, when the train comes . . ."

"*Ja,*" said Herr Wattenbarger seriously. "Edelweiss will not late let me be."

25

GOOD FRIDAY

Rachel rolled over in bed and opened her eyes in the pale dawn light. Moshe still slept soundly beside her. Both had been awake half the night, worried for the Arab girl.

Rachel frowned and propped herself up as a strange sound penetrated the glass of the window. For a moment she imagined she had heard the bleating of sheep in the courtyard below where they slept.

"What is it?" Moshe asked.

Rachel held up a finger. "Shhh." The noise sounded again.

The distant bells of the great Church of the Holy Sepulchre rang rich and resonant from the Old City. "It's just the bells." Moshe closed his eyes again and rolled over.

"No. Something else."

"It is Good Friday." Moshe yawned. "The bells will ring all day today." He wrapped his arms around her and pulled her near him. "Are you all right?"

She knew he was also thinking about Sarai. "I lay awake for a very long time and wondered about her. . . ."

"Me too. But I was not surprised she left."

Again the bleating noise filtered into the room. Now Moshe sat up. "What was that?"

"You see?" Rachel slipped from beneath the covers and lifted the shade of the window.

Below her in the courtyard, a little nanny goat stood tied to a fig tree. Sarai Tafara sat beside her with a small bowl beneath the udder. She sang softly as she milked the goat.

"Moshe!" Rachel said in wonder. "Moshe! Come and see!"

Moshe joined her at the window. Both stared down in total astonishment at the black-robed figure of the young woman and the shaggy goat.

"A goat!" Moshe exclaimed. "I thought I would never see such a thing in the Jewish section of the city until the Messiah came!"

Rachel pried up the window and shouted joyfully down to Sarai, "You have come home!"

"Good morning!" She smiled up at them. Her veil lay on the pavement, and her face shone with delight. "I have brought a playmate for Tikvah!"

"A goat!" Rachel cried. "And you know how to milk it, too!"

"I am an Arab," said Sarai. "Descended from the Bedouins. Milking of goats is in the heritage." The bluish liquid hit the metal bowl with a tinny sound.

Moshe and Rachel looked at each other in bewilderment. The girl's surly defiance had melted. But how?

"Where have you been?" Rachel called as the clang of other bells joined those of the great church.

Sarai did not answer for a moment as she concentrated on her task. "I have been to purchase a goat. There is only canned milk for Tikvah on this side of the barricades, and it is not the way of an Arab to fail to return a kindness. Even to an enemy."

This time there was no bitterness in her words. There was no sharpness in the word *enemy*. The dark hatred that had hovered over Sarai since she had come to live with them seemed to have vanished.

"It used to be so good," Moshe said wistfully, "when Arabs and Jews were friends. But now peace seems so far away—"

"Peace is here," Rachel said quietly, touching her heart. "It is nowhere else." She nodded toward Sarai. "She is loving her enemies, Moshe. That is peace. At least in this house this morning."

The sound of Tikvah's hungry bawling interrupted. "Well, if loving her enemy brings fresh milk for Tikvah, that will mean peace . . . and quiet this morning." Moshe gestured toward Sarai and the goat. "So, I'll change the baby. You go down and find out how to operate that machine." He swatted Rachel playfully and sent her off to learn the finer points of herd management from Sarai.

General John Glubb, British commander of the Arab Legion of Jordan, sat across the table from King Abdullah. Abdullah was a small man, polite and unobtrusive. He was, thought Glubb, quite unlike his father, who had defeated the Turks in 1917 with the help of T. E. Lawrence of Arabia. Now Glubb held the reins of command for the Arab Legion, like Abdullah, who reigned as absolute monarch of Transjordan, just east of Palestine.

"Jerusalem is of no significant strategic benefit to us, Your Highness," Glubb patiently explained.

"Jerusalem is of the utmost importance if we are to annex Palestine into our nation," the king said after a thoughtful pause. "The rest of Palestine is simply more land." He waved his hand as if to dismiss it. "Haj Amin Husseini has seen the significance of the Holy City. That is why he has fought so hard to control it."

"But the rest of Palestine must come into our hands first. Jerusalem would be better left under United Nations control as the plan is now drawn. The Jews are begging for that—"

"First they demanded that Jerusalem remain in a Jewish state. Now they call for the United Nations to internationalize the city. Why do you suppose they have changed their minds?" The question was rhetorical, and the king answered it himself. "Because they see that the city will fall when the English are gone. And if it does not fall to the Arab Legion of Jordan, then it will fall to the fanatical Jihad Moquades of Haj Amin's Irregulars. Haj Amin is our mortal enemy. Have you forgotten?" the king insisted.

Glubb Pasha frowned. "I have not forgotten. But why waste men and ammunition on Jerusalem when we might so easily capture the rest of Jewish territory? Let Haj Amin have Jerusalem. It is a small kingdom for him."

King Abdullah smiled. "Some say it is the center of the universe. If we leave the battle of Jerusalem to Haj Amin, then we certainly have given him what will be the center of our kingdom." He pressed his fingertips together. "No, we shall not abandon Jerusalem."

"And if the United Nations does take the city under its wing as a trusteeship?"

The king gave a short laugh. "I do not believe that this will come to pass. The United Nations talks and talks. . . . The Jews request this because Jerusalem is the weak point for them. They realize that they will fall to us. I tell you, while the other Arab nations advance against the Jews in Galilee and Golan and Gaza, we must take Jerusalem. He who rules in Jerusalem will eventually rule over all of Palestine."

"I wish to register my disagreement with this matter," General Glubb said softly. "We should be concentrating our forces elsewhere. All of Palestine—"

King Abdullah held up his hand to interrupt. "Ah, John Glubb, you are a general. You are Glubb Pasha, and most of your officers are also British officers. But I have another gift. I am not a warrior as my father was. I am a statesman. And I tell you that we may yet win a victory of diplomacy if you will listen to my plan. Jerusalem! Jerusalem!

Jerusalem! There is the key!" He raised his voice not in anger but in conviction. "Do you think the world cares about Golan or Gaza or Haifa or even Tel Aviv? Most of the world has not even heard of such places . . . but Jerusalem!"

The king paused, then looked out the high-arched window into the dusty streets of Amman. "Today I will meet with the American Thomas Kane. He is sent here by President Truman. You will stay with me for the audience, Glubb Pasha, and then you will know my mind. . . . First you must also know the minds of these Americans and then you will see . . . Jerusalem."

The red-and-white-checkered keffiyehs of King Abdullah's Arab Legion were the most coveted uniform of all armies of the Middle East. The Arab Legion was the elite of all fighting forces. Commanded by British-trained officers and descended from the armies of Lawrence of Arabia, they were also well equipped by the British government. Tanks and trucks and mortars were in rich supply. This fighting force was the key to Arab military victory in Palestine.

Tom Kane sat on the hard stone bench outside the audience room of King Abdullah. He had met the little king before and had found him to be a true statesman, reasonable and diplomatic in his dealings. Kane fiddled with his hat and looked down the long marble hallway at the dozens of Arab soldiers who stood casually chatting as King Abdullah held private audience with ordinary citizens of his kingdom. No petitioner, no matter how insignificant, was denied a personal meeting with the king. Kane had always admired Abdullah's personal style of governing his subjects. He hoped now that the gentle reason of the little monarch's personality would prevail over the cries for war.

The massive copper doors swung open, and Kane looked up with a start to see Abdullah escorting the petitioner out to the corridor. Grateful and ecstatic, the peasant man bowed a dozen times and then knelt to kiss the hem of Abdullah's robe. *He is still the Bedouin sheikh, governing his tribe,* thought Kane as the peasant was led from Abdullah's presence.

At that, Abdullah noticed Kane sitting on the bench. "Ah!" he exclaimed, walking quickly toward him. "You see, it is Tom Kane!" He stretched out his hand. "How very good to see you again, Mr. Kane!" The ruler's accent was decidedly English in pronunciation.

Kane bowed low. "*Salaam,* Your Majesty," he said. "I am honored."

Abdullah called for a samovar of coffee and trays of food, which were placed on a carpet in the center of the room. Together they sat on mounds of pillows, and Abdullah dismissed all but two servants, who stood at attention behind them. A large, ornate screen depicting the victory of Suleiman the Magnificent over Jerusalem stood off to one side of the room. Kane guessed that there were others who now listened to their words hidden behind the screen.

"And how am I honored by your visit, Tom Kane?" Abdullah asked as he munched on a rolled grape leaf.

Kane plunged into the topic head-on. "My government perceives that you may hold the key to peace here in the Middle East."

"Too kind, too kind. My poor nation."

"Your army is very rich. The other members of the Arab Confederacy look to the Arab Legion for the backbone of the army that will invade Palestine."

"This is so. Perhaps. We have had a good army since before Partition, Tom Kane. We have not built our forces for fighting Jews, but first the Turks and more recently the Germans. It is not King Abdullah who has first considered fighting the Jews. It is the folly of the United Nations that we are thrust into such a positiion."

"Folly." Kane said the word as though he did not understand it. "When your father fought the Turks, this kingdom was given to him by the British. The Jews were also promised a homeland at that time. Your promise was fulfilled long ago. You have known these things. You have never been hostile toward the Zionists, King Abdullah."

"No. They are quite brilliant. Possibly they have much to teach us as they reclaim the desert. But the boundaries of Partition are quite unacceptable. Quite."

"And you alone of all the nations recognize that the Jews have a right to exist."

"This opinion makes me suspect in the Legion. Many of my brothers doubt my loyalty to the Arab cause."

"Yet you are the backbone of their plans to invade Palestine."

The ruler contemplated Kane with amusement. "A paradox, is it not?"

Kane nodded. The scent of lamb drifted up, but he was not hungry. "It is well-known that you and Haj Amin Husseini are mortal enemies."

"He fought with the Nazis. I, with the Allies. Of course we have nothing in common. Nothing."

"And yet he is the spark that has ignited the Palestinians. He is the flame that burns in Jerusalem—"

"Words, it is said, are mightier than the sword. Especially if they drive men to the sword . . . or away from the sword." Abdullah let the thought linger. "You have come a long way to see me. What do you propose?"

Kane toyed with the food on his plate. "Haj Amin wishes for an independent homeland in Palestine. One without Jews and with Jerusalem as his capital."

"Common knowledge . . ."

"Our government believes that there is a way that this issue might be settled without war."

King Abdullah smiled, as if he had anticipated Kane's comments, and stared into his cup of thick black coffee. "And how can this be? How can this be with all the Arab Confederacy shouting for war against the Jews?"

"They will not fight without you."

"No. They would not win without me, I think. No one wants to die alone. The Irregular Army of Haj Amin has shown itself a mass of peasant bunglers. No. Without my Arab Legion, you are correct . . . the others will not fight. Except among themselves."

"Quite," Kane said with satisfaction. "If there is some way to avoid hostilities further—"

"To the point."

"Suppose the lands mandated to be Arab lands in Palestine are simply annexed into Jordan . . . without a battle?"

"A political settlement?" Abdullah appeared to mull it over. "And what of Jerusalem?"

"The Jews are requesting that the city become an international trusteeship—"

"With the UN as joint government, I presume? A large concession for us Arabs. We could capture the city with ease, you know. As well as all of Palestine."

"At what cost? The Jews are prepared to die to the last man, woman, and child, Your Highness. I believe this. I have seen their determination myself."

"Yes. I also believe. Heads of stone, these Jews. Heads of stone like the walls of Jerusalem itself." He sighed. Pursing his lips, he looked again out the window as the bawling of camels drifted up from the souks of the city. "If I considered your proposal, Mr. Kane, would not my brothers—the Arab Confederacy—consider me a traitor? I already have a large number of soldiers in Jerusalem. We have only to gently squeeze and the city will fall to us. Why should I give up Jerusalem to the United Nations? If the city is in my hands anyway, all of Palestine will be mine. Jewish lands and Arab lands will be the nation of Transjordan. Why should I consider a proposal that would weaken me in the eyes of my brothers? I am already in the positiion of strength."

"There is only one reason I can think of, King Abdullah. You are the only man who can prevent further bloodshed. The only man who can stop Haj Amin and put an end to war."

Abdullah signaled for more coffee. "Perhaps these are matters that I will contemplate, Tom Kane. The Jews would be willing to talk, I presume. Jews are always willing to talk. We Bedouins are the warriors. Fight first and talk after the dead are buried." There was no pride in the comment. "Perhaps I will consider what you say, although such a move could be quite dangerous for me personally, you understand."

Kane nodded, feeling a twinge of compassion for the ruler. Most certainly, any diplomatic settlement of the situation after so many vows to utterly destroy the Jews would seem like a betrayal of the other Arab nations involved. "If you would simply refuse to fight . . . others would lose heart."

"Not all others, Mr. Kane. You must not forget those. But I shall consider your words." Abdullah lifted his chin slightly, as though he could hear a faraway voice. "My grandfather . . . a wise man . . . he told a story of two young boys in our tribe. One said to the other, 'My father is the greatest man in the tribe because he alone knows how to set broken bones.' And the other boy said, 'My father is greater because he knows how to keep bones from being broken.' "

Kane nodded in understanding. He knew that, one way or the other, King Abdullah had decided he would rule in Palestine. Whether it was he who set the broken bones or kept bones from being broken was the only issue at hand. "There is so little time for this matter to be resolved, Your Highness. Would you be willing to send a representative to talk?"

"Jerusalem is the issue here, Mr. Kane. My Arab Legion has headquarters in the Old City. Surely you know this already. We talk from a position of strength. We will talk to the Jews secretly and with certain conditions."

"That is understood. Whom will you choose to represent you?"

The monarch rested his chin in his hand. "Our commander of the Old City garrison now in Jerusalem is a man of education and reason. His name is Fawzi Tell. He is a colonel trained under Glubb Pasha. I shall let him choose."

Abdullah paused, his eyes burning intensely into Kane's. "This must not become common knowledge. News of such a conference must not reach the ears of Haj Amin or his Arab High Committee. This is a matter for consideration between the Jewish Agency and those whom they consider worthy representatives. Someone from the British government should also be in attendance and, of course, yourself. . . ."

He frowned and leaned forward, lowering his voice. "If word of this reaches my brothers of the Legion, I must, of course, deny that I had knowledge of it."

Kane nodded. "Certainly." He was filled once again with the realiza-tion that he was dealing with a culture in which assassination of rulers was quite commonplace. Kings had toppled for far smaller reasons than the settlement of the Palestinian issue. Kane cleared his throat before addressing one more issue. "Your men have once again closed off the convoy route into the Old City. The Jews have requested—"

Abdullah laughed and waved his hand. "It cannot hurt to allow food in. Once a week?"

"Once a week. Good."

"As long as we are discussing the issues—there may come a time when there is nothing to discuss." He cocked his head slightly. "I am not a man without compassion, Mr. Kane. My soldiers are not like the rabble of Haj Amin. The Jews would have little to fear under my rule." There was hope in his voice.

Kane did not answer that the Jews would never submit to Arab rule willingly. He simply nodded and hoped that the question would be put to rest once and for all.

26

GOING HOME

The jagged peaks of the Nordkette towered six thousand feet above the Inn River and the city of Innsbruck. Standing on the crowded sidewalk outside the Office of Tourism, Ellie felt small and vulnerable in the awesome shadow of the mountains. She clung to David's arm as visitors surged around them. Everywhere she looked there were couples and groups of people laughing and talking in the babble of a dozen different languages. After a week of quiet seclusion in the farmhouse above Kitzbühel, the noise was jarring and intrusive. Ellie longed for the hushed whisper of the wind and the chatter of birds that sang, unseen, in the branches of the trees.

"You okay?" David asked, as though he felt her tension where she touched his arm.

She shook her head and looked back over her shoulder to where the statue of the Virgin Mary stood atop a tall marble pillar in the center of Maria Theresien Strasse. A red trolley car packed with people clanged around the base of the pillar and turned the corner.

"I want to go home," she whispered, feeling like a kid on her first day of school. "Back to Kitzbühel."

David's eyes were shadowed with concern. He tugged his cap low on his forehead as a group of noisy Americans strolled by. *He's edgy, too,* Ellie realized.

David tried to smile. "I know what you mean." He pointed down the street, toward a small shop. The glass was spotlessly clean, revealing a display of cameras. "Go on." He nudged Ellie. "Maybe it's better if we're not together. Why don't you go window-shop?" His voice was reassuring.

She smiled up at him and leaned her head against his arm. "You know what will happen if I find a good camera!" Then she let go of his arm and walked through the tide of pedestrians toward the camera shop.

The display was full of cameras. Some were as simple as American-made Kodak box cameras; others, like the Argoflex twin-lens camera, were more sophisticated. Almost every model, Ellie noted with disappointment, was manufactured in America. A result, she guessed, of the terrible effects that the war had reaped on manufacturing in Germany.

With regret, she thought of the precious Speed Graphix camera that her parents had given her for graduation. She got mad all over again when she remembered the way the brutal Arab had knocked her to the ground on Partition night and smashed the camera. David had purchased her another one for Christmas. Now that, too, had been destroyed.

She exhaled loudly and stared longingly at the various models. *It would be wonderful to make a record of our stay here. Pictures of Herr Wattenbarger at the workbench. Frau Wattenbarger kneading bread. And maybe one of Wilhelm and Olga's bed to show our grandkids someday.* That thought made her smile again. She shielded her eyes against the glare of the reflection in the window as she scanned the display for price tags.

Behind her, people strolled by arm in arm, their forms caught in the glass like images in a mirror. Ellie could also see the shops across the street and the stony ramparts of the mountains behind the onion domes of the churches. And then she saw herself—hair tucked beneath a stocking cap, freckled face, and happy green eyes. For a few minutes her fear and apprehension had vanished. She was just another Feriengaste, window-shopping in Innsbruck.

The moment of pleasure was short-lived, however. Another shadow moved in the glass. In a world of smiling couples and boisterous groups, a solitary man waited.

Ellie stared at the reflection. Her stomach knotted and her breath grew short with fear. She could not make out the features of his face. He stood across the street, half concealed in the shadow, and he did not move as he looked directly at her.

Can he see my face? Ellie asked herself, raising a hand to her cheek. She looked away and then back to the dim form who stared into the inadequate mirror. Her first impulse was to run back to find David at the tourist office, to bury her face in his chest and hide like a shy child behind the strong legs of Daddy. *No. The man will follow you! And if he is after David . . .*

Ellie fought her impulse to panic and run. She closed her eyes for a second, hoping that when she opened them, the watcher would be gone. Still he remained rooted under the arch of a florist shop. His arms were crossed in confident determination as he stared at the back of Ellie's head.

The blood pumped loudly in Ellie's ears. She bit her lip and looked back toward the tourist office. David did not appear. But surely he would.

What if the man has a gun? Unable to think clearly, she moved quickly toward the door of the camera shop. When she yanked it open, she was startled by the clanging of a cowbell. She rushed in, certain she was pale and out of breath.

The shop smelled of developing chemicals, and an old man sat hunched over a counter as he worked on a camera. When he turned at the sound of the cowbell, Ellie thought how much the old fellow looked like the Walt Disney version of Geppetto, the toy maker in *Pinocchio*. Wire spectacles hung low on his nose. A lock of gray hair spilled across his lined forehead, and he wore gray wool knickers and an embroidered vest.

His welcoming smile faded when he saw Ellie. "You ist pale, Fräulein," he said, standing up and crossing to the counter.

Ellie did not dare look out the window of the shop. She scanned the cluttered shelves and stacks of merchandise and enlarged photographs of the surrounding mountains. "A little winded, I guess." She moved toward the back of the shop, only then daring to glance back.

"American?"

"Yes. Waiting for my husband. At the tourist office. Food coupons, you know." The words came out in a jumble. "I'm a photographer." *You're saying too much! Shut up, you dope!* "I mean . . . I like to take pictures. . . . I mean, I would like to learn so we could have pictures of this place." She glanced back nervously. The shadowed alcove of the florist shop was deserted. She looked at the bemused shopkeeper then. "Have you got a telephoto lens?" she asked grimly, letting the pretense drop. "Wide angle."

The old man raised his eyebrows at her question. It certainly was an unusual request from an amateur interested only in snapshots. *"Ja."*

"Could I borrow it a minute, *bitte?*"

He rummaged in a wooden cupboard and produced a German-made camera, obviously army issue. Ellie shook her head at the swirling letters on the lens: *Leica.* She took it from him respectfully and stared through the viewfinder to focus on the doorway of the florist shop. The watcher had vanished. Ellie could clearly see the small sign on the door announcing the shop hours. A portly woman in a green wool suit stepped out the door, but the man was nowhere to be seen.

"This, she ist a fine camera," the shopkeeper said as she continued to search the street outside.

"Yes," Ellie replied almost curtly. *Just your imagination.*

"But she ist not just for everyone, Fräulein." He chuckled. "American Kodak a gut camera for Feriengaste ist."

Ellie frowned and lowered the camera. She stood with her back to the little Geppetto. "Why don't you keep this on display?" she asked absently as she continued to scan the street.

The man shrugged. "The camera Deutsche ist. Americans still the Deutsche do not like."

"How much for this?" Ellie's voice was flat and preoccupied, but she was not about to walk out without at least making an offer on this precious prewar camera.

"A fine camera, Fräulein."

"And nobody wants it. It ought to go cheaper than a Kodak."

Fifteen minutes later, as the shopkeeper finished wrapping Ellie's purchase, David walked into the shop. His face was blanched and his eyes wide. He wiped beads of sweat from his brow. "Come on," he said gruffly.

Ellie tucked the package beneath her arm. Something was terribly wrong, and she knew it. Perhaps the watcher had not been her imagination after all. "What is it?"

The cowbell rang out their departure.

David swallowed hard and removed a rolled-up newspaper from the pocket of his coat. "It's in the papers," he said grimly. "Names. Dates. Places. It's all in the paper."

Her eyes grew wide. "Us?" she asked with dread.

He took her arm and propelled here along the sidewalk. "Everything but us. Everything but our names!"

"Someone was watching me," she said. "I think. Standing in the door to the florist shop."

David walked faster. "We gotta get back. To Kitzbühel." His voice was tense, and his fingers dug into her arm.

Muffled drums beat mournfully as David pulled Ellie through the crowds that lined Friedrichstrasse to watch a solemn procession weave through the streets of Altstadt, the Old Town of Innsbruck.

Men in lederhosen and flowing medieval robes formed ranks with women dressed in dirndl skirts. They followed a large wooden crucifix that towered above the parade. The drumbeat matched the cadence of Ellie's heart, as if the mournful sound were drawing them toward their own funeral.

"Bitte!" David cried, passing through the spectators. "Bitte!"

"What is this?" Ellie cried, imagining an enemy in every face.

"Good Friday!" David replied above the din.

A giant wooden effigy of Maximilian I, dressed in crown and coronation robes and kneeling in prayer, was carried on the shoulders of two dozen men behind the crucifix. They passed beneath a balcony that was roofed in gilded copper tiles. The Golden Roof—Frau Wattenbarger had told them about it. From this box, the real Maximilian and his sixteenth-century court had looked down on jousting knights, troubadours, and jugglers in the square.

Now, as Ellie glanced upward, she recognized the uniforms of American and British officers as they shared the glory of conquerors and watched the procession with smiling faces and exchanged comments. One, Ellie noticed, removed his hat as the image of the crucified Christ passed below the balcony. For the others, it was no more than a quaint Tyrolean custom of little significance. Ellie wondered if they noticed that the emperor Maximilian, who once stood where they stood now, was kneeling to a greater King?

David also looked up, then lowered his eyes quickly and tugged his hat farther down on his brow. "Come on!" he hissed. "Come on, Els." His words were urgent. "That guy up there in the balcony. The colonel next to the British officer. That's John Greely. He was with the Ninth—in North Africa."

"He knows you?" Ellie could not help but look back toward the gilded box.

"You could say that." David pushed his way through a group of nuns. "My squadron commander."

Ellie felt herself pale. There was no safe place. Not here, at any rate. All of Europe was occupied. David was well-known for his exploits. If it were not for his wool knickers and beard and Tyrolean hat, no doubt someone would have spotted him already.

He guided her away from the parade into a narrow street of three-story houses that resembled those out of a book of fairy tales. The thump of the drums seemed to follow them.

Almost involuntarily, Ellie glanced over her shoulder, expecting to see the watcher following them. She saw only the backs of spectators who stood like a wall at the end of the lane.

"We'll lay low at the farm," David said without looking back. "We'll be safe there, Els." He was trying to reassure her, she knew, but his voice betrayed his doubts. "We'll stay there as long as it takes. Until we can get back."

"Back where?" She could hardly breathe. It seemed that every shuttered window must conceal their pursuer.

"Palestine. After the English are out. There's no place else." He looked her in the eyes. "We'll be okay when the English are gone. We can go home then."

"Home," she said bleakly. "Santa Monica? The States, David?"

He shook his head grimly. "No. Not for a long time, probably. I mean Israel, babe. That's all that's left for us now."

The train back to Kitzbühel was nearly half empty. Most of the other tourists would wait to return on the late train after the Good Friday processions were over. Herr Wattenbarger had expected the same from David and Ellie and would not be there to meet them, but David figured he could hire a sleigh for the three-mile ride back to the farmhouse.

They passed the trip in silence. Both of them stared out the window toward the high peaks of the mountains. They seemed like craggy islands in the middle of a river of racing clouds. White glaciers glistened in the sunlight.

Ellie did not think even once of unwrapping the precious German-made camera. Instead the package sat in the empty seat beside her to ward off any strangers who might wish to sit down.

David had placed his hat and the untouched picnic basket beside him for the same reason. Now they sat across from each other, knee to knee, and neither dared to look at the other for fear of betraying their emotions. They would talk in the privacy of the little bedroom above Frau Wattenbarger's kitchen.

Ellie imagined the warmth and safety of the thick log walls. The house seemed far away . . . too far away. Towering ruins of once-great castles glided by. Behind their massive walls knights and barons had planned their great Crusades into the Holy Land. By the thousands they had flocked to join the quest to recapture the Holy City of Jerusalem from her Muslim conquerors.

They had murdered and pillaged their way across the Continent in what had been a Christian version of the jihad. And when enough blood had been spilled in the name of Christ, when the walls of Jerusalem had fallen to their onslaught, they had built castles like these in the land of Palestine. Great towering edifices had been carved in the Pass of Bab el Wad. Holy relics had been discovered and brought back for barter and sale. Enough pieces of the true cross had been sold to forest an entire mountain.

But in all of that, the One who had died on that cross had been forgotten. Like the men on the balcony today, the conquerors had not bowed their hearts to the greater King. In their thirst for blood and search for sacred sights, they had forgotten that the King they pretended to fight for had willingly given His life for the sins they committed. And when His own disciple had drawn a sword to defend Him, Jesus had turned to him and said, *"All who draw the sword will die by the sword."*

The thought brought a wave of cold doubt into Ellie's mind. She looked at David, who simply stared out the window.

"What are you thinking?" he asked quietly.

"About the castles . . . the men who built them."

"What?"

"The same men who built these built places like Kastel. In Bab el Wad."

David gestured toward a mound of broken stones where an ancient castle once towered. "Looks like Kastel, all right. They must have had the same architect." He frowned. "I haven't thought about Moshe and Rachel in a week. Until today, I forgot about Crusader castles and holy wars and everything but you." He lapsed into silence as the train chugged up a long slope, climbing out of the valley.

"It has been beautiful," Ellie said wistfully. "Wonderful to forget about all we left behind."

"You sound like it's over."

She looked toward the folded newspaper. "The Crusaders had one advantage—the printing press hadn't been invented yet."

"Yeah." David rubbed his temples. "This guy Crabtree is a real headache. Would you know him if you saw him?"

"No. I don't have the vaguest idea what he looks like. The guy in front of the flower shop . . ." She groped for words. "I thought maybe . . . but that is impossible. Impossible."

"We'll just have to lay low at the farm, Els."

"How long can we keep that up?"

"In a couple of weeks, the British are leaving Palestine. Then we'll have a country of our own again. A place to go home to. We'll stay in Kitzbühel until then—stay with the Wattenbargers." He winked. "You're learning how to cook, after all. I don't want to throw you out of ground school before your first solo flight." With those words, his face suddenly clouded.

"What? What's wrong, David?"

"Ground school . . ." He ran his fingers through his hair in frustration. "We've got those ME-109s. I haven't thought about them, either. Anyway, Scarecrow and I picked a couple dozen fighter pilots when we were back in the States. I'm not worried about the C-47s. Martin Feinsteinel has got that part of the operation all wrapped up in Panama. All those guys have to do is get to Prague and pick up the cargo, then fly to Palestine—"

"They can do that without you. They don't need you for that."

He fixed his eyes on hers. "No. But they need me to train the fighter pilots in the ME-109s."

"Why?"

"I'm the one who suggested we buy the planes. I picked the crew. . . . They're probably on their way to Europe by now."

"Where in Europe, David? We've been left high and dry. Without hope of a contact. Surely they can find someone else to teach them."

"Not unless they hire an ex-Luftwaffe pilot, babe. I'm one of the few Americans qualified in those birds—and Martin is going to need fighter cover when they start flying cargo runs into Palestine. The Arabs are hiring British pilots—RAFs. And they've bought up every Spitfire available."

"Where are your pilots going to meet?" Ellie's voice was flat with resignation.

David sighed. "That's just it . . . I don't know. I landed in Palestine and took off again and we just never discussed it." He shrugged. "I don't know. I don't know anything." He flipped the newspaper onto the floor of the train. "This Crabtree guy seems to know more than we do. I'll bet he could tell us how to reach Mossad headquarters."

"If he knew, it would be in the paper," Ellie said glumly. "And if he knew where we are—"

"Nobody knows where we are. Not even the people who should know." He stooped to retrieve the paper. "So I guess all this worry about the pilots is useless . . . useless. If they want me—if Avriel wants me, he'll have to find me . . . before someone else does."

THE
TRUCE

John Glubb furrowed his brow at the words of King Abdullah. "Then what is the point of this meeting, Your Highness? You have gone to the trouble of consulting the American—"

King Abdullah smiled. "What is the point? My dear Glubb Pasha!" He spread his hands in exasperation. "We have no choice but to confer with the Americans. We have no choice but to confer with anyone who appears to have a reasonable solution to this matter!" He seemed elated.

"Then you are for the internationalization of Jerusalem?"

"Never!" He snapped his fingers for coffee. "Jerusalem will belong to Jordan and to me as its sovereign . . . that is established." He raised his eyes to the heavens. *"Insh' Allah."*

"Then such a meeting is a waste of time." Glubb slapped his hat against his knee in impatience.

"You are a soldier, Glubb Pasha. I am a statesman." Abdullah's words were patronizing. "Haj Amin is a butcher and my only real threat. The Americans do not recognize him as a power. The Jews cannot put an end to him. The British will not put an end to him. And so, I will use him to my benefit."

"How can he be of benefit to anyone?"

"You will see very soon. There will be at our little conference tomorrow morning a representative of every major faction in the dispute for the city. The American. Someone from the Jewish Quarter of the Old City. A representative of the Jewish Agency. Of course, an Englishman, and then a member of our forces and the Syrians and Iraqis. I have contacted the Egyptians, but they are not interested in Jerusalem in the least. There is only one major faction that will be missing."

"Someone from Haj Amin's faction."

"Let us simply say that they will not be there as *diplomats*!"

"I still do not understand, Your Majesty."

"Does the world hope that we will find a permanent solution to the question of Palestine?"

"Yes."

"And all hope we might make Jerusalem the center of the universe at last! The international city!"

"That is the purpose of the meeting, is it not?"

The monarch leaned forward and gazed intently at Glubb. "You still have not heard me, Glubb Pasha! Jerusalem and all of Palestine are fruit ripe for the plucking! They will belong to Jordan; I am certain of that. Now, this Palestinian madman must be finished soon. . . . Then perhaps we truly may annex Jerusalem and Palestine into Jordan by simply *talking*. We must be the voice of reason! Let Haj Amin be the butcher of the Middle East. The Western nations do not negotiate with butchers."

John Glubb considered the policy of King Abdullah. "So you are suggesting that we might win Palestine without a battle?"

"Quite!" The king sat back, satisfied that at last he had communicated his goal. "Everyone needs a . . . bad guy, as the Westerners say. Haj Amin fits the role quite well. I will take care of him, and then the Western world will look to me—"

"But the negotiations in the Old City?"

"The Christians have been kind enough to open their quarter to the lofty goal of peace through negotiation. Haj Amin will not be represented because he refuses to negotiate. The rest of us will be there, and . . ."

"Yes?"

"The eyes of the world will center there. It is a Christian holy day, remember?"

John Glubb remembered clearly the ancient traditions of the Saturday before Easter. "Yes. I thought you chose that day because the holy places would be open to pilgrims. There is a one-day truce."

"Haj Amin has not agreed to a truce. Nor will he."

"He will not know of the meeting."

Again King Abdullah smiled. "Oh, but he must hear of it!"

"But that will lead to violence, surely."

"Surely. Yes. It will lead to violence—and then the world will be convinced that Jerusalem cannot be made an international city."

"But—" John Glubb considered the king's words. He was trying to understand. He was a soldier—a good one—but he had no taste for the intrigue of politics. "And then what?"

"Then you will see the Holy City pass into my hands. Perhaps the Jews will end up negotiating with me alone. Or we may have to fight for Jerusalem. But Haj Amin and his Palestinian fanatics will be finally discredited among our brothers in the Arab Confederacy, and even more certainly throughout the world. My hatred of Haj Amin makes me a close brother to the Jews!"

He clapped his hands. "There is no other nation that can administer the lands of Palestine. I will be kind and benevolent to the Jews. You will see, Glubb Pasha. They will request peace. They will come to me and ask for my protection . . . which I shall gladly give them."

A light dawned in Glubb's eyes. "Well, that is one way to fight a war. If you can win it by seeming to be the only reasonable fellow in the whole brawl, I suppose—"

The little king nodded eagerly. "So. Now you understand."

"What are you going to do about Haj Amin's Irregulars tomorrow?"

"I think we should simply let news of the meeting leak out discreetly to the proper sources. I am certain that Haj Amin has men who will take it from there." He frowned and thoughtfully tugged his goatee. "Send some minor official of the Legion to the meeting, however. Knowing the Mufti, he will strike at the heart. I do not want anyone valuable hurt."

The evening meal was a cautious feast of fresh fruit and lamb stew that Rachel prepared from the food that Sarai had brought home from the Old City. When she had asked the young woman where she had gotten the money to purchase the food and the nanny goat, Sarai had simply shrugged and said that she had sold something of great value. She had not explained what that something was, but then she had produced a stack of gold sovereigns that she placed on the table. "This is for my lodging," she said. "And perhaps you will allow me to purchase other things to eat when I go back into the Old City."

With a puzzled look, Moshe had gone off to the Jewish Agency and left the two women at home alone.

Rachel stirred the stew, lifting the fragrant ladle to her lips to taste the garlic and sweet onions that simmered with chunks of lamb. It was the best meal she had tasted since she had come to Palestine. She smiled. It was, in fact, the most delicious dish she had tasted in many years.

Sarai entered the kitchen, her dress making a swishing sound. Rachel turned to see the young woman framed in the doorway and drew her breath in sharply. Sarai wore a long lavender dress that reached to her ankles. The full sleeves were embroidered, and thousands of tiny stitches graced the neckline as well as the hem, almost to the waist. Rachel found it difficult to believe that an old woman had ever worn the garment. It seemed to have been created for someone young and vibrant . . . and very beautiful.

Sarai had draped a silk scarf over her cropped hair and wrapped it around her neck to frame her perfect oval face in a deep purple. Her olive skin had a smoothness like the gleam of polished wood. Her eyes, such a deep brown that they were almost black, complemented her white teeth, sparkling behind full lips.

"You are . . . so beautiful," Rachel said appreciatively.

"You think so? Truly?" Sarai was flustered. She seemed self-conscious.

"Oh yes! Truly!"

Sarai put a hand to the scarf. "My hair . . ."

"You would never notice! Not ever," Rachel consoled. "And did I tell you that among the Orthodox of my people it is sometimes custom for a married woman to cut her hair short? You would fit right in—only you are much lovelier!"

"The black dress," Sarai said quietly. "I tore it when I climbed the fence. And then there was the goat . . . I can mend the dress tomorrow, but I could not wear it to table smelling like the goat."

As Sarai smiled broadly, Rachel was once again struck by her beauty. "Well then! I am glad for the smell of goats, because it has made you put on the dress! Miriam would be proud to see you in it. You are . . . like a flower garden."

"I should like to meet this Miriam." Sarai touched the soft fabric of the dress. "Her work is . . . she has created from something beautiful inside her soul, I think. Only the old ones stitch like this. And . . . I had never seen such beauty among the Christian embroidery."

"You can tell she was a Christian?" Rachel asked in wonder as she wiped her hands and touched the sleeve of Sarai's gown.

"Oh yes . . . you can even tell from which village she came. You see—" she pointed to a profusion of lupines that bordered her left shoulder— "she writes of Bethlehem here. . . ."

"She did? Of Bethlehem?" Rachel studied the swirls and dots of the flowers and wondered how it was that Sarai could see such things.

Sarai swept her hands over the dress as if to show her. "Yes. She loves the stories of Bethlehem. This one, you can read, is the story of a woman called Ruth. A beautiful story. I had never read such a lovely story before. We were only allowed to read the Koran, and it is not nearly so beautiful."

Rachel was still staring into bouquets of blossoms and sheaves of wheat that shimmered in golden thread. "The story of Ruth?" Rachel was incredulous.

"Yes!" The girl was exuberant in her explanation. "As I read it a while ago I thought perhaps somehow it had been written for me! Here"—she pointed to another row of deep purple flowers—"here the story tells of the woman Ruth. She was not a Jew. Not at all. She was from the land of Moab." She pointed eastward. "Moab is where Jordan is. And Ruth was an Arab of Moab who married a Jewish man."

"Please tell me, Sarai," Rachel said in an awed voice. "Where do you see all these things?"

The girl looked at her as though she were a child. "In all the letters. Do you not see the letters?"

Rachel shook her head. "No."

"You do not read?"

"Not Arabic," Rachel said, just beginning to distinguish the flowing cursive script among the patterns.

"Then I shall teach you." Sarai took her hand and led her to the chair. "Sit."

Rachel obeyed. "Teach me, then."

"This story of Ruth was written for us, my beloved enemy." Sarai's voice became tender. "It is the story of two women—one Arab and one Jewish. First their lives were united by grief . . . and then by love. They lived together in Moab, an Arab land. Still they loved. And both lost their husbands. . . . May Allah keep such heartache from you!"

Rachel watched as Sarai's brown finger traced the beautiful story of Ruth and Naomi. Rachel sat in silent awe at the realization that old Miriam seemed to have created this work of art especially for the broken heart of the young Arab who now seemed somehow transformed.

Sarai continued, "And when I read this part of the story, Rachel, I knew that this was my story. And for you as well. Here you see the words of Ruth's heart when Naomi told her to go back. But Ruth could not go back. She had no place to go, no family—like me."

Her finger traced the lines of an arabesque tower that was shaded in hues of red into deep blues and purples as she read: "*And Ruth said, Intreat me not to leave thee, or to return from following after thee: for whither thou goest, I will go; and where thou lodgest, I will lodge: thy people shall be my people, and thy God my God: Where thou diest, will I die, and there will I be buried: the Lord do so to me, and more also, if ought but death part thee and me. . . .*"

Sarai fell silent then, although the story of Ruth wove on and on.

"That is beautiful," Rachel said at last, as if she had never heard the words before.

"I have worn this dress tonight because of those words," Sarai murmured. "If those two women of old could be such friends—a Moabite and a Jew—then perhaps there is also hope for us." Her dark eyes sparked with tears of hope.

Rachel looked at Sarai and put out her arms, gathering her up like a small child. "Oh yes! Yes, little sister! Let it begin here, with us. We who have suffered know what a need there is to put away hate forevermore!"

Sarai cried softly on Rachel's shoulder. "Such a beautiful story," she said with difficulty. "And a happy ending."

"And it was the woman of Moab who loved first, Sarai. You have loved your enemies well." Now Rachel cried with her. "Sister," she said at last, "we begin here."

Haj Amin was quite pleased with himself. Breaking the fast of Ramadan, he passed the heaping platter to the Iraqi general who sat beside him.

"A fortuitous occasion, General!" Haj Amin said. "Tonight I not only celebrate the birth of the prophet but also a great victory for the Jihad of Palestine."

Two dozen others sat around the thick Persian carpet with him. The sounds of drums and cymbals and a reedy flute accompanied the celebration.

"What victory, Haj Amin?" the general asked.

"My agents in Europe have located the Jewish terrorists who sank the *Trina*," Haj Amin said nonchalantly.

"What is the difference?" a jowly Syrian growled bitterly. "This will not bring back the *Trina*."

"You cannot complain," offered another Iraqi officer as he stuffed his mouth full of rice. "The weapons have been salvaged."

"The ammunition was utterly destroyed!" snapped the Syrian.

Haj Amin lifted his hand serenely. "Gentlemen! Brothers! We must not forget the will of Allah! The will of him who gave us the prophet and the words of the Koran."

"It is not the will of Allah that we make stupid blunders!" The Syrian glowered at the religious leader.

"But Allah the Merciful sees all things, my brother." Haj Amin broke his bread and dipped it, leaving the men to wonder what Allah had seen and what Haj Amin Husseini knew that made him so confident tonight.

"That is so," conceded the Syrian.

"He is all-knowing and all-wise," said the Iraqi general.

Haj Amin smiled. "And all-powerful."

The men around the Mufti shifted in their places. Each man waited for the bit of news that Haj Amin was obviously holding just beyond their reach.

Finally the Iraqi could stand it no longer. He wiped his lips with the hem of his keffiyeh and blurted out sarcastically, "And what do Allah and Haj Amin know that the rest of us do not know?"

"Those Jewish terrorists," Haj Amin said with confidence, "are soon to lead us to the source of the Zionist organization in Europe."

A silence fell on the group. Drums and cymbals continued to beat out a happy cadence. "You have not killed them yet, then?"

"Not yet," Haj Amin said, taking another mouthful of lamb. "But no matter. We know where they are, and there is time. We simply wait."

The Syrian was unimpressed. "And while we wait, King Abdullah is bargaining with the Jews for Jerusalem! And for Palestine!" He scowled. "Abdullah will not fight if he can win the battle with words! What good will it do for you to find the Zionist headquarters in Europe? Even if you destroy them all, you will then be Mufti of nothing!"

Haj Amin simply stared at the man in disbelief. "How do you know this?"

The drums fell silent. Men stopped chewing and stared at the two men.

"How do you know this?" Haj Amin shouted. "Answer!"

"There is nothing to be done for it, Haj Amin. King Abdullah has tricked us all. He will take Palestine. He will make friends with the Zionists and have Jerusalem himself."

"How have you come by such news?" the Mufti hissed.

"A captain. In the British forces in Palestine. He is to be present when they meet tomorrow."

"And there are other representatives who will be there?" Haj Amin stared at each man at the table. Their eyes spoke of knowledge of the rendezvous. "But no one from the Palestinian Arabs, I am certain." He looked back at the now-shaking musicians. "Play, then," he said with resignation. "It is the feast to end Ramadan. We should be joyful."

28

HOPE

The young messenger boy ran through the souks of the Arab Quarter of Jerusalem on his way to the shabby room of Fredrich Gerhardt. The boy carried in his hand a sealed envelope from the head muhqtar of the Palestinian Arab High Committee.

It was very dark in the streets, but the boy knew his way. He stumbled once on the stone steps of the Street of the Patriarch and cut his knee, but there was a reward for him if he quickly found Commander Gerhardt in his lodgings near the Muristan.

He ran panting up the unlit stairs, past unpainted doors and laundry that dripped over the railing of the balcony. At last he came to the door at the dark end of the corridor. He raised his fist but hesitated before knocking. It was late but also urgent, the old muhqtar had told him. The talents of the great commander Gerhardt would be needed in the morning. The boy banged his hand against the peeling paint of the door. Then he knocked again, more loudly.

Nearly a minute passed before the door was opened slightly and the grim face of Gerhardt glowered down at the messenger. "What do you want?"

Gerhardt had not been asleep, the boy noticed. A cigarette was burning in an ashtray on the table behind him.

"The muhqtar—" The boy's voice trembled. He held out the envelope. "Word has come from Damascus. A message for you, but you have no telephone, they say. So the muhqtar has sent me."

Gerhardt snatched the envelope from the messenger and tore it open as the boy crossed his arms and waited in the hallway. He squinted as he read the words. "I will send a message back."

Gerhardt scribbled a few lines onto a blank sheet of paper. He tore it off and folded it, not bothering to seal it in an envelope. He thrust it into the boy's hands with a small coin. "Take this to the muhqtar. Tell him I said to send it to Haj Amin." He gave the messenger a shove. "They will pay you."

The boy pocketed the slip before scrambling back down the rickety stairs and into the street.

Two lights winked on in the upstairs apartment of Gerhardt. The beams puddled in the street where the boy passed. Even without reading the message, the boy knew that Commander Gerhardt was about to make another legend for the Jihad of Jerusalem. Something was going to happen . . . something terrible and wonderful for the great cause of the Holy Strugglers—and he himself had delivered the command to Gerhardt! The boy felt proud as he ran back along the crooked course. But he reminded himself that he must tell his friends to stay off the streets of the Old City until something—some great explosion—signaled an end to Gerhardt's mission.

Yehudit carried the large basket of sandwiches from the kitchen of Tipat Chalev to the barricade at the end of the Street of the Stairs.

"*Shabbat Shalom!*" she called loudly to answer the Haganah challenge in the darkness. "It is Yehudit! I have brought you supper."

The shouts of the Arab mobs seemed very far away tonight. They would not turn down this street so readily now that the Jews carried their weapons openly at the night watch.

"Come ahead," Dov's voice called to her. "*Shabbat Shalom!*" The greeting of Sabbath peace seemed a strange paradox to the nightly sound of the riots that emanated from the Muslim Quarter.

She lugged the heavy basket to the dozen men who crouched behind the sandbags. In carrying the burden on Friday night, she had broken a Sabbath regulation prohibiting work. Living under the iron hand of Rabbi Akiva, she never would have dreamed of such a violation. Now the very act of defiance gave her a sense of delight. She was free at last, and for the first time in her young life, the oppressive burden of her father's tyranny was lifted from her shoulders. She was a welcome and needed member of the Haganah in the Old City now. They all—and especially Dov Avram—treated her as such. She had even considered that one day she might wish to carry a rifle instead of just a basket of food for the sentries.

"You are early," said Dov as he took the basket from her.

"I thought I was late," Yehudit said breathlessly as she sat down on a sandbag. She raised her chin toward the racket. "The Arabs have begun their routine early tonight."

"It is the last night of Ramadan." Dov handed out the sandwiches. "They are celebrating—letting off steam ahead of time."

"Ahead of time?"

"Yes. They will have to control themselves now until after Easter. There is a short truce . . . just long enough for the Christians to make their pilgrimage."

"Brave souls they are," said a young soldier with his mouth full of bread and stale cheese. "Brave they are to come into the Old City."

"So!" Dov smiled and Yehudit saw his teeth flash in the darkness. "Our rowdy neighbors will have to control themselves for a short time. Maybe we can all take a nap for a while," he joked.

But Yehudit sensed that an official declaration of the Easter truce would not stop the violence of the Palestinian mobs. After all, Haj Amin had not declared a truce.

"I wonder each night"—she gazed toward the dark hump of the Dome of the Rock—"why they simply do not attack in force and end it."

Dov pointed toward the roof of a low-domed building. The silhouettes of the British soldiers were barely visible. "Well, the English are not gone yet. They are not much help to us, but I think the Arabs fear an Englishman might accidentally shoot in their direction!"

"And maybe hit an Arab by mistake!" There was a ripple of laughter.

"They are not feeling a need to rush," Dov continued. "They will know where to find us when the English leave, *nu*?"

"*Nu, nu!*" said a voice in the darkness.

"Well, they might find a surprise when they do finally come." Yehudit crossed her arms defiantly.

"If they are surprised," offered another of the soldiers, "they will not be half so surprised as we are!" A fresh chuckle erupted from the sentries, and then the rattle of gunfire burst from the Arab souks. "Maybe they will find they used all their ammunition celebrating the birth of Mohammed! *Oy*, such a surprise!"

Dov looked into the clear night sky. Yehudit's eyes followed his gaze. The stars seemed close enough to touch. She was glad she was sitting here with Dov.

"I see the Arabs have not knocked down any stars," Dov said quietly.

"Still, God must not like it! Every night the Arabs aim up at His windows!" one of the men called. Another burst of machine-gun fire sounded. "See?"

For a minute the group listened to the cries of hatred that swelled from the souks. "Sticks and stones, eh?" Dov said at last. Then he took Yehudit by the arm. "You should be going back now. Old Shoshanna will worry for you if you are late." His words were tender.

"You said I was early," Yehudit protested, not wanting to leave Dov's side or the vicarious excitement of the outpost.

"That was *before*. Now you will be late. Come on," he urged. "I will walk you to the corner."

"Hurry back, Dov," called a voice. "Shemuel will eat your Shabbat meal!"

As Dov took Yehudit's hand, a shiver of delight went through her. Together they walked beneath the shadows of the buildings.

"I am glad you came," Dov whispered, his eyes intent on her.

"And I am glad you are glad." Yehudit looked at him and smiled, then squeezed his hand.

"Have you heard any word from your father?" he suddenly asked.

"My father? How can one who is dead hear from her father? You do not know him if you think his heart will soften. He counts me among his enemies now. I will not hear from him."

"I am sorry for him, then," said Dov. "He has thrown away such a treasure."

"Dov!" Her cheeks felt warm in the darkness.

"No. No. Please . . . it's true. You are . . . a treasure. A good Jewish girl. Kind. Gentle. With a heart for Zion. You are . . ." He searched for words. "A . . . soldier!"

"Well then." She was still flushed with the excitement of his nearness. "And you are a good Jewish boy. Learned in the Talmud and in the use of a Sten gun." She laughed.

Dov spun her around suddenly, pulling her against himself and kissing her as they stood in the arch of a doorway. She could feel the bulge of the revolver beneath his Hasid coat. Warmth surged through her. She had never been kissed before, and the experience left her feeling faint.

Dov stepped back from her. "I'm sorry." He hung his head guiltily. "I should not have done such a thing."

Yehudit put her hand to her pounding heart. "Why not?" she breathed as the world and the stars whirled in opposite directions.

"It is not fitting that I should . . . that we should . . . kiss. Unless—"

She stepped toward him. "Unless what?" She gently put one finger under his chin and raised his head. What she saw in his eyes took her breath away.

"Unless we first stand beneath the chuppah . . . ," he finally managed.

"Well then?"

"Whom shall I ask for your hand?" Dov's voice sounded desperate.

She thought for a moment. "Perhaps the good Rebbe Lebowitz?" she offered gently. "He could find us a canopy to stand beneath and say our vows, if you can find a minyan of ten men to witness."

"Yes!" Dov embraced her clumsily, stepping on her toes. "*Oy!* Excuse me."

She laughed at him. "It's all right. I'm glad you stepped on my feet, Dov. . . . I was about to pinch myself anyway to see if I was dreaming." She raised her face to his and closed her eyes.

He kissed her cautiously at first, and then with more enthusiasm.

"No," she whispered, "I am not asleep. You do love me. . . ."

"We should go see Rebbe Lebowitz," Dov said in a voice almost pained. "Tonight."

It was nearly midnight before the armored car dropped Moshe off. Sarai had long since gone to bed, but Rachel sat up in the parlor and watched for his return.

Even in the dim light she could see that his face was exultant as he bounded up the steps. Quickly she unlatched the door and let him in. Without a word, he slipped his arms around her and held her close.

"What is it?" she asked, catching his excitement. "Tell me!"

Moshe pulled her around the corner of the foyer into the parlor and touched her face. Then he kissed her long and hard. "The meeting I told you about," he whispered as he looked furtively over his shoulder. "Kane and King Abdullah—"

"Yes?"

"There is hope, Rachel . . . hope for peace!"

"Oh, Moshe!" She returned his embrace as visions of peace filled her brimming heart. Perhaps the miracle of God's love had begun among others besides her and Sarai. "Tell me!"

"Where is she?" Moshe asked.

"In bed. Sleeping."

"You're sure?" He slid the paneled doors of the parlor shut as Rachel lit a kerosene lamp.

"She would be as glad for this news as we are," Rachel said.

He continued to whisper. "Kane met with Abdullah. The conference was a success. Abdullah hates the Mufti as badly as we do. He wants a peaceful settlement!"

"Praise to the Eternal!" Rachel closed her eyes in the joy of such a thought.

"Tomorrow the truce begins for Easter. We will go into the Christian Quarter of the Old City with the pilgrims."

"We?" she asked, her heart falling.

"Me. The others who will negotiate," he rushed on. "I am multilingual,

so I will go with Golda Meir for the Agency. We will meet with representatives of England, Jordan, members of the Old City Jewish Quarter
Council. Kane will be there. A few others. This is what we have been
praying for!" He held her hands tightly and looked into her eyes.

"You will be safe?" she asked, wishing that another could go, yet
proud that Moshe would be part of such an important event.

"I promise." He stroked her cheek, then tugged her gently toward
the floor. "You know what I have been thinking about all night while
all this was going on?"

"What?"

He put his hand on her womb. "This . . . and you. And us! I have
been imagining what it would be like to simply live!"

"I thought the same thing that afternoon in your classroom at the
university." She put her hand on his and played with his fingers. "It will
happen for us, Moshe! It is too sweet a dream not to come true! A happy
ending for us, yes?"

He did not reply. For a long time he gazed tenderly down at her face
as though the dream were already reality. "I will call in sick"—he grinned
and his dark eyes sparkled—"and we will stay in bed all day and make
love." His lips brushed hers and she giggled.

"Shame on you, Professor! They will fire you!"

"No." He traced the slim line of her throat with his finger. "I will be
the president of the university." He kissed her again, more insistently.

"You cannot lie to them," she mocked.

"I won't be lying," he said in a husky voice. "Haven't you read Song
of Solomon?"

"What, my king?" Her breath caught at the warmth of his touch.

"*If you find my beloved,*" he whispered, "*tell her that I am sick with
love. . . .*"

"*His mouth is most sweet—*" Rachel drew him to her. "*This is my beloved,
and this is my friend, O daughters of Jerusalem.*"

29

COMPANY AT KITZBÜHEL

Clutter. Chaos and confusion.

The fat Italian directed the beam of his flashlight around the tiny one-room apartment of L. C. Crabtree. Heaps of books and papers tumbled from the desktop. Piles of books were stacked on the floor like crooked pillars. Shirts and trousers were tossed over the backs of rickety chairs, and ashtrays made of tin cans overflowed with ashes.

The fat Italian turned to the Englishman. "Someone has been here before us. The place has been ransacked."

The Englishman shook his head. "No. He simply lives like a hamster, old man." He grimaced and began a careful excavation. "What safer place? What safer place to hide it than this, eh?"

The Italian shrugged. "But how will we find anything?"

The Englishman knocked a pile of newspapers to the floor, then removed each drawer from the desk, upending the contents until the level of debris climbed steadily. He stood in the center of the mess and turned slowly around, his eyes finally resting on a makeshift end table covered with a sheet and topped by a lamp and a small porcelain statue of Mary holding the crucified Christ.

Without ceremony, the Englishman lifted the edge of the sheet and gave a tug, mimicking a magician pulling a tablecloth from under fine china. The lamp and statue crashed to the floor. Beneath the sheet was a square cardboard box. The Italian knelt and lifted the lid. Rows of file folders were inside, each neatly labeled with names and current addresses.

"You see," said the Englishman with satisfaction. "In a hamster cage the thing that stands out is organization!"

Fists slammed against the door. A stream of angry Italian curses filled the hallway. The fat Italian called over his shoulder, "Never mind! He is drunk again! I put him to bed!"

The curses were accompanied by one more thump on the door, and then footsteps retreated, leaving the two men to marvel over their discovery. "Names!" The Englishman examined a file. "Look! *Look*, Pietr! And there are six in Jerusalem now!"

"Yes." Pietr narrowed his eyes. "And I am certain that I saw her on the train . . . it had to be."

"Of course it was her, you fool!" The Englishman flipped through the Jerusalem file. His eyebrows went up as he examined its contents. "Crabtree was—is—on his way to Palestine after his excursion to Kitzbühel. And look what he takes with him, eh?"

The Italian held the beam of light steady on the pages. "So the journalist goes to the Holy City to pay homage to the Saints—a dirty business. Dirty." He closed the file and sat back against a mound of laundry. "Ah, well. For the glory of Allah."

"Can you carry the whole box?" asked the Englishman with grim satisfaction.

"Yes. And another."

"We won't need any more than this. My countrymen and the Americans will pay dearly enough." He jammed the folder back under *J* before he closed the lid.

"And Haj Amin? What will he pay?"

"My dear fellow," the Englishman answered, thumping the box, "this is his entire Swiss bank account—a king's ransom, Pietr—all found in the confessions of a saint and tucked away in the cage of a hamster."

The two men glanced around the room at the chaos they left behind. It was not so very different than when they had first entered, after all.

The hired sleigh followed a narrow road, bordered on one side by a snow-covered meadow and on the other side by a thick forest of evergreens whose branches sagged beneath the weight of the week's snowfall. They passed a covered, life-sized crèche where Mary and Joseph stood watch over a small wooden cradle. Ellie had to remind herself again that it was April . . . Good Friday, not Christmas.

The jingling bells on the harness added to the illusion, and every mile closer to the old farmhouse renewed her sense of peace. She and David snuggled close under a heavy woolen blanket. The young man who drove the sleigh did not look back at them or even speak during the drive from Kitzbühel to the Wattenbarger farm.

Above them, glistening white peaks blended into the blue and purple hues of twilight. Ahead and to the left, up a long, sloping hill, the lamps of Frau Wattenbarger's kitchen gleamed a golden welcome. Wisps of smoke rose from both stone chimneys to drift into the mountain mists that swirled among the branches of the trees. The scent of woodsmoke carried with it the aroma of fried potatoes, and for the first time since they had left the safety of the house this morning, Ellie was suddenly hungry.

"They will be surprised to see us an hour and a half early," David said quietly. His voice sounded more relaxed. He put a hand to his stomach. "I hope the Frau has cooked enough supper for us, too."

Ellie nodded in agreement. The door of the farmhouse opened, flooding the front of the house in light. She squinted as the tall, lean silhouette of Herr Wattenbarger stood framed in the doorway. Then another man stepped out beside him.

"Who is that?" Ellie sat forward in alarm. But the door closed in that instant, and the view of the second man was lost to her.

"What?" David's eyes followed her trembling finger as she pointed.

"There was a man there," she said, her brow creased with a frown.

"Where?" David searched the gloom in front of the house.

"I saw another man. Herr Wattenbarger came out the door just now, and someone was with him."

"Probably Frau Wattenbarger." David sat back, as if satisfied with his explanation.

"No," Ellie insisted. "It was a man. I saw a man with him."

Was it possible for someone to pursue them in Innsbruck and know about this place and beat them home? she wondered. After all, they had taken the first train back to Kitzbühel.

The driver, his fair cheeks red with the cold, turned for an instant. "Ja, Fräulein. I myself have Touristen brought here today. They wish not at the Golden Griffin to stay. So here I bring them." His smile faded as he stared at David's and Ellie's faces.

The window of their bedroom was unlit. The one next to it glowed brightly. Ellie sighed. Their refuge must now be shared with other tourists.

"This is the Easter week," said the driver. "Then come students of the university, ja?" His face was more somber.

"Are they German?" David asked.

"American. Like you." He smiled again, more broadly. "They bring skis—"

David gripped Ellie's hand hard, as if to say, *Everything will be all right . . . remember the sparrow.* She leaned her head against his arm in exhaustion. The sleigh bells now seemed distant, like something out of a dream, and Ellie found herself wishing that the ride were longer.

The horse pulled up before the door of the farmhouse and Frau Wattenbarger bustled out the door, her arms wide in greeting, while a young couple hung back, smiling self-consciously at their arrival.

"Home early, children!" Frau Wattenbarger embraced Ellie, while Herr Wattenbarger, his pipe in clenched teeth, shook David's hand warmly.

"Innsbruck ist today a busy city! The parades, did you see?" He did not wait for an answer, instead turning toward the young couple who stood with their arms around each other's waists. "From America also. They ist here on holiday. They have come for the last snow . . . like you, ja?"

"So, Papa, introduce! Introduce!" Frau Wattenbarger led Ellie to the couple. "This ist Ted und Maryanne Samson. Just married!" she said with delight in her eyes. Ellie wondered briefly if they should give up the big bed for a night. "Und this, James and Sue Madison." The old woman used their false names with an ease that Ellie had been unable to master.

The young man had the kind of fresh-faced, homey look about him that made Ellie think of her own kid brothers. He had an easy grin, red curly hair, and a smattering of freckles. A thin mustache struggled to grow on his upper lip, and Ellie thought that surely he must be much older than he looked. His wife was a fair-skinned brunette with a shy smile. She seemed to huddle under his thin arm. Ted was at least as tall as David but had the slight build of a runner rather than the muscles of his namesake, Samson.

With relief Ellie noted that there was not even a glimmer of recognition in the young man's brown eyes. "Good to meet you." Ellie's words were genuine.

"And good to meet y'all!" Maryanne spoke with a heavy Southern accent and an enthusiasm to match.

As they walked into the warmth of the house, a flood of conversation erupted from the young woman. Ellie guessed that in conversation with Maryanne, there would be very little to do but listen and answer in monosyllables.

"Ted got a degree in languages down at U of Texas. We was childhood sweethearts, an' I swear I never did know what that boy was talkin' about!"

"I know what you mean." Ellie nodded politely and exchanged looks with David, who was listening to the less pronounced accent of Ted, who also seemed eager to talk.

"James Madison!" Ted slapped David on the back. "Who thought that one up? Of course, being named for a president isn't bad. Down home we knew two gals by the last name of Hogg, and their daddy named them Ima and Ura!"

"Ima Hogg and Ura Hogg!" Maryanne picked up on the story. "The names fit, too, I can tell ya! Though nuthin' else ever fit 'em! They was big as a house! Their daddy had to use a truck to haul 'em in!"

"So!" David said loudly after Ted and Maryanne stopped laughing. "How long have you been in Europe?"

"Oh, Teddy's been here nigh onto three years. Now he's workin' in Rome as an interpreter. He can sweet-talk me in four different languages, an' I don't know what he's sayin'!"

"That's right. She doesn't even know if it's sweet talk!"

"Interpreter?" Ellie asked.

"Sure!" Maryanne said. "Why, he knew jus' what to say to get us here. I didn't have to even open my mouth!"

That must've been difficult for you, Ellie thought. *It hasn't been closed since we met you.* Ellie did not look at David, certain that he was thinking the same thing. "And how long have you been here, Maryanne?"

"Three weeks. An' me an' Ted found us a Baptist army preacher an' got ourselves hitched the day after I got here. My mama would've liked to be here, but I sent her a wire tellin' her it was all legal and proper and done by a Baptist preacher, so she don't mind too much. She always jus' loved Teddy to pieces! Jus' loved everythin' about him! Daddy hoped he'd go into the hardware business with him, but Teddy got it in his head he wanted to be an interpreter, an' I don't mind. I get to see the world. Visited Vatican City and, my *goodness*! All them statues! That Michael Anglo fella carved everybody stark naked! And in church, too! I didn't write Mama about that. Can you imagine goin' t'church surrounded by all them naked statues!" She paused for a breath. "Well, Ted says I need educatin'!"

"I'm goin' to teach her to ski," Ted added more quietly. "The work of Michelangelo is lost on her." There was a touch of embarrassment in his voice, Ellie thought. Then he spoke in quiet German to Frau Wattenbarger. It was a compliment, most certainly.

The old woman blushed slightly and bowed, then looked at Ellie. "He asks what we will for dinner have. Because it ist Freitag und we already went to Mass, we will have fresh trout that Papa has caught today here. You like to learn to cook trout?" Her twinkling eyes revealed that she, too, was amused by the garrulous young American bride.

Maryanne raised her hands in enthusiasm. "Trout! Holy mackerel! I ain't had a good mess of fried fish since last month. I'll show you how to cook 'em Texas style!"

Frau Wattenbarger raised her chin in kind but firm resolution. "No, my dear. When I someday come to Texas you show me. Here in Kitzbühel, I show you how we cook fish on a holy day after Mass." She smiled and led the two young women into the sanctity of her kitchen.

The men remained in the Stube, smoking pipes and discussing politics. Their voices drifted into the kitchen. Ellie was relieved to hear Ted and David exchanging pleasant conversation and genuine laughter after a time, while Herr Wattenbarger practiced his English with them both.

Frau Wattenbarger was definitely the mistress of her own kitchen, and it took only a few minutes before even Maryanne had settled into a sort of respectful attention.

"Today ist holy day," Frau Wattenbarger said. "The day our Lord was crucified. It ist the same in America, I think. My daughter writes that Mass there is much the same—"

"You don't say!" Maryanne sounded amazed. "Where does she live?"

"The same place as you . . . Texas."

She gasped. "Why, I never knew there was Roman Catholics in Texas! Least not enough to have a church of their own an' all. 'Course, Texas is a big state—the biggest!" There was an edge of pride to her voice. Perhaps even homesickness.

"Ja," Frau Wattenbarger said as she seasoned three enormous trout. "There ist a few Catholics in Texas. Only after Mass, my daughter says the trout she must cook are very, very much smaller than here . . . und fried crisp like so much potatoes."

Maryanne drew back slightly, uncertain if she had been somehow insulted. "Well, maybe she ought to cook up some catfish. We got catfish with mouths so big they'd plumb swallow up one of those trout of yours."

Frau Wattenbarger nodded and smiled, winking gently in Ellie's direction. "I do not doubt. . . . Und how many can you eat, Maryanne?"

30

THE MIRACLE
OF HOLY FIRE

The Christian Arabs of Bethlehem and Nazareth had joined the thousands who now gathered in the predawn light outside the walls of Jerusalem. Compared to the usual multitudes who came for Easter week, this year's assembly was a pitiful few thousand. From around the world, the clergy of various sects had come to witness again the miracle of Easter.

There were few laymen among them in the procession as they marched slowly toward the Lion's Gate and onto Via Dolorosa, the ancient Way of the Cross. Hymns rose in every language as men and women hoisted wooden crosses onto their shoulders and walked on the stones where Christ was said to have walked to Golgotha.

Moshe and other members of the negotiation team were pressed in among the pilgrims now, and as they passed the Antonio Fortress, Moshe looked to the rooftops. He was surprised that only a few soldiers were on duty and they were all of the British forces. The red-and-white-checkered keffiyehs of the Arab Legion were nowhere to be seen. The fighting, it seemed, was to stop as men remembered once again the blackness of the tomb near Golgotha.

Moshe walked just behind a troop of French nuns. Their sweet voices blended with a hundred other songs until the discordant notes merged into one unutterable hymn of harmony with words understood by God alone. This was the first time in his life that he had been a part of the solemn processional to the Church of the Holy Sepulchre, and he felt amazed that it had taken a war to finally lead him to this path. As he passed beneath the Ecce Homo Arch, the music swirled around him, echoing back from the colonnades with such sweetness that he marveled that violence and destruction would not shrink back from it.

Ahead of him were other members of the negotiating team. All of them had melted into the obscurity of the crowds and would not come together again until they were safe at the great church.

The sky was deep violet with streaks of pale pink clouds where the sun would rise soon. A flock of white pigeons broke from the shelter of a tall minaret and swirled out in one unified pattern like a banner in the wind. Moshe followed their flight as he joined the Christian hymns with a soft baritone melody of "HaTikvah"—"The Hope." Right now it seemed more than a song of hope for the Jewish nation. The Hebrew words blended beautifully with the other choruses, and Moshe raised his voice louder so that the Hope of Israel could be well represented in this pilgrimage to the tomb of the Messiah of Israel.

This morning he wondered if he was the only Jew in the world who sang praise for the el-Kiama of Yeshua Messiah . . . the Savior and deliverer of the Jewish people and all the world. Now it seemed that the world had forgotten that Jesus had come as a Jew to fulfill all the ancient prophecies of the Jewish Holy Scriptures.

He looked about him at the dress of those he walked among. Of course there were no prayer shawls, no talliths in the group of pilgrims, but Moshe wished that he had his.

What prayers can I pray this morning to remember that the Son of God came as a Jew to carry the cross down the Via Dolorosa? The answer came easily to his mind. He remembered the prayers of the morning service . . . the slightly swaying image of the rabbi cloaked in the tallith as he read from the Jewish prayer book.

Moshe began to recite the ancient words from the *Siddur* as every observant Jew was doing even as he walked now. He prayed the prayer in Hebrew:

"O look down and have compassion, we beseech You, upon Your people for the sake of Your name. In Your abundant mercies, O Eternal, our God! have pity and compassion, and save the flock of Your pasture. . . ."

Had not Yeshua called Himself the Good Shepherd? Was not Israel still His flock? Moshe wondered.

"Have compassion on us for the sake of Thy covenant. . . ."

This was an ancient covenant, made when Abraham had offered his only son to God.

"We beseech you, O King, gracious and compassionate!"

Moshe recited the words of the *Siddur* loudly, although not one of the Gentiles around him understood.

"Remember and regard the covenant between the divided sacrifice, and hold before Your throne the memory of the only Son, a victim, ready bound, for Israel's sake. . . ."

"So, God, Abraham offered his only son, and two thousand years later You finished the covenant by offering Yours! Yes. A covenant sealed between You and Abraham here on this very place! And it will never be forgotten. A Jewish Scripture, yes, Lord?"

No one heard Moshe or replied, so he spoke again from the midst of the Gentiles of the nations. *"But thou, Bethlehem Ephratah, though thou be little among the thousands of Judah, yet out of thee shall He come forth unto Me that is to be ruler in Israel.* Micah 5:2!" Moshe said with satisfaction.

Although the ancient prophecies had been discarded by more recent rabbis, Moshe remembered clearly what the rabbis of old had known and believed about Messiah. And those who had filled the broad hillsides of Palestine to hear Him preach and watch Him heal . . . they had seen and known.

Some had feared Yeshua because He saw the hearts of men. When the religious leaders had thrown the Law at Him, He had preached love and compassion, which was a more difficult road to travel in the end. He had quoted Isaiah and called them hypocrites: *"This people draweth nigh unto Me with their mouth, and honoreth Me with their lips; but their heart is far from Me. But in vain they do worship Me, teaching for doctrines the commandments of men."*

And so, Yeshua had come to be the governor of men's hearts, to teach them of God's love as the first commandment. Then men had crucified Him.

As they had crucified one another for thousands of years.

As they still shouted for blood!

Moshe thought of the young Arab woman Sarai. He had mistrusted her because she was an Arab. And in this moment, he knew again that he was no better than the hypocrites Yeshua had spoken to with such honesty. "I have drawn near to You with my mouth," he whispered, "but not with my heart. Not in the matter of the girl. When they crucified You, You forgave them. You loved them even as You bled and died. I have not loved my enemy, Lord, so my heart has still cried for the blood of war and revenge.

"Change my heart today," Moshe prayed. "Cleanse me from secret faults and make me as Yeshua was on this earth. Give me wisdom today, and help us find peace in our hearts. . . ." He prayed aloud, but no one heard him. He looked down at the flagstones and thought of the feet of the Messiah and the weight of the cross He had dragged to Golgotha.

Yeshua had carried the sins of the world—hatred and lust and greed—with Him to put evil to death. He was betrayed for thirty pieces of silver, as the prophet Zechariah had predicted. Then they crucified Him as the psalmist had written they would in the twenty-second psalm. They gambled for His clothes and spit on Him and mocked Him, and in the end, the words of Isaiah fifty-three had been true. *"By His wounds we are healed,"* Moshe quoted, raising his hands to the last light of the morning star. *"The Lord had laid on Him the iniquity of us all."*

A lightness filled Moshe's heart as he walked. He knew he would find some way to speak to Sarai of what he felt. They would find some way to love each other, even as enemies. And in that, they might begin to knit a fragment of peace. He smiled as he remembered what Rachel had told him about Miriam's secret, ongoing testimony. The story of Ruth and Naomi was a beautiful one.

Ruth the Moabite was given a place of honor in the ancestry of Yeshua, the Jewish Messiah. Could it be that someday the Messiah would unite the hearts of men in peace and love? Moshe almost laughed out loud at how far men had come from the simple teaching of Yeshua. On every corner of the Old City there stood a different church. Even those who professed to believe in the teachings of Yeshua could not get along.

"Their hearts are far from Me," Moshe said softly. It was little wonder that Jews and Arabs alike rejected Christianity. It was fragmented by dissension and bitterness. . . . It was far from the teachings of Yeshua.

The great dome of the church towered over the procession. Men and women crowded closer to the heavy metal doors to wait. Hours before, the lights inside the church had been extinguished, and a deathlike darkness filled the interior. Silence rippled through the crowd as they held unlit candles aloft and prayed for the light of faith to come again this year.

Moshe closed his eyes a moment. When he opened them, he thought he caught a glimpse of Sarai, beautiful and shining in the lavender dress. She stood across a wide gulf of jostling pilgrims and was nearer to the door than Moshe. Her eyes searched eagerly for the approach of the patriarch of Jerusalem who would soon come to open the doors of the church and the sealed tomb where Yeshua had been buried.

Moshe considered raising his hand to call her, but the silence seemed profound and holy in the deep shadows of the street. There was no hope of reaching her now. The crush around the door was too intense, and more people gathered in the back. Instead he continued to watch her as she would appear and disappear behind a portly Greek Orthodox priest. Her face was alight with hope in el-Kiama, just as Rachel had told him it had been the night before when the two women had sat together and Sarai had read the story in the stitches of Miriam's dress.

Moshe did not need to speak to her in order to know that she believed. The glow of her countenance was enough to tell him that the story had healed her shattered life. Now she had come to see for herself and remember that death had been swallowed up when the crucified Messiah had stepped from His grave.

There was no more time to think about it. With a sigh, Moshe pushed through the crowd and inched his way toward the patriarchate, where three members of the negotiating team had already entered the building in which they would meet. As much as he felt drawn to the mysteries of this morning's ritual, Moshe could not stay to watch.

At that moment, Sarai looked toward him. Her face lit with recognition; then, as she waved, she looked puzzled. He read it in her eyes: *"Why is he going away from the church? Why does he enter the side door of the patriarchate?"*

Moshe averted his eyes, pretending that he had not seen her.

Golda Meir moved toward the entrance of the church, ahead of Moshe Sachar. Her eyes scanned the parapets and rooftops above them. She was uneasy and preoccupied, impatient to begin the talks before the tumult in the streets began in earnest. They would have only two hours at best to lay some foundation for peace here this morning. It was not enough time for such an important beginning.

Tom Kane looked back over his shoulder and spotted Golda. He nodded in greeting, satisfied that she had made it, then slipped quietly into the building.

Fredrich Gerhardt and three other Palestinians stood together at the railing of the tall minaret of the el-Omariye Mosque just opposite the Church of the Holy Sepulchre. From their high vantage point, they had a clear view of the solemn processional as it wound through the streets toward the Christian shrine.

One of the men with him pointed at the British soldiers who patrolled the rooftops on either side of the route of the pilgrims. "The English are many."

Gerhardt shrugged. "It does not matter. Many or few, they cannot stop what will happen."

"What if they find it?" asked the Palestinian.

Gerhardt raised the field glasses and looked toward the domed roof of the patriarchate, where the meeting between the Jews and the Jordanians was soon to take place. He knew the room and the time and the circumstances exactly, and he had prepared a surprise for the participants. "Even I, who know where to look for the bomb, cannot see it," he said simply. "The English are not looking for anything. They cannot imagine that we might disrupt the little Christian ceremony at the Dunghill. After all, they have reasoned that our war is between Jews and Arabs. They are not looking for trouble today."

"The Christians have asked for this," said a second man, likewise raising field glasses to gaze down at the people. "They should not have allowed this meeting . . . not without us."

"The Christians do not care who rules Jerusalem, whether it be King Abdullah or the United Nations."

"I think they would prefer the United Nations."

"Then they will be surprised to learn that we are the power that will decide the fate of Jerusalem," Gerhardt said grimly. "Without the Mufti, there will be no peace here, and even then it will be a peace of his own choosing."

The bomb he had planted on the roof of the patriarchate was a cruel device, packed with chunks of sharp metal scraps. Gerhardt had salvaged the metal from the shop of a man who made iron grillwork for the windows of shops in the city. Explosives had been packed around the shards of metal and set to detonate a half hour after the negotiations were scheduled to begin. The device would then rip downward through the support beams of the roof, and if any were lucky enough to escape the red-hot shrapnel, they still would not escape the collapse of the structure above them.

It was a bomb similar in destructive power to that of the explosion that had destroyed the wing of the King David Hotel two years before. Over eighty civilians had died in that explosion, and the foundation of the British Mandate had also crumbled, leading to the Partition vote.

Today, the day before Easter, as Christian pilgrims traveled to the tomb of Christ under the illusion of safety and truce, Gerhardt hoped that his bomb would once again shatter the confidence of the Christian world. Without the Mufti at the helm of power in Jerusalem, all the talks and plans of peace devised by other nations would amount to nothing. Great armies crumbled in the face of even a small band of terrorists.

Let them talk of peace, Gerhardt mused. *Still they will die. Let them sign*

their pacts. The paper will be torn to shreds. Let them pray! Their prayers will
soon be turned to screams of grief and agony.

The minaret where they stood was a literal stone's throw from the
great church.

"What if the English see us here?" asked the youngest of Gerhardt's
recruits.

"What if they do? I am certain they have already seen us. As they have
seen ten thousand other curious Arab eyes watch the Christians salute
their Christ."

The question irritated him. It was a question born of vulnerability,
and Gerhardt had come to believe that he was immune to detection
or suspicion or capture. Perhaps that was what made him truly seem
invulnerable to his small band of terrorists. He walked the streets in the
open like everyone else. He moved among the souks with confidence,
like a man without conscience or guilt. And all feared him in his boldness and held him in awe for his accomplishments in the cause of the
jihad of Haj Amin Husseini.

After the death of Ram Kadar, the faint of heart had drifted away
with the women and children. They were chaff on the wind. Now those
who remained behind were the true of heart—men of steel who were so
committed to the end of the Jews that they thought less of life than of
dying in glorious martyrdom to the holy cause. Those men were drawn
to Gerhardt like fragments of iron pulled from the sand by a magnet.
Now they clung to the magnet while the sand of Palestine's Arabs was
blown away from the rock of Jerusalem in the whirlwind of fear. They
alone would liberate Palestine, and they alone would rule beside their
leader in the end.

Gerhardt stared down at the bobbing heads of the pilgrims and tried
to spot the negotiators who had entered the city among them. Their
eager faces seemed as close as his hand in the focus of the binoculars.
Smiling and whispering, they stared at the great doors and waited for
them to open in the emerging light.

Just to the left was the entrance to the patriarchate. A tall, thin man
in a gray, double-breasted suit knocked twice and then slipped into the
building. *Most certainly British*, thought Gerhardt with amusement. He
was followed by two other men who were dressed more like the pilgrims
around them, and then a large, big-boned woman entered. She was obviously Jewish. Once again, Gerhardt scanned the crowds for the faces of
others who moved toward the patriarchate. His gaze fell on a young
woman dressed in lavender who waited pensively outside the church.
She swayed among the crush of the crowd like a bright flower in the
midst of a dark meadow.

Gerhardt frowned and focused his field glasses to draw her face nearer to him. "The sister of—" He did not finish. He was still not able to comprehend that the sister of Yassar Tafara could be standing among the Christian pilgrims. And yet it had to be her! He remembered her, filthy and sobbing on the road through Bab el Wad the morning after the massacre of Deir Yassin. He had assumed that she had been quietly eliminated by some relative of Haj Amin. Yet now she waited outside the church! "Sarai," he said flatly.

"Who?"

"Sarai Tafara. The sister of Yassar. She is down there." Gerhardt's voice was gruff and impatient. "See for yourself. Two meters from the church doors just to the left. A purple scarf on her head and a lavender dress."

"She is not dead?" one of the men asked in amazement. He, too, had seen her trembling and nearly naked on the road. "Her cousin Ahkmed was chosen to put her away, I heard."

"And I heard that Ahkmed was killed," another man said. "They found him dead in Sheikh Jarrah."

"No matter." Gerhardt turned away to descend the stairs of the tower. "She is alive and among the Christians, it seems. The Mufti will want to know how. And why."

Sarai stood on her tiptoes and tried to follow the progress of Moshe Sachar through the crowds. At first she had been uncertain that it was he. Then he had looked at her with a spark of recognition and glanced away. Now he moved through the difficult press of the people away from the gates of the church.

Why does he not stay? she wondered. *Has he also come to see the miracle of the holy fire? Then why does he not stay?*

Moshe was still fifty feet from the meeting place when the Greek Orthodox patriarch, surrounded by a host of priests, came out among the people on the street. A murmur rippled through the crowd, and Sarai turned her eyes from Moshe to watch as the great doors of the church were unlocked and swung open. The throngs parted for the bearded old man dressed in sparkling white vestments to pass.

From the time she was a child, Sarai had heard whispered stories about this Christian tradition: *"Lamps of the basilica extinguished in the early hours of Saturday. The deathlike darkness as the tomb is sealed. The patriarch enters the tomb to pray and wait until heaven sends down a spark, a flame to relight the torch he holds. Then amid the crash of bells and shouts of joy, the flame is passed from one candle to another until the whole church is ablaze with the light of the faith of resurrection!"*

Today Sarai had come to witness the miracle of the holy fire for herself. She had read the story among the flowers, and hope had illuminated her soul like a bright flame in the darkness. She wanted to sing out these songs she heard, but she did not know the words, so her heart sang its own melody.

As the patriarch approached, Sarai glanced back toward Moshe. She hoped that he would look at her . . . if only to see in her face that she did not hate anymore.

As the crush of the crowd ebbed, she felt the strong grip of hard fingers dig into the flesh of her shoulders. She gasped and looked up. "Gerhardt!" she cried, but her voice was lost amid the noise of the multitudes.

He smiled and encircled her with his arms. "Sarai Tafara. Your brother is worried for you. You might get hurt out here today." He nodded toward the building, where Moshe was about to enter. "So, Sachar is in on this today."

She kicked against him and struggled briefly. But in the surge and shouts of the streets, no one noticed as Gerhardt carried her through the jostling pilgrims. "What do you want with me?"

"Your brother and cousin are worried for your safety," he said again, moving toward the edge of the excitement and nearer to the mosque.

"Please!" Sarai struggled, but he held her tightly, her feet just off the ground. *"Please!"*

Moshe had just reached the side entrance to the building when he turned for one final glimpse of Sarai. In that instant he saw her face filled with revulsion and horror as Fredrich Gerhardt dragged her from where she had been waiting.

"Gerhardt!" Moshe shouted, but it was like trying to outscream a gale-force wind. "Stop him!" He tried to push his way past a solid wall of human beings who all shoved back with equal force, straining for a glimpse of the old patriarch of the city.

When Moshe stepped up onto the base of a pillar, he saw Gerhardt's strong arms wrapped around the girl. Gerhardt's face was amused as he gazed toward the roof of the building where the negotiations would soon take place. Suddenly Moshe knew it was no coincidence that Gerhardt was among the Christian pilgrims. The presence of Gerhardt had always meant death. Always!

Moshe examined the roof where he had seen Gerhardt look. Gerhardt's head was almost out of sight. *How much time?* Moshe wondered, jumping down and clawing his way to the side entrance where the others had entered.

"God!" Moshe cried. Gerhardt was planning to send down his own brand of holy fire! "God! *Help* me!"

Moshe made a choice that tore his heart. There was little hope of catching Gerhardt and the girl. His first duty had to be to those of the negotiation team. He threw open the door and stumbled into the foyer of the building. Outside the noise was still deafening as he ran through the marbled hallways to the heart of the church offices.

Breathless and trembling, he flung open the walnut door where his companions had already taken their places at a long polished table. Moshe looked up into the dome of the cupola above them.

The face of Tom Kane was lined with concern. "Moshe . . . ?"

"We must get out." Moshe tried to steady his voice. "We must—"

"Now?" asked the British government official.

"What is it?" Golda Meir stood.

"We must—," Moshe gasped, pointing upward. "The Mufti's men," he panted. "I saw them . . . a bomb—get *out!*"

Moshe held Rachel very tightly as she wept against his chest. He had not told her the identity of the man who had taken Sarai. That would have been more than she could bear.

"What will become of her?" Rachel sobbed.

"I do not think . . . that she will be coming back here to us." He spoke gently, trying not to say what he believed would happen to the girl.

"Will they kill her, Moshe?" Rachel's words were anguished, her eyes red from weeping.

"I . . . perhaps not. Not now. She is no longer grieving. Maybe they will leave her alone."

She covered her face with her hands. "She said she wanted to go to el-Kiama," Rachel said softly. "To the Resurrection."

Moshe grimaced, remembering his choice not to follow Sarai. When the British soldiers had disarmed the bomb, there had been less than three minutes left on the timer. The cheering hordes of people had never known how close they had been to tragedy. In the sacrifice of Sarai, Moshe had made the right choice. He was certain. But still that knowledge did not take away the pain he felt for the young woman . . . or Rachel, who now grieved so deeply.

"Her presence saved a lot of people today," he said carefully as he stroked Rachel's hair. "If I hadn't seen her . . . seen him . . ."

"You know who it was? You recognized the man who took her?"

Moshe nodded. "Someone I have fought before. One of the Mufti's men. His being there could only mean one thing. Only one thing. But I never would have seen him if I hadn't first seen her, Rachel."

"She was so happy. So *happy*!"

"Yes. I saw it in her face. I . . . I don't know what to say. Not about any of it, Rachel. The British guards searched the streets for her . . . searched the mosque . . . but you know the Old City. It is a labyrinth. No one could find her in all that mob. We can only hope and pray that since she is a cousin to Haj Amin, maybe someone will take care of her."

"God must—" her voice caught when she tried to speak—"He must take care of her."

31

SAMSON'S MISSION

The days at Kitzbühel passed more or less peacefully, with David and Ellie avoiding the Samsons as much as possible. Maryanne Samson proved to be as much a washout on the ski slopes as she was viewing the great treasures of the Vatican. After only one cold morning on the slopes, she went to bed, crying and moaning whenever she turned over. Frau Wattenbarger patiently cared for the obnoxious young American woman, fixing her hot salt baths and bringing the food to her room.

Ted, on the other hand, did not seem to mind his freedom. When he was not talking politics with David, he was constantly hitching up the mare and taking a drive into Kitzbühel, where a roulette wheel had recently been installed in the Golden Griffin. Maryanne's whimpering voice would be heard through the thick log walls after he returned, and though the words were muzzled, the sentiment was definitely unhappy.

" . . . You got yourself a gal in town? What you doin', Teddy Samson?"

His reply was always much quieter than her questions, and as soon as the scene began on the other side of the wall, David would switch on the radio and listen to music and news on the American Armed Forces station.

Tonight, as the Andrews Sisters belted out a rendition of "Boogie Woogie Bugle Boy," the Samsons verbally battled it out in their room.

"I wanna go hoooome! To Texaaaas," Maryanne bellowed.

David looked at Ellie with a wry smile. "I'll bet ol' Teddy-boy wishes she would go, too."

"She's just a kid." Ellie tried to find some excuse for the young woman's obnoxious behavior.

"Yeah. Well, he's my age and a pretty intelligent guy. That—" he jerked his thumb toward the racket—"would drive any guy nuts."

"Well, he doesn't seem that much more mature than she, if you ask me. Running off to Kitzbühel at the slightest provo—" The slamming of a door and footsteps retreating down the hallway interrupted her sentence but conformed her point. "You see, there he goes."

A loud caterwauling vibrated the walls as Maryanne broke into sobs of misery.

"That's why I married you," David said with a grin. "You cry softly." Then, more seriously, he added, "You better warn her about men, or she'll find herself on a one-way boat back to Texas."

"I tried to talk to her." Ellie shrugged. "When you and Ted were skiing. She told me I was *in cahoots*—"

"In cahoots?"

"Uh-huh, and that I should mind my own business and let her die of misery and heartbreak."

"Yeah? What did you say?"

"Okay. And I left. She *wants* a one-way ticket, David. She hates everyone but her sweet ol' mama back in Texas. Or haven't you noticed?"

"Well." David sniffed and rolled his eyes as the sobs receded into a soft *eh-hoooo, eh-hoooo*, broken by hiccups. "Ted's a good-enough kid. Must've just been lonesome over here for a piece of home."

"Now that he's got it, I wonder what he's going to do with it. Frau Wattenbarger said she doesn't even think Maryanne is hurt all that bad. Sore muscles, sure, but not enough to send her to bed for *days*! She's crying wolf."

"Meanwhile the wolf goes to town." David leaned forward and turned the volume of the radio up as the news crackled over the receiver:

> *"The situation has intensified again after the mediation between Jews and Arabs in Jerusalem. A Jewish convoy loaded with food for Kfar Etzion was attacked and totally destroyed by Arabs. Jews have retaliated by forcing unarmed residents of the Arab sections of the city from their homes. Meanwhile, correspondent Lawrence C. Crabtree of the New York Times European edition seems to be hot on the trail of the Jewish terrorists who blew up the Arab arms ship in Italy two weeks ago. . . ."*

David sat forward, staring at the radio. "Speaking of crying wolf!" he mocked, but Ellie could tell he had instantly become tense.

> *"Two saboteurs remain alive of those who shared in the exploits of Bari Harbor. In a copyrighted story from the Times morning edition, Crabtree claims that the American Jews are hiding out somewhere in the Alps of Switzerland. . . ."*

"Switzerland. See? He's off by hundreds of miles."

*"Correspondent Crabtree's own whereabouts are as yet unrevealed,
but his stories keep American GIs hooked like a Saturday matinee
serial. . . ."*

Ellie swallowed hard. "David," she said pitifully, "turn it off. I'd
rather listen to Maryanne cry. At least that doesn't have anything to do
with us."

"Neither does *this*. I mean, the guy's in Switzerland. Interlaken or someplace. Probably knocking on doors and asking everyone if they've seen a
couple of Jewish terrorists. Forget it, babe. I won't turn the thing on again.
Just a few weeks more, and we are citizens of a brand-new country."

"Right now I feel kind of like Maryanne does. . . . I just want to go
home to Mama."

Ted Samson arrived at the Golden Griffin Hostel just after dark. The air
was filled with a pleasant blend of polka music and the aroma of cooking food. He tied the mare to a long hitching rail and rubbed his hands
briskly together against the cold.

Several battered army jeeps were parked haphazardly along the street.
Light from the high windows of the old stone building shone brightly
on the snow. A golden griffin, claws outstretched and jaws wide, marked
the sign, as it had for over three centuries. It had served as a landmark for
weary travelers and bored farmers and men who came for other, more
secret reasons.

Inside, the head of a giant stag hung on the wall above a main dining room. A great carved-oak banister wound up toward the rooms. The
room was crowded, and a pall of smoke drifted over the heads of a
boisterous crowd that sang along with the polka music and raised their
frothy beer steins in one toast after another.

Ted removed his heavy army-issue parka and walked through the
main dining hall toward a closed door at the back of the room. There the
subtle click of the roulette wheel held the attention of a dozen men who
sat around the table with stacks of chips growing or diminishing before
them. Finding a place on a hard wooden table, Ted tossed ten dollars
onto the table. A stack of ten blue chips was passed across to him. He
tapped the stack against the green felt table and looked at the numbers
before him. Then he shoved the entire stack onto the double zero.

"Bettin' with the house?" a weary-looking American asked.

"Bets?" said the bored young man who manned the wheel.

Chips were placed on the numbers, some in smaller stacks than others, and the wheel was spun. The tiny ball bounced and clicked within the spinning circle until it slowed and stopped.

"Number seventeen red! Seventeen red!" The croupier raked in the chips. "No winners."

The weary American cashed in his winnings and rose from the table, but Ted tossed another ten dollars on the table. Ten more blue chips were passed to him, and he laid out another double-zero bet.

"Again?" asked the American, shoving his fedora back on his head.

Ted did not reply. Instead he kept his eyes riveted to the tiny clicking ball as it rattled toward number 26.

"Not my night." Ted shrugged.

"Come on," said the American. "I'll buy you a beer. Teach you a little something about gambling."

The American left the room as Ted placed one more bet. "Twenty bucks on number one," he said glumly as the wheel once again began to spin.

"Number fifteen! Fifteen!"

Ted rolled his eyes and got up, making his way into the crowded dining hall. He scanned the ruddy faces of those in the room until he spotted the crumpled fedora of the American, who occupied a table near the back of the room beneath the huge stag's head staring out through the smoke. Dodging buxom barmaids and rowdy hotel guests, Ted worked his way through the tables.

The man with the fedora sat quietly sipping the suds from a mug of beer. When he saw Ted coming, he held up his hand and snapped his fingers at a barmaid to order another. The oompah of a tuba nearly drowned out his voice as he called to Ted. "Double zero, huh? Can't you do better than that, Stripes?"

Ted felt angry—angry at the nickname and at his own failure. "Look, Tree," he said impatiently, "you couldn't do any better."

"Ah, come on now. Why so surly? I'm the one footing the bill here, not you." Tree's eyes narrowed as Ted sat across from him. "And you bet I could do better than a double zero!" His voice became instantly hard. He swigged his beer and slammed the stein on the table. "Finding the right number is what good reporting is all about."

"Then why don't you do this yourself?" Ted shot back.

"I would." Tree nodded thoughtfully. "But maybe she knows what I look like. . . . I don't know. I've been around a long time. You're just another pretty face as far as she is concerned."

"Well, the only thing I can say about this whole setup is that they don't suspect anything. I'm sure of that."

"Good for you, Stripes. You haven't shown them your press pass yet?" Crabtree was a little drunk. A silly grin accompanied his insult.

"No," Ted spat. "And Maryanne is—"

"Yeah." He leered. "How are you and Maryanne getting along, anyway? Any progress?"

Ted put a hand to his head and waited to answer as the barmaid placed a stein in front of him and refilled Crabtree's. "I'm sleeping on the sofa," Ted answered curtly.

"Don't admit that to the guys in the pressroom."

"Look, we're doing everything we ought to be doing. Maryanne hangs around all day listening. When they leave with me, she's going through their clothes and papers. There's nothing. Nothing, I tell you. I think you're on a dead-end hunt."

Crabtree waved his stein in front of Ted. "Naw. I smell blood. Stick around long enough and we're going to hit pay dirt. Number seven, Stripes. I can smell a story a mile off."

"Well, I can read one all the way from Palestine. That's where the story is, Tree. Have you kept up on all the stuff?" He sipped his beer in frustration.

"Look, kid, my articles are still front page. Right up there. On the trail of Jewish terrorists. A few days away from discovering the source of the Jewish European operation. I tell you, I didn't come this far to go back empty-handed."

"What if the Mossad is done with Meyer—finished? Man, he's nothing but a hot potato to them now. They'd probably just as soon see him buried."

Tree held an instructive finger in the face of his young protégé. "What is this?" he mocked. "Jimmy Olsen telling Superman what to do? You gotta trust me. Those two aren't double zero—we're gonna hit the number, kid. David Meyer is their best flier. They aren't gonna let him rot in some Alpine dump while the Arabs bomb Tel Aviv. And when Meyer makes his move, we make ours—pure, unbiased investigative reporting. In the meantime, you and that little Texas tart of yours—"

Ted bristled. "You could have picked Ellen instead of her. She drives me nuts."

"Ellen has to run the office." Crabtree smiled. "And don't underestimate Maryanne, boy. Other men have, and they've lived to regret it. That act of hers is a great cover—but that's all it is. Beneath that slushy Texas accent, she's sharp enough to slit your throat before you know it. Besides, if you can't stand her, it's more natural . . . like you're really married."

"Yeah. She plays that junk to the hilt." Ted took a longer swig as if to erase the memory.

"She's nosy enough," Crabtree said firmly, "and plenty smart enough to handle this plan. Just hang on, kid. You'll see this old man knows what he's talkin' about. The Jewish Mossad is gonna be making a call, kid, and we're gonna be right in the middle of it." Crabtree gave Ted an encouraging slap on the shoulder, spilling his beer. "You'll see, Stripes. It's a little like fishing. Just takes patience . . ."

The wedding canopy of Dov and Yehudit was held aloft by four rifles. As Rabbi Lebowitz read the service, Rabbi Vultch lifted the cup and recited the blessing for the young couple. Ehud stood behind Dov, and Shoshanna and Hannah stood to the left of Yehudit. Yacov was thoroughly embarrassed by the vows to love and cherish. He blushed when Dov finally lifted the veil to kiss his new bride.

A mighty cheer arose from the small group of guests gathered in Tipat Chalev. Then Dov took the glass from the hand of Rabbi Lebowitz and smashed it beneath his heel.

"*Mazel tov!*"

Tiny sips of cognac were passed around the room; then toasts were given in spite of the fact that there was no wine in the glasses. These days, water in the Old City was as precious as wine and rationed from the cisterns in minute quantity. Water had come to symbolize life as much as the fruit of the vine, and so, at this particular hour of history, the toast "*L'Chaim*—To life!" was made with water.

The music played and dancing began, even as the witnesses slipped out to take their shifts at the barricades. Joy was intensified and life seemed precious. The shadow of death towered over the tiny Jewish Quarter, but love still triumphed in the simmering depths of the cauldron.

The soldiers of King Abdullah's army froze in their conversations and raised their heads to listen to the songs of the condemned as they celebrated in these final days of their lives. The end was a forgone conclusion. . . . It was simply a matter of time.

Captain Stewart marched through the Jewish Quarter. The threats and accusations of Rabbi Akiva were fresh in his mind. How he hated Akiva for forcing him to come here now! Yet Stewart had to keep their bargain. He motioned to his sergeant, who ordered soldiers to kick open the door of the Jewish home.

The wedding music fell silent as the wooden door splintered and the British captain Stewart and his men entered. Resentful eyes stared at the captain and his dozen men as they interrupted the celebration. Yacov clenched his fists as the two factions faced off. A line of black-coated Hasids stood between Dov and Yehudit and the uniformed soldiers.

Stewart raised his chin and addressed the crowd. "A wedding is not normally the place for a police action," he said stiffly.

"At least he is not so stupid as he looks," Yacov said in Yiddish, and the Jews laughed.

Stewart flushed with anger. He hesitated. "The girl is underage."

"She is a married woman now, Stewart," Rabbi Vultch announced loudly. "You have no right—"

"*You* have no right! According to civil authority, the girl is underage and has not received permission from her father," Stewart yelled back as the clamor grew.

"Her father—may God be merciful even to him," said Rabbi Lebowitz as he stepped forward, "has declared her dead to his household. He has declared her dead, you see—" He gestured toward Yehudit, nestled beneath Dov's arm.

"Well, she is very much alive." Sweat poured from Stewart. "And Rabbi Akiva is her father according to civil law—the laws of the Mandatory Government. Headquarters were contacted. Rabbi Akiva believes the girl was abducted. I have orders."

"Abducted!" shouted Ehud. "Like the night of Passover?"

"She is underage," Stewart repeated. "I am required, as a representative of the civil government under which you live, to return the girl to her father. Anyone hindering this action will be arrested. Anyone arrested will be removed from the Old City. Anyone resisting arrest will be shot."

Silence fell heavy on the room. Even the four rifles that had held the wedding canopy had been brought without bullets. The clack of British rifle bolts was ominous. It seemed like a replay of the night Stewart had arrested Chaim and Shimon. To be taken from the Old City by Stewart's guards might mean being turned loose among the Arab souks. Ehud did not speak again.

A thin, high voice called from the back of the room. "Yes! Yes! He is right. I am underage. If my father says I must go back—"

Someone cried out a protest. "No, Yehudit! No! You cannot go."

Stewart looked momentarily relieved. Perhaps this distasteful duty would be easily accomplished. He looked up as a door slammed.

"No. He is right. I am underage. So my father says." There was a deathly silence as the crowd parted and Old Shoshanna stepped through the wall of black coats into the center of the room. "Yes. Take me to my father!"

As laughter rippled through the guests, Stewart narrowed his eyes. "Enough!" His face reddened at the sight of the wrinkled old woman.

Shoshanna continued to call loudly, "Underage! Yes. Take me back now."

Even a few of Stewart's troops suppressed an amused chuckle. Rabbi Lebowitz stepped up beside her. "I suppose I shall have to give up my little kichel if her father demands it," said the old rabbi, planting a kiss on the wrinkled cheek of Shoshanna.

After the laughter subsided, the rabbi moved closer to Stewart. He stopped and appraised the weapons of the soldiers, then moved within inches of the bitter, thin-lipped officer.

Stewart leaned back from the nearness of the old rabbi, but he did not step backward, even though the rabbi's face was nearly touching his.

"You will have to go over me to reach the girl," Rabbi Lebowitz whispered.

Stewart drew himself up ramrod straight. "What makes you think I won't, old man?"

"Because"—the rabbi gave him a soft, pitying smile—"I am flesh and mind and soul. As you. A human . . ."

"What has that got to do with anything?" Stewart said loudly. "I have a job to do! And do it I will!"

Rabbi Lebowitz reached a bony hand out and, rooted before the officer, beckoned to those who stood behind him. Yacov came first to his side, and then the black-coated line advanced. Women and children followed until all of them crowded up against the soldiers—nose to nose, chests pressing against the hard metal of the guns.

Then the old man spoke again. "Will you kill us all, then?"

Stewart lifted his chin higher and stared at the old man. He was beaten. With one backward step, he pivoted on his heel and gave the order to his troops: "About-face!"

Yehudit and Dov had long since slipped down the basement stairs and out into the labyrinth of tunnels beneath the Old City. They had emerged to the seclusion of a little room set aside for them by Ehud and Rabbi Vultch, and in that secret place they celebrated *L'Chaim* in the shadow of death.

PART III

The Sacrifice

*Greater love hath no man than this, that a man
lay down his life for his friends.*

JOHN 15:13

SARAI'S
UNION

President Harry Truman sat deep in his big leather chair and clasped his hands on the desk in front of him. The walls of his office were cluttered with packing crates for the move to Blair House while the White House was being remodeled. "Well, Mr. Kane," he said in a clipped voice. "Excuse the mess. Looks like the Easter bunny brought more than eggs to Jerusalem this year."

Kane wondered if he should laugh at the president's words, but Truman looked dead serious and quite unhappy about the events of recent weeks. "Yes, sir. Not as we'd hoped."

Truman slapped the desktop and swiveled around to look at the large globe, which could be seen protruding from boxes of books beside his desk. "The world is changing so fast, Kane, I'm going to have to ask Congress to buy me a new globe. If I stuck a red pin everywhere there was trouble, this would be the largest pincushion on record. First we lose Czechoslovakia to the Reds; now Moscow has its furry cap set for Berlin—not to mention what's happening right here at home. A Jewish state seems like mighty small potatoes compared to all this." He looked quickly to see Kane's reaction. "Well?"

Kane cleared his throat and chose his words carefully. "Not if you consider that a Jewish state would be the only democracy in the entire Middle East."

Truman considered Kane's words. "That's a point, Mr. Kane, but Secretary of State Marshall is still worried about the Russians coming in—"

"That is why we can't waver in our support."

Truman held up a manila folder jammed with news clippings that protruded from every angle. "Have you read the reports, Kane?" He flipped open the file. "Especially the ones by this Lawrence Crabtree fellow." He began to read: *"Zionist connections with the Communist regimes now sweeping Eastern Europe are apparent with the volumes of arms sales. . . ."*

"Sounds sinister enough, I'll grant you. But my understanding is that arms deals were made in Czechoslovakia before the Communist takeover. The weapons I saw—the few the Jews have—are German war surplus."

"Here's another one." Truman held the clipping up to the light. *"With the aid of Bulgarian Communist terrorist Mikhail Gregovsky, an Arab arms ship was sunk."* He arched his eyebrows.

"Also a Crabtree dispatch." Kane shrugged and smiled. "The man has a flair for the dramatic and sinister; I'll grant you that."

"You're the expert on the Middle East, Mr. Kane." Truman continued to scan the clippings. "Are you saying that in your expert opinion this link to the Reds is exaggerated?"

"I don't know who's paying Crabtree, Mr. President, but the biggest foreign assistance to the Jews seems to be coming from Americans."

"Hmmm. Yes. Fifty million dollars, to be exact," Truman conceded. "Golda Meir—she's quite a woman. Wish it were that easy to appropriate funds from Congress, Kane."

"It's not just American money. It's American volunteers. My first visit into the Jewish Quarter of the Old City was held mostly with Americans from Brooklyn. Of course, there are a dozen other nationalities, but the preponderance are American." He grinned sheepishly. "All of them asked me to remind you it's an election year."

"They did, did they?" Truman sat back and shook his head. "Is that the only message?"

"No, sir."

"Well?"

"There was also an old rabbi who wanted me to tell you to remember the Alamo."

Truman laughed in earnest. "The Alamo!"

"He said that was the only American history he knew."

"Well, that's enough, Mr. Kane! I have had a few moments lately when I felt like Davy Crockett myself. Franklin didn't do me any favors leaving me with this job, I can tell you." He shook his head in amusement. "Okay, Mr. Expert, what about the Arabs? this Abdullah fellow in Jordan?"

"The Arabs have an old saying: 'Me against my brother . . . my brother and I against my cousin . . . my cousin and I against the infidels. . . .' " Kane opened his briefcase and pulled out a thick file, which he handed to Truman. "That is precisely what is happening right now in the Arab League. The Mufti and King Abdullah are bitter enemies, but when it comes to the Jews, all the Arabs seem to agree that the Jews are the infidels, if you get my meaning."

"So King Abdullah is not interested in a peaceful settlement?"

"I didn't say that. He is interested more in having Jerusalem as his capital. The Jews are hoping for an international city in Jerusalem. They will not simply hand the government over to Abdullah."

"Give it to me short, Mr. Kane." Truman tapped his fingers on the lengthy report.

"In a nutshell, Jerusalem is the issue. Abdullah would be happy to annex the Arab lands of Palestine into Jordan and avoid war. He would even grant the Jews their small corner of Palestine. But he will not agree to allow Jerusalem to be governed by the UN. The Jews will not let Jerusalem be absorbed into Jordan—not without a fight."

"So. The war will be fought over Jerusalem if it is fought?"

"That is the entire issue. And unless Abdullah changes his mind, he will bring all the Arab powers into the war with his Arab Legion. While he attacks Jereusalem, the others will take on the rest of the Jewish settlements."

"And what will the outcome be, in your opinion?"

"The British continue to sell surplus arms to Jordan while we have placed an embargo on the entire Middle East. The British have also allowed Jewish Jerusalem to come under siege again. No convoys, and the Old City is virtually starving to death."

"The Alamo."

"Exactly."

"Maybe we can put a little diplomatic pressure on Great Britain and even this up a bit," Truman said thoughtfully. "The English are counting on our aid to rebuild their country, after all."

"Passive assistance to the Zionists," Kane agreed. "An excellent idea, Mr. President."

"So all the Arab brothers and cousins have joined up on this one. What chance do we have of convincing Abdullah to give up Jerusalem to the UN government?"

"It depends on how much pressure he can stand from the other brothers and cousins pushing on him now. If he is a strong and independent ruler, then we may avoid war. If he falls into the Arab rhetoric that the only good Jew is a dead Jew, then war is certain. We must stall, in any case."

"And where do we fit in this?"

Kane did not answer immediately. President Truman stood and went to the window. "Well, sir—" Kane rummaged in his case again and pulled out a clipping from the editorial page of the *Post*—"did you

278 BODIE & BROCK THOENE

happen to read the letter Howard Moniger wrote a few days before he
was killed?"

"You mean the American professor?" Truman took the paper.

"Yes. Very clear, I think." Kane fell silent as Truman held the clipping
up to the light of the window and began to read. A deep frown furrowed
his brow as he skimmed through the facts that had led to this terrible
impasse in Palestine. Then he began reading out loud:

*"Any move to revise Partition would be a blow to UN prestige—a climb
down in the face of force. Moreover, it would probably increase the fighting. Stalin could then maneuver over to the side of the ex-Grand Mufti
and try to stir up the whole Arab world. This could be disastrous to the
U.S., the UN, and the 800,000 Jews in Arab lands."*

Truman adjusted his glasses.

*"With English arms filtering through to the Arabs of Palestine, the
Zionists are being bloodily penalized by the embargo."*

Truman placed the clipping in the thick file and sat down heavily. After a thoughtful moment, he looked up at Kane. "The man was
an archaeologist, not a political scientist. What do you think about
this? Does the real Communist threat come from the Arab side of this
thing?"

"If the Mufti were at the helm of Palestine, I have no doubt that
Comrade Stalin would be the power behind him. Howard Moniger was
right. The Russians voted for a Jewish homeland not because they have
a heart for the Jews but because they would love to bring their troops in
to settle the issue."

"On behalf of their own interests."

"Let's face it . . . it is much easier for Communists to overthrow a king
than it is for them to destroy a democracy."

"What you are saying is that our only hope in the Middle East is a
strong democratic Jewish homeland?"

"That is my opinion, Mr. President."

Truman stared at the globe, his face tight with worry. "Czechoslovakia.
Now they're cutting off Berlin. Vienna is threatened. For them to have
even a toehold in the Middle East . . ."

"Don't you know Stalin is worried about the same thing in reverse?
The Russians voted for Partition because they did not believe the Jews
had a chance of surviving."

"Then we've just got to take the other side of the issue, Mr. Kane."

He hesitated and frowned. "Do the Jews think they have a chance of surviving?"

"I think they might appreciate a word of encouragement from our direction, Mr. President."

Truman clapped his hands as if to say he had made a decision. "Some sort of pledge of our good faith, is that it, Kane?" He nodded, not waiting for Kane to reply. "I've got just the thing." He took out a pen and began to scratch out a personal note to David Ben-Gurion.

The events of recent weeks had been good for Haj Amin Husseini. Gerhardt's activities in the Old City had once again brought to the attention of the Arab nations that the Mufti still exercised power in the back alleys and villages of Palestine. Even a small Palestinian force, armed with explosives and daring, could accomplish with terror and uncertainty what negotiations and artillery could not guarantee.

Terror could erode the will and confidence of those who were terrorized. That had been the contention of Fredrich Gerhardt since his days with the Nazi SS, and people had not changed since those terrible times. Even though the bomb on top of the Greek patriarchate had been detected and disarmed, a half-dozen other bombs had been successfully detonated around the Old City. Haj Amin and Gerhardt had made their point and made it well. Once again the rulers of the Arab League included the Palestinian leader in their plans. Now it was King Abdullah who found himself a target of their anger.

"You have done well for us, Gerhardt." Haj Amin tossed the latest newspaper across the desk to where Gerhardt sat.

"Our brothers see that King Abdullah has tried to usurp what is rightfully yours, Haj Amin." Gerhardt rubbed his chin as he continued. "This enlightening is to our benefit. Abdullah will *never* rule in Jerusalem, no matter how much he talks and bargains with the Jews! Unless it is our way, then terror will be the law for the Zionists. Even now, my bombs have them all looking under their beds before they fall asleep at night."

"Yet still the Zionists hope that King Abdullah and the Arab Legion will refuse to fight when the English leave." A hint of concern remained in the voice of the Mufti.

"Abdullah will have more to fear from the Arab nations if he does not fight than he should fear from the Zionists." Gerhardt lifted his chin in proud satisfaction. "We have done more to show our brothers the way to fight than all the armies of Abdullah put together. Blood and fire, the

Jews say, will cause Zion to rise again." He laughed. "Their blood and my fire, eh?"

Haj Amin smiled and sighed with pleasure at the turn of fortune. "Yes. You truly have done well in this private war of yours. And you train your young men well on our behalf." He appraised Gerhardt with renewed respect. The madman had channeled his hatred into a constructive and deliberate campaign against both the Jews and the members of Abdullah's Arab Legion. The number of explosions that had ripped through the Legion's ranks were equal to those that had destroyed Jewish outposts.

Abdullah's men blamed Jews, just as the Zionists claimed that Abdullah's talks were simply meant to trick them and lull them into complacency right before the British evacuation. No matter which side held up the white flag, the flag became spattered with blood.

Terror was the wedge that Haj Amin had driven deep between the Haganah and the Arab Legion. Now he was confident that King Abdullah's plans would fail.

"We will liberate Palestine," Gerhardt said. "And then I will wish to command your armies."

Haj Amin did not reply. They were still a long way from that day. "Until then," the Mufti said with a smile, "perhaps we can offer a small reward?"

Gerhardt shrugged. "You speak of the girl," he said flatly. "The sister of Yassar Tafara . . ."

"She is also our cousin." He spoke in the royal *we*.

"I have her already," Gerhardt said with an air of boredom.

"And does she please you?"

"She does not speak at all. And yet she obeys. She does whatever I tell her."

"You see, she is a good woman." Haj Amin tapped his fingertips together. Word that Sarai Tafara lived as the harlot of Gerhardt had filtered back to Damascus and to the family in Beirut. It had been assumed that she was dead and thus out of disgrace. Now her angry father had contacted Haj Amin and wished the matter settled. No Husseini woman could live unmarried with a man, and somehow Haj Amin would have to resolve the issue. "Might you wish to marry her?" he asked in an off-handed way.

"Marry!" Gerhardt cursed. "Why should I marry her when I have her at my will?"

Haj Amin fought to control himself. He continued to smile with serenity. "You must marry her because she is a Husseini."

"And raped by a dozen Jews!" Gerhardt scoffed. "She is not fit to marry. Only to serve."

"She is a widow to a Jihad martyr, Gerhardt!" Haj Amin drew himself up. How he hated these petty family disagreements!

"She is chattel."

"Does she please you?" Haj Amin asked again.

"She is . . . amusing. I had thought when I was finished with her I would share her with my men."

"That you will not do." Haj Amin narrowed his eyes, and his voice became hard. "You *will* marry her. The Koran says that you may have four wives. It is fitting that you be linked with the family of Husseini. You may use her however you like once you have married her. You may marry three others and have her serve them if it is your will . . . but it is *my* will that the disgrace be finished. She will not live as a harlot. If that is to be, then she shall not live."

Gerhardt looked away from the icy blue eyes of Haj Amin. To Gerhardt, it did not matter if Sarai Tafara lived or died. She bored him with her silent tears and cold looks and trembling limbs. Even when he beat her, she did not resist or cry out. But here was some use for her—her name was Husseini!

"Her father shall pay me for taking her as my wife. Six hundred pounds was the mohar young Basil paid to marry her. She was a virgin and worth it. Now she is worthless."

Haj Amin nodded in agreement. "I shall pay you myself. Then I can report to her father that she is wed to the commander of my armies."

Gerhardt smiled at the words. "Commander. Yes. Payment enough, even for damaged goods."

"Then it is settled?"

"And I will be *brother* to Yassar!" Gerhardt laughed loudly at the thought. "I wonder what he will say to this . . . *union!*" he mocked.

"Yassar will not disagree. He is also faithful to serve us."

"A bungler!"

"A patriot!"

"And where is *my brother* now?"

"Still in Europe." Haj Amin tapped his fingers on a file folder. "He does well for us."

"Is he still killing priests with their pants down?" He laughed more loudly.

Haj Amin answered by sifting through a stack of clippings and choosing one, which he handed to Gerhardt. "You see, it is confirmed that they were members of the Jewish Mossad. Yassar did well for us. He has taught our Zionist enemies a lesson."

Gerhardt scanned the article that identified the two murdered men as Jewish terrorists connected with the Bari Harbor bombing. "It says here that there are other Jews who participated in the action. Will my *brother* also murder them in a toilet?" He tossed the clipping back with disdain. "He had better guard himself. He has the look of a Bedouin peasant."

The Mufti's blue eyes glinted. "Not like you and I, eh, Gerhardt? With our Crusader beginnings—"

"Thick lips and dull face. He will be recognized and picked off by the Mossad if he follows too closely. To find these . . . *priests* . . . was pure luck! Now he plays with the fire of the European Mossad. They will not be caught with their pants down."

"You worry unnecessarily, Gerhardt. Your brother-in-law has hired someone else to do the hunting for us. He has paid well, and you will see; we will make an end to the Jews in Europe. They play at making themselves powerful. We know the truth: The Jews have nothing but noisemakers."

Haj Amin gathered the clipping back into the stack. "The hounds are baying even now, yet the little foxes believe that they are safe in their den. It is only a matter of time, I say . . . then all Yassar will have to do is pay the rest of the retainer to our mercenaries. In the meantime, we are patient and confident that the end is near. Very near."

The news made little difference to Gerhardt. He was content to work in the dark shadows of Jerusalem's alleys. He was content to eliminate the enemies of Haj Amin, whether they were Jews or Arabs. Blood and fire were the butter on his bread, the meat he thrived upon. He stood, aware that the meeting was also near an end. "When he captures these Jews," Gerhardt said thoughtfully, "send my congratulations to my brother . . . and also tell him that his beloved sister lives . . . by my mercy and under my protection." The words dripped with sarcasm.

As Gerhardt left the room, Haj Amin decided that he would say only that Sarai had married a hero of the liberation of Palestine.

THE MOSSAD'S
MESSAGE

Propped up in the big bed, David studied the contents of the wallet for the hundredth time while Ellie slept soundly beside him. The candlelight cast a large shadow on the wall as he lifted each item up to search for some hint of where they might find a contact. By now, he was certain, the fighter pilots he and Michael had hired would be arriving in Europe. But *where* in Europe? And now that the Communists were firmly in control of the government of Czechoslovakia, would they still be able to get to the fighter planes?

David held one hope on that score—the Soviets had, after all, voted in favor of Partition and a Jewish state. No doubt they had done so just to create a rift between the United States and Britain, but as long as the issue kept the allies squabbling, Russia was still standing firm on its decision. Perhaps this pro-Partition stance would hold long enough for the pilots to be trained in the 109s and fly them out of Prague.

Unfortunately, there was little hope of David and Ellie entering Czechoslovakia alone with their American passports. Avriel would have to make some sort of under-the-table deal with a Communist government official for the pilots to enter the country, David reasoned. Certainly, after Golda Meir's fund-raising drive in the U.S., the Jewish Agency would have plenty of cash on hand for a few well-placed bribes.

The men David had hired to fly the planes were all good pilots, but not one of them had any airtime in the German-made 109s. Without instruction, the American fliers would fly the tricky planes right into the ground.

No one knew this better than David. He had learned what he needed to know in a Messerschmitt cockpit from a German pilot he had captured over Italy. *"This little 109 ist like a woman, Herr Meyer. If the hand ist too strong, then she will rebel. If too little control, then you are a dead man also, ja? But when you know her good, the speed—she will your breath take away."*

The trick was staying alive long enough to get to know the plane. David was one of the few American pilots who had ever attempted to do that. And he was certainly the only one available to pass this knowledge along to the recruits.

Ellie sighed and turned over. "What are you doing, David?" she whispered in a husky voice.

David held the small photograph of the girl up to the light. "Looking at this stuff," he answered without looking at her. "They would have had to put a message in here somewhere . . . somewhere. . . ." He tossed the snapshot onto the blanket and picked up the laundry tickets.

Ellie sat up beside him. "Maybe there is something at the laundry. Something we could claim that would lead us . . . like a treasure hunt."

"Yeah." David tossed the tickets down. "Well, the laundry is in Rome. They kill priests in bathrooms back there, remember? I still have nightmares about that guy watching us on the train. I'm not going back to Rome." Yet, even as he said it, he knew that he might not have a choice. If every road led to a dead end, at least he might leave Ellie here and try to make it back to the airfield in Rome.

"I'm going to hold you to it," Ellie said through a yawn. "David, we've been through this stuff a thousand times." She absently picked up the snapshot of the pretty young woman. "There's nothing here. Nothing." She peered at the smiling face, the long blond hair, and the flowering bush behind the petite figure. She held it close to the light and searched for some hint of tiny letters concealed in a shadow. There was none. "This is one you can get rid of." She half smiled. "Unless you think she's gorgeous enough to carry around in your wallet."

"I don't know." David's eyes were heavy with weariness. "I thought she might be a contact. You know, somebody we were supposed to meet along the way."

"Hmm," Ellie mused, smiling. "Not bad-looking. You don't think you'd recognize her if she came up to you on the street and kissed you hello?" Ellie turned the picture over and stared at the back of it. "How frustrating. They didn't even put her phone number on the back."

David was in no mood for jokes. He snatched the photo from Ellie and held it out to the flame of the candle. "So much for gorgeous blonds," he said with disgust. "So much for fighter planes and the Mossad." The edge of the photo curled and browned, and a tiny flame blackened the edge. He held it up for Ellie.

"Don't catch the bed on fire," she warned with an amused smile.

Then, as the paper of the picture darkened, Ellie shouted, "Put it out! David! Put out the fire!"

He held it up playfully. "Nothing doing . . ." Then he saw what Ellie

THE KEY TO ZION

285

must have seen—a thin scrawl of ink had begun to appear where nothing had been before. The flame licked away the top word and had begun to eat away the second line before he gasped and blew it out. "What did it say?" he asked, laying the charred photo down carefully. "What was the first word?"

"Salzburg, I think. . . ." Ellie was on her knees staring at the rest of the message. "I think it said Salzburg." Slowly she read the words out loud. "*Gasthof zur Post Hallstatt May 3* . . . oh, David!" she whispered in an awed voice. "This is it! We aren't too far from Salzburg, are we?"

"No. No, I don't think so." He continued to stare at the parched letters. "You're sure it was Salzburg?"

"Salz . . . *something*. Look." She followed the bottom of the missing letters with her fingertip. "*S-A-* and maybe that's *L* and *Z*. The rest is gone. You didn't blow it out in time, but—" She closed her eyes as if to picture the flaming letters in her mind again. "Yes. I think Salzburg."

"All this time and here it was," David said in frustration. "All along we had it right here!" He looked hard at Ellie. "What was the date for the rendezvous?"

"May third. Two days. We have two days, David. "We're *not* late!" She breathed a prayer of gratitude. "*Salzburg*. A day by train."

At that instant there was a sharp, insistent rap at the door. "Hey, open up!" the voice of Ted Samson interrupted. "I smell smoke!"

He was joined by the worried voice of Herr Wattenbarger. "We ist smelling smoke here. Haf you fallen to sleep in your pipe, James?"

David answerd to the name of James almost naturally now. "*Nein,* Herr Wattenbarger." He jumped up from the bed while Ellie placed her hand carefully over the snapshot. He opened the door a crack and peered into the hallway. Ted was still dressed. Herr Wattenbarger wore a nightshirt and a drooping nightcap.

"Was ist das?" Herr Wattenbarger frowned at a thin cloud of smoke that hovered over the bed. "I am smelling smoke und here ist standing Ted by the door—"

David frowned slightly at the thought that the young American might have overheard their words. "Sorry. Sorry, Herr Wattenbarger. My wife just found an old photo . . . in my wallet . . . an old girlfriend . . . it was nothing, really. Didn't mean to frighten you."

The old man cleared his throat loudly to express his disapproval. "We have a stove for such burning." He turned and padded back down the corridor to his room.

Ted continued to stand by the door. "An old girlfriend, huh?" he said with a slight edge of triumph in his voice. "Glad to know I'm not the only one with a jealous Hausfrau."

Ted's gait was light, and a tiny smile tugged at the corner of his mouth as he returned to the room next door. He jerked the door open and leaned against the doorframe.

"Where you been, Teddy?" screeched Maryanne. "You just up and leave, and I never know where you're goin'! Leave me all alone here in this godforsaken—"

"Can the act, sweetheart," Ted ordered smugly, slamming the door behind him.

Maryanne's countenance and tone of voice changed instantly. "What did you get?" Her voice was low, and all trace of her Texas accent vanished.

"They found a message. And"—he smiled—"I got it all, too. Right through the door. Wait till Tree hears about this!"

"Tree!" spat Maryanne venomously. "I could care less about what he wants. It's David Meyer I'm after. After what he did—" She broke off abruptly and sat up, cross-legged, on the bed.

"Where you goin' now?" she howled in perfect Texan, loud enough for David and Ellie to hear her through the wall. "You goin' back to that drinkin' and gamblin' place?" She broke into wails and sobs.

Ted grinned and shook his head as he shrugged into his coat. "I gotta hand it to Tree," he muttered. "You *are* perfect for this part." He put his hand on the door latch, then turned. "But why do you have it in for Meyer? What's he to you?"

"Never you mind, Teddy darlin'," Maryanne whispered, lying back on the bed. "It's family business, that's all."

"Lucky number seven, Franz." Ted Samson tossed his chips onto the table.

"No double zero today, Herr Samson?" The croupier spun the roulette wheel with a flourish that sent the little ball clattering over the numbers.

"Not today." Ted glanced around the room. Crabtree was not among the usual crowd of gamblers.

A sigh of disappointment arose from the group when the wheel slowed and the ball bounced to a stop. "Double zero!" cried the croupier. "Ah, Herr Samson! On this day of all days, you change your bet! A pity!" He raked in the chips as Ted shook his head and shrugged, then left the room in search of Tree.

He took the stairs to Crabtree's room two at a time. At last, the waiting had paid off! Just as Crabtree had predicted, David Meyer had finally played his hand. This would ultimately lead to the heart of the Zionists' European operation, and Ted could not conceal his excitement at the thought that he was part of such an incredible undercover operation. It had indeed been like going fishing. Ted had set the hook, and now Crabtree would reel in the really big fish.

Through the heavy wooden door of Crabtree's room, Ted thought he heard the murmur of voices. He hesitated, then knocked softly. The voices grew silent.

"Yeah?" Crabtree called.

"Tree," Ted whispered. "It's me. Stripes."

A long moment passed before the door opened, revealing half of Crabtree's face. He looked sick . . . or drunk. "Okay, kid," he said hollowly as he stepped back. "Come in."

Ted's broad smile faded as he stepped into the room. Crabtree's eye was nearly swollen shut. Lamps were overturned, and his papers were scattered everywhere. "Tree!" Ted said in horror. "Wha . . . ?"

Crabtree stared moodily at the floor. He did not answer or look up as a large man stepped from the tiny bathroom. He held a Walther pistol in his hand. His massive bulk nearly took up the entire doorway, and he pointed the pistol directly at Ted as another man stepped from behind him. He carried a red-leather address book in his hand.

The smaller man wore a tweed jacket of English cut and held a pipe clenched in his teeth. "And you must be Ted Samson?" he said in a crisp British accent.

"What is this?" Ted demanded, stepping forward. The aim of the large man's gun stopped him. "Tree? Who are these guys?"

Crabtree did not answer. He gingerly touched his swollen eye and continued to stare at the floor.

The big man narrowed his eyes menacingly. "You're in dangerous work, boy," he said, shifting his massive bulk. His suit and appearance seemed Italian, but his accent was unmistakably American. "Both of you are in dangerous work." He looked at Crabtree and a slight smile curled his lip. "Going to lead the way? Going to show the world the inner workings of the Jewish Mossad?"

"Tree?" Ted felt suddenly afraid. "What is this? Who—?"

"Shut up," said the Englishman quietly, and Ted obeyed. "So"—he directed his question to Crabtree—"this is the young man staying at the house with them? The woman has stayed behind, as usual. Afraid of *us*?"

"Yeah." Crabtree nodded. "Like a snake's scared of a mouse. She's not the type to be scared."

The Englishman appraised Ted. "Stripes, you call him?" He did not expect a reply. "Well, Stripes, what news have you brought from the front lines, eh? Where are David and Ellie Meyer staying?" He smiled. "What has Maryanne told you?"

Ted backed up a step as the huge dark man advanced. "Same as always," he said nervously. "Nothing. Nothing. They're staying put. Going nowhere—"

"Do not attempt to lie to us," said the Englishman as he lit his pipe. "We have come too far, followed you too long. Now you will work for us."

Ted drew himself up. "Who are you guys?" he demanded. "You are tampering with members of the American press!" His words were belligerent.

The big man took another step forward and waved the gun barrel slightly.

"And who do you think you are tampering with, Mr. Samson?" The Englishman smiled again at the fear that flashed across Ted's face.

Ted looked at Crabtree as if he might somehow communicate the identities of these hostile intruders. Crabtree seemed resigned to whatever fate awaited them. He did not speak.

"What do you want with us?" Ted asked.

"You have done a magnificent job tracing the movements of an essential member of the Jewish operation this far. The whole world awaits your next revelation, *Stripes*." There was a touch of ridicule in his voice. "We simply wish to accompany you on your long journey . . . be there as the story unfolds . . . make sure the news is accurate and exciting."

"And then," said the fat Italian, "if you're real good boys, maybe we'll turn you loose. If you cause trouble, you're dead."

Stripes blinked in disbelief. "We're . . . we're newsmen," he protested. "We don't *make* things happen. We just write about them when they do."

The Englishman struck another match and puffed slowly on the briar pipe. "That is where you are wrong, my friend. Perhaps you *were* newsmen, but your latest investigation marks a definite change of career. Now, we have a small assignment for you. . . ."

Herr Wattenbarger knocked softly on the door, then opened it without waiting for an answer. David looked up, startled at the unusual intrusion.

"Herr Wattenbarger?" he asked quietly. Ellie was still sleeping, and David glanced toward her.

The Austrian put a finger to his lips. "She must now get up," he whispered hoarsely. "And both of you come now down the stairs." His face was lined with concern.

"What?" David asked.

But again the old man put a finger to his lips in warning. Then he left the room and shut the door behind him.

Five minutes later, appearing sleepy and somewhat disheveled, David and Ellie entered the kitchen, where Frau Wattenbarger stood over a big skillet, frying sausage. She frowned, then nodded toward the door that led to the stable. For the first time since they had come to the farm, there was no cheerful *"Guten Morgen"* to greet them. The Frau put her finger to her lips and raised her eyes toward Ted and Maryanne's room.

Something had happened . . . or was about to happen, David thought. Neither he nor Ellie spoke but slipped through the stable door to where Herr Wattenbarger waited in the dim light.

His mouth was turned down at the corners, and his brow was furrowed deep. He stood gently stroking the face of a sweet brown milk cow, who blinked her eyes in lazy appreciation. The sled and the Haflinger mare were gone.

"Herr Wattenbarger," David said after he shut the door from the kitchen. "What is . . . ?"

A man stepped from the shadows behind the farmer. The man was dressed in work clothes like those of Herr Wattenbarger. He wore a green hunter's cap, and his face was serious, almost angry. He was about the same age as David and at least two inches taller.

"You are David Meyer," the stranger said slowly, pronouncing his words with only a slight accent.

"David!" Ellie cried fearfully, grabbing David's arm.

David pushed her behind him, then stepped forward. "What of it?" His words were belligerent. He clenched and unclenched his fists.

Herr Wattenbarger continued to stroke the nose of the cow. "You must go." His voice carried a note of sadness. "David and Ellie Meyer. You must for your own sake go away—now, this morning. Now."

"What is this?" David looked from one man to the other. "Who is this guy, Herr Wattenbarger?"

The stranger continued to study David, allowing the old farmer to speak. "Wilhelm Grieg, he ist. A friend."

The stranger's face did not change. "You must get out," said Grieg.

"Tell dem, Wilhelm, what you haf seen," said the old man.

The stranger nodded. "For some time this Samson man, he has come into the village. There he meet with an American man often—"

"Samson?" David asked. Then it occurred to him that these men knew their true identities. "And how do you know our names?"

"We have for some time known," said Grieg. "And we think that you are safe here until yesterday . . . and then last night the American who staying is at the Golden Griffin, he has visitors. We watch and wait and they do not come out."

Herr Wattenbarger turned to face them. "David Meyer." He said the name kindly. "You must go. This Ted Samson has early this morning gone to town. The woman Maryanne who is with him here, she stays to watch you, I think. . . ."

"Ted has the horse." David was almost overwhelmed. *How long have they known? And why did they not turn us in?*

"Wilhelm will you take," said Herr Wattenbarger. "He has the sleigh bells taken off from the sleigh. The Samsons' room ist on the far side of the house. She will you not see, I think."

"Our stuff," said Ellie, still in a state of shock. "My clothes . . ."

The door creaked open, and Frau Wattenbarger slipped in quietly, carrying the two smallest bags. She set them in the straw and put out her arms to Ellie. "My dear." She hugged Ellie tightly. Tears had streaked her face. "Gott go with you, my dear."

Wilhelm had already opened the door that led outside. He motioned with his hand. "We must not to Kitzbühel go," he whispered. "I will you to St. Johann take, and there you will the train catch."

34

"CAUSE THE TRUMPET TO RESOUND"

Although the route to the Wailing Wall had been closed to Jews these many months, Rabbi Lebowitz still donned his tallith and phylacteries and turned, with Yacov, to face toward the ancient stones.

"Morning prayers, Yacov," said the old man, "especially are important nowadays, *nu*?"

"*Nu*, Grandfather."

"Are you praying with your heart, from your neshoma? Eh, my little kichel?"

Yacov scuffed the toe of his worn-out shoe on the stone floor. "Yes, Grandfather. But I would pray better if you would not call me your little cookie anymore." He touched his stomach. "It makes me think of food, and . . . I am hungry, Grandfather."

"*Oy*," said the old man, reaching out to cock the boy's yarmulke off to one side. "Yes. It's a good thing God does not say to love Him with our whole stomachs," the old rabbi agreed. "Ours here in the Old City are so empty." He let his breath out slowly. "So. We pray for breakfast. And I will not call you my kichel, lest Rebbe Akiva sprinkle you with sugar and gobble you with his tea."

The boy nodded and straightened his yarmulke, then snapped his fingers and called to Shaul. "*Oy*, Grandfather. Every night I dream that Shaul goes into the Arab Quarter and steals us a chicken."

"This morning we will pray for a chicken."

"No, Grandfather. Only one chicken would not be enough. We would have to share with all our friends. I am content with a piece of suet from the butcher shop." He ran his fingers along the dog's bony sides. "He grows so thin, Grandfather. The Arabs must have pity on him. Yesterday there was even a small sliver of meat on the fat."

"Send him off now, boy," the rabbi gently urged.

Yacov laid his head against that of the large, gaunt animal. "Go now,

Shaul. Butcher!" He snapped his fingers and opened the door, and Shaul galloped out toward the barrier. Yacov watched him for a moment, then closed the door. "Ehud asked me what I would be if I could be anything," Yacov said softly. "I told him I would be a dog."

"A dog! Why, Yacov?"

"Because the Arabs are nice to dogs."

The thought of what the boy had said stung the old man. Yes, often men were kinder to animals than they were to their fellow men. He did not reprimand the boy for his honest words. "But dogs cannot pray, Yacov. Men may still speak to God, even when they are surrounded by evil and fear."

"And God?" Yacov asked. "Do you think He hears, Grandfather?"

"Come." The old rabbi gathered the boy into the folds of his tallith. "Open the *Siddur,* and we will pray."

The words of the morning service circled upward from the Holy Place of Jerusalem as they had for thousands of years. Millions upon millions of lives had come and gone, and this simple prayer had not been answered. The old rabbi did not, however, believe that the prayer had been unheard. The boy read from the little prayer book, but Rabbi Lebowitz closed his eyes and recited by heart . . . from his heart:

> *"Cause the great trumpet to resound for our liberation, and the banner to be reared for the gathering of our exiles, and do Thou bring us together from the four corners of the globe. Blessed art Thou, the Eternal—who collecteth the outcasts of His people Israel. And unto Jerusalem, Thy city, in mercy mayest Thou return, and dwell within as Thou hast promised. Oh rebuild it speedily, in our days, as an everlasting structure, and the throne of David do Thou full soon therein set up."*

Young and old, they prayed the ancient prayer from the Jewish prayer book as one. And for the first time in his life, the old rabbi believed that he might indeed live to see it answered!

Today, as the sun beat down on the canvas awnings of the Old City shops, Gerhardt had gathered some tools and left Sarai alone in the tiny apartment. As always, he turned the key and locked her in.

Flies seemed to own the air of this reeking neighborhood, where lamb carcasses hung from beams in shops. *How fitting that Fredrich*

Gerhardt would choose to live in such a place! thought Sarai. She lay down on the narrow bed and covered herself with a thin veil against the host of buzzing insects. In spite of the heat of the day and the locked door, she was thankful—thankful to be alone, free for a few hours from the brutality of this man who was a hero of the Jihad.

Yassar had once told her of him, how he had rigged the car that Basil drove for the American Embassy. She herself had seen the damage to the Jewish Agency. She had been glad then and filled with a sense of awe for the name of Gerhardt. Now, this afternoon, he had gone to strike the Zionists yet another time. Tomorrow he would go, and then agaZin the next day. Sarai would lie in this prison beneath her shroud and be thankful that he had gone to turn his vengeance on someone besides her.

Somewhere in the city, the earth would rock and the air crack with the explosion of one of his toys. Men and women would die. They were not Jews or Arabs to Sarai anymore. They were simply people now.

Sarai lay in the stifling darkness as the flies hummed about her. She thought of her mother and her sisters. The smiling faces of their children. Were they safe? Were they happy? Did they remember her dressed and blushing in the beauty of her wedding veil? The whole world seemed huddled on the threshold of the grave now. She hoped that her family was well. She prayed that if they thought of her at all, it would be of happier times when laughter came easily.

She sat up, still holding the veil across her face. There, among the garments of the man they called Death, hung the pretty lavender dress. It was the only bright thing in the room. Gerhardt had torn the shoulder the first night he had brought her back, but Sarai had repaired it as if she were nursing a sick friend. Once again she reached for it, taking it down with care and laying it across the ragged blanket that covered the bed. She wept silently now as she read the story. . . . It had begun with such hope for her and Rachel.

"*Where thou diest, will I die.* . . ." Sarai read the words slowly before burying her face in the garment. "El-Kiama! I heard Your voice that night beside the tomb! I heard Your story in the garden of the old woman's stitches! You must help me now! You must give me courage to believe! El-Kiama! Where You have died, there I must die!"

She did not know how much time had passed before the sound of a distant blast caused her to raise her head and look toward the bars that covered her window like a prison. A thin plume of smoke spiraled up near Zion Gate.

Gerhardt would be home soon.

The water truck seemed like the most inconsequential target for an Arab bombing, yet now it smoked in a twisted heap on Jaffa Road by Zion Square.

Rachel had seen the dreadful explosion from a distance as she and Tikvah had gone to fetch the daily water ration. Dozens of Jewish women and children had been standing around the vehicle before the blast, and now they lay in writhing, weeping heaps in the square. The water in the tank of the truck had absorbed much of the blast and probably saved lives. Rachel had looked down at Tikvah, and then, unwilling and unable to aid in the tragedy, she had returned home with the empty bucket.

The child lay on a blanket in the front room. Her wide blue eyes could not grasp the grief and weariness of her mother. Tikvah happily sucked her fist and gurgled at Rachel's approach. When Rachel sank to the floor and lay very still in the heat of the day, Tikvah soon fell asleep and remained beside her until Moshe unlocked the door and found them there together.

Moshe's faraway voice awakened Rachel. He cried her name, rushed to her side, and knelt beside her.

She opened her eyes and blinked up at him.

"Are you all right?" he said, gathering her into his arms.

She put a hand to her forehead in confusion. She did not remember lying down beside Tikvah. "Yes," she said weakly, "I am all right." She shook herself awake. "I . . . truly I am all right." She struggled to sit upright.

"I thought you had—" His eyes were clouded with worry. "There was an explosion, and I came straight home."

"Yes," Rachel said slowly. "The water truck." She looked up sharply, as though he could tell her why it had happened.

"I couldn't believe it," Moshe said angrily. "People in line for *water*. We still don't know how the bomb was attached. Or who did it. No one was killed, thank God! I was afraid you might have been there." He looked at the empty water bucket.

"No." Rachel followed his gaze. "We only saw it far away. Like a slow film. A burst of fire and people falling, and then the water gushing everywhere." She sighed. "I didn't try to help, Moshe. Tikvah was with me. And I was afraid also for the baby. Then I felt so dizzy. I think I just lay down here."

There was a slight bump on her forehead. Moshe touched it and frowned. "The doctor was right. Jerusalem is no place for a pregnant woman." His voice was grim. "I want you . . . I'm going to arrange for you to go to Tel Aviv. You will be safer there. At least you will have good food and water."

"No!" She sat erect and defiant. "I have run away too much in my life! I cannot go now. There are other women among us who are—"

"You want me to spend my days in worry about you?"

She touched his arm. "Do you want *me* to spend my days in worry for *you*?" she repeated the question. "Moshe. My darling, please . . . I cannot live apart from you any longer."

He grimaced at her words and sat cross-legged on the floor as Tikvah awoke and Rachel picked her up. "I . . . we . . . do not know what is going to happen here in Jerusalem. If this negotiation works, then all our worry is for nothing; but right now there is reason to worry. I only wish I could think of you as being someplace safe. You and Tikvah . . . and the baby."

"Moshe," Rachel said in a soft voice, "what of Sarai? Have you heard?"

Solemnly he shook his head. "I keep asking. I won't stop, but—"

"I keep praying that she will come back. That somehow she will come back here to us." She smiled at the thought of the goat. "Like she did that morning. Her heart full of gifts and . . . *knowing!*"

"There was a truce that day. She could not come back so easily as that. And, Rachel—I just don't believe she will come back. You cannot stay here on that hope."

"I do not stay here on that hope, my husband." She frowned and searched his face. "I stay here for the pleasure of being with you." A flicker of doubt appeared in her eyes. "Please," she said haltingly. "Have you . . . grown tired of me?"

"Tired of you!" Moshe bellowed. He wrapped his arms around her and laughed. Then he held up his foot to display the flapping sole of his shoe. "I just ruined a pair of shoes running here to make sure you are all right!"

"You must tell me if—"

Moshe put a finger to her lips. "Stop this. It is *meshugge, nu?*"

She kissed his finger and then his palm, laying her cheek against his strong, calloused hands. "Then you must never think of sending me away, because without you, I would surely die."

Moshe debated telling Rachel who had taken Sarai, but he could not. The brutality of Gerhardt was still too fresh in her mind. And Moshe could only assume that it was Gerhardt or his confederates who had just reaped a harvest of Jewish wounded.

35

THE GREAT SALT MOUNTAIN

The fat Italian kept his pistol carefully concealed inside the deep pocket of his overcoat as Stripes spoke quietly to Herr Wattenbarger outside the stable door.

"Gone? But gone where? When did they leave?" Stripes was attempting to appear calm, but he knew he must look like a man who had just seen a ghost.

"To town they have left." Herr Wattenbarger's smile was curious. "After you have left, so did they." He turned his gaze to the stern-looking Italian who towered over Stripes. "They have gone for business. They are with a new airline here in Europe." There was no reply, only a long and thoughtful silence from Stripes and the Italian.

At last the Italian nodded curtly. "Yes. He has business with me."

"Perhaps you catch them in Kitzbühel, *ja*? Such a pity that you all the way here have come and they are gone. We have still one room to let." Herr Wattenbarger stuck out his lower lip and scratched his head.

Maryanne emerged, carrying her large handbag. She looked startled for a moment, then smiled calmly.

The Italian frowned slightly, then nudged Stripes. "This must be your wife, Ted. I will settle your account. We might catch him in town. Excellent.

"Allow me to help you, madame." He took the handbag from Maryanne. "Indeed, this is a good place to conduct business, mein Herr." He spoke in flawless German as he peeled off a dozen banknotes. "Our company will no doubt remember such a secluded place as this for meetings."

"*Sehr gut!*" Herr Wattenbarger replied.

"But our *baggage*, Teddy . . . ," Maryanne protested. "I ain't goin' no place without my *suitcase*!"

"Herr Wattenbarger will watch your belongings, madame," said the Italian with a slight bow.

Maryanne must have spotted the bulge of the gun in the Italian's pocket, for her face paled.

"We have need of your husband's services, madame. As an interpreter," the Italian replied.

Ted grasped the protesting Maryanne by the arm. "We gotta catch James and Sue, *sweetie*," he said in a thick Texas accent, as if he were speaking in a foreign language and had to get the pronunciation right. "So *come on!*" He propelled her away from the Italian. "Forget about the Texas sweetness," he growled through his teeth. "Keep your eyes open, and for once keep your mouth shut!" He tried hard not to look at the bulge in the pocket of the fat Italian's overcoat as he silently cursed L. C. Crabtree.

They had missed the afternoon train, and the Italian was angry and gruff as he followed Maryanne and Stripes back toward the Golden Griffin. "You are certain they mentioned Salzburg?" he menaced.

Maryanne did not reply. Once confronted by the cold blue steel of the Walther pistol, she had fallen into silence.

They passed unnoticed through cliques of vacationers who gathered with skis in the lobby of the hotel. Twice Ted felt the gun press against his back as they climbed the broad staircase that led to Crabtree's room.

In the dim light of the hallway, Maryanne's already pale skin seemed almost ghostlike. They stopped a few feet from Crabtree's door, which was slightly ajar.

The Italian frowned and nudged Stripes once again after a moment of hesitation. "You open it," he said harshly.

Maryanne stood beside him as the door swung slowly open. Her eyes grew wide, and she put her hands over her mouth as if to scream, but no sound came out.

The expression on her face matched that of the Englishman who lay in a pool of his own blood in the center of the room. Ted had never seen anything like it. Eyes wide and fixed, the dead man stared toward the open French doors that led to the balcony. Maryanne's face reflected the same expressionless blankness—no terror, only a calm acceptance of the murder and mayhem before her.

Curtains billowed in the cold breeze that swirled around the room, rustling loose sheets of typing paper like leaves in the wind. Stripes shook his head, unable to comprehend the scene. "Gone," he said again and again. "Crabtree. Tree. He's gone!"

"Wait here," David said, stepping out from the shelter of the train station in Salzburg.

Ellie nodded and held her hand out to catch a raindrop as David pulled up his collar and dodged puddles on the cobbled street.

A light drizzle did not dampen the beauty of Salzburg. A forest of onion-domed churches was overlooked by the high-walled palace of the bishop of Salzburg, whose residence had been built by the revenue from the precious salt of the surrounding mountains.

Ellie's heart pounded with excitement and hope when David hailed a horse-drawn hack outside the train station. She looked into the gray sky. *So close. So close to our own men. Please, God . . .* She prayed silently and peeked back over her shoulder, remembering the watcher in Innsbruck. The train chugged slowly away, and the small crowd on the station platform raised umbrellas against the rain and dissolved into the streets of Salzburg as David spoke quietly to the driver of the carriage.

Dripping wet, David stepped back from the hack and stared disconsolately at the soggy slip of paper containing the address. The driver clucked his tongue, slapped the reins against the scrawny horse, and drove away, leaving David in the street. He turned, and the disappointment on his face caused Ellie to shudder involuntarily.

"What?" she asked. "What's wrong?"

The carriage disappeared around the corner.

David climbed the steps of the platform more slowly. His hair hung in damp strands on his forehead. "Wrong place," he answered quietly, and the sense of excitement and security evaporated.

"What do you mean?" She could scarcely breathe. *"Wrong place?"*

David's normally playful eyes flashed with anger. "You heard me," he snapped, pocketing the slip of paper. *"Wrong!"*

"Well . . ." Ellie read the sign above the station. *Salzburg.* "Well, then, where—?"

David took her by the arm and pulled her into the wet street. "Come on." He was still angry, and she felt suddenly very vulnerable. "Think," he said harshly. "Look at the sign, Els."

She glanced back at the sign once again in bewilderment. "What?"

"Spell it."

"S-a-l-z-b-u-r-g," she complied.

"Right. Salzburg with a *U*. So. You remember what you saw on the back of the picture?"

"You mean before you burned it up?" She returned his irritation.

"Just think!" His voice was loud.

Ellie frowned and restructured the image of the flaming photo: edges curling around the frail letters to devour them only a moment after they appeared. She put her hand to her head. Again she spelled the first word as it burned in her memory. *S-a-l-z-b-e-r-g.* She gasped. "David. It was spelled with an *E*, not a *U*!"

"Right." He turned up a nearly deserted lane of pastel-colored houses and leveled his gaze on her. "Right," he said again, and this time his voice sounded apologetic. "It's not a city." He was whispering the explanation now. "It's a *salt mine*! In the mountains above a little town called Hallstatt."

"Then Hallstatt is the town?"

David nodded and took her hand as they walked up a steep incline. "No train to Hallstatt until tomorrow morning."

"What about the other words—*Gasthof zur Post*?"

"It's a kind of hotel. A little way station, really."

"How far is this . . . salt mine?"

"Not far. This whole region is built on the salt trade. About forty miles. But no train."

"Taxis?"

"All horse-drawn, I'm afraid. The gasoline problem is so bad."

"Could we hitchhike? I mean, surely someone must be going there? Hallstatt." Ellie said the name thoughtfully. "You know how the roads are crowded with army jeeps. Maybe we could get a ride. We are supposed to be there tomorrow, David!" Ahead, the lane opened into a small square with a large fountain where bronze horses spewed streams of water from their nostrils. A line of weary-looking horses and small carriages were tied in a row.

"We'll need to find a room here for the night. I don't want to chance it . . . being recognized. We'll get a room. Take the train in the morning."

Across the square, a short, stout man in a brown overcoat huddled beneath an arch out of the rain. Nearby an old Austrian with a drooping mustache fed oats to his horse. He glanced toward David and Ellie as another young couple passed near the fountain and walked quickly toward the entrance to a cathedral.

Ellie shivered, but not from the damp. Suddenly every face seemed unfriendly. Each person who passed through the square became a potential enemy. She thought of Mikhail and Bernie, of the fat Italian on the train. She remembered the watcher in Innsbruck and the articles that had been splashed across the pages of the European newspapers. The warmth and safety of the Wattenbarger farmhouse seemed a whole lifetime away. There was no going back today, no going forward. There was only this purgatory of gray skies and misty rain that hung over the glowering fortress of Salzburg. And in the distance, the towering peak of Salt Mountain was lost in the clouds.

"Salzberg," David whispered. "Not a town . . . a mountain."

David pulled off his boots and lay wearily across the sagging bed. The springs groaned, and Ellie could not help but think about the warmth of the soft feather bed back at the farmhouse. David sighed and closed his eyes, evidently oblivious to the worn furnishings of the tiny room they had rented for the night.

Ellie pulled back the lace curtains and looked out the dingy window-panes onto the Salzburg street on which Mozart had been born. Across the narrow street, a huge Austrian flag hung from a freshly painted four-story house to announce the birthplace of the famous composer. A small queue of tourists gathered outside in the rain to wait for a tour. British, Ellie guessed from their tweed coats and umbrellas.

Below their room was the Mozart Café, where legend proclaimed that a young Mozart had sipped wine and found inspiration. The soft strains of quartet music drifted up through the floorboards along with the scents of coffee and apple strudel. At any other time in her life she would have felt near to heaven in such surroundings, but now her heart thumped wildly and her hands were damp with perspiration. The intensity of the music matched her anxiety.

"You hungry?" David asked.

She jumped, startled by his voice. "No," she answered, still staring out the window toward the parapets of the bishop's palace and the forest of green-copper church spires.

"Well, I am." He raised his nose to the aroma of cooking food.

Outside Ellie saw a young boy carrying a sack of long loaves of bread slung over his shoulder like a quiver of arrows. Her stomach growled in spite of her denial of hunger. "Maybe I am." She shrugged. "But I'm scared to go out . . . *scared*, David."

"You want to go back to Kitzbühel?" he asked seriously. "You'll be safe with the Wattenbargers."

"I'll be safe," she said glumly, "while you go on to meet Avriel and your pilots."

"That's the idea. You think it was some kind of lucky break that we found the address on the back of the picture? We'd still be back there in peace and quiet—"

"Not exactly peace and quiet with Ted and Maryanne." Ellie rolled her eyes.

"Well, you get my point. Here we are, forty miles away, right where we're supposed to be—almost—and almost on the exact day, right?"

Ellie nodded reluctantly. "Wrong Salz-*whatever*, though."

". . . berg," David finished. "This is the town, and we're going to the mountain," he instructed. "Look, back there I was a grouch about this whole thing, but then I thought about it . . . and I tell you, Els, we just have to quit thinking there are accidents. I mean, I can't figure out why we're here instead of there right now, but maybe we don't need to know. See? So let's relax and enjoy the music. It ain't Benny Goodman, but it'll do. And that's real coffee I smell, and strudel. You ought to be taking pictures out the window."

She looked at the camera that sat forlornly on a rickety bed table, then back at David, who was grinning broadly. "You won't even let me stay depressed!" She attempted a pout but chuckled in spite of herself. "I wanted to be depressed."

"Am I right or what?" he said, tucking his chin in innocence. "But, yeah, if you want to be depressed . . . I mean, if it makes you happy, go ahead. Me? I'm going to sleep for about half an hour, then go downstairs and have dinner. You wanna come along?"

"I'll let you know," she said coolly, pulling back the lace of the curtains again.

"Suit yourself." He lay back down. "Wake me at five, will you?"

Within minutes, David was sleeping soundly; his snores rattled a strange counterpoint to the string quartet. Ellie sat at the window for a long time, then retrieved her Leica camera and opened the window as the afternoon sunlight broke through the clouds and light and shadows played over the rooftops of Salzburg. For a while, she forgot her tension and even giggled when David's snoring fell in perfect time to the music.

The clop of horses' hooves sounded on the cobbles, and Ellie focused her camera on the driver, who sat hunched against the cold as he guided his horse up the street. Then, as the carriage pulled away, she saw something that made her gasp and step back from the window. Across the street stood a lone figure. *Overcoat. Brown fedora.* But his face was obscured behind a camera as he focused his lens on the window where Ellie stood.

"Probably he was just taking a picture of the café," David had said irritably when Ellie woke him to report the man with the camera. "Right now, I would take a picture of a café. Or food. *Come on*, Els, you're just imagining!"

But his words had not calmed her, so he had left her with the pistol as he stole downstairs to order their meal and carry it back on a tray.

She did not sleep soundly that night, and long after the strains of Mozart's chamber music had ceased, she lay awake in bed listening for footsteps outside their room. When she did sleep at last, her dreams were filled with frightening images.

The watcher at Innsbruck was there and the fat Italian on the train. The great arch of a train station towered over her like the huge iron rib cage of some terrible creature. Light filtered through the skeleton as voices called out destinations, and she wandered through crowds of faceless strangers in search of David, in search of home. And always, just behind her, the footsteps of someone ominous and terrifying echoed louder than the scream of train whistles, louder than her own scream when she saw David in the distance as he was pushed beneath the wheels of a locomotive. . . .

Drenched with sweat, calling David's name, Ellie sobbed in his arms as he held her in the predawn light.

"Hush now," he soothed. "Hush, Ellie. It was just a dream. Only a dream." His voice sounded far away as she struggled to separate the nightmare from reality.

She laid her head against his chest and sobbed as she listened to the soothing beat of his heart. "Oh, David! It was like we had been swallowed by some monster . . . and we were trapped inside and all the trains were there—never slowing, but we had to catch a train . . . *some* train! Then I got lost from you, and the man came after me."

He patted her back and rocked her. "Just a dream. A nightmare. You're safe. I'm here. Hush now."

She squeezed her eyes against the final terrible vision of the wheels rushing toward David. Again and again she replayed the scene, finally forcing her mind to finish the drama by remembering how they had rolled out from under the train in St. Michel. "I was so afraid," she said weakly.

"It's okay," he whispered, stroking her hair back from her tearstained face. "You're just seeing all the places we have been. Rome Central Railroad Station, remember? I said it was like being swallowed by Jonah's whale. Iron arches like ribs. Remember? But we're *here*. Salzburg. In a little hotel on Mozart Strasse."

He checked the clock and stifled a yawn. "Of course, if you holler any more, they're likely to kick us out." There was a hint of amusement in his voice.

She pushed him away and dried her eyes.

"In three hours we'll be on the train to Salzberg—*berg*—the mountain," David added. "And we'll have a whole troop around us. Then you can sleep like a baby buffalo in the middle of the herd." He lifted her chin and kissed her gently. "You okay?"

She nodded gratefully. "Glad I'm awake."

"Me too." He kissed her again and pulled her closer. "And we have three hours before we have to catch the train."

Ellie lifted her face to his and relaxed in the gentleness of his touch. "Well then?" She smiled as he pushed her back on the bed and the springs groaned loudly. "Only three hours, David . . . ," she repeated, wrapping her arms around his neck.

36

CRABTREE'S GHOST

British colonel Halloway faced off with Tom Kane as the second convoy in a week wound its way to Zion Gate and the Jewish Quarter under British escort.

"My thanks, Mr. Kane." Halloway's voice dripped with sarcasm. "I thought you understood our situation here! Understood our policy of British lives first!"

"I reported to my government what I saw here on my first trip to Palestine, Colonel. Nothing else." Kane spoke confidently.

"And now we get a dispatch from our government saying that the United States will suspend Marshall Plan aid to England just as our country begins to rebuild after the war."

"That's right, Colonel. I have a confirmation memo to that effect also in my briefcase. The decision was made that unless Great Britain stops providing military aid to the Arabs of Palestine—"

"We have never aided the Palestinian Arabs!" Halloway protested, whirling around to face the window.

"Well, then, let's be precise, Colonel. I was fortunate enough on my journey to Jordan to catch a glimpse of a military depot just over the border from Palestine. The insignia on the British vehicles had not even been removed yet. Hundreds of trucks, tanks, jeeps—and, of course, the Spitfire fighter planes."

"Jordan is an independent nation!"

Kane lowered his gaze and smiled slightly. "Yes. You're right, of course, Colonel. I don't suppose you have been in the Muslim Quarter of the Old City lately?"

The British officer looked uncomfortable. Tom Kane knew that the officer had to be fully aware that thousands of Jordanian Arab Legion soldiers now lived in the Old City and prayed daily at the Dome of the Rock for a swift victory over the Old City Jews and all of Palestine.

"What has the Old City got to do with anything?" he snapped.

"Come now!" Kane was irritated and allowed himself to become patronizing. "Fair is fair, Colonel. None of this is being done in secret. King Abdullah wants Jerusalem. The British like King Abdullah. After all, it was you who installed him as king, and now you have fully equipped his army."

"So"—the colonel clasped his hands behind his back—"your government requires that in these last days of our occupation we assist the Jews?"

"Just make sure they get supplies."

"Or America cuts off aid to Britain."

"That's about the size of it."

"The Russians must be quite happy." The words were accusatory.

"No doubt." Kane did not argue with that. He could not. The Allies were definitely divided on this issue. "But they might be surprised, Colonel Halloway. There are many good men in your government who may not be a majority. However, they stand firm on Britain's pledge to establish a Jewish homeland in Palestine. Remember, Colonel?"

The officer looked away as if he did not hear. "That was 1917," he said, as though time had made the Balfour Declaration worthless.

"Hmmm. Yes. That promise was made thirty years ago, wasn't it? It has taken thirty years too long to be accomplished, in the opinion of my government and the other nations in the UN. So, here we are at last."

"What about Jerusalem?" Halloway asked, less belligerent now but definitely worn out.

"If King Abdullah will agree to allow the city to remain neutral with the United Nations governing, we may well avoid a war."

"And if he does not?"

Kane hesitated before answering. "The Zionists will never allow Jerusalem to be ruled by Jordan. No. If Abdullah will not agree to international government in the city, then there will be war."

"Over Jerusalem." Halloway gave a tight-lipped, angry smile. "He will not agree." There was a perverse satisfaction in that for the colonel. "But I will not be here to see the massacre when the Jews fall." He inclined his head slightly as though he were picturing the green hills of home. "No. And I may not even bother to read it in the news, either."

Kane picked up his hat and smoothed the crease. "Well, in the meantime, Colonel, I understand your government has sent you orders."

"Blackmail. Extortion," Halloway said. "Risk British lives—for what?"

"For American aid for the rebuilding of England, Colonel." With that, Kane stood and tipped his hat. There would be no handshake between old friends. Partition had divided more than land.

Captain Stewart watched with satisfaction as the last meager supplies destined for the Jewish Quarter were thoroughly searched. Not a sack of beans or a can of salt went past him unopened. He was confident that the Old City Haganah would receive not one more bullet among the supplies.

He stood over a barrel marked *kerosene* and shouted at the Jewish Agency driver who was helping unload the supplies. "You! Jew! Get over here . . . now!"

The driver looked up angrily and wiped sweat from his brow. "Me?" He pointed to himself.

"Yes! Get over here!"

The hot afternoon sun beat down on the stones of Zion Gate. Several other men from the Jewish Agency stopped their work for a brief minute to watch the encounter between the British captain and their fellow worker.

"Right, Cap'n," the Jewish man said with a cockney accent that betrayed his English birthplace.

"Open the drum." Stewart stood back and clasped his hands behind his back.

The worker looked at him blankly. "Why?" he asked.

"Open it, I said!" Stewart rocked on his heels and tapped his riding crop against his thigh.

The Jew shrugged and unscrewed the dollar-sized cap, then handed it to Stewart, who sniffed it, then plunged the crop into the barrel. To his surprise, it went all the way down and came out wet. Drops of liquid fell on the hot pavement as Stewart screwed the lid back onto the container.

Stewart looked down at the liquid. Drops of kerosene should have remained on the stones. But these drops had simply evaporated. He started to kneel.

At that moment, a small, pedantic-looking man, who seemed too frail to work as a stevedore, stepped up to Stewart. "Captain Stewart," he said haughtily, "I have a message for you." He handed him a yellow slip of paper, then climbed back into the truck.

Stewart turned from his task and opened the note. What he saw made him completely forget the now-vanished liquid on the cobbles.

A. SAINT 34b Halisal Cairo.

Stewart stood silently blinking at the words, then turned to find the little Jew who had handed the paper to him. The man was gone, like the liquid from inside the drum. He opened the paper . . . and closed it again. Without another word, he waved the barrel through the gate.

The Jewish Agency worker breathed a sigh of relief when Captain Stewart allowed the barrel to go through the gate. He knew the drum did not contain kerosene for cooking but a wealth of small-arms ammunition packed in a tight circle around the inside wall of the container. The center of the drum was filled with water. Kerosene had merely been sprinkled on the top for odor.

The early morning train into the Salzkammergut wound northward through a patchwork of newly cultivated fields and broad pastures. Nestled between mountains were broad blue lakes that glistened in the sunlight like sapphires. White sails billowed as small boats scudded across water ringed by tiny villages. It seemed like something out of a storybook.

As the course moved east, the farmland was replaced by a dense mantle of green fir trees that climbed upward toward the snow lines of the tall peaks. Hours passed as the train snaked its way toward their destination.

What had appeared as forty miles on the map stretched into a hundred and more along the twisting route. Mountains towered above the calm blue of Traunsee, where a fairy-tale castle perched on an island in the center of the lake.

Ellie had held an image in her mind of a vast mountain range of white salt piled up in great heaps. Instead, the conductor gently explained to her, the Salzkammergut held its ancient treasure buried deep beneath the forests. Steep-pitched roofs of wooden shakes and half-timbered exteriors seemed to blend into the mountains themselves, and again Ellie found herself wondering if time had stopped here and they had wandered into another century. Placid teams of oxen pulled their loaded carts past big, rough-hewn chalets, while children in lederhosen played beside the Traun River, where salt barges had once floated from Hallstatt and the great Salzberg, ultimately to the Danube.

Ellie took a dozen photographs as these sights passed by the window of the train. She had forgotten her nightmare, and the sense of being pursued had vanished. Most of the passengers detrained at Bad Ischl, the elegant town that had served as Emperor Franz Josef's summer capital.

Here, the talkative conductor explained, Franz Josef had issued his imperial ultimatum to Serbia and began the First World War. It was difficult
for Ellie to imagine that in a place of such beauty anyone could contemplate war. She herself had almost forgotten that the reason for their own
journey was, in fact, to join forces with a few handpicked warriors who
would soon be fighting in the faraway skies over Palestine.

"How much longer?" Ellie asked as the noon sun sparkled on the
river.

"Not so far, madame." The conductor bowed with Prussian courtesy.
"Just beyond." He pointed out the window to where craggy rock walls
soared up thousands of feet. "The Hallstattersee, the lake, is through this
valley ahead at the base of those mountains. Around the lake you go to
Obertraun and off the train. Then you go across the lake until at last you
come to Hallstatt the village, *ja?*"

"*Danke.*" She smiled brightly up at the man.

"*Bitte schön!*" He bowed again before leaving the nearly empty car.

"Sounds like the jumping-off place of the world," Ellie whispered
to David. Only then did she look back at the few who remained on the
train. All of the other passengers were men. All were dressed in Austrian
clothes—wool jackets with stag-horn buttons, hunting caps, and wool
trousers. They stared back at her with obvious curiosity.

At last, as the lake came into view, a man of about sixty got up and
walked toward them. He tipped his hat and spoke in surprisingly good
English. "You have come for the reunion?" he asked politely, taking the
empty seat behind them.

"Reunion," David said flatly, with no hint of a question in his voice.

"*Ja.* I can see an American when I know one." There was a sparkle in
the man's eyes. "You have come for the reunion of the 101st Airborne,
ja? It was you and your comrades who have saved the art the Nazis put
into the Salzberg to hide." The words were definite and meant to inform
David, not question him.

"Of course," David said. "The reunion."

"Amazing how the Nazis hid their treasure and then planted bombs
into the mine shafts, is it not?" He shook his head in disbelief. "Wicked
fellows, I think. If they could not have the looted artwork of Europe
for themselves, they wished to destroy it." He sighed. "And so now,
the reunion. You have come with the others who have saved the great
masterpieces."

David stuck his lower lip out and nodded thoughtfully. "Of course.
Really something."

"And you are staying at the Gasthof zur Post, I am thinking?"

Ellie and David exchanged a glance. Could this man be the contact they had been waiting for? Ellie wanted to throw her arms around the man's neck and hug him in her relief.

David lowered his voice to a whisper. "Is Avriel there?"

For an instant the man looked confused. "Avriel?"

"How many of the guys made it?"

The man shrugged. "I do not know. We simply heard that there was a reunion. Americans come back to the Salzberg. I am not from Hallstatt myself, but news travels fast here in the mountains. You fellows saved the Salzberg and the mines. I am from Goisern. The next stop." He smiled broadly and extended his hand. "I wish you well."

David reddened as the train clanked to a stop and the man got off in the tiny village. Another peasant also disembarked, leaving only David and Ellie and one Austrian man who slept soundly against the window-pane with his hat pulled low over his eyes. His arms were crossed, and a hand-carved pipe was tucked into the pocket of his jacket.

At last they were nearly alone, and every imagined enemy had failed to appear. Avriel had sent the American pilots into this remote corner of Austria under the guise of ex-GIs who had come to a reunion. It was brilliant in its simplicity. There was no other reason for anyone to visit Hallstatt. Any other strangers would be spotted immediately in the tiny village. Here they would be safe from intruders. David studied an old map of the area as the train crept along Hallstatt Lake and finally arrived at Obertraun.

"It is here you get off the train," the conductor told them quietly before he moved down the aisle to shake the shoulder of the sleeping man. "Herr Tannenbaum," he said softly.

The man woke with a start, knocking his pipe to the floor with a clatter. "*Ja?*" He blinked into the bright sunlight that reflected on the glassy smooth lake. "Obertraun?"

"*Ja.*"

"*Danke*, Franz," he said with familiarity as he rubbed a hand over his eyes and groped for a small satchel. He followed David and Ellie onto the platform of a chalet-style train station.

"The boat you find this way." He smiled warmly at David and pointed across the narrow lane to a small boat dock, where a half-dozen boats were tied up. They bobbed in the water as the boatmen stepped onto the dock.

Their fellow passenger said quietly, "A good fare I will bargain." He held up three fingers. "Three will a cheaper price pay."

David shrugged and stepped aside to let the short, muscled man dicker with a boatman for the fare. Ellie studied the man's thick arms and strong, untanned bulldog face. *He is a miner,* she deduced, feeling somewhat like Sherlock Holmes. And then she breathed a quick prayer of thanks that no one had followed them and every stranger had been helpful to them.

"Twenty minutes and we're home free," David leaned over and whispered as the miner clasped hands with the boatman on the price of the fare across the lake.

In the distance, beyond the crystal water, the little village of Hallstatt clung to the slopes of the mountain. The tall white spire of a church pointed skyward, and the green peaks of Salt Mountain towered above.

"Perfect," said David. "Perfect."

The peasant man cocked his head and pointed to the bow of a little fishing boat. "One American dollar for each. Today this is expensive for the reunion, *ja*?"

"The reunion," Ellie repeated, climbing into the boat.

"You have come for this also?" asked the peasant, taking his place beside her.

"Yes." Ellie looked at David, who was smiling broadly as the boat slipped away from the dock and the breeze caught the sail. Canvas flapped loudly and then billowed full, catching the boat and pushing it toward Hallstatt.

"You are a miner?" Ellie asked, exaggerating her words.

"Of a kind," the man said. "I am also come for the reunion, *ja*? Only two years ago we have found this great treasure in the tunnels of the Salzberg."

"You were there, too?" Ellie asked in fascination.

"*Ja*. Such an event was this. All the greatest treasures of Europe. Michelangelo, Pollaiuolo, Raphael . . ." He smiled at her. "To see such things rescued—" He shook his head. "The salt within the mines preserved the paintings and tapestries. To every museum in Europe one should have to travel to see what came from those shafts, Fräulein."

"And you were there?" Ellie asked in wonder. She nudged David in the ribs. "David, he was actually there when they took all that stuff out of the mine shafts. Imagine! What a story."

David did not speak.

And then Ellie saw his face. It looked grim and pale, as if he were seasick.

David stared hard at the peasant who shared their passage.

"David, are you okay?" Ellie asked as the boat neared the shoreline.

He did not reply. His eyes hardened, and the muscle in his jaw twitched as he clenched his teeth. "Tannenbaum," he said at last.

"*Ja?*" asked the man.

"That means 'Christmas tree,' doesn't it?"

"*Ja.*"

"Yeah. I thought so. We used to sing the song when I was a kid . . . about the Tannenbaum. And you're here for the reunion, too?"

The face of the peasant flinched slightly. "Just as yourself. And what ist your name, *bitte?*"

David looked toward the Hallstatt dock. His eyes widened as the massive figure of the fat Italian stepped from the boathouse. A Walther pistol was in his hand. David quickly pulled his own revolver from the waistband of his trousers. He hesitated only a second before pointing it at the peasant. "Come on now, Christmas Tree. You know my name."

The peasant smiled ruefully. "*Ja,* I know your name." He glanced toward the dock and cursed at the sight of the Italian.

"Wait a minute!" Ellie cried. "There isn't *really* a reunion *is* there?" She was genuinely bewildered.

"Bright girl." The peasant shoved his forester's cap back on his head, and all pretense of an accent dropped away.

"Then . . . then . . . who *are* you?" she stammered as the boat slipped into the dock. The huge hands of the fat Italian grasped the rope, securing the boat to the pilings. Ellie covered her mouth with her hand and gave a cry of fear as the Italian pointed the Walther into the boat.

"L. C. Crabtree is his name," said the Italian in perfect English as he reached down to grasp Crabtree by the collar and drag him out of the boat. The gun barrel went immediately into Crabtree's ribs. "And now he's writing the news for us."

"But who are *you?*" Ellie held tightly to David's free arm as he kept his gun leveled on Crabtree.

"Ask your husband, Ellie Meyer," said the Italian with a short laugh. "He's probably got most of it figured out by now." He shoved Crabtree roughly along the dock, calling back over his shoulder, "Come on, Tinman, you're late."

The Gasthof zur Post was the only hotel in Hallstatt. It had been built several centuries before to accommodate Hapsburg officials who traveled to oversee the great salt mines above the village. Now Ellie and David sat in a small room with Bobby Milkin and Avriel as they explained the desperate search that had been conducted by the Mossad since they had slipped from the train.

"And so, you see," Avriel said patiently as he poured tea for Ellie, "when you left the earlier train at St. Michel, our man lost you altogether. He could have gone back to St. Michel, of course, but at the time you were also being trailed by an Arab agent. Our man thought it better that he give you time to find refuge while he led the Arab elsewhere."

"So," David said, rubbing his chin thoughtfully, "the Italian was our contact?"

"Correct," Avriel said with satisfaction. "The whole train was crawling with officials looking for the perpetrators of the Bari Harbor bombing, however. Each time he tried to make contact, someone interfered. It wasn't until later that he remembered the woman—"

"You mean Maryanne?" Ellie asked, unable to believe that the scatterbrained bumpkin could be in the least bit dangerous.

"She was on the train with some thick-lipped, scruffy-looking chap," Avriel said. "He looked Turkish, possibly Arab. . . . Anyway, the two of them together looked mismatched, and both of them had a compartment in the same car as you. He stayed out of sight the entire ride—we can only assume he might have been worried that David might recognize him and make a run for it. *She*, on the other hand, was in and out of the compartment two dozen times, looking for an opportunity—"

"An opportunity to what?"

Avriel reached down and picked up a large handbag. Ellie recognized it as belonging to Maryanne. He upended it on the bed, and a German Luger bounced out. "An opportunity to use this."

"Maryanne?" Ellie gasped.

"Yeah," said Milkin. "And she would have used it, too, if the Italian hadn't stayed right there."

David frowned deeply and put a hand to his forehead. "Wait a minute! Hold it! So how come she didn't knock us off at the farmhouse?"

"She was simply waiting. Someone obviously realized that you were much more valuable to the Arabs alive than dead. After all—" Avriel spread his hands to indicate that they had arrived—"you led them here."

Bobby Milkin worked his cigar and puffed with enthusiasm. "Crabtree was hired by her. He's just been guiding them along. She would have killed you yesterday if you hadn't left Kitzbühel when you did, Tinman—you get it?"

Ellie pondered the information. "*They?* You keep saying *they*. Who are *they*? I mean besides *her*?"

"You mean Ted Samson?" David asked.

"Naw." Milkin grew impatient. "Ted Samson don't know schmooze from shoeshine. He's the schlepper."

Avriel rolled his eyes at Milkin's explanation. "Please, Bobby."

He silenced Milkin with a withering look. "As I was saying, she hired Crabtree . . . not the other way around. And we know now that Lawrence Crabtree is not above doing investigative reporting—for the highest bidder. The Italian spotted her their first day in Kitzbühel. I can only assume that's why she did not come out after that. She and Crabtree used Ted Samson as their go-between."

"That putz!" David said, feeling a sense of pity for Samson.

"Right," agreed Milkin.

"L. C. Crabtree has been serving as the Mufti's public relations department, you might say. He has broad influence and has managed to advertise that the Jews are up to sinister plots in Europe, which he promised to uncover."

"And how did our men know when to move in?" David questioned.

"Ted Samson had always played a certain number on the roulette wheel. He broke his usual pattern. Got careless, you see.

"There's more you should know. We went through Crabtree's Rome apartment and"—Avriel held up a small, red-leather-bound address book—"among other things, we found this." His finger marked a place, which he held open for David to read.

There, in a cramped scrawl, were the words *A. SAINT 34B Halisal Cairo*.

David stared at the name for a moment; then his face flooded with anger. "You mean he knew *her*?" he demanded.

"Who, who, who?" Ellie asked in confusion.

"Angela Saint Martain," answered Avriel quietly. "The Arab agent who murdered Michael Cohen—and almost killed David as well. There is a possibility that Crabtree might have simply been acquainted with her in a professional capacity," he conceded. "But it was this link that led Maryanne to him. She was . . . she and Angela knew one another quite well."

Ellie furrowed her brow. "I don't remember anyone at all like Maryanne at school."

"It goes further back than that," Avriel said with a wry smile. He reached into the big handbag again and pulled out a passport, which he handed to Ellie. "She went by the name of Samson, pretending to be married to Ted. But as you can see—"

Ellie gasped and stared hard at the picture and the signature. "Maryanne Saint Martain!" She almost choked on the name.

"They're related," Milkin said with authority. "Ain't they, Avriel?"

"Yes. Sisters. Quite infamous sisters, too, I might add. Between the two of them they have—had—enough information to blackmail a good many of the British officers stationed in Cairo during the war . . .

several who are still in Palestine. The connection has worked well for Haj Amin."

David wiped sweat from his brow. He looked even more sick. "Sisters," he said in a choked voice. Turning to Ellie, he added, "And to think, we've been sleeping next door to the sister of Angela Saint Martain." He swallowed hard. "Are there any more of them?"

"No. Not that we are aware of." Avriel's voice was unamused at the question.

"Well, what are you going to do with her?" Ellie frowned.

"She has come in quite handy," Avriel said with smug satisfaction. "When we went through Crabtree's apartment in Rome, we found almost all of the documents she held for blackmail. We have them now. We also have her."

"In a *real* safe place," Milkin laughed.

"We have notified the British—at least one middle-level officer in Jerusalem—of our find. He will be delivering a half-track to the Haganah tonight."

"Yeah!" Milkin rubbed his hands together in glee. "With the gun turret stuffed with ammunition and Sten guns."

"Everyone has his price, it seems." Avriel poured himself a cup of tea.

"And Ted Samson?" David asked. "After all, he didn't know what he was in with."

"We have taken that into consideration." Avriel nodded. "He is on his way to Afghanistan."

Ellie squinted as though she were trying to see the reason for the location. "Afghanistan?"

"Yeah," Milkin said. "I picked it. He don't know the language and there ain't an American Embassy there. So we're just gonna sorta turn him loose up there—"

David nodded and shrugged. "Perfect. Only you, Milkin."

Ellie wanted to know more. "What about Crabtree?"

For a moment, neither Avriel nor Milkin spoke. Then Avriel chewed his lower lip and peered over his spectacles at Ellie. "He murdered the Italian's partner," was the only explanation.

"Murdered?"

"Killed him. Back in Kitzbühel," Avriel elaborated.

Ellie looked from the face of one man to another. "And?"

Milkin stretched his neck up and drew a soggy cigar across his throat. "So . . . this!"

"You mean . . . he's . . . dead?" Ellie gasped.

"Quite," Avriel said, dusting off his hands.

"If there were any other Arab operatives in Kitzbühel, your little side trip to the city of Salzburg threw them off. Quite clever," Avriel said with admiration. "Any questions?"

"About a million." David shook his head in disbelief. He did not admit that their side trip to Salzburg was totally unplanned.

"What about the boatman?" Ellie grimaced. "Didn't he see the guns? Won't he be the least bit curious?"

"One of our guys," Bobby said dryly. "He had a gun on Crabtree most of the way over."

"Crabtree is an internationally known journalist. . . . You just can't—" Ellie faltered.

"Oh, we intend that L. C. Crabtree continue to write for quite some time." Avriel smiled and directed his gaze at Ellie. "And with your help, Mr. Crabtree will do a great service for the cause of Zionism."

Ellie attempted to figure out yet another twist in the story. "Okay. I'm waiting," she challenged.

"Crabtree has been writing stories about the sinister Jewish operation in Europe. Actually, he has been doing us a great favor. For the purpose of drama and journalistic flare, he has made us sound considerably more dangerous than we really are." Avriel chuckled. "The effect in Arab political and military circles has been marvelous. Arab morale is quite low in spite of the rhetoric. Arab civilians have been instructed to evacuate Palestine in anticipation of a dreadful force of Jewish partisans who will swarm the country after evacuation."

"Well, aren't the Arabs building up their own forces to meet this imaginary army?" David asked.

"Yes," Avriel conceded. He looked to Milkin for further explanation.

Milkin puffed the cigar with confident vigor. "Sure. Them blanket heads is givin' us all kinds of trouble. But they're scared—at least the civilians are. We've been able to move in where they left, see?"

"And here is the best news of all." Avriel lowered his voice. "There are certain Arab leaders who are willing to negotiate now. As long as they thought they could parade in over the top of us without a fight, they were confident and ready to wipe us out. Now they are having second thoughts, you see. If indeed the Jews have massive stocks of men and supplies waiting to be airlifted into Palestine from secret European bases, if indeed we have an enormous air force of fighters and bombers—"

"But we *don't*," Ellie protested.

"That is the beauty of it, Ellie." Avriel spread his hands in rejoicing. "If the Arabs *think* we do, then it is like Gideon standing on a mountain with three hundred men holding nothing but clay pots! Remember the story? They lit their lamps and broke their pots and shouted together,

and the enemy—thousands of men—ran away! Regardless of his intentions, L. C. Crabtree has been the noise of those breaking clay pots for
us. The Arabs are worried. And confused. And ready to negotiate."

"So what do you want me to do?" Ellie frowned.

"Write the news."

"Write?"

"*You* send in Crabtree's dispatches." Avriel brightened as understanding
flooded her face.

"A lot of sound and fury, in other words." She smiled.

"Not in other words," Avriel chuckled. "*Exactly.*"

Milkin interrupted. "Scare the pants off 'em."

David stared into his cup. "I don't want to be a wet blanket, but what
if it doesn't work?"

"We don't think that far ahead." Avriel dismissed his comment.

"Okay. But we need to be more than all show." David's voice carried
a warning.

"Sure, Tinman." Milkin slapped him on the back, spilling tea onto
the floor. "That's why we're *here*—here at the Salzberg, buddy!"

"Well, where are the rest of the guys?" David gestured around the
room. "Did the pilots we hired in the States make it here, or what? And
how are we going to get from here into Czechoslovakia to train on the
ME-109s, anyway?"

Avriel and Milkin exchanged triumphant glances.

"Details, Tinman," Milkin laughed. "You always was the one for
details. . . ."

IN THE SALT MINES

By four o'clock in the afternoon, all of Hallstatt was in the shadow of the great Salt Mountain. A towering crescent of peaks encircled the tiny village, and for months at a time it received no direct sunlight at all. A single street threaded through a row of tall, sharp-gabled houses that climbed the hillside and were linked by a network of steep wooden steps.

In the false twilight of late-afternoon shadows, David and Ellie followed Avriel and Milkin up a staircase that led to a cable with a metal cage attached. On a heavy timbered platform they were given carbide lamps by an elderly attendant, then locked into the swaying cage for a slow ride above the spruce trees to the top of the Salzberg, three thousand feet up.

The lake, far below them, became a silver plate of sunlight, and the houses of Hallstatt looked like tiny miniatures in a toy world. The air was cold, and Ellie was grateful for the down parka and thick wool trousers Avriel had provided for her. A pair of sturdy leather hiking boots had also been purchased for her days ago in hopes of their arrival.

Ellie studied the scholarly appearance of Avriel as the breeze ruffled his graying hair and reddened his thin cheeks. He squinted behind the wire rims of his glasses and looked small and vulnerable next to the craggy features of Bobby Milkin. She could not help but feel a sense of astonishment that this small, frail-looking man was the genius behind the entire Jewish operation in Europe. Through his ability and persistence, weapons had been purchased and were now being readied for shipment. His calm, unruffled exterior made her feel confident in the plan that had been laid out for them in the room of the Gasthof zur Post.

She closed her eyes and listened to the rush of the wind and the moan of the diesel engine that pulled them upward along the cable. High above them an eagle soared, and she remembered the Scripture in Isaiah that Uncle Howard had repeated a thousand times: *Those that wait upon the Lord shall mount up with wings as eagles. They shall walk and not be weary, they shall run and not faint . . . or something like that,* she thought, determined that she would find out soon exactly what the Scripture was and memorize it.

She focused her camera on the outstretched wings of the eagle. *Hovering, soaring, seemingly without support. Spread your wings and trust that the wind will hold you up. Trust . . . and wait. Trust, and God will renew your strength and give you hope to put one foot in front of the other . . . walk and not be weary, or at least not fall down.*

She studied David through her lens. *My eagle. Strong and confident. Spread your wings, David . . . you and the rest of the guys. There is a mighty wind blowing for Israel, and it will hold you up. It has brought us this far. So very far since the beginning.*

David caught her eyes and held them with an expression that said, *"I love you. We're going to make it."* Then he looked up toward the top of the Salzberg, where a small opening to a mine shaft was cut in the face of a cliff.

"That is only one shaft," Avriel explained, pointing. "There are dozens and dozens of ways in and out. A perfect place for our purposes. The Nazis thought of it first, you know. I think it is rather fitting that one of the key operations of the Jewish Mossad will take place in a location that was so vital to the top brass of the Third Reich, don't you?" He appeared rather smug as he shouted the words over the wind.

"How did you find out about it?" Ellie questioned.

Avriel laughed loudly. "I was here when the art treasures were brought out of the shafts."

"But you aren't American. Were you part of the 101st Airborne?"

Avriel raised his eyebrows to mock her naïveté. "You are sweet. No. I was not part of the armed forces."

"Well then, how did you get in on such a top-secret operation? Were you in charge of returning the artwork to the museums?"

He shook his head. "No, no, my dear. My occupation might have been better listed as art connoisseur . . . and thief. Eleven of the great masters are missing from the lists . . . eleven. And I alone know where each of those eleven has found a home."

Ellie was flabbergasted. She eyed David to see if Avriel was joking.

David shrugged and nodded. What Avriel had said was evidently true.

"You mean you actually *stole* them?" Ellie's jaw dropped.

"In a manner of speaking," he replied. "Stole them from the Nazis and sold them back to private owners. It was all excellent training, and it managed to buy a few thousand Jewish lives in the bargain. But that is another story. . . . In the meantime, I made some fine connections here that will serve our purposes quite well." He nodded toward the end of the cable. "You will see what I mean."

Each of the foursome carried a rucksack of provisions as they hiked up the steep trail toward a more secluded entrance into the mine shafts. Ellie stopped beside a tiny rivulet and splashed her face with ice-cold water.

"Taste it," challenged Avriel.

She hesitated, then put a drop on her tongue. She grimaced. The flavor of salt was strong. "Salty."

"Yes. And now we follow the brook, and it will lead us where we must go." Avriel shouldered his pack again and walked another quarter of a mile through the spruce trees, finally arriving at an abandoned opening of a mine shaft. Bootprints muddied the water that streamed out from a wall of wooden planks blocking the entrance.

"They should have covered the tracks," said Avriel with irritation as he pried a board loose and stepped aside for David and Ellie and Milkin to enter. Then, with the same plank, he smoothed the prints in the mud and stepped into the shaft.

Milkin lit the carbide lamps with the butt of his cigar. David held his light aloft, but it penetrated the oppressive darkness only a few feet ahead of them. Indeed, the faint flicker of the lamps only served to emphasize the utter blackness of the tunnel.

The little brook flowed down the center of the path as they ascended a slight incline. The air was cool but warmer than the cold winds of the mountain. It seemed to Ellie that she could feel the heaviness of tons of rock suspended just above their heads. Avriel trudged on, confident of the way they would take. Ellie flashed her light toward the ground to see the imprints of a dozen pairs of boots in the thick mud.

"You sure you know where we're going?" David asked Avriel in a hoarse whisper that reverberated through the shaft.

"We have been in the mine only ten minutes." Avriel chuckled. "We have walked down this one shaft not even a half mile. Wait a few hours, and then you may ask me if I am lost."

"Hours!" Ellie felt her hands get clammy. She was ready for a good healthy dose of sunlight. "How long will we walk?"

"All night." Avriel's voice was matter-of-fact. "The shafts are twenty-five miles. Interconnected galleries . . . twelve different levels about a half mile high. We must stay clear of the working galleries. Not too difficult, I think. These shafts have not been used for years. We are at least two miles away from the working mines."

"But how do we get from one shaft to another?" Ellie asked in a child-like voice as she contemplated the honeycomb that they had entered.

"That is the fun part." Avriel lifted his lamp toward the smooth timbers that braced the ceiling. "Number thirty-seven," he said, and his voice echoed as the ceiling suddenly expanded and opened to a high gallery above their heads. "Right this way." He bowed slightly and directed the beam of his light to the side of the wall where two polished wooden rails protruded from the blackness. Their shadows seemed like giants behind them. "Your carriage awaits, madam." Avriel nudged Ellie slightly toward the rails and the black hole.

Reluctantly Ellie walked forward. The banisters dropped off into sudden nothingness. "What am I supposed to do?" she asked fearfully.

"Twelve galleries," Avriel explained. "All are connected by these down shafts and ladders. I will sit in front, like so—" He sat astride the banisters and began to pull on a pair of thick leather gloves. "You sit behind me, David behind you, and then Bobby. Hold on tightly to me."

Ellie obediently sat on the rails behind Avriel. Her heart thumped in her ears. David and Bobby likewise boarded. "Now what?" she asked timidly.

"And now, this . . ." Avriel grasped the heavy ropes on each side of the banisters and pushed himself forward. Instantly they were plummeted down the rails into the darkness of the shaft like a human bobsled, twisting and turning at incredible speed.

Ellie screamed loud and long as they ripped through the blackness and finally landed with a thump at the bottom as Avriel tightened his grip on the side ropes to slow them.

Avriel was instantly on his feet, but the other three lay panting in the gravel at the foot of the banisters. Avriel held his lamp aloft and grinned at the ashen faces of his companions. "Nothing to it," he said.

David coughed and thumped his chest. "Nothing to it," he squeaked. "Like a dive from ten thousand feet right into the pitch-black of the ocean."

"I don't want to do that again." Ellie pulled herself upright.

"There are twelve galleries." Avriel extended his hand to her. "You will get used to it."

"I lost my cigar," Milkin mumbled as he brushed himself off. He said nothing else for the next half hour as Avriel led them through a narrower chamber and then onto another set of banisters to repeat the wild plunge into darkness.

Ellie clung tightly to her rucksack in the next descent and, at the bottom of the down shaft, noticed that a tiny trickle of the brook had also branched off to follow their steadily downward progress through the great Salzberg.

Avriel extended his hand to offer them each a small lump of salt to suck on as they started down a wide, tall corridor. "*Salzkammergut* is the word for Salt Crown Lands," he explained as their light faded away in the height of the ceiling. "Romans and Celts were latecomers here to the mines. Down in Hallstatt they have collected things that go back to the days of Solomon. Who knows?" His voice echoed. "Maybe even Jewish slaves mined the salt here. By medieval times the government controlled the whole area. Travelers had to have permits to enter. This kept smuggling at a minimum."

"You mean people smuggled salt?" Ellie asked wearily. "Why don't we sit down here and you tell us about it."

Avriel ignored her plea as they trudged relentlessly on. "Salt was one of the most valuable items in the world then. Worth more than gold. To preserve things, you see, there was nothing else. Only salt. Men fought wars for this salt. Some Hapsburg count once said that these mines had become a tidbit for every helmeted dog in Europe to snap at . . . and so they did. And then the Hapsburg Dynasty ended, and eventually along came Hitler and his helmeted dogs. The first time I saw these shafts they were stuffed with furniture and tapestries and artwork such as the world has never seen together in one place."

"And you stole eleven paintings," Ellie repeated.

"I only wish I could have taken more from the Nazis." Avriel shined his light down a side tunnel that was blocked by a pile of rubble. "There are good men buried down there beneath that," he said. "Friends of mine . . ."

Moshe remained in the deep shadows beneath a cypress tree as the thin slits of a British armored car's headlights slowly turned the corner of Jerusalem's Street of the Prophets. An old familiar shudder coursed through him, and he wished that he had not been the man chosen for this errand. He clutched the manila envelope close to him and remembered the amused faces of the men as they had gathered around him for the briefing.

"Why me?" Moshe had asked.

"You know him."

"Yes! And he knows me! He knows me well!" Moshe had protested.

"Good. Then you can both identify each other. Besides, should he try anything, we will have a backup man with a rifle aimed at his head."

"And if he also has a backup man?" Moshe had taken the brown envelope even as he asked.

"He knows that you are only giving him half . . . only half tonight.

He's not going to kill anyone until he has the other half. And after tonight, he will not want anyone in the British government to know what he has done."

"Besides," Shimon had quietly added, "you should have seen his face when I gave him the slip of paper. It is . . . it is . . . poetic, Moshe! To think that you will be the one to meet him . . . after all, you spent a good number of weeks in the hangman's shadow because of him."

Now, as the armored car approached the arranged meeting place, Moshe wondered again if he was not moving into the shadow of the noose once more. Shimon Devon, one of the Haganah men, had been right, however. There was a certain amount of satisfaction in meeting Captain Stewart under these circumstances—especially since Moshe had read the complete file.

Captain Stewart and his brother had been small cogs in the wheels of the Saint Martain sisters, yet they had provided information enough to result in the deaths of a thousand men over the course of a year. Perhaps Stewart had never realized what he had fallen into. Certainly, he had no money to give to pay off the blackmailers, but he was in a position to pay by way of favors—favors to the cause of Haj Amin in Jerusalem.

It was all quite clear to Moshe now, and he could not help but pity the man he was about to meet with. Stewart was hopelessly, irretrievably caught in the center of two forces. To Shimon and members of the Jewish Mossad, it had become a wonderful joke that Moshe should confront Stewart. The irony of the meeting was too rich to pass up. But Moshe knew that tonight he would witness the final stroke of Stewart's moral bankruptcy, and he wondered if there would be any semblance of remorse or humanity left in the British captain.

The car slowed and stopped in front of the dark windows of Mrs. Bett's bakery. Lights flashed and blinked off. A moment later, Stewart climbed from the vehicle and stood at the front-right fender as instructed. His hands were in plain view, and his face, illuminated by the soft glow of the night sky, seemed tortured.

Moshe stood slowly and stepped from the shadows.

Stewart strained to see him as he walked across the street. Then his anguished face darkened with rage and resentment. "They didn't tell me it would be you!" he snapped.

"They told me it was you," Moshe answered calmly, remembering the rifle of the backup man. "As a matter of fact, I read the whole file. All of it."

"So what? We didn't know who they were! Terry and I didn't know. I thought they were . . . just girls."

"Come now, Stewart," Moshe said in a patronizing voice. "A judge and jury would never believe that."

"Just give it to me!" Stewart reached for the envelope. He was shaking and wild-eyed.

"Your brother, Terry." Moshe held the envelope out of reach. "Killed in the explosion of the King David—"

"Give it to me!"

"He was the one, wasn't he, Stewart? You just went along with your big brother."

"Shut up! Let me have it," he pleaded. "I kept my part of the bargain."

"And all this time you pretended to be the vengeance of God. I read the file, Stewart. You're not an Englishman anymore. Terry would have been court-martialed and hanged. You—maybe just prison!"

"Shut up!" Stewart lunged, and Moshe smelled the rank odor of whiskey on his breath. "Shut up!"

"So, all this . . . not for home and England, Stewart, is it? You have no money, so you were ordered back here. After your brother died, you were ordered back—not to serve England, but to serve . . . others."

"What do you want from me?" Stewart began to weep.

Moshe's eyes narrowed as he appraised the pathetic quisling before him. "*This* will do for a start." He indicated the armored car. "Although it's supposed to be a half-track."

Stewart was panting with fear. He looked over his shoulder and then grasped at the envelope. "They'll be here! Don't you know? The patrols . . . I . . . I couldn't get a half-track. This is . . . my car. I . . . that's all I could do!"

"And guns? Ammunition?"

"Yes! Yes! And I'll have to tell them . . . that it was all stolen. That the Jews stole my car, and—"

Moshe held up a finger. "No, Stewart, not this time!" he warned. "This time it was the *Arabs* who stole your car."

An engine groaned two blocks to the north. Stewart clutched at Moshe's shirt. "Right. Whatever . . . now, please—"

Footsteps sounded behind them, and a rugged young Haganah soldier emerged from the shadows. "Come on, Moshe, let's go."

"Is this all of it?" begged Stewart, clutching the envelope.

"Only half." Moshe looked toward the backup man. "All right." He nodded. The soldier raised the rifle butt and, with a swift, unexpected thrust, smashed it against Stewart's face.

With a cry, Stewart crumpled to the ground, where he lay bleeding and clutching his broken nose.

"Not enough to knock him out," said the backup as they roared away in the armored car. "Just enough to make it look real for the patrol."

Moshe nodded agreement, then exhaled loudly. "Drop me off at the corner of Rehavia," he said wearily.

Avriel fell silent among his memories, and the time passed slowly in the bowels of the Salzberg. In the darkness, Ellie lost her ability to judge the passage of hours, and even minutes seemed endless. David took her rucksack from her and carried it with his own. The distance between down shafts and banisters was about forty-five minutes. They had been down five before Avriel finally called a halt beside the entrance to a huge cavern of white crystal that glittered in the light of their carbide lamps.

"We will stop here," he said removing his pack. "I like it here." He glanced around with an air of familiarity. "It is far past suppertime now. Are you hungry?"

Ellie had already stretched out beside a boulder and removed her boots. "I'm going to feel this hike tomorrow," she moaned.

"If we stay here longer than a few minutes, you will feel it tonight," Avriel chided.

David sat beside her and pulled out a loaf of fresh white bread and cheese from the pack. Avriel extended a wineskin full of cold apple cider, and they ate in ravenous silence.

"It is time." Avriel shined the lamp on his wristwatch. "Put on your boots."

"How much longer?" Milkin lit a cigar, his first since the initial wild ride down the banister.

"We will arrive just before dawn." Avriel was already on his feet and looking toward a particularly low-ceilinged shaft opening.

"We might arrive without our feet." Ellie pulled the heavy footgear over her swollen feet.

"One moment," Avriel said kindly. "Why didn't you say your feet hurt, eh?" He pointed at David. "Pull them off again. Five minutes will fix her." He flashed a beam of light on a small, shallow pool. "This salt makes the salt baths at Solbad. Soak your feet. Five minutes and, like magic, you will walk all night."

Ellie doubted the veracity of his claims, but five more minutes was still five minutes, so she peeled off her socks and plunged her aching feet into the cold puddle. With sighs and moans of delight, David and Milkin followed suit; soon they all were not only fed but also refreshed. Avriel seemed proud of his prescription, but the instant five minutes had passed, he ordered them out of the pool and back into socks and boots.

For another hour, Ellie's feet tingled as she trudged along behind David. And then, after two more descents, she began to cast longing glances at every puddle on the floor of the mine shaft.

"Five minutes," she pleaded with Avriel.

A rumble like thunder echoed far behind them. Instead of stopping, Avriel quickened his pace down a damp and dripping shaft with timbers crusted in ancient brine. "This way." His voice was low. "No one has come this way for many years."

Again the rumble sounded . . . closer now. "What is it?" Milkin whispered, but even his whisper seemed too loud.

"We must be quiet." Avriel held a finger to his lips. "For a while. We have come close to the working mine. I did not realize. . . . Our voices will travel."

So for another hour they walked in total silence until the distant rumble in the heart of the great Salzberg grew faint. Only then did Avriel turn into a wide gallery where a half-dozen shafts led out from a circle like spokes on a wheel.

A larger briny pool sparkled in the center of the cavern. Water dripped from the ceiling into the water with loud echoing plops. "Now," said Avriel, wiping water drops from his glasses, "five minutes."

He sat beside the pool with them with his pants rolled up, the icy salt water soaking his calves and knees while he studied a chart drawn onto darkened oilskin. Five minutes passed, then ten, but he did not urge them to their feet. Ellie was grateful for the time to rest and did not question Avriel until David finally asked, "Shouldn't we get going? We've been here twenty minutes."

Avriel nodded and chewed his lip thoughtfully as he continued to study the chart on his lap. "A honeycomb," he said quietly.

There was something in his voice that caused Ellie to sit up straight. "You know where we are . . . don't you?"

"Possibly not." Avriel smiled and folded the map, shoving it deep into his pocket. "But I have been lost here before."

"Don't joke," Milkin menaced. He pulled on his boots.

Ellie looked for the tiny brook and the bootprints of the men who had gone before them. Neither was in sight. "How long has it been since you were here?" she questioned.

"Here? Never. I have never been here in this place exactly."

Milkin cursed. "This is somethin' like outta *Tom Sawyer*. Injun Joe's cave or somethin', ain't it?" He cursed again. "You mean you don't know where we are?"

Avriel grinned. "I didn't say that. We have simply taken a little detour. Are you all soaked and refreshed? Nothing quite like a good soak in salt. Ellie, you may not even feel the hike."

"Cut it out, Avriel," Milkin said. "I need a drink and a good bed. I'll settle for a little fresh air, even. *How much longer?*"

David stood with his hands on his hips and gazed at each of the openings that led from the central room. He lit a match and held it up. It sputtered in a slight breeze, and Avriel chuckled softly. David looked at Avriel with a curious smile. "That way?" He pointed.

Avriel nodded. "About a hundred yards, I think. It should bring us out an hour early. Maybe a mile above camp."

Bobby Milkin rushed ahead of the other three as they picked their way carefully down the final tunnel. A mighty shout of victory echoed as he emerged out of the back side of the Salzkammergut. They were far above the hidden valley, where the fliers of David's command were safely tucked away. Their wooden barracks had once served as the station for a small contingent of Luftwaffe fighter pilots protecting Germany from the great onslaught of Allied bombers during the war. Now the same barracks housed Jewish pilots who would fight to end the oppression Hitler had begun.

In the predawn half-light, David gazed down at the green meadow and the cracked pavement of a narrow airstrip. Two shacks. Barracks and a small airplane hangar.

Avriel stepped up beside him. "I have known about this place for many years. Göring used the airstrip to bring his looted treasures into the Salzkammergut. And, of course, there were the fighter planes stationed here."

"We flew over this route a hundred times protecting B-17s, and the 109s would just appear out of nowhere. We never suspected. Never saw this little place," David said in wonder.

"The Alps are full of such secrets, I am sure," Avriel added as he watched Milkin scramble down the slope toward the camp. "This is a secret I have long kept to myself for a day such as this. A few of the Hallstatt miners know. But no one comes here. No one." He pointed at the hangar. "And inside there is our greatest treasure." He looked at David. "Two Messerschmitt 109s, Captain Meyer—two. I assume that will be enough to train our pilots until we can get them into Czechoslovakia to their aircraft."

David nodded thoughtfully. He looked up into the clear early morning skies, where the last radiant stars dimmed against the approach of morning. "Yep. Two should do it for now. A week here and we'll be ready."

38

GIDEON'S TRUMPETS

Not a day passed that Moshe did not ask if some news had been heard through channels about the fate of Sarai Tafara. The answer was always the same: a shrug, a slow shake of the head. The world was too pre-occupied with the worries of feeding the Jewish population of a hundred thousand souls to spend much time worrying about one young girl . . . and an Arab, a Husseini, at that.

Bab el Wad was once again sealed against Jewish convoys when the British pulled back from Ramaza at the mouth of the gorge and the Arabs moved in in force. The final convoy of food to the isolated kib-butz of Kfar Etzion on the southern flanks of Jerusalem had been totally destroyed—no survivors. Now the tiny Jewish settlement was surrounded by the Legion and holding on only with the aid of airdrops, which often fell into enemy territory.

Bombings around Jewish Jerusalem were so commonplace that hardly a family had remained untouched. If death or injury had not yet come into a household, it had at least touched a friend or relative of a friend. In these final days of the occupation, the violence intensified as a foretaste of what was to follow immediately on the heels of British withdrawal.

Haganah gains in the Arab Quarter of Sheikh Jarrah had been elimi-nated this morning by British military order.

"Your men," the Haganah had been told, "have occupied Sheikh Jarrah. This is directly in the path that the British military has chosen as our route of evacuation. You will remove your forces within the next six hours or we will bring in our artillery and blast you out!"

When the field guns had been moved into position after five and a half hours and then were loaded and ready, small bands of Haganah and Palmach straggled out of Sheikh Jarrah to surrender the deadly ground beneath Mount Scopus and Hadassah Hospital. Mount Scopus had been reinforced and was somewhat prepared for the Arab onslaught, but the Jewish officers knew they were no match for the British artillery that was now aimed at Sheikh Jarrah. A strategic withdrawal seemed in order until, on May 14, the Haganah would sweep back over the area from Mount Scopus while they held off the Arab armies in the east.

The withdrawal was accompanied by Jewish shrugs and brave sentiments that this was only a temporary setback, but they knew that the retaking of Sheikh Jarrah would ultimately cost many Haganah lives.

On his way home that day, Moshe carried a heavy burden of hopes and doubts with him. And the heaviest burden of all was the one that he had to give to Rachel: *"Sarai is lost to us. Lost in the terrible uncertainty of these days. She is forgotten in the midst of daily tragedy that has engulfed thousands . . . thousands! What can one life mean in all of this? We must forget her, Rachel, and go on with the business of surviving!"*

He found Rachel in the shade of the courtyard as she milked Naomi, the little nanny goat, as Sarai had taught her. When he told her the news—that there was no news of the girl, nor was there likely to be—Rachel bowed her head and wept for her lost sister. He put his hand on her shoulder to comfort her, and wordlessly, she drew herself up and continued to milk Naomi.

"I will not stop praying for her," Rachel said at last when she could find her voice again.

"I am sorry." Moshe frowned and looked to the east, where the Old City bristled with armed men. "There is nothing to be done. Nothing more. It is easier to call Paris than it is to get a call through from our west side of Jerusalem into the Arab east side. We live on different halves of the moon now."

She nodded in understanding. There was no bitterness in her, only sadness. "And is there any news about the internationalization of the city, Moshe?" she asked hopefully. "Might the United Nations come in and stop this?" She waved her hand toward the walls of the Old City.

He sat down on a rock below the fig tree and leaned wearily against the trunk. "Yes. Hope. Ben-Gurion, all of us have agreed that this is the most sensible solution. Maybe the only solution for the Yishuv. If, after the British leave, Jewish Jerusalem should fall to the Arabs by force, then it will break the back and will of the rest of the settlement. International occupation of the city seems the only reasonable answer for us right now."

"And what do the Arabs say?"

Moshe laughed a short, bitter laugh. "They are not interested in solutions. They are aware of how fragile our hold is here, and publicly they refuse to admit the possibility that the UN is a reasonable answer to war."

"Privately?"

"Privately we are all praying for negotiations with King Abdullah—if he will see reason. And, Rachel, he talks to the Americans as though he wants to avoid war. If we can negotiate a separate truce with him, then maybe there is hope."

"What has Tom Kane got to say about it?"

"He . . . he still believes that we have hope through negotiations with King Abdullah. In the meantime the Mufti's men are wreaking havoc on all of us." He held his hands up in frustration. "King Abdullah's Arab Legion has the force and arms and men to perhaps take all of Palestine. We are, of course, putting up a smoke screen—"

Rachel smiled. Moshe had told her of Ellie's articles that now flooded the newspapers abroad with news of the great Jewish army being prepared in secret locations around Europe. "And do the Arabs believe all that they read in the papers?"

"Perhaps they believe enough to be uncertain. . . . Uncertainty may confuse them . . . delay them . . . make them want to negotiate. They have been slinging threats like stones, claiming that it will take them only a matter of days to sweep over all of Palestine." He leaned forward and clasped his hands together. "Rachel! If only we can hold them long enough on that day so that for every grenade we throw, they think we have a thousand more! Do you see?"

She nodded. "Yes. Then even when we throw our last grenade, they will think they have more to face."

"Yes! That will make them hesitate! Just a day . . . two days . . . until we have a chance to get our men out of the camps of Cyprus and put rifles in their hands. David is training the fighter pilots right now. There are sixteen of them. We can make sixteen seem like a thousand if only they can get here in time! The cargo planes are all assembled, ready to bring the men and equipment we will need. But delay and Arab hesitation are what we must have! We must be able to stop them at a hedge, hold them with the threat that there are tanks behind that hedge."

"Even if there are no tanks."

"Exactly!" His face was fired with hope in this impossible illusion. "We are Gideon, Rachel, against the great armies. We bluff, and they wonder and fear. Ellie is doing a magnificent job in her writing. We sound like the Allied armies preparing for the invasion of Europe! Her tales about the fighter pilots . . . I read them and found myself almost believing, even though I know the truth!"

Rachel laughed then, her mind full of the lively red-haired shiksa who delighted so in playing at the game. "I especially liked the picture you brought of David standing on the wing of the plane."

"Ah yes! The one with the Tin Man painted on the wing!"

"Yes! The Tin-can Man with the Star of David painted on his chest! It is—"

"It is Ellie." Moshe shook his head, and the sense of hopelessness lifted. "The newspapers carried it as far away as America, we heard. The Mossad has been approached by dozens of pilots who wish to join us! And we have heard—through channels—that it is driving the Arabs mad! They are having blackouts and air-raid drills in Cairo and Damascus now."

Rachel removed the bucket from beneath Naomi and untied her, leaving her to graze the garden freely. "The world does not side with the weak, Moshe," she said as they walked into the house. "No. We have learned such things the hard way from Hitler. And so we must not show them how truly fragile we are. David. The Tin-can Man. He is so wonderful, *nu*? A man of chutzpah in a world of paskudneh!"

"You should send these words to Ellie!" Moshe said with enthusiasm.

"And what words will we use to frighten King Abdullah?" Rachel frowned in mock seriousness.

Moshe thought a bit, then brightened. "*Shtup zikh nit vu men darf nit!*" he exclaimed.

Rachel threw her head back in delighted laughter and gave Moshe a kiss. "You will tell him, '*Don't be so pushy*'? That's *it*?"

"He doesn't know Yiddish," Moshe teased. "If I say it fast he will think I said, '*Look out! Six million Jewish men and a dark night!*' "

"Even with my terrible English I cannot translate the Yiddish to that!" She put her hands on her hips and peered at him in amazement.

Moshe shrugged. "No, I suppose not. But it certainly sounds ominous." He embraced her playfully, pinning her against the kitchen counter. She smiled up at him, catching the glint of appreciation in his eyes.

"And how is our pitseleh today?" he asked, changing the subject.

"He is . . . fine." Rachel raised her chin to meet Moshe's kiss.

"Who says it is a he? I want another beautiful little girl," he whispered as all the cares of the terrible times diminished in Rachel's presence. "Another . . . beautiful . . . like bookends—one on each side of their mama. And then I want all the time in the world to read the one in the middle."

"You have read me." She kissed the palm of his hand. "And you know me line by line."

"Sigh by sigh." He touched her cheek. "And the words are so beautiful that I want to read them again and again."

Captain Stewart stood for a moment in the center of the souk and stared at the man in the yellow-and-black-striped keffiyeh. The man dickered with a Copt priest who told him his tomatoes were no good and too expensive, anyway. The Arab vegetable merchant argued loudly and lowered his price as the monk raised his ever so slightly. They would eventually reach agreement, and the monk would walk away, satisfied that he had purchased the finest tomatoes in the market.

Stewart checked the slip again. *Yes. Yellow keffiyeh. Tomatoes. Yes. This is the man.* He waited for the bargaining to end, then approached the unshaven, dirty vegetable merchant.

"Ah Captain Allah be praised he sends us fine tomatoes to sell today in the souk you will buy?" The merchant said it all in one breath, without pause or punctuation.

"You are Halidi?" Stewart asked.

"Ah Captain Allah be praised you have heard of the tomatoes of Halidi who sells thanks be to Allah here in the souks."

"Yes," Stewart said. "I have heard of you." He handed the man the paper and watched as the peasant looked furtively over his shoulder, then pulled the canvas tarp over the narrow opening to his stall.

"Come with Halidi Captain Allah is merciful to send you we were knowing you are coming." He put a cracked, dirt-caked finger to his lips. "The great commander awaits you this way this way."

Stewart followed the peasant through the back alleyways of the Muslim Quarter until at last he stood at the doorway of a decrepit building that looked as though it housed twice as many souls as there was room for.

The peasant pointed up to the second story. "He is there with his new bride Allah be blessed she is a Husseini." The old man lowered his voice to a hiss. "A strange young woman Allah be merciful we have heard rumors."

Stewart stared at him for a moment. Then, as the leathery hand extended palm up, Stewart flipped a coin to him and pushed past the enthusiastic thanks that gushed from his mouth.

Stewart made his way carefully up the leaning staircase. He stepped around piles of garbage and discarded furniture until he came to the door where paint flaked onto the ground. He knocked twice and waited. Then the knob turned and the haunted face of a young Arab woman appeared in the crack. She did not wear a veil. Her skin was smooth but slightly sallow, and dark rings circled her eyes, making her appear almost old. "You are Mrs. Gerhardt?" Stewart asked crisply.

The woman lowered her eyes and simply stepped back, opening the door to let Stewart pass. The room was clean and tidy but poor in its furnishings. The clothes were hung on a metal rack near the foot of an iron-framed bed. Dresses numbered only two. The black and dreary one she wore, and the other, among the man's clothing, was lavender, ringed with flowers.

Fredrich Gerhardt sat at a splintered wooden table across from where Stewart stood. His face was amused. His thick jaw jutted out in a half smile as he appraised his visitor. The young woman went immediately and sat on the edge of the bed. She placed her hands in her lap, and Stewart could see her tremble. Stewart looked first to Gerhardt, then to her, and back again, just as Gerhardt raised a gun from under the table.

"You are Stewart," Gerhardt said without intonation.

"Yes, Gerhardt. I know you by reputation."

Gerhardt laid his gun on the table and pointed to the only other chair in the room. "Sit. The girl will make you tea." Then he whirled around and cursed the young woman in Arabic until her eyes grew wide and she stood hurriedly to put her veil across her face and get to the task of preparing tea.

"You have taken a new wife." Stewart licked his lips nervously at the outburst and the terrified reaction of the girl.

"A convenience. She is stupid and slow," Gerhardt said, narrowing his eyes in disdain as she passed his chair.

Stewart eyed the back of the girl. "Can I speak freely in front of her?"

"She does not know any English. Barely her own tongue. I have considered cutting it out, for all the purpose it serves. What an ornament, eh?" He smiled.

Was the man joking? Stewart was uncertain.

"For a man to wear his wife's tongue. Surely such a thing would be admired," Gerhardt added.

Stewart cleared his throat. "It seems an empty gesture to me since she talks so little." He shrugged. "There are women to whom such an event would be a blessing to the world. But when one is already without speech—"

The amusement left Gerhardt's face. "I suppose. Yes." He tapped his fingers on the grip of the gun. "I was told you would come. Told you had some item that might interest us. And that you also had shown your hatred of the Jews. So—"

"I know we are, shall we say, skilled in certain things, Gerhardt. I am willing to trade you information if you in turn will help me."

"We bargain in the souks. What is it you wish?"

"The death of a man. A Zionist. This is a man who is your enemy as well as my own."

Gerhardt drew his breath in like a man bored with conversation. "Yes. So? I am a man of many enemies."

"What if I told you I could deliver into your hands the life of one man whom you hate more than others?"

"I would ask you how you know whom I hate."

"I have heard we share hatreds. I have heard . . . that you would pay dearly for the life of Moshe Sachar."

Behind them, a cup clattered to the floor with a loud crash. The girl stood back in horror at her clumsiness. Stewart figured that such behavior normally would have resulted in a beating. But today, Gerhardt seemed not to notice the splintered china on the boards.

Gerhardt stared hard at Stewart. "It was you who arrested him—by order of the Mufti, I have heard. There is much you have done for the cause of the Jihad, and your own causes. The women of Saint Martain. They helped you as well, Stewart. This is known."

"Now Sachar has the file. And I have a way to get rid of him if you will listen."

The girl set their cups on the table and slowly poured the steaming brew. Her hands still trembled.

The men spoke for a long time, then drank to the end of enemies.

David stood beside the ME-109 and watched as Bobby Milkin skimmed the top of the mountains, then dipped below the rim of the gorge on course for a perfect landing on the little airfield. A cheer arose from the other pilots, each of whom had checked out in the plane before Milkin.

David wiped his brow and turned to Ellie. "Well, ol' Crabtree is going to have something to say about this, isn't he?"

She laughed, but he could barely hear her above the roar of the engine and the rush of the wind caused by the single propeller. Bobby Milkin taxied to a stop, then unlatched the cockpit, standing up and raising his fists in victorious salute. The cigar still dangled from his lip.

Ellie snapped a picture and laughed again. "Crabtree is going to be famous for the photographs one day," she called up to David. "Recording the birth of the Jewish air force."

"Don't tell anyone these mugs have had only eight hours' of flight time each in these little jinglebobs." David patted the *Tinman*.

Avriel sauntered out of the barracks and raised a hand, motioning to David. His face was serious and concerned.

As David hurried toward Avriel, he glanced back and saw the exultation of the pilots as they gathered around Milkin and lifted him from the plane.

Inside the sparsely furnished little room, Avriel poured David a steaming mug of coffee, then pointed toward the radio. "Your C-47s are on the way from Panama," he said, but his voice lacked enthusiasm.

"Great!" David said, wondering if Avriel was simply tired or perhaps sick. It was not like him to seem so gloomy with good news. "Martin Feinsteinel, huh? And the rest of the guys?"

"Yes. We lost one transport on takeoff. Killed four crewmen."

David stared at the swirling black liquid in his cup and thought of other crack-ups, other comrades' lives snuffed out in a moment of carelessness. "Who?"

"I don't know. The message was brief. Said the load shifted . . . and, of course, the planes were—are—still not up to standard."

David clenched his fists and thought of Angela Saint Martain and her part in obtaining mechanics and crews. Had his message gotten to Feinsteinel in time to root out any potential saboteurs? "This wasn't—?" He almost couldn't bring himself to say it. "Do they think it was caused by someone? You know what I mean, Avriel."

"The cargo shifted," Avriel said flatly. "It was secure on the last check, but it shifted. Feinsteinel is not sure if the ropes snapped or maybe somone cut them. But it rolled the plane on takeoff. Flipped it back, and—"

David peered out the grimy panes of the window to where the men pushed the two Messerschmitts toward the hangar. "Yeah," he said. "Tough break." He resolved not to think about it anymore. This was war. Tragedy would become commonplace in the days ahead. He exhaled loudly. "Okay. So when do we get out of here?"

"I'm not sure." Avriel sounded even more gloomy.

"Well, Czechoslovakia is only seventy-five miles north as the crow flies. A few minutes of flying time, and we'll be able to pick up the rest of the 109s."

"Here it is." Avriel put down his mug and leaned toward David. "It's a question of timing, you see."

"What are you talking about? Timing?"

"The world is full of question marks."

"Avriel!" David laughed. "It's already May tenth, buddy. Four more days and the British are gone! And the Egyptians have ex-Nazi pilots who are flying Spitfire fighters—"

"I read the report," Avriel said quietly.

The fact that American pilots were flying German-made planes against Germans flying Allied fighters had made for a lively discussion over the supper table. The irony of it was enough to make heads spin.

"The point is . . . well . . . there is a chance that all this—" Avriel motioned toward the planes—"we are hoping . . . praying . . . that it will not be needed."

"Okay," David said. "That's fair. So what's going on, Avriel? What's in the works?"

Avriel reached into his pocket and pulled out a slip of paper with a decoded radio message on it. "I just got this."

David scanned the note, and the words nearly took his breath away. "What? Talk of delaying the declaration of statehood?" he exclaimed, reading the note over and over.

"Just for a short time. Negotiations are still going on. Even with our planes and weapons, what little we have may not be enough. There is thinking that maybe a few weeks' delay—"

"What do you think of this?"

"Well"—Avriel spread his hands in helplessness—"I . . . I don't know. But this is what it means to us here. If the planes come into Palestine too early, before statehood is declared, then they could still be confiscated. If there is talk of peace through negotiated settlement, and you fly in, it could upset everything. You see?"

David scratched his head. "Yeah. Even a blind man could see this one." He handed the slip back to Avriel. "We're stuck either way we do it."

"Quite. We may not know the decision of the Jewish Provisional Government until a few hours before the British leave."

"And if negotiation fails, we will arrive too late to make the opening round of ex-Luftwaffe pilots strafing Tel Aviv."

"Exactly. I don't want to lose these planes, Tinman," Avriel said solemnly. "It is the threat of a Jewish air force that has driven the Arabs to consider peaceful settlement." He smiled ironically. "Our dear *Crabtree* has bluffed very well, I think. If only our enemies knew the truth of it, eh?"

"Yeah." David tapped his fist nervously against his palm as he sat in thoughtful silence. "Okay, Avriel," he said quietly. "You don't want to lose the planes, huh?"

Avriel nodded eagerly, as if hoping David had a solution. "We are not exactly the Allies invading Europe," he said dryly. "To have the planes impounded would be fatal to us."

"We've got sixteen pilots here besides me and Bobby, right?"

"Sixteen competent pilots, and twenty-five planes waiting in Czechoslovakia. When the transports come we will dismantle the fighters and carry them to Palestine to be reassembled."

"And Martin Feinsteinel is bringing a C-47 to carry the pilots to Czechoslovakia to get the other 109s." David slowly pieced together the entire picture. "Okay. How about this? Put these sixteen guys on ice in Prague until we see whether statehood is declared or delayed. After it's settled—"

"*If* it's settled."

"Okay. *When* it's settled, those sixteen can fly out to Palestine while the remainder of the planes are shipped."

"Of course. That is what we planned all along."

"That leaves two planes, Avriel . . . the 109s on our roster." He stood and gazed out at the little airstrip. The Tin Man was emblazoned on one plane, and a likeness of the Scarecrow graced the other fighter. "I think Scarecrow would like to be the first Jewish fighter plane over Tel Aviv," he said softly.

"You want to go ahead? Before the rest of your squadron?" Avriel mulled the plan over.

"Right. Milkin and me could make those guys think they've flown smack into a hornet's nest, see? If this talking doesn't do the trick, Avriel, our men are going to appreciate a little fighter cover."

"Even if it's only two planes?"

"Two planes. Yeah." David frowned at the thought of the odds. "We can hold them long enough—as long as you don't take too much time getting these guys headed to Palestine. And if you lose only two planes, what have you lost? Not everything. You'll still have sixteen crack pilots and twenty-five 109s on the way."

Avriel grimaced. David knew what he was thinking, though he didn't say it: two planes lost would also mean, in all probability, the loss of David and Milkin.

"Yes, I see your point." Avriel cleaned his glasses on his shirttail and joined David at the window. "Timing. That is the key. To send them all before statehood is declared would mean all were lost. But only two—if you arrive early, you can hide at Beit Darras until the matter is decided. If war is declared against the Yishuv, at least we will have two—"

"That's the spirit." David clapped Avriel on his back. "Just do me a favor, will you, Avriel?"

"Anything."

David watched Ellie out the window. She was talking with a group of fliers near the hangar. The wind blew her hair back from her face. Colors sparkled in her auburn curls, and David's heart ached at the thought that he would have to leave her. "Just don't tell Ellie, will you?"

"She'll have to know something."

"Yeah," David muttered, worried over how to tell her. "I'll just have to make it gentle."

39

THE LAST SUPPER

On the afternoon of May 11, Milkin and two other pilots returned to camp lugging a string of trout and the carcass of a stag they had shot on the Salzkammergut. The atmosphere of the little training camp was one of anticipation. By midmorning of the twelfth, it was rumored, Martin Feinsteinel would be landing to take them north to Prague, where they would await orders to pick up their own fighters.

Now, as the air swirled with laughter and the delicious aroma of "The Last Supper," as the meal had been dubbed, David tied a blindfold over Ellie's eyes. He took her by the hand and led her a distance before he opened a door and nudged her forward into a cold building.

"What? What? What?" She giggled.

David's voice was full of amusement. "Hold it!" he protested as she reached up to take off the blindfold. "Not yet!" He guided her hand toward the wing of an airplane and left her standing there.

She heard the hiss of a match being struck, and then, from outside the darkened window, a dreadful caterwauling began as the men from the Oz Squadron started to sing:

"You must remember this . . .
A kiss is still a kiss,
A sigh is just a sigh. . . ."

"Oh, David!" Ellie cried. "You didn't."

"The fundamental things apply
As time goes by-y-y-y-y!"

"Yeah," David replied, enjoying the moment. "Take off the blindfold."

Ellie lifted it from her head and gasped at the sight in front of her. Illuminated by the light of two slightly crooked candles set precariously on a wooden crate, Ellie saw tin plates filled with a meal of venison and potatoes. Draped from the wing of David's 109 was a large banner that proclaimed, *HONEYMOON SUITE, KING DAVID HOTEL!!!*

Beneath the wing of the plane David had made a soft bed for them with blankets laid across a mattress of fragrant pine needles. He took her in his arms and danced in a slow circle with her.

"And when two lovers woo,
They still say . . ."

David sang the words off-key: "I love you-u-u. . . ."

"You know"—Ellie leaned her head against his chest—"Humphrey Bogart didn't try to sing to Ingrid Bergman."

David smiled down at her and lifted her chin. "You disappointed? I know I promised you a piano player next time."

"No, no. This is more memorable." She raised her voice and directed it toward the window. "Especially listening to Milkin sing with a cigar in his mouth!" she laughed.

Milkin's disreputable baritone wavered, and he coughed.

"That's better, Milkin!" David shouted as they continued to dance.

Ellie glanced toward the bed. "Isn't this like counting your money in front of a poor man?" She inclined her head.

"Who, them? They aren't going to hang around. I only paid them for this one song!"

"No matter what the future brings,
As time goes by. . . ."

"Second honeymoon," Ellie whispered. "Sweet, Tinman, really sweet."

"Well," he said, clearing his throat, "you've been such a good sport about all this." He looked momentarily self-conscious as the song ended and the choir called out to them,

"Night, Tinman."

"Sweet dreams, Tinman!"

"Sleep tight, Tinman!"

"Don't be late for breakfast, you two!"

Laughter and footsteps retreated, leaving David and Ellie alone in the candlelight.

"Really sweet." She kissed him lightly.

His love for her reflected in his eyes. "Yeah. Like you."

"Only last time we were saying good-bye, remember?" She kissed him again and started to pull away. He held her more tightly. "David? Supper will get cold."

"Just a minute," he said in a barely audible voice. "This is . . . all too perfect. I want to make it last a minute longer."

She laid her head against him again and listened to the steady thump of his heart. "Yes." She sighed. "No need to hurry, I guess." She opened her eyes and gazed at the bright silver of David's aircraft. She smiled back into the face of the gangly caricature of the Tin Man proudly wearing the bright blue Star of David.

Then she almost lost her breath with the realization that David would be over the skies of Palestine in this little plane. The machine guns were real. The bullets tearing into the skin of the 109 would be real, too. "David?" she asked in a small voice. "This isn't . . . good-bye, is it?"

He guided her toward the makeshift table. Then, in his best Bogart imitation, he said, "Of all the joints in all the woild . . . she had to come inta mine. . . . Your venison is getting cold, sweetheart."

"You're not saying good-bye to me, are you?" she asked more insistently as she searched his face for the answer.

"You're going to Prague in the plane with Martin and the guys," he tried to reassure her. "Me and Milkin are just going a little ahead, that's all."

"Ahead? To where? Are you going to meet me in Prague?" Ellie held tightly to his hands.

He hesitated only an instant. "Will you stop the worrying? I'm going to meet you."

"In Prague?" Her face was intense. "Say it to me . . . 'I'm going to meet you in Prague.' *Say it!*"

He stared at her, defeated in the attempted deception. "I'll meet you," he said quietly. "At the King David Hotel."

She bit her lip. "You're going on. Ahead of the rest. Oh, David, why?"

"We can't risk taking the rest of the squadron in until we know if statehood is going to be declared. We may not know that until the fourteenth. Somebody needs to be there—just in case."

Ellie stared at the plane. "You . . . you have to promise me." She sank down on the blanket beside the crate.

"Anything," he said, kneeling beside her.

"You have to be careful, David, in that tin can of yours, and come home to me. . . ."

He kissed her cheek. "I'm not planning anything else, babe," he said gently. "You know how I hate good-byes."

The sun had not yet topped the ridge when David leaned his back into pushing the 109 onto the runway. David, Milkin, and Avriel had already been up for hours, plotting the route they would take.

"Two refueling stops, anyway," David had said. "Even with the belly tank we can't stretch the operating radius more than six hundred and fifty miles."

"Okay. Two stops." Milkin looked concerned. "Where we gonna stop that they ain't gonna throw us in the clink?"

"Yugoslavia," Avriel had suggested. "Or Turkey."

"The British have their brand on just about everything in the Mediterranean. I don't want to repeat the experience we had in Cyprus."

"Athens," Avriel said flatly. "There is only a small contingent of British there."

"Right." David had marked it with a finality that ended the discussion.

He had already kissed Ellie one last time, and she had left the runway, climbing high onto the rocks of Salzkammergut. They would not say good-bye, they had decided, so she had not stayed to watch as he and Milkin now climbed into the tight cockpits of their planes.

"Avriel," David called as the engines sputtered and then roared to a start. "We've got three 20 mm cannons and two machine guns on these babies. They aren't going to mean a thing once we're out of ammo," he shouted over the din.

Avriel nodded and raised his hand in acknowledgment. "Right!" His words were nearly drowned out. "I'll get a C-47 on the way to Palestine with that in mind! Scheduled for Beit Darras!"

David grinned and waved. Beit Darras was the same airfield where he had crash-landed two months before. He hoped this transport would have better luck. "Take care of my girl!" He jerked a thumb to where Ellie had last been seen. "Tomorrow in Jerusalem!" he called, then slid the windows of the cockpit down until he was alone with the thunder of the engine and his thoughts of what awaited him.

"Okay, Lord, it's You and me," David prayed. The plane began its taxi down the short runway. *If I rise on the wings of the dawn, if I settle on the far side of the sea, even there Your hand will guide me, Your right hand will hold me fast.*

He pushed the throttle forward. As the wheels lifted from earth, the power of the plane jammed him back against the seat, and he rose on the wings of dawn.

Far below him on a rocky ledge, a small figure stood with upraised arms. And the morning light caught her auburn hair in one shining, last embrace—*"Shalom!"*

Athens rose from the Aegean Sea into the hills like tiers of tiny houses carved from alabaster. The broken temples of the Acropolis were unchanged for thousands of years.

David glanced toward Milkin, a mere wingspan away. A cigar hung from his lip, and he was pointing at his nearly empty fuel gauge. David gave him the okay sign, then banked sharply and circled in toward the small Athens airport. Refueling had gone well in Yugoslavia, and David had no reason to think it would not also go easily in Athens.

Permission to land was quickly granted, and within a few minutes David and Milkin taxied down the runway to a stop beside the large refueling truck. David flipped the latch on the cockpit and was immediately hit by a blast of hot air. His ears were ringing from the constant roar of the engine. Milkin had already jumped to the ground and stood shaking his head as if to retrieve his hearing.

A small, thin, shabbily dressed Greek sauntered out of the hangar. He was wiping his hands on a greasy rag. "Fuel, bubby?" he called in heavily accented English.

"Right. And be sure and fill the belly tanks. Got a ways to go."

"Ho-kay! You wanta Coke? Go in and sit." He jerked a thumb at the hangar. "We got real American Coke!"

Milkin was still wriggling his finger in his ear and had missed the entire conversation. David took him by the arm and guided him toward the Quonset building that had in its time housed a flock of German 109s.

David's legs felt a little shaky, and he was grateful for the chance to walk around for a few minutes. The offer of a Coke sounded close to heaven.

"Where we goin'?" Milkin asked.

"You want something to drink?" David shouted in his ear.

"Yeah!" Milkin yelled back. "And a toilet!"

When they entered the gloom of the hangar, it took a moment for their eyes to adjust from the bright sunlight. Then the doors clanged shut behind them, and the building became very dim.

Milkin squinted and shouted, "What the—?"

David whirled just in time to see a dozen dark shapes emerge from the shadowed corners. He reached for his revolver, but already strong hands grasped him and Milkin, grappling them to the ground.

40

DARKNESS

Sarai sat quietly on the edge of the bed as the British captain Stewart reviewed the chosen route. Gerhardt was smiling broadly. It was one of the few occasions Sarai had seen him do so.

"Good!" Gerhardt declared. "You have done well. The negotiators will be without escort, you say?"

"One of Abdullah's own men is supposed to drive them over the border from Jordan into Palestine. He has been paid and will let them off about a hundred yards too soon." Stewart pointed down at the map. "So. You will be here." He tapped his finger. "Two birds with one stone, as we say."

"King Abdullah will be blamed for this," Gerhardt said. "Haj Amin shall be pleased." He stood and stretched. For three hours the two men had pored over the plans. Now it was Gerhardt's turn to show Stewart the device. He picked up a wooden crate from under the table. In it was a homemade bomb, almost laughable in its crudeness. But Sarai noted that Stewart did not laugh. The killing power of such a weapon was well-known, and Gerhardt's skill at assembling these harbingers of death was legendary.

"Antipersonnel?" Stewart asked.

"This is more than that," Gerhardt said proudly. "If you find even small pieces of them, you will be lucky. And you see here . . . if one should attempt to disarm it, the end is the same. To pull any wire leads also to death. The shrapnel will tear to pieces anyone within a twenty-foot radius."

"How many will you plant?"

"Four." Gerhardt pointed to the path Moshe would be taking. "Connected by a wire grid just beneath the sand. When the grid is broken by a footstep, they will all explode at once."

"Brilliant!"

Gerhardt looked pleased. He smiled proudly. "You wish to come watch?"

"I cannot, alas, Commander. There is packing to do. We will be leaving Jerusalem on schedule tomorrow . . . one last parade through the Old City."

Gerhardt seemed disappointed that he would not have an audience. "You will miss a great show."

Sarai leaned forward and cleared her throat. "My husband," she said haltingly.

This was the first she had spoken in days and the first time she had ever used words of familiarity with Gerhardt.

He turned, startled at her voice. "What?" he barked.

"Such plans. Such skill, my husband. Always you leave me behind as you wreak vengeance against my enemies. May I not go with you? May I not see with my own eyes the skill of your hand?"

Gerhardt laughed and looked at Stewart in amazement. "The woman has a voice!" he mocked.

"And words of admiration for her husband," Stewart added. "I would not cut out such a tongue if I were you."

"So!" Gerhardt exclaimed, stepping near Sarai. She looked quickly at the floor. "You wish to join us on our campaign?"

She put a trembling hand to her veil and nodded silently.

"It cannot harm," Stewart said. "It will be in Jordan. No Jewish guards to trouble you. Two Jews alone in the dark on foot. I would take her. Much better there than Jerusalem."

Gerhardt fingered the bullets on his bandolier. He reached out and lifted Sarai's chin. "And how will you reward your brave Jihad Moquade, my woman?" He mocked her, but she smiled shyly, then looked away, unwilling that he should see the fear she carried in her heart.

"Your desire, my husband," she said softly.

Gerhardt laughed again and turned to Stewart. "You see! You see, Stewart! Even the women hate the Jews, eh?"

Stewart gazed down at the deadly device before him. "Make sure you stand back from the explosion."

"Always! Always! I do not like the mess."

Haj Amin paced the length of the suite and then back again as Yassar Tafara sat staring forlornly at the brass samovar. Dressed only in his bulletproof vest and the baggy trousers of his shoub, the Mufti looked surprisingly thin and frail.

"And so we have been paying this . . . this . . . newspaperman! For what? He has already declared that the Jewish air force is as mighty as a new Luftwaffe! He claims a Blitzkrieg will annihilate all of Cairo! And possibly Damascus! Look!" He motioned to the drawn shades. "The city is blacked out!" He whirled around to face Yassar. "And *you* were sent to destroy these Zionists in Europe."

Yassar clasped his hands together. "Crabtree was hired by Maryanne Saint Martain." He pronounced the name slowly. "Always the Saints have chosen well their confederates. My cousin, I had nothing to do with this fellow. He was paid to find them. Which he did—"

"And then the Zionists paid him more to work on their behalf!" the Mufti roared. "And the Saint has also gone to the other side. The Führer once told me of the fickleness of humankind. They turned against him also when the Allies rose up with guns and tanks and endless men. The Americans are behind this all, and now King Abdullah negotiates for peace in earnest." He threw a vase against the wall. The crash made Yassar jump. "And all simply because these Americans—" He did not finish.

"You have said often yourself that the war against the Reich has not ended." Yassar tried to comfort him. "You are the only rightful ruler of Palestine and Jerusalem."

"But Abdullah will rule in my place. And he will be content to occupy only the portion of Palestine that the UN has given to the Arabs." He paused by his cluttered desk and snatched up a newspaper. "Two hundred fighter planes the Jews have. And mercenaries to fly them."

"We have also hired German pilots—"

"So the Germans and the Americans will fight again." He smiled at the irony. "And there will be war! Oh yes, Yassar! There will be war. We have made certain of that. But there will not be a Palestine for us when it is done. There will not be Israel, but there *will* be the land that Abdullah swallows up."

"Perhaps we may yet praise Allah," Yassar said thoughtfully. "Abdullah and the others will annihilate the Jews all the same."

Haj Amin shook with fury at the statement. "What difference does any of it make if I do not have my nation? if I do not rule in Jerusalem as Suleiman once ruled? What difference?"

Yassar considered his words. "Then we shall simply say the war has not ended. May it never end until the House of Husseini rules in Jerusalem."

Haj Amin put his hands to his head and sank into the large brocade chair at his desk. "Yes. Of course." His voice grew quiet, and some measure of calm returned. "Your brother, Gerhardt, still works to that end."

"My *brother*!" Yassar scoffed.

"Yes. Your brother," Haj Amin said threateningly. "Tonight he will put an end to negotiations between the Jews and Abdullah."

Yassar raised his eyebrows in surprise. "Yes? How can he do such a thing?"

"He has received information about the route of the Jewish negotiators. And the time. He will make an end of them tonight. The Zionists will assume it was a trap set by King Abdullah. That should end the talks of peace."

"How has he gotten this information?"

"Through an Englishman . . . a British officer who hates the Jews even as we do. He and Gerhardt have one particular Jew in mind, and your brother plans to settle this matter personally."

All of Czechoslovakia now lay beneath the shadow of the Communist hammer and sickle. The city of Prague was dirty, melancholy, and hungry when the small band of fliers arrived to take up residence in the massive Flora Hotel.

Ellie looked out from the window of her room on the litter of Wenceslas Square where only two months earlier Communist Premier Gottwald, riding in a Russian limousine, had come to announce his victory. Now Russian soldiers were everywhere, and the scaffolding that climbed the faces of war-damaged buildings gave the city the atmosphere of a prison. Great red banners were draped everywhere, and enormous portraits of Stalin hung alongside one of Comrade Gottwald in the lobby of the once-grand hotel.

The Americans were uneasy and anxious to get to their planes. Speeches blared over the radio denouncing opponents of Communism as "agents of foreign reaction."

"What does that make us?" Martin Feinsteinel had asked Avriel.

Avriel had put a finger to his lips and simply replied that the Russians had also voted for Partition and that it was important that no word of criticism be uttered. "The walls have ears," he whispered.

Purges had already begun. Arrest of opposition leaders had proceeded. Now Avriel could only hope that the arms deals he had transacted before the Communist takeover would still hold up in the face of the new and deadly regime.

Ellie exhaled loudly and looked around the seedy room. *Surely David must be home by now,* she thought. Then she smiled at the realization that Palestine had become *home.*

Avriel had warned her that she must keep her camera hidden, and that any news reports she wrote in the name of Crabtree must not mention the terrifying reality of the situation in Czechoslovakia. After all, they must attempt to remain on good terms until all their defense materials had been moved out of the country. That could be weeks, and until then, they would have to smile and nod and bribe.

The thought of it seemed almost revolting to Ellie, and suddenly she had a sense of being cut off behind enemy lines. She shuddered and sat down on the sagging bed. Like Dorothy in *The Wizard of Oz*, she wanted to click the heels of the ruby slippers and be home . . . home with David and Ben-Gurion and Moshe and Rachel and— "Uncle Howard and Miriam," she whispered aloud. "Dear God, I'm so homesick. . . ."

She resisted the urge to cry and held her chin high. "I feel alone in this terrible place, but I'm not, am I?"

A soft knock sounded on her door. "Ellie, it's Martin and Avriel. Are you decent?"

She opened the door and was surprised to see that they looked as worried and depressed as she felt. "What's wrong?"

Avriel put a finger to his lips and motioned toward the bathroom. She followed the two men into the tiny cubicle, where Avriel opened the taps and let the water rush out noisily.

"We were assigned these rooms," Avriel said. "Probably they've hidden microphones. We can't be too careful."

"Is David all right?" she asked with a sense of foreboding.

"We won't know that for a while," Avriel answered. "The only news we have now is that our people are still—even at this late hour—uncertain."

"Afraid of the armies massed at the borders," Martin added.

"We could be here for weeks," Avriel said gloomily. "Weeks in this place . . ." He looked toward the water-stained ceiling. "Anyway, we have two fighters in Palestine, and David asked that the first transport to Tel Aviv bring ammunition and spare parts for the 109s."

"I'm leaving tonight," Martin said so quietly that his words were nearly lost beneath the rushing water. "The C-47 can make it fifteen hundred miles nonstop. Be there by morning. The guys were talking. . . . We thought—" He looked at Avriel.

"Palestine is probably a whole lot safer place for an American journalist right now than Prague is," Avriel replied.

Ellie could see the concern in his eyes, even though his glasses were fogging up in the now-steamy bathroom. She couldn't help but laugh at the ridiculous conference. "You mean . . . I can be a spare part?" The relief was delicious. She was to be bound for Palestine within a matter of hours!

"You are no spare part." Avriel took off his glasses and grinned. "The Old Man will have plenty to keep you busy once the bombs start to fall!"

The C-47 had not departed from Prague in time. Loaded with ammunition, spare parts, and Ellie, it had hacked and coughed so badly after takeoff that Martin had been forced to circle and return immediately to the field.

Mechanics had checked and rechecked the complaining engine, and now, a dozen hours after its scheduled departure, it was taxiing onto the runway to wait for clearance for takeoff.

"Hold a moment, Service Airways," the tower responded over the radio as the propellers hummed a perfect harmony.

There were no other planes anywhere to be seen. Martin sniffed indignantly and turned to Ellie. "How long do they want us to wait, anyway?"

She shrugged. "Until the next war."

Again the voice crackled over the radio. *"Sorry for the delay, Service. Uh . . . we need to check the papers of one of your passengers— "*

Martin screwed up his face. "He's got to be kidding." He flipped the switch on the radio back and forth several times as he spoke. His transmission reached the tower something like this: "Rag . . . Prague tow . . . thi . . . Servi . . . C-four . . . clear . . . nd . . . eady . . . ake . . . off." Then he simply taxied forward and eased the big plane into the air as the tower shrieked protests over the radio.

"He didn't really mean it," Martin said to Ellie as he turned the radio to the off position. "If they really wanted to check your papers, they would have shot us down by now. That's a fundamental rule."

Within a few minutes they passed over the border of Austria, and Ellie was lost in sweet memories that seemed a long time ago.

Moshe helped Rachel pack for the journey.

"We will meet up with Golda Meir at the power station on our side of the border. You will wait there with the Haganah men while she and I cross over to speak with King Abdullah."

Rachel knew she could not go with Moshe on this last desperate attempt to avoid war, but she was afraid to remain behind while he traveled on such a dangerous mission. She nodded. "Tikvah and I will pray for you while you are gone."

"It is not even safe for you to go to the power station." His face reflected the weight of his concern. "But we will be going from there immediately to the Old Man in Tel Aviv to tell him of Abdullah's decision. And I will not leave you alone here in Jerusalem the night before Partition ends. Already the battles rage throughout the city."

Rachel carefully folded a small stack of Tikvah's clothes. "You said you wanted me in Tel Aviv." A slight smile was in her eyes. "This is an elaborate plan to get me there."

"More elaborate than I would like, I'm afraid." He did not laugh at her joke. "Look at you . . . so thin, and you expecting. If there had been any way at all, I would have had you there months ago. Now this seems like the best way to get you fed, *nu*?"

She frowned. "Moshe. Please do be careful. Please. I was frightened when you only went into the Old City. Now you travel to Amman—"

"Abdullah is a man of honor . . . the sort of honor Bedouins have, at any rate. We will have his protection as long as we talk. This is a council of enemies before the battle. Tomorrow, after the Mandate ends, will be another story. That is why I want you far from Jerusalem."

"What about Grandfather and Yacov?" Rachel said quietly. "They are in the heart of it. You have said that the Old City is the key to our state."

"We have slipped in enough small arms now, thanks to Stewart looking the other way. The Old City will be able to hold the Legion for a while anyway. And that is what we need—time! Time for the rest of the Yishuv to truly arm!"

"What about my grandfather?" Rachel pleaded. "And my brother?"

He held her by the shoulders. "You saw the tunnels. The shelters. Dov and the others will hold the Legion. The rabbis and children will pray. Far belowground, out of reach of the bullets and the bombs, your grandfather will pray until we break through Zion Gate from the outside."

He searched her face. "Rachel, you must pray also. Your grandfather went back into the Old City knowing full well what the end might be. He went knowing that they remained there to buy us time . . . precious time! A few days would be enough to bring in the weapons we need! And perhaps in a few days we will be able to save the Old City."

Rachel stared down at the small suitcase. "When can I return to Jerusalem, Moshe? When will you bring me home?"

Moshe embraced her. "If Abdullah agrees to allow Jerusalem to be governed by the UN, then there will be no war. And I will bring you back right after statehood is declared. Tomorrow or after the Shabbat."

"And if not?"

"We will not think of that until we have to."

❂

Gerhardt had stepped out, muttering that he needed a fuse and another detonator.

Dusk was falling over the city as Sarai stepped to the barred window to look out one last time. Pigeons rose like a plume above the great dome of the Church of the Holy Sepulchre as the evening bells rang out. *They are locking the doors now, but Your tomb is still open and empty, is it not, el-Kiama? I will cling to that hope. As You whispered to my heart in the garden that night. I will remember how You, innocent, died for me. How You saw me from Golgotha. And I will follow You. El-Kiama. Resurrection. Yes. It is right that I follow You.*

She bathed herself and dressed in the bright lavender dress, the field of flowers stitched in love. And then, before Gerhardt returned to ridicule and tear and rave, she traced the bouquets with her fingertips. How she longed to meet the old woman who had created such a garden. . . . How she ached to speak with her in their own tongue and recite words of love and joy that they shared el-Kiama, their Savior.

"Perhaps I will meet her," Sarai said aloud. She sighed and pulled the long black dress over the garden so she would not be seen in the night.

ANY RISK
FOR PEACE

In the Old City, Ehud and Dov huddled together with Rabbi Vultch as they studied the map Stewart had provided. In precise detail, the map of the Old City showed the exact position of the British outposts along the perimeter and the order and time of scheduled withdrawal. More incredibly, the strength and position of Arab Legion outposts were also noted in red. The time of withdrawal had not been announced officially, nor would it be. But thanks to the map, the men of the Old City Haganah were ready to take British positions the minute they pulled out.

Although many others believed that the city would immediately be saved by United Nations intervention, the men in the little basement headquarters would not trust that hope.

"As Stewart pulls out, we move forward." Dov traced a line along the rooftops. "Here. Four men."

"Only four, Dov?" Ehud stuck out his lower lip in concern.

"There are a dozen forward positions," Dov said, tapping each one. "The most important is Zion Gate. If we can swarm the Armenian Quarter and hold Zion Gate, then our troops outside the walls will be able to come in and reinforce us."

"A miracle." Ehud clapped his hands good-naturedly. "We will maybe even survive awhile! *Oy!*" He raised his eyes to heaven.

Rabbi Vultch was not laughing. "And if Zion Gate should fall?"

"Then the Arabs will have us here. Ducks in a puddle," Ehud said with a calmness that belied the seriousness of the situation.

"Yes. So everything else must be a holding action, *nu?*" Dov marked the perimeter. "Our main force must be to keep the gate open!"

"How many men do you think they will send against us?" Rabbi Vultch stared hard at the marked Arab fortifications.

"How many do they have, Rebbe Vultch?" Ehud laughed. "That is how many they will send."

"The gate—" Vultch pointed toward the position of Zion Gate.

It seemed so far from the Quarter, Dov thought.

"There is a chance if we can keep the gate open." Rabbi Vultch repeated the words as though they were a comfort to him. At last, the precarious buffer of British forces was being withdrawn. What they had planned for in these tunnels, what they had lived for and feared, was about to come upon them.

"More than a chance," Dov comforted. "Our friends in the New City will not abandon us." Then a terrifying thought came to him. "What . . . what if the English lock the gate when they leave? What if we are locked in and our comrades are locked out and—"

"Then we will blast it open." Ehud frowned.

The thought of such an action was disturbing. Certainly it would cost precious lives to accomplish it.

"At least we have much more now than we had two weeks ago." Dov mentally checked off the list of explosives that had been slipped in with the convoys. "Stewart has not checked a manifest in the last four deliveries."

"Reason to wonder if the bullets have gunpowder, if you ask me." Ehud grimaced.

"You are joking!" Vultch looked stricken.

Ehud thumped his chest. "*Oy!* Me joke? Never."

"He *is* joking, and the point is that we have enough to last a whole week. We can hold the Arabs a week. That should be enough time—"

"For what?" Ehud and Vultch asked in unison.

"To . . . hold them! That is what!"

"Meshuggener!" Ehud cried, slapping his forehead. "Why didn't I think of that?"

"This Alamo that Rebbe Lebowitz speaks of—" Rabbi Vultch scratched his head—"has he ever told what became of the men who fought there?"

"Yes." Dov answered with a smile. "They held the gate open and their comrades rode in and rescued them."

"Truly?" Vultch looked relieved.

"Certainly." Dov grinned broadly. "And if you don't believe me, just ask the Americans." *Why should he know the real story?* Dov mused. *One lie—a little one—to calm the good rabbi's jangled nerves. What can it hurt?*

Later he took the American volunteers aside one by one and asked them to rewrite history with a happier ending. Such illusions would be needed, Dov decided, for the long days ahead.

Sarai's eyes grew wide as Gerhardt drove east from Jerusalem to descend the mountains of Palestine that towered above the Dead Sea. Jericho, with its brown rooftops and little stone houses, was already alive with the roar of Arab Legion tanks and armored vehicles as they moved west toward Jerusalem. A few miles beyond, Gerhardt was waved easily through Legion checkpoints and into the Wadi Shuieb, where the Allenby Bridge crossed the Jordan River into Jordan.

Darkness was thick by now, and they had to wait on the west bank of the river as two tanks creaked and groaned across the bridge. Gerhardt cursed and honked and finally threatened until traffic heading into Palestine was held for them to pass.

It is all too late, too late, Sarai thought. If Moshe had indeed gone to negotiate with the king, it was a useless, futile gesture—one that had drawn evil nearer to him with every mile they traveled.

Sarai looked at Gerhardt. His angry eyes were fixed on the rutted road that now wound north toward his target. *He is scarcely a man. So consumed by his hatred is he that he has become hatred.* He was as one possessed, and the knowledge of that filled her with fear. *Suppose he hears my thoughts?* She shuddered and tried to think of her mother and her sisters and the shady courtyard of her home in Sheikh Jarrah. Life had been pleasant then. A wonderful moment of sunlight that now had passed away.

She stared out the window. The land was desolate—a land of scorpions and vipers. It was no wonder King Abdullah coveted Jerusalem!

Sarai closed her eyes and remembered the sweet scents of flowers on the summer air. There had been no bars on her windows. No fear in her heart. She called up the image of her mother's face and held it high between her and Gerhardt. *If he hears my thoughts, he will see only Mother. He will not kill me for thinking of her.* Pretending to sleep, she laid her cheek against the seat as Gerhardt rushed through the black night toward the northern bridge across the Jordan.

The wind came from the west and swept up the pass and into Jerusalem. Moshe held tightly to his hat as he helped Rachel into the flimsy Piper Cub. It shook and rattled in defiance, as though it did not want to fly in such a gale.

The pilot was a worried-looking young man from Tel Aviv. David

Meyer had taught him to fly, he told them, but he had never flown in such a wind.

Moshe frowned and climbed in bravely beside him. "We have no choice," he instructed the young man. "We have to meet Mrs. Meir at the power plant by nine this evening. She cannot go on to Amman without me. And we must go to Amman!"

"We may find ourselves some place besides Jordan if we take off in this!" The little plane shuddered.

Moshe was insistent. "I would go through hell if it meant saving Jewish lives!" he shouted above the roar of the engine.

And so, as Tikvah squalled at the top of her lungs, the Piper coughed and sputtered into a reluctant takeoff against the wind that had sought to ground it.

They flew northward toward Galilee. The land below was mostly Arab land. Ramallah. Nablus. Jenin. The pilot ticked off the names, but all the land below was lost in inky blackness.

"The Arabs are afraid of our air force!" The young pilot laughed as the engine coughed and sputtered. "That Crabtree fellow has made them all duck when the shadow of a bird passes overhead! Quite a good chap! They're all cowering in their little houses now at the sound of our plane!"

He chatted and laughed most of the way as though he were grateful for the company. Rachel's heart was heavy with a foreboding that had come with the wind, so she was glad that she did not have to answer questions or talk.

"Fifteen minutes!" the young man called over the noise of the bucking plane.

Rachel felt sick and near tears. *"Fifteen minutes, and I will have to say good-bye,"* her heart seemed to say. She tried to think of other things, like dear Ellie writing her outrageous columns in the name of Crabtree. But nothing helped.

Minutes slipped by until finally a single light beckoned from the ground. Seconds later, a row of headlights illuminated a dirt strip, and the plane dipped down for a landing.

Moshe helped Rachel from the plane. The blackness of the night was profound, broken only by an arch of stars that swept from one side of the horizon to the other.

They stood for a moment, then turned instinctively toward the sound of rushing water and the thrumming beat of a mammoth's heart.

"The turbines," Moshe said. "The power plant."

Soon they were surrounded by dark, whispering figures who glided from the surrounding field and led them toward the pulsing hum.

"She is already here, Professor Sachar—"

" . . . arrived by car from Haifa an hour ago."

" . . . impatient to be off."

Rachel held the baby close as they topped a rise and looked down on the dark building of the plant that crouched beside the Jordan River just below the Sea of Galilee. The power station was in Jewish hands for now and provided electricity to both Jordan and Palestine. It would undoubtedly be a prize hotly contested by both sides—and tonight Haganah soldiers were everywhere along the ravines and wadis that surrounded it.

The main building was on the west bank of the river, officially on the soil of Palestine. The roar of waters became louder as they walked along a path that led to the three-story plant. It was made of corrugated tin, which seemed to vibrate with every wind of the turbines. Rachel gazed across the inky black waters of the Jordan River. Power lines stretched from conductors to imposing towers that led straight from this place to Amman, the capital of Transjordan.

"Tonight King Abdullah's palace will be illuminated by this power," said the voice of a faceless soldier. "You must think of us here on the west bank. . . . Our prayers go with you."

Moshe nodded, and in that instant, the black-cloaked figure of an Arab woman stepped from the shadows. It was Golda Meir, veiled and disguised in traditional Arab dress. "*Shalom*," she said to Moshe.

Someone handed him a keffiyeh and white shoub to put on over his clothes. He dressed quickly. In the end, he looked like a Bedouin sheikh standing beside his wife.

"How do I look?" Moshe turned to Rachel in final farewell.

"Convincing." She kissed him lightly. "Be careful."

He nodded. "Remember the hand that guides me," he whispered in her ear.

The deep voice of Golda Meir said insistently, "Abdullah has sent his most trusted servant to pick us up. He will be waiting for us now." She pointed across the river. "The king sent word that our visit is entirely at our own risk. He has not warned any member of the Legion that we are coming. We cannot miss our ride."

There was no more time. Rachel wanted to hold Moshe tightly, to keep him from going . . . or she wanted to go with him. He embraced her quickly. There was no more time for words. He appeared briefly as a ghostly apparition, stark against the black waters as they crossed the river on the footbridge, and then he was gone.

Rachel's heart cried out to him, *"Come back! Do not leave me!"*

"The risk is great," said a soldier who stood at her side. "But if they might bring peace back with them . . ." His words held the hope and prayer of every heart in the Yishuv tonight.

Rachel swallowed hard and touched the face of their sleeping child. *He goes for you, Tikvah. And for the child of our love.* "Yes," she said, still searching the darkness of the eastern bank of the Jordan for one last glimpse of Moshe. "Yes. Any risk for peace."

The black sedan was parked beside the dirt road, just beyond a hill over-looking the river. At the approach of their footsteps, the driver opened the door and stood beside the vehicle.

"Salaam," Moshe said as he bowed in traditional greeting, and then he added, *"Zurbati."*

"Salaam, Professor Sachar, Mrs. Meir," came the whispered reply. He opened the rear door. "Get in. We must hurry. You are late."

The man who drove them was an Iraqi by birth and the most trusted of all King Abdullah's servants. Moshe could only hope that they were not too late—too late to stop the advance of the armies now assembling on the desert of Transjordan. Ahead was the first of many military check-points along the long, bumpy road to Amman.

Red-checked keffiyehs glared in the headlights. A tank was parked alongside the road, its cannon pointed toward Palestine like the needle of a compass. "Are those Iraqi soldiers with the Arab Legion?" Moshe asked as he spotted a different uniform among the more familiar Jordanians.

"Yes," said the driver, almost with irritation. It was as though the out-come of these talks was already settled. "Now you must keep silence!" he hissed as they pulled to the roadblock.

The beam of a flashlight shone in Moshe's eyes as the Legion guard scrutinized the passengers of the car. A quiet exchange took place between the driver and the soldier, ending with the word *"Zurbati."* Then machine guns were raised, and the automobile was allowed to pass.

The mutual hatred between the Mufti and King Abdullah had been growing since the early days of the British Mandate in Palestine. Abdullah was fond of reminding his followers, "My father always told me to beware of preachers."

The issue with Abdullah is not a matter of a holy war, Moshe thought as they traveled over the black and desolate countryside, *but rather one of simple politics.*

Once this dusty kingdom had been a part of Palestine. Winston

Churchill had awarded it to Abdullah as a consolation prize after his family had been driven, first by the Saudis, from their rightful throne by the Red Sea and then from Damascus by the French. The little nation was, as Churchill boasted, "created with a stroke of a pen on a Sunday afternoon in Cairo." In effect, the creation of Transjordan had also vastly cut down the area the British had promised to the Jews as a homeland, so all concerned had been disappointed.

Now there was some hope that Transjordan could be rejoined with at least part of Palestine, and on this proposal the Zionists hung their fragile hope for peace—that is, if King Abdullah would not cast his eye on the Jewish lands and lust after them also. And then there was the matter of Jerusalem! This was the capital that King Abdullah longed to call his own.

Golda Meir sat rigidly beside Moshe as they approached another military checkpoint. A long line of armored vehicles moved west as they moved east. The good woman did not speak, but Moshe was certain that her thoughts matched his own. *There are so many! How will we ever face such a force? How?*

Again the flashlight shone on them. *"Zurbati,"* whispered the driver, and they were waved through.

Golda heaved a sigh of relief; then her eyes followed the long line of headlights that faced them. "So many," she whispered.

Moshe pulled his thoughts from the terrifying reality of what they faced. He thought of topics that might take their minds away from the certain loss of Jewish lives if they failed in their mission tonight. "When we arrive, there will be ceremonial cups of coffee to drink and afterward a large meal. You must eat."

"I cannot think of eating."

"You must, or they will think that you scorn their hospitality."

She nodded once, then continued to look at a troop truck full of Iraqi soldiers as it moved toward the border. "God help us," she muttered.

Moshe shook his head to clear it. "Eat with your right hand," he instructed as though he did not hear the pounding fear in his own heart. The truth was that he could scarcely think of eating either. His thoughts returned to Rachel and the baby waiting at the power station—waiting and hoping for a miracle.

42

WAITING AND HOPING

Still miles from their destination, Gerhardt parked the car and sat silently. He lifted his head as if to sniff the wind for the scent of his prey. Sarai heard the distant throb of the power plant.

"They are here," he said. "Come."

He shouldered a heavy pack and set out on foot without regard to the young woman who struggled to keep pace with him. The pulse of the power plant became stronger as they climbed the bank of a ravine and moved through a stand of rushes.

Far away, Sarai could see the silhouettes of the towers in vivid relief against the starlit sky.

"They will follow those lines," Gerhardt said. "The driver will let them out early beside the road. Then they will walk along those towers back toward the footbridge."

Sarai did not answer as she held the hem of her dress up from the dust of their trail. Her breath was short, and her sides ached with the exertion. The brush tore at her legs and ankles until she could feel warm blood trickle into her shoes. Although she felt as if her lungs would burst, she did not protest, lest Gerhardt leave her and go on with his mission without her.

Twice more Gerhardt paused to sniff the wind like a wolf in pursuit of a deer. Clutching her dress, Sarai glanced at his shadow. With the pack he seemed hunched and deformed—the inhuman image of a beast in the night. Tears of fear stung her eyes. *I must not let him hear my thoughts. El-Kiama! Help me! He is the very shadow of death!* She conjured up the face of her father, eyes full of sympathy, stroking her head when she lay ill. *"The pain is only a little while, Sarai. You will be well again soon. Do not weep, my little Sarai. Do not be afraid."*

Gerhardt climbed a knoll ahead of her and stood above her, looking out across the land. He seemed not to notice when she stepped up behind him.

"There it is," he said at last. "The footbridge. They will return to Palestine by that route. There is no other way." Then, pointing to the dark line that crossed the Jordan, he added, "Of course, they shall not return to Palestine at all."

After passing through ten blockades, the car reached the outskirts of Amman. The driver turned right and drove up a long, winding road that led to an ornate stone house at the top of the hill.

"You shall not meet at the palace," said the driver, "but here. It is too dangerous for you to be seen at the palace."

They were ushered into a pale green, circular room, dominated by a huge, black-tiled fireplace. A pleasant Turkish woman offered them cups of tea in welcome, and then they sat in silence to wait.

Twenty minutes passed. Their tea was scarcely touched. And then at the head of the staircase appeared the thin, frail man they had come to see. Moshe was startled by the sadness that etched the little monarch's face. He descended the stairs carefully.

Golda and Moshe stood.

"*Salaam*," King Abdullah said in a quiet voice.

"*Shalom*," Moshe and Golda replied.

Both words meant simply "peace," and Moshe could not help but reflect on how alike the two greetings were. As they were led to a smaller room where coffee was served, Moshe noticed how pale and strained Abdullah seemed in the light.

"It has been a long time since I have seen you, Habibi, my dear friend," Abdullah said to Moshe. "Since together we fought the Germans."

Moshe smiled, aware that small talk was an important part of the custom. "Amman has grown up since last I was here, Your Majesty," he said in perfect Arabic. Golda Meir did not speak even a word of the language, so she tried to smile calmly through an extended conversation from which she was excluded.

At last the moment came when the point of their visit was addressed. Abdullah looked directly at Golda and, as Moshe translated, began to speak. "You have journeyed here at great peril to your life."

"Have you broken your pledge to us after all?" she asked.

"When I made that pledge, in hope of peace, I was in control of my own destiny and could do what I thought was right. But since, I have learned otherwise. Before I was alone. Now I am one of five."

"But you are the most powerful of the Arab League."

"The League is a sack into which have been thrust five heads," Abdullah said carefully. "I am but one of those."

"Do you not understand? We are your only true allies in the region."

"And so we can be allies," said the king. "Why are you in such a hurry to proclaim your state? There might still be peace. Why are you so impatient?"

"We have waited two thousand years. One cannot call that being in a hurry."

Abdullah listened as Moshe translated. Then he shrugged. "Yes. I understand. But it is not up to me."

"You could annex the Arab portion of Palestine, and war could be avoided. Jerusalem would not belong to either state."

Abdullah smiled slightly at her remark. "Jerusalem," he said, "where the caliphs of Suleiman ruled. I am myself of the blood of the prophet. It is not fitting that Jerusalem be handed over to the infidels to rule."

Golda frowned slightly as Moshe translated. Moshe understood her frown. Abdullah had made up his mind. Jerusalem would be his. "You know that if war is forced upon us, we will fight and we will win."

Abdullah sighed. "I know it is your duty to fight. But why don't you wait a few years? Drop your demands for free immigration. I will take over the whole country, and you will be represented in my parliament. I will treat you very well, and there will be no war."

"That is not possible," Golda responded through Moshe. "You know how hard we have worked and all we have done. Do you think we have done this just to be represented in a foreign parliament?"

"Listen to the cry of the young men in my souks! They cry for war! Can I deny this if you resist my help?"

"You know who we are and what we want. You know to what we have aspired for two thousand years. We cannot deny our hearts. If you can offer us nothing more than you have just done, then there will be war, and we will win it—"

"Tonight you have seen our tanks," King Abdullah said in a tired-sounding voice.

Until then, Moshe had simply repeated the words of one leader to the other. Now he spoke from his own heart. "You put too much reliance on your tanks. You have no real friends in the Arab world, and we will smash your tanks with our air force." These were brave words considering the true state of Jewish defenses, but Moshe was certain the "Crabtree dispatches" had also alarmed the little king. Thick fabric covered the windows to keep any light from escaping in the event of an air raid.

Abdullah looked grave and unhappy at Moshe's words. He hesitated.

"You must do your duty as I must bow to mine. The events of tomorrow are in the hands of Allah the Merciful. All of us shall someday know what fate has in store for us."

There was no more to say. They had run the perilous gauntlet only to reach a dead end. For all of Moshe's brave thoughts and words, the tanks of the Arab Legion were real.

They filled their plates at a table heaped with food, but neither Moshe nor Golda ate more than a few bites. They were heartsick at the news they would have to bring back. The journey ahead of them was long and dangerous, and there were no hopes of peace to boost their spirits. There would be war—that was certain and irrevocable, and King Abdullah had marked Jerusalem as the capital of his nation.

Jammed in the back of Martin's C-47, Ellie arrived in Palestine with the rest of the spare parts. She felt thoroughly rattled by the nine-hour non-stop flight from Czechoslovakia, and worse, as she stood at the end of the airfield, Sam Baker, one of the Americans David had hired, explained to her that neither David nor Bobby Milkin had arrived.

"But they should have been here yesterday!" Martin exclaimed. "Have you got feelers out on this? When were they last seen?"

"They refueled in Yugoslavia. After that—well, we just haven't heard from them or anybody who ought to know."

Ellie felt sick and dizzy from the heat and the terrible disappointment. She put her hand to her head. "Not here," she said softly, as though the words were too brutal to be believed. "David. Not here."

Martin mopped his brow, then put an arm around Ellie's sagging shoulders. "It's not likely that both of them would have engine trouble," he tried to reassure her. "I mean, they wouldn't *both* disappear over the ocean or anything terrible like that—"

"There haven't been any reports of plane crashes, Ellie," Sam added, looking worried for causing her undue concern. "We think they're someplace."

"Well, of course they're someplace!" she flashed, suddenly too exhausted to hold up well. She covered her eyes and bowed her head. "He's just not here! Oh, David! Tinman! Why aren't you here?"

Sam shifted uncomfortably in the face of Ellie's obvious distress. He peered at the huge aircraft and shook his head. "So. We have a planeload of 109 spare parts and ammo, and no 109s."

"That's about the size of it," Martin said grimly.

"What a way to come into a war." Sam shook his head. "Come on, you two." He walked toward a waiting vehicle. "The Old Man wants to see you in Tel Aviv."

In Ben-Gurion's cluttered study in Tel Aviv, Ellie and Martin sat across from the Old Man and listened as he explained the situation.

"David and Bobby Milkin have been arrested."

Ellie bit her lip. She was relieved that David was only locked in a cell in Athens instead of lying in the rubble of his plane as she had imagined the last few hours. "Can they do that? Can the British just pick him up like that?"

"There are warrants out on him in a dozen different languages," the Old Man said. "As there are on you." He looked at Martin. "It was good you brought her here. A dispatch from Avriel said that the Secret Police tore her room apart shortly after you left."

Ellie could scarcely believe it. She felt the furthest thing from a desperate international criminal. "What will they do with David?"

"The Italians have been contacted. Extradition is being requested, but they'll have to stand in line, I'm afraid." He rubbed his forehead wearily. "The U.S. State Department is going to do what it can. A fellow named Tom Kane is quite a fan of your husband's." He directed his stern gaze at Martin. "You'll have to carry on. We've unloaded your plane. Are you able to fly back?"

"Tonight?"

"I cannot tell you how important it is that the flights begin when we give the word. We need you there, loaded and waiting. I'm afraid that the cargo you brought us is of little use—that is, with the exception of Ellie."

"Most of the transports are already in Europe," Martin said, reaching for his hat.

"David Meyer left you in command." Ben-Gurion stuck out his hand. "That is good enough for me." The two shook hands. *"Shalom."*

"Shalom," said Martin; then he winked at Ellie. "He's a tough guy. I wouldn't worry about him too much. With the State Department working on it—"

Ellie's words caught in her throat. "Be careful, Martin," she called after the young pilot as he left to repeat the nine-hour flight.

The Old Man had not slept for days, Ellie knew. Sam had told her. For a moment, his eyes glazed with exhaustion; then he caught himself and looked up. "So much to do. And tonight is the hardest task of all . . .*waiting!*"

Gerhardt remained deep in the shadows by the road. He had time—lots
of time—and he was in no particular hurry to spread his net for the feet
of his enemies. It had been arranged that they would be late.

He gazed up at the black windows of the power plant. There would be
sentries there, staring out into the darkness even now. But he, Gerhardt,
had become a shadow long ago. Darkness was home to him. He moved
most easily beneath the very noses of his prey.

The engines of the power plant drummed a primitive rhythm, like
drums of war in ancient battles. Gerhardt closed his eyes and rejoiced
for a moment in that god of war.

Sarai watched Gerhardt with fear.

"Sit!" he hissed to Sarai.

She obeyed instantly, dropping to the ground.

Gerhardt laid the pack beside her. Then, crouched in his black robes,
he moved away in the darkness. Sarai's eyes tried to follow him as he fit
himself into the shadows that fringed the road. His form seemed to melt
into the patterns until even she could not tell which was he and which
was the night. He moved among the ancient demons of her Bedouin
forefathers, and her breath became short with the terror she felt.

El-Kiama, she prayed silently, *see me here and help me! El-Kiama!*

Only a few yards from the footbridge the road dipped, creating a
shallow depression where the blackness of Gerhardt poured into the
shadow. *He will put his web there.* Sarai studied the small mound that
was just high enough to conceal him as he worked. *There, where they are
certain to walk, he will spread this net of wire and plant the mines. And they
will step into the shadow and dissolve in the light.*

She prayed that the rush of the water would drown her thoughts so
that Gerhardt would not hear. She looked at the pack and remembered
what Gerhardt had said about the mines: *"They cannot be disarmed."* She
remembered Moshe with his arms around Rachel, the way he looked
when he held the baby.

"They will not hear me," Gerhardt said, emerging beside her.

She jumped at the sound of his voice.

"You are frightened?" he asked, and the question was full of scorn.
"You have not seen a Jew in pieces," he said lightly, pulling the pack
toward him.

She could barely speak. "Will . . . will we remain here to see it?"

"You would like that?" His teeth glinted.

Sarai did not answer his question. Instead she thought of her mother for the thousandth time. She could not let him see Rachel or Moshe in her eyes. She could not show him the baby or the goat—or the Voice in the garden that had given her such joy.

"The revenge of Deir Yassin, for you?" he asked.

Jewish soldiers. Laughing. Tearing. Hurting. Killing. Yes, I will remember the evil of Deir Yassin. For that is what I face tonight. The death of the innocent. Arab. Jew. Innocent. And evil lies in wait to kill the innocent! A net of wire in the sand!

"Yes," she answered, knowing full well that the evil that had robbed her was crouching beside her at this moment. *The same! The very same!* "Yes, Fredrich Gerhardt," she said, "tonight I will have revenge for Deir Yassin."

The clock above the desk in the power plant supervisor's office read 1:07. Tikvah slept happily to the hum of the engines while Rachel sat in quiet consternation in the midst of a group of young Haganah soldiers from nearby Naharayim. They spoke in hushed whispers about what they would face if tonight's mission failed.

Rachel could think only of Moshe. They were late coming back, and on that one life, her entire world seemed to hang.

"Moddy, go up to the top, will you? See if you can spot anyone out there."

"I just came down. I tell you, nothing is on that road—not even a spider."

Rachel raised her chin slightly. "May I go? I am . . . I would like to see, please."

"There's nothing to see," said the one called Moddy. "But let me finish my coffee and I'll go up with you."

Up meant a series of metal ladders that led to the catwalk at the top of the whining turbines. The precarious third-story perch boasted a row of windows—the best lookout available. Throughout the long watch three men stood sentry duty at that lofty post.

Moddy stared at Rachel's long, embroidered Arab gown. "Not much for climbing ladders."

Rachel simply returned his look. "I can go up alone if you like."

He grinned and shrugged. "We're going to be crowded up there." He stepped onto the ladder and began his ascent as Rachel held her dress above her knees and climbed after him with stern resolve. Tier after tier they climbed until they reached the dizzying height of the catwalk. The heat was intense up here, and all of the dozen windows were open to let the hot air escape. The concrete floor was a long way down, and Rachel gripped the flimsy rail of the catwalk fiercely.

She peered out into the pitch-black of the night. No light reflected on the surface of the river. No movement was seen in the solitary land beyond it. Rachel wondered how the sentries could see, anyway. The territory was shrouded in the night.

Moddy had sauntered confidently down the narrow walkway and with a flourish returned to offer Rachel a pair of heavy binoculars. "For seeing at night." He smirked. "A little something I picked up from British Intelligence. Go on! Have a look! They work pretty good."

Rachel nodded her thanks to him. The noise of the turbines seemed too great to talk over. She held the binoculars to her eyes and peered over the Jordan again. "A miracle!" she exclaimed in delight at the sudden detail that had been obscured moments before.

"Look over toward the power lines," Moddy directed her. "They'll be coming that way. When we see them, Paul will pull the switch and turn on the floodlights."

Using the glasses, Rachel stayed at the window, tracing and retracing the rocky road along the power lines. *They will come that way. . . . They must come that way!* While the sentries chatted amiably above the roar of the plant, Rachel remained rooted on the narrow metal catwalk, at last feeling as though she was doing something useful. Moshe would not be happy at the thought of her three stories above a concrete floor, but the waiting had nearly driven her mad. Now they were late, and if the power of hope and love could draw them somehow nearer to safety, Rachel wanted to stand as the highest beacon.

She did not know how many minutes had passed before Moddy asked for the binoculars again, but in that time she had memorized every rock and rut on the road. With regret she returned the glasses, but still she stood in the heat and the noise even after Moddy offered to help her down.

"No, thank you," she called above the din.

"When you want down," Moddy returned, "tell Paul or Jonathan." He pointed down the catwalk. "It gets hot up here, Mrs. Sachar," he warned. "You won't pass out or anything?" He seemed suddenly doubtful that he should leave her.

Rachel glanced out at the blackness. Without the binoculars, there was little use in her staying. She bit her lip at the memory of her sudden dizziness the day the water truck was bombed. Heights always made her feel woozy. "Maybe I should come down." She changed her mind and stretched out her hand as Moddy helped her onto the ladder.

The temperature cooled with every step downward. Still Rachel's hair pressed against her neck from the perspiration. Her legs felt shaky even after she put her feet on the solid floor of the plant, so she hung on to the ladder for support.

"Please," she asked the concerned Haganah guard, "can I go outside?"

Again he looked doubtful. "It may be better if you wait in here." He frowned at her pale skin. "Are you all right?"

Yes, she thought, *only pregnant.* But she did not say it. "I could use some fresh air, if you please."

He nodded reluctantly and led her to the side door that faced the river and the footbridge. A blast of cool breeze washed over her, and she threw her head back in relief to look up at the stars. Moddy stepped out with her, but she said to him, "I would like just a minute by myself."

"This is not a summer camp, Mrs. Sachar," he warned. "I am supposed to look out for you. Don't go anywhere." He disappeared back into the thundering building.

Only a dozen feet from her was a boulder overlooking the bridge and the river. Rachel walked to it, choosing her path carefully. All around her were the sandbagged outposts of the frontline Haganah of Galilee. Rachel sat, leaned her back against the hard stone, and clasped her knees to her. The air felt good against her damp skin. The sound of a night bird called from the rushes by the riverbank, and Rachel bowed her head and prayed that Moshe's delay meant good news for these who waited with her—peace to the Yishuv!

43

LIGHT IN THE DARKNESS

A different driver took Moshe and Golda Meir west, back toward the Jordan River. Through the windows of the car, they saw Iraqi forces massing at Camp Mafraq. In hushed whispers they spoke of what would happen later that day. A sense of failure and disappointment rested heavily on their shoulders.

"If we are lucky—and victorious," Moshe said to Golda, "we might lose only ten thousand men. If we are unlucky, we could have up to fifty thousand casualties."

Golda shook her head in despair. "Please—" she held up her hand—"no more words." And so the rest of the journey passed in silence ringed by terror as they slipped through the enemy lines back to the power station.

The closer they got to their destination, the more fearful their driver seemed to become. He uttered the password with a shaking voice and did not answer when Moshe asked him how far they were from their destination.

Always they followed the route parallel to the great power lines that linked Jordan to Palestine. When they at last drove through the tenth barricade, the driver pulled to the side of the road. He turned and placed his arm on the back of the seat. When he raised his hand, Moshe and Golda found themselves staring down the barrel of a gun.

"Get out!" the man demanded.

Golda narrowed her eyes. "Why don't you just shoot us and make an end to it now?" She was angry and defiant. "You turn us out too far from the border."

"Get out!" the man shouted. "I am not paid to shoot, only to drive. And I am not paid to drive any farther than this! Your border is there!" He waved the gun. "And I *will* shoot if you do not get out now!"

Had King Abdullah arranged this? Moshe could not believe that. The monarch had given them a message to take back to the Yishuv. This was not his doing.

"What are you afraid of?" Moshe asked. "We are still a mile from the river! You cannot let us out here."

"Get out!" said the trembling Arab, as though those were the only words he knew to speak.

Moshe opened the door and helped Golda out onto the deserted stretch of road. The car roared away in a billowing cloud of dust, eating the distance in half the time it had taken to arrive.

"Well," said Golda in a shaking voice, "I guess we should have eaten more of the king's dinner."

Moshe laughed, even though he did not feel like it. Perhaps they had left the last enemy blockade behind them, but it still was a long way to the footbridge. They were already nearly an hour later than they had anticipated. The soldiers who guarded the plant would be concerned, and worst of all, Rachel would be waiting and frantic with worry.

"If we follow the power lines"—Moshe pointed up and tried to sound reassuring—"we will be there in a few minutes." He wished now that he had brought a gun.

The dust died away, and they began their slow trek through the darkness. The crunch of the gravel beneath their feet seemed too loud, and the night sounds of the desert called an ominous warning of what was to come from the east. Moshe could not help but think that lives were now measured in hours, that death pursued the Yishuv along this very road.

He looked at the starlit heavens and could find no peace or beauty in the sight to satisfy his soul. Abdullah had said that each would know soon enough what fate held for them.

Gerhardt worked with skilled fingers, laying the web ten feet across and five feet wide. It was deeper than the stride of a man, and the wires were close enough together that even one footstep would break the current and trigger the mines. He lay on his belly in the gravel and hissed for Sarai to pass him a needed tool or another coil of wire from the pack. The Jews could not hear their whispered words. The thrum of the power plant concealed them.

"How heavy must one be to break the current?" Sarai whispered.

He rose slightly to consider the question. "Not heavy."

"A rabbit? A mouse?"

"The wire is thin, like thread. Not a mouse. Maybe a dog." He twisted and clipped and laid the grid of fragile wire as he spoke. "I shall teach your brother this."

"Poor Yassar," she said quietly.

"What?" he demanded.

She faltered and hesitated. "Poor Yassar . . . he . . . is not so clever as you. . . ."

"You have found your tongue, girl, and become a cousin of Haj Amin!" He enjoyed her flattery. "Perhaps you will make a warrior."

She touched the hem of the lavender dress, still totally concealed beneath her outer garb. *Light and color. Not darkness and shadow.*

Gerhardt spoke again, irritated by her silence. "You may learn tonight to be a Jihad Moquade."

She answered, "A Holy Struggler." She paused, then added, "Yes. Tonight I learn."

"And your greatest enemy is destroyed."

"Yes." Her voice sounded hollow. "The Shetan of Deir Yassin."

"What? What are you thinking, girl? What is wrong with you?" He crawled toward her.

She shrank back. "I . . . was remembering . . . it frightened me."

Her answer evidently satisfied him, for he returned to his work. "Then watch and see them in pieces."

"How long?" she asked, uncertain that she could stand much more. "How long until you finish?"

"Fifteen minutes," he answered, then asked for another roll of wire.

Moddy came out and called Rachel's name, concerned when he did not see her by the door.

"I am here," Rachel said, standing and brushing herself off.

He strode toward her quickly. "Are you ready to come back in?" he asked impatiently. He was worried enough about the safety of the professor and Golda Meir. He did not enjoy the added worry of Professor Sachar's wife bounding about the plant grounds.

She asked quietly, "Is the baby awake?"

"The baby? No. Not the baby. She is sleeping like a . . . like a baby," he finished, feeling foolish. "No, I just think you are safer indoors and I—"

Rachel smiled and put a hand on his arm to calm him. "I was just sitting here praying."

"Oh." He looked surprised.

"And it is much nicer to pray when I am here under the stars instead of . . . in there; don't you think so?"

"I suppose."

"So. Also I want to wait here. Near the footbridge, so that when my husband comes, I will be able to kiss him hello."

Moddy had no argument for either of the two reasons she wanted to remain where she was. "Well . . ." was all he could say.

"Are you going back aloft to keep watch?" she asked gently.

"Yes. Just going. They should be here," he worried. "Yes. I'm going up."

"Then you watch, and I will pray." Rachel's calmness soothed him. "And when you see them coming, turn on the lights as you said you would do."

He exhaled loudly and looked up into the myriad of stars that splashed across the sky. "You won't go anywhere? Our sentries might shoot you. Everyone is nervous, you know."

"I promise, Moddy. I will stay right here by the rock. Close to the bridge. *Nu?*"

"*Nu,*" he said grudgingly, frowning in the direction of Amman.

Rachel watched Moddy disappear in the darkness of the plant before she sat down beside the boulder again. She gazed into the vast skies and remembered how far she had come.

From the Warsaw Ghetto. Auschwitz. The hands of my enemies. Brutal days of slavery. The end of war and the beginning of wandering. Homelessness among the million homeless. And then, God, a miracle. You brought me through the sea and to this . . . this land of promise and deliverance! Hear my heart, O mighty God of my father Abraham!

She raised her hands to the heavens. *We are Your bride, Israel, and You have brought us home! Do not forsake us in the days that come. Have pity on us and on Your other children*—her mind filled with thoughts of Sarai—*who are also descended from Abraham. Unite our hearts in Your love. One at a time, Lord, make us beloved to one another and give us peace.*

Hope welled within, and she thought she might burst with the joy of it. Jerusalem! Grandfather and Yacov! Ellie and David! Sarai! And last of all, her own precious ones: Moshe and Tikvah and the child she carried beneath her heart.

Rachel was not the same sad soul who had landed on a cold beach in Palestine six months before! Her heart and hope had been reborn. Her life had been resurrected in seeing God's great love for her. He had loved her even in Auschwitz, as He loved all who died there. And now He had brought her from the grave. Today, like Rachel, Israel would be reborn. Just as Yeshua had stepped from the grave, so this little nation would breathe again as He promised in His Word.

"And I," Rachel said loudly as she stood to search the road beyond the river, "I am alive to see the promise fulfilled!"

"Fredrich Gerhardt, do you believe in el-Kiama?" Sarai asked as he worked feverishly to finish.

"The Resurrection?" He scoffed. "No, I believe in el-Kamama. The dunghill. Return to the dunghill."

"Is that all life is to you?"

"What else?" He was irritated by her words. It was better when she said nothing at all. "I send the Jews to el-Kamama."

"How much longer?" she asked quietly.

"It is alive now." He lay in the shadow, already imagining the devastation his creation would bring.

"I believe in el-Kiama." Sarai's voice was confident.

Gerhardt looked up to see her standing opposite him with her foot stretched out over the grid of the deadly net of wires and mines.

"What are you doing!" he almost shouted.

"Do not move," her voice threatened, "or you are a man for the dunghill."

He had not seen her rise and take off the black garment that covered her bright dress. He cursed her. "The Jews will see you!"

"Do not move or you are dead!" she warned. "You said not a mouse, but a dog. How many times did you call me a dog and beat me?"

Gerhardt lay rigid in the dirt, his eyes wide and fixed on the dainty foot and the flowered hem of the dress that hovered only inches above the first mine. She had watched him. She had asked him every secret, and he had told her.

"Fool!" He cursed again. "You have gone mad! Do not step down!"

"Do not move," she answered. "El-Kiama has given me courage! Even if I die, I am not afraid!" She filled her lungs and lifted her voice in the high, shrill, undulating cry of Arab victory. "El-Kiama!" she cried, and the foot wavered a fraction above the mine. "Twenty feet, you said. Everyone for twenty feet will be torn to shreds! Look at you, Fredrich Gerhardt! Four mines, and one lies within a foot of your face!"

When Rachel heard a piercing Arab cry, she swiveled toward the sound in fear. A woman stood on the road near the footbridge. A man cowered at her feet.

A few seconds later Moddy and the sentries on guard duty around the perimenter must have spotted the same thing Rachel had. The floodlights of the great hydroelectric plant clicked on as rifle bolts slid into place and sentries plastered themselves behind the protection of the sandbags.

"It's a woman!" The cry resounded as the woman again released the Bedouin trill.

The lights reached the distance of a soccer field, illuminating two figures on the road, far beyond where the young Arab girl held her foot in the air, as if poised to step on something. She wore a beautiful lavender dress.

"Look!" someone shouted. "It's Mrs. Meir! And the professor with her!"

"Don't shoot!"

"Keep your rifles trained on the girl!"

Rachel stood then, her eyes unable to take in both the sight of Moshe walking slowly up the road and the slim lavender flower that wavered in the center. "Sarai!" she whispered in awe. Then she shouted to the others, "Do not shoot her! She is a friend!"

Sarai Tafara's voice called out to Moshe, and he stopped in the center of the road, fifty yards from the girl.

"Do not come close here, Professor. He has mined the road! Come no closer!"

The curses of Fredrich Gerhardt grew louder. "You have betrayed your people!" he screamed again and again.

Her face seemed to glow with the answer she hurled back at the monster who lay before her. "Who are my people?" She waved her foot in a threat over his own deadly net. "Are you my people, Gerhardt? You? Men like you?"

Rachel moved slowly toward the footbridge. "Sarai," she said, and then she said the name again. "Sarai, my beloved enemy! Sarai!"

Moshe called to Rachel, "Go back! Come no closer! Rachel!"

At the mention of Rachel's name, Sarai looked away for just an instant. And in that instant Gerhardt grasped his revolver and shot.

Rachel screamed. The lavender petal hovered in the air for a second, then crumpled forward as Gerhardt tried to escape. Then the vision, the lavender garden, vanished in a roar of light and sound. And in her bright wake, the dark form of evil dissolved before their eyes.

44

KEY TO
A NATION

It was dawn. May 14, 1948. The last day of the British Mandate in Palestine.

British troop transports jammed with duffel bags and men were parked along the Tel Aviv wharf like trumpeting elephants in a circus parade.

Inside the administrative wing of the King David Hotel in Jerusalem, minor British officials said their good-byes to clerical workers as they burned documents and stripped the offices.

Pictures of Churchill and Bevin and Allenby had come down from the walls, leaving faded squares of plaster and empty nails. The British Mandate, which had begun with such high hopes, was now finally, irrevocably crashing to an end. The future of Jerusalem would now be decided by war. For this reason Tom Kane met with David Ben-Gurion, Golda Meir, and half a dozen others in Tel Aviv today.

Moshe stood to the right of Kane, prepared to serve as interpreter for those among the staff who did not speak English. The American diplomat himself had the look of a Jewish Zionist, Moshe thought. His tie had been discarded for a plain white shirt, open at the collar, and his lean face was tanned from weeks in Palestine. Those in the stuffy office knew that he had done much to aid them, but it was probable that what had been done was still not enough.

The meeting had begun informally and now proceeded through gallons of lukewarm tea. There were dozens of important issues to be addressed before statehood was declared this afternoon, and one in particular occupied the minds of those present. The American people had shown their support of a Jewish nation, but what of the United States government? Conflicting statements still continued to flood from the State Department, leaving everyone concerned awash in a wake of confusion.

"On every front," Ben-Gurion said solemnly, "we are being urged to wait. Wait! Wait! Declare statehood later. Would that guarantee that we will not be attacked and annihilated by the Arabs anyway?"

"Of course not." Golda lit her fifth cigarette. "They already attack everywhere the British have withdrawn. Last night Moshe and I traveled to speak with Abdullah. The only thing that would have prevented war was to compromise with him and his withdrawal from the Arab League. Obviously our hope in that was futile . . . *tragic!*" She shuddered at the memory of the long night.

Tom Kane cleared his throat and nodded. "Faced with the Arab Legion at arms against you, perhaps you have a fifty-fifty chance of survival."

"And since we decide to take that chance anyway," someone asked from the back of the room, "will the United States stand with us? Or will they waver as they have done since November?"

Kane chose his words carefully as he opened his briefcase and removed a cylinder eighteen inches long and about the size of a rolled newspaper. He looked toward Moshe, whose eyes grew wide at the sight of the object. "Professor Sachar?" he asked, carefully placing the object on the table.

Moshe stepped forward. Layer by layer he stripped the newspaper off until, finally, the golden brown leather of the scroll of Isaiah was revealed. Men and women pushed in for a closer look. Hushed whispers and questions buzzed among them.

"What does this mean?" Moshe asked Kane.

"The president accepted this as collateral for an air force," Kane answered quietly as he handed a piece of monogrammed stationery to Ben-Gurion. "He asked me to return it in the event negotiations with Abdullah failed. He requests that you accept it as our pledge of faith."

The top of the clean white paper read *Harry S. Truman.* Below that was a simple message. "He says," Ben-Gurion said, "'*Read Isaiah chapter forty-one again. Best Regards, Harry Truman.*'" Ben-Gurion looked up at Moshe. "Can you find it?"

"It is not numbered, but—" Moshe carefully rolled out the ancient scroll until he came to the Scripture portion he recognized as chapter forty-one. "Here," he said, and his voice held a sense of awe. He was reading from Scripture copied two thousand years ago, as Israel fell before the legions of Rome. Now the promise seemed clear and certain, like the unwavering hand that had written it on the leather.

Moshe searched the eager faces who leaned in, waiting for the promise. "Look," he said, "a teardrop stained the ink here." He pointed to a small smudge and began reading there:

"But you, O Israel, My servant,
*   Jacob, whom I have chosen,*
*   you descendants of Abraham My friend,*
I took you from the ends of the earth,
*   from its farthest corners I called you.*
I said, 'You are My servant';
*   I have chosen you and have not rejected you.*
So do not fear, for I am with you;
*   do not be dismayed, for I am your God.*
I will strengthen you and help you;
*   I will uphold you with My righteous right hand.*
All who rage against you
*   will surely be ashamed and disgraced;*
those who oppose you
*   will be as nothing and perish.*
Though you search for your enemies,
*   you will not find them.*
Those who wage war against you
*   will be as nothing at all.*
For I am the LORD, your God,
*   who takes hold of your right hand*
and says to you, 'Do not fear;
*   I will help you.*
Do not be afraid, . . .
*   O little Israel,*
for I Myself will help you,' declares the LORD,
*   your Redeemer, the Holy One of Israel."*

Moshe stopped reading there and once again looked up at the awe-struck faces of his companions. It was as though a mighty voice had been heard in the room. As if these words had remained unwritten by the hand of God until this, the moment when the mighty promise was most needed.

Ben-Gurion held up the slip of paper. "There is a postscript here. Truman says, *'U.S. foreign policy—written in the Book.'* "

Shortly after sunrise, the sad skirl of British bagpipes echoed hauntingly through the labyrinth of Old City streets. Rabbi Lebowitz stood with Yacov and a small delegation of rabbis on the steps of the Great Hurva Synagogue as the British began their final march through Jerusalem.

Rabbi Lebowitz lifted his eyes to the domed rooftops where, even now, Dov and Ehud led their men to the forward positions being evacuated by the British. As the pipers played, Yacov stood at attention and saluted the men of the Haganah. Then he turned and saluted the tattered remnants of the flag that still waved atop the dome of the synagogue.

Along the Street of the Jews, past the Yeshiva schools and sacred halls of learning, the men of the Suffolk Regiment marched. Their thirty-year reign in the land of Palestine had been filled with turmoil. Now they were like the others: soldiers of Babylonia, Assyria, Legions of Rome, Persians, Arabs, Crusaders, and Turks.

Where are they? the old rabbi wondered as the English soldiers rounded a corner with Colonel Halloway at their head and Captain Stewart behind him. *Where are they all now? Gone. Gone. Gone. But still we are here. Still we are Jews, waiting for the return of Your Holy One!*

As if some invisible signal had been given, the bearded old scholars kissed the fringes of their talliths and covered their heads with the ancient garment that had been the sign of their faithfulness for thousands of years. *"Hear, O Israel: The Lord our God, the Lord is one. . . ."*

Yacov recited the words of the Shema with the old men. Then he looked up into the face of the old rabbi. "They are coming, Grandfather. Coming to us!"

The men of the Suffolk Regiment marched to the steps of the Hurva. The command was given to halt, and the pipes fell silent. Rifles were slung, and the soldiers stood blinking in the morning sunlight as the aged rabbis looked back at them.

Colonel Halloway saluted smartly and clicked his heels at attention. Then he extended his empty hand to the side, and Captain Stewart stepped forward. He placed a rusty iron bar into the colonel's outstretched hand and stepped back.

Yacov's eyes grew wide as the British officer climbed the steps and stood directly before Rabbi Shlomo Lebowitz. With a nod, he offered the bar to the old man. Yacov drew his breath in sharply. It was the key to one of the seven gates of the Old City of Jerusalem. It was the key to Zion Gate.

The colonel cleared his throat as emotion filled the old rabbi's eyes. Rabbi Lebowitz grasped the key tightly with both hands and bowed in thanks.

"From the year AD 70 until this moment," the colonel said, "a key to the gates of Jerusalem has never been in Jewish hands. This is the first time in nineteen centuries that your people have been so privileged." The colonel stood to attention and saluted.

"Blessed art Thou, O Lord, who has granted us life and sustenance and permitted us to reach this day," said Rabbi Lebowitz quietly. Then he addressed the colonel. "I accept this key in the name of my people."

The Englishman turned, barked an order to the regiment, and marched his men from the walls of Jerusalem for the last time.

From the black depths of the British military prison in Athens, David Meyer and Bobby Milkin listened as news of the final British evacuation of Palestine blared over the radio.

David sat forlornly on the narrow bunk and listened to the voice of David Ben-Gurion, speaking from a Tel Aviv museum:

> *"With trust in the Rock of Israel, we set our hands in*
> *witness to this proclamation. . . ."*

For fifteen minutes he spoke, and David's heart crowded with emotion. He imagined Moshe and Rachel Sachar standing among the assembly of witnesses. If Martin Feinsteinel had brought in the load of ME-109 parts, probably his dear Ellie was there, too. Certainly she was listening! Her ears were hearing the fulfillment of a dream . . . the fulfillment of a prophecy: *"I took you from the ends of the earth, from its farthest corners I called you."* The importance of this moment in history filled him with wonder—and with despair. *They will need us come morning. They will need our little fighters.*

The inflection in Ben-Gurion's voice rose as he finished the proclamation:

> *"Accordingly we, the members of the National Council, representing*
> *the Jewish people in the land of Israel and the Zionist movement,*
> *have assembled on the day of the termination of the British Mandate*
> *for Palestine, and, by virtue of our natural and historic right and the*
> *resolution of the United Nations, do hereby proclaim the establishment*
> *of a Jewish state in the land of Israel—the State of Israel!"*

The Old Man's voice cracked with emotion as he continued:

> *"The State of Israel will be open to Jewish immigration and the*
> *ingathering of exiles!"*

A spontaneous roar erupted from the crowd that was there. Its sound echoed through the corridor of the jail.

"The State of Israel," Milkin said in awe. "What'dya know!"

"They'll be dancing tonight." David smiled wistfully.

"And bombing tomorrow," Milkin added.

The sound of the jail warden's keys floated down the corridor. He was an amiable British officer, pleasant and unassuming in his duties. Unsolicited he had brought in the radio so David and Milkin could listen. David watched as he marched jauntily toward their cell. His mustache curved in a perpetual smile, he beamed as he stood outside the bars of their cell.

"*Mazel tov,* lads! Why so downhearted? Got yourself a state, after all, and our laddie bucks are comin' home quick march, as they say!"

"Thanks, Captain Culpepper." David smiled halfheartedly.

"Well, come on! Brighten up, boys! Commanding officer wants a word with you!"

When the kind captain unlocked the door, David noticed that an armed escort of a dozen men waited down the hall.

"Come on, peaceful like!" the captain urged. "No funny business!"

In the background, David could hear Ben-Gurion's words:

"Even in the midst of attacks launched against us for months past, we call upon the sons of the Arab people dwelling in Israel to keep the peace and play their part in building. We extend the hand of good neighborliness to all the states around us. We call upon them in peace. . . ."

"*Mazel tov,* lads," the warden called as they were loaded into the back of a military paddy wagon.

"Where you think we're goin'?" Milkin asked gloomily as they wound through the streets of Athens. "Kinda feel like they're gonna shoot us or somethin', y'know?"

"They can't do that." David felt angry. Again he thought of Moshe and Rachel and Ellie with their arms around one another in rejoicing. All David wanted was to be there with them.

"I could sure use a good cigar," Milkin complained. "Think they'll grant us some kinda last wish? A cigar, maybe?"

"Knock it off," David threatened. He was in no mood to hear any more.

The van stopped. David and Milkin listened intently to voices at the back of the vehicle. Their words were muffled and indistinct. ". . . don't see that we have any choice . . ."

As David pondered the meaning, the doors clanged open, and they were blinded by the unfamiliar sunlight. The roar of an airplane engine passed overhead. Two officers waited outside the van.

"Come on now," said a colonel with a trace of an Irish accent. "Get out of the van."

David and Milkin complied, shading their eyes against the sun. "Where are you taking us?" David asked the Irish colonel.

"Taking you?" His lilting brogue sounded amused. "Well, I'm afraid you'll have to take yourselves, now won't you?"

"Huh?" Milkin turned around and gasped. The two 109s sat wingtip to wingtip on the tarmac in front of them.

"Yours is the one with the Tin Man, isn't it?" the colonel asked David. "I always admired your exploits. . . . You strafed a German Panzer division for my company when I was up against Rommel in North Africa. Knocked a few of their birds out of the sky as well."

David staggered forward. "You mean . . . ?"

"That was when you were serving with the American 9th Air Force. In Benghazi, I believe." He tugged his ear.

"Isn't this going to mean your head?"

"No. You were arrested before Israel was a sovereign state. Now you are an officer in the Israeli Air Force, from what we're told. To arrest you and hold you constitutes an act of war against the new State of Israel."

David laughed out loud and clapped Milkin on the back. "We're free!" he said, throwing back his head in laughter again.

The colonel drew a deep breath. "You must have friends in high places, Captain Meyer." He saluted in admiration. "Word is that order for your release was arranged by the U.S. threat to withhold Marshall Plan foreign aid to Great Britain. I hope our friends in Northern Ireland don't try to recruit you!"

David and Milkin scrambled into the cockpits of their fighter planes. Engines coughed once and turned over with a powerful roar.

The Irish colonel saluted as they taxied down the runway and lifted off. The Star of David glistened proudly on the shiny metal *Tinman*.

"*Mazel tov* . . . Israelis," the colonel called as the ME-109s rose powerfully into the skies.

EPILOGUE

Within hours, the newborn State of Israel was plunged into war with five Arab nations. The skies over Tel Aviv were defended only by two Jewish warriors flying German war-surplus planes, but their actions permitted the arrival of critical military supplies and additional fighter aircraft.

The Old City held out heroically against the Arab Legion's onslaught for a week before surrendering, thus giving the Yishuv time to arm and consolidate its positions. The Old City and the revered Wailing Wall were declared off-limits to Jews, and for the next nineteen years, Jerusalem was divided between Israel and Jordan.

The voice of Arab moderation, King Abdullah of Transjordan, was assassinated by the Mufti's henchmen. Eventually the mantle of Palestinian Arab leadership passed into the control of Haj Amin's successors, including his real-life cousin PLO chieftan Yasser Arafat.

During the recapturing of Old City Jerusalem in the Six Days' War of 1967, Israeli tank commander Yacov Lubetkin was wounded. He was carried from the battle to safety by two young men of his command: Ehud Luke Sachar and Michael Howard Meyer.

AUTHORS' NOTE

Twenty years ago this day, we traveled to Montreal to see the exhibit Children of the Holocaust. We sat on a park bench as members of the Jewish community flocked to attend services for the holy day of Yom Kippur. Young men stood in the sunlight with their talliths billowing. Old men stood in knots and talked quietly.

A woman, perhaps sixty years old, came and sat quietly beside us. She had a kind face and was dressed in a well-tailored burgundy suit. Her gray hair was pulled back in a bun beneath a lovely hat. She greeted us with a soft accent, and we began to talk—first about the weather and then other things. She was from Poland, and she told us her story . . . not with bitterness but with radiant peacefulness. She felt that the hand of God had preserved her life, and by a miracle He had brought about the return of the children of Israel to their homeland. Now she lived with her own children, and she had come to the synagogue to remember.

"We all need atonement," she said.

Research for the Zion Chronicles series has been an ongoing task. Hundreds of men and women have offered their own stories and reflections on the events surrounding the miracle that is Israel. Some are still living; others have left their stories through news accounts or The National Archives. George Orwell once remarked that the magazines and newspapers of the day are like a time machine. In this case it is true. During the three years we wrote this series, we lived in 1948 through news accounts and personal testimonies. We are grateful to the people who took the time to leave a record for those of us who were yet unborn. Their accounts tell more of the truth than any history book.

On a personal note, we want to thank those who have walked with us through this series. Bodie's parents shared their memories of this time, and her mother was always on the lookout for copies of old magazines that touched the events found in The Zion Chronicles. Bodie's brother, sisters, and all our family provided tremendous support and listened patiently and with love to endless hours of conversation about plotlines and historical events. Our love to each of you!

Thanks also to our little community up here in the California mountains. God could not have given us a more wonderful place to call our home. And then there is Margaret Tait and her cello . . . her music and that of our friends with the San Francisco Symphony have provided an incredible backdrop for every chapter and inspiration even in slow times of writing. *Mazel tov* and blessings!

Our children—Rachel, Jacob, Luke, and Ellie—deserve tremendous credit for their roles in these three years of work. They unselfishly shared their parents with piles of research and a typewriter that tapped for endless hours, months at a time. Their patience resulted in five novels and nearly three thousand manuscript pages in thirty-six months. We are proud and grateful to God for such love and support and that God has allowed our family to be "of one heart."

We love you and thank you all, our dear ones. From those who offered a story without a name to those whose names are as familiar to me as my own . . . I hold you up in praise before *the One Lord, the God of Israel*, who has made us all!

There are a hundred stories yet to be told, and so the work continues. . . . Shalom!

DIGGING DEEPER
INTO
THE KEY TO ZION

> "There is a greater enemy. . . ," Rachel murmured. "One who would keep us imprisoned in our hatred, one who delights in the bitterness that divides us."
> "Yes. And he is the enemy we must defeat within ourselves."
> "Perhaps," Rachel offered, "we defeat him by loving."
> —RACHEL AND MOSHE SACHAR, pp. 153–154

Do you struggle with bitterness or hatred toward another? Do you bear scars from being wounded by hatred and bitterness? Have you experienced a broken relationship? Are you held captive by fear?

Rachel Sachar, Sarai Tafara, and Yehudit Akiva—women of vastly different backgrounds—all bear scars (emotional, physical, or both) due to mistreatment. All were held captive by fear.

Rachel, terribly wounded at a young age by the enemies of her people, lived for years in the torment of hatred and bitterness. But as she came to believe in God's great love for her, her heart changed. She was able to return good for evil by extending compassion and love to Sarai, her "enemy." Although Sarai at first refused Rachel's kindness, Rachel kept trying.

Sarai, an Arab, had been taught to hate Jews. That passion was fueled when she was raped by renegade Jews. It was no wonder she was suspicious and angry when Rachel and Moshe took her home with them. It took the beauty of a deceased Arab's soul—old Miriam and the message she had embroidered on a lovely purple dress—to change Sarai's heart.

Yehudit was abused for years by her demanding, authoritarian father. She had accepted the treatment because she didn't know anything else and lived in fear of her father's wrath. But when a child's life was in jeopardy, she acted, knowing the consequences. She was shunned by her father and held captive in his home. At one point, she wished to die. It wasn't until the Jews at Tipat Chalev embraced her as part of their "family" that she found purpose, meaning . . . even love!

Each woman's heart and life were transformed because someone chose to love her. "Remember what I was not so long ago. And see what miracles the love of God has done in my heart," Rachel says. "The world is always full of one more lonely person in need of hope. No. We cannot touch them all. But what about those whom God brings to us? . . . We can think of them one at a time! *One* person! *One* life!" (p. 190).

Change may not happen all at once. We are like the famous statue of Michelangelo that was chiseled free bit by bit, "one chip of stone at a time" (p. 121). God does the same for us daily, if we are willing.

You may still carry the marks of others' hatred—on your body or your soul. But why not allow those marks to be ones of compassion (see p. 153), as Rachel does? Why not choose to end the bondage of hate on your own soul? Why not choose to love, just as Messiah loves you?

It is only through el-Kiama's transforming love that all people—regardless of race, nationality, social status, or age—can be united . . . and that peace can reign on earth.

Yet we live in the meantime, when hatred abounds. As you search for answers to your daily dilemmas, we trust that the following questions will help. You may wish to delve into them on your own or share them with a friend or a discussion group.

Most of all, we pray that you will "discover the Truth through fiction." For we are convinced that if you seek diligently, you will find the One who holds all the answers to the universe (1 Chronicles 28:9).

Bodie & Brock Thoene

SEEK . . .

Prologue

1. If you were Eli bar Yehuda, what would you think as you watched people die in the Temple courtyard and realized that soon you would die, too?

   _____

   _____

2. "Why have You abandoned us, O Lord?" Eli asked (p. vi). "All is lost. All is ended." Has there been a time in your life when you felt abandoned by God? when you've wondered if "all is lost"? Tell the story.

   _____

   _____

PART I
Chapters 1–2

3. "I have lived too long. Too long. To see the innocent die thus. . . . Better you should take an old man, *nu*, instead of those with hope and joy left to spend," Rabbi Lebowitz says (p. 4). Why do you think some people die young and others live to an old age? Is it better to offer hope and have it taken away than to have no hope at all? Why or why not?

   _____

   _____

4. "I want to go back to the way it was before," Yacov tells his grand-father (p. 4). Have you ever expressed this sentiment? When?

   _____

   _____

5. Rabbi Lebowitz is determined that he and Yacov will return home to the Old City of Jerusalem (see p. 5). When have you returned home after a long journey? How did it feel to be home at last?

   _____

   _____

6. "I say that a sacrifice is in order. To save many, we eliminate a few," the young Jewish Mossad agent says (p. 12). Do you agree? Why or why not?

_____

_____

Chapters 3–4

7. "'He told me not to hate them,' Rachel whispered, forgetting for a moment the presence of Dr. Rimsky. . . .

   "'Not hate the Arabs,' the doctor repeated bitterly. 'An impossible request'" (p. 18).

   If a person you love was hurt or killed (such as Professor Moniger—a man who truly was a "friend of the very world"— p. 18), would you be able to not hate the person who caused that event? Especially if the death seemed "senseless and without reason" (p. 18)? Why or why not?

_____

_____

8. Moshe, a Jew, thinks of the many Christians, Muslims, and Jews who worked shoulder to shoulder in archaeological digs "in the dust of Palestine to uncover a common past. . . . They had been his friends, his brothers. Now they were his enemies" (p. 21). Has a friend of yours become an enemy? What came between you? Has there been any move toward reconciliation? Why or why not?

_____

_____

9. _"War makes barbarians of us all,"_ Moshe realizes (p. 22). What historical events can you point to that prove the truth of this statement?

_____

_____

Chapters 5–8

10. After her rape, Sarai Tafara is in extreme emotional and physical anguish. Per Arab custom, her disgrace is also her family's disgrace, and the only way to remove the shame is to end Sarai's life. Her cousin Ahkmed is assigned the task of "rescuing" her (see pp. 29, 31).

Do you think it is ever right to help someone in pain end his or her life? Explain your perspective.

_____

_____

11. Journalist Lawrence Crabtree was on a mission to discover the answer to his burning questions:

    *Who are the good guys, and who are the bad guys in this little Middle Eastern drama? (p. 34)

    *Why had the Jews of Europe gone like sheep into the extermination camps? Why had they not fought back? Why had they offered themselves as victims to a nation gone mad with hatred? (p. 35)

    How would you answer these questions?

    _____

    _____

12. "'Lord . . . help me now, or I will break! Some word from him. Some word of his safety . . .' " Rachel prayed. "Not knowing what to do, she turned to find even some small task to take her mind off Kastel" (p. 48). When have you been concerned about a loved one's safety? Did "tasks" take your mind off the anxiety? Why or why not?

    _____

    _____

    Chapter 9
13. In 1948 there were many opinions, even within the U.S., about what (if anything) should be done to help the Jews establish their homeland. Reread the conversation on pages 59-65 between Tom Kane, Secretary of State Marshall, Undersecretary Lovett, and President Truman.
    Consider the facts:

    *God promised the land to the Jews thousands of years ago in the historical record of the Bible (which has remained unchanged since it was written).

*There has never been an Arab nation in Palestine.

*The British ruled Palestine from 1917 until May 1948. Before that, the Ottoman Turks ruled there for many hundred years.

Do these facts impact your opinion in any way? If so, how?

_____

_____

14. President Truman's decisions are swayed by the actions of individual American voters who have given $50 million, 70,000 flares, 50,000 helmets, farm tools, etc. (see p. 64) to help stop the massacre in Palestine and to have a small part in establishing peace in the troubled land. You may only be one, but your vote does count. How might God be calling you to fight injustice or to help the hurting today?

_____

_____

15. "Her father had not come for reconciliation or explanation. That much was immediately obvious to Yehudit. And so he had come because he wanted something from her" (p. 65). Have you ever experienced a situation similar to Yehudit's—where someone has used you to get something without caring about you, as a person? How did you respond?

_____

_____

Chapters 10–11
16. Reread pages 73-76, where Rachel compares her memories of the prewar days in Germany and Poland to what she is hearing Haj Amin Husseini say over the radio. Dov also compares this time in Palestine to his fight against the Nazis in the Warsaw Ghetto (see p. 84). What similarities and differences can you identify between these experiences?

_____

_____

17. If you were Ehud, and an old rabbi and a young boy asked to go along on the dangerous journey through Zion Gate (see p. 80), how would you respond?

_____

_____

18. If you believed what was written—"Out of blood and fire Judea will fall! . . . And out of blood and fire it will be reborn!" (p. 85)— would you choose to be a part of those who would "give birth" to Zion for the Jews? Why or why not?

_____

_____

Chapters 12–15

19. "It is important that we maintain our image of fairness in all this. Justice is the thing, isn't it? We'll let the Jews and the Arabs take one another's eyes, and we'll be the only ones left who still can see," the British colonel Halloway says (p. 91). How does this statement impact your view of the events that transpired in the British Mandate of Palestine in 1948?

_____

_____

20. "These are the ashes of Jews, and soon all who still live will also be ashes," Ahkmed tells Sarai.

Her response? "And when they are all dead, will that then return to me my husband? my village? my life?" (p. 92).

Is revenge ever worthwhile? Why, or why not?

_____

_____

21. What factions can you identify among the Arab League nations for the conquering of Palestine (see pp. 113-117)? Compare Haj Amin's strategy with the other Arab nations'. Why do you think Haj Amin's strategy is so different from the others?

_____

_____

Chapters 16–18

22. When Moshe and Rachel bring the injured Arab girl to the hospital, the nurse refuses to treat one of "them" (see p. 125). If you were the nurse, would you find a place for the girl? What pros and cons would you consider while you were deciding?

_____

_____

23. Why does Rachel, a Jew, feel such deep empathy for Sarai, the Arab girl (see pp. 127-129)? When have you felt empathy for someone who has suffered as you have? How did that empathy impact the other person? impact you?

_____

_____

24. "I figure the Lord is watching us. He knows everything from beginning to end. He even knows how scared we are," David tells Ellie (p. 134). Do you believe God is watching over you? What evidence have you experienced to back up your conclusions?

_____

_____

25. "For two thousand years we have said, 'Next year in Jerusalem,' true? Always we Jews have looked to the future . . . to Jerusalem. Now the future has waited long enough. If _we_ do not grasp it, other hands . . . will," Rabbi Lebowitz claims (p. 146). What have you waited to do? Could _now_ be the time to grasp that future?

_____

_____

PART II
Chapters 19–23

26. What conflicts do Moshe and Rachel experience (see pp. 152, 167) as a result of taking "the enemy" into their home? Which side would you take—Moshe's or Rachel's? Why? Could you continue to love someone who rejected your offers of kindness? For how long?

_____

_____

27. How did Rachel break the ice with her beloved enemy, Sarai (see pp. 155, 163–167)? And what does Sarai do as a result (see pp. 191–196, 197–199, 218)? What can you do, practically speaking, to encourage an enemy to become a friend?

_____

_____

28. "*Hope*. All the world lives and feeds on that one word," Rachel tells Moshe (p. 188). In what ways can you keep hope alive in your small corner of the world?

_____

_____

29. Do you believe in el-Kiama (the Resurrection) or el-Kamama (the dunghill)? (See p. 194.) How does that belief affect the way you live—and your thoughts of death?

_____

_____

Chapters 24–27

30. When Sarai returns with the goat, "the dark hatred that had hovered over [her] since she had come to live with [Moshe and Rachel] seemed to have vanished" (p. 218). What has happened to Sarai? Have you or someone you know experienced such dramatic life change? If so, tell the story!

_____

_____

31. "Do you think the world cares about Golan or Gaza or Haifa or even Tel Aviv? Most of the world has not even heard of such places . . . but Jerusalem!" King Abdullah tells General Glubb (p. 220). How does this statement impact your thinking about the events happening in Jerusalem in 1948? about what's happening there today?

_____

_____

32. Why is the biblical story of Ruth a good parallel for Rachel and Sarai's relationship (see p. 236)? What similarities do you see between the two stories? (If you have never read this beautiful story of a transformed heart, why not read it now?)

_____

_____

Chapters 28–31

33. In a time of uncertainty and pending war, Yehudit—a young woman who has never known love—finds love in the eyes of Dov, the "Bear of Warsaw" (see p. 244). For the first time in her life she is free from her father's tyranny and is a welcome and needed member of the Haganah. How has someone's love transformed your life?

_____

_____

34. Because of Sarai's transformation, Moshe prays, "Change my heart today. Cleanse me from secret faults and make me as Yeshua was on this earth. Give me wisdom today, and help us find peace in our hearts" (p. 255). Dear reader, how does your heart need to change today? What secret faults are you harboring? In what areas of your life do you need wisdom? peace?

_____

_____

35. Miriam's beautiful embroidery was a "secret, ongoing testimony" of her life (p. 256). If others looked at your life, what ongoing testimony would they see?

_____

_____

PART III
Chapters 32–36

36. "Men and women would die. They were not Jews or Arabs to Sarai anymore. They were simply people now" (p. 293). Although Sarai is living daily with the abuse of Gerhardt—"the man they called Death"—her heart has changed forever. What difficulties do you

live with on a daily basis? How have those difficulties affected the status of your heart?

_____

_____

37. Have you ever struggled to separate a nightmare from reality, as Ellie did when she dreamed of David being pushed under the wheels of the train (see p. 303)? As you evaluate your dream, what under-the-surface fears are revealed?

_____

_____

38. Tom Kane and President Truman play a very important card: They insist that the British government has to make sure the Jews get supplies in these final days before the end of the British Mandate of Palestine or America will cut off aid to Britain (see p. 306). They are only asking that Britain stand firm on their own pledge to establish a Jewish homeland in Palestine. Have you ever had to play an important card to remind someone of their promise? If so, what happened?

_____

_____

Chapters 37–39
39. How was Captain Stewart caught in his own trap (see p. 324)? When has an enemy of yours received his or her comeuppance? When have you received your comeuppance? What did you learn from both situations?

_____

_____

It's fascinating to see the changed response of Captain Stewart later, on pp. 334–335, when he observes Gerhardt's abuse of Sarai.

40. *"Sarai is lost to us. Lost in the terrible uncertainty of these days. She is forgotten in the midst of the daily tragedy that has engulfed thousands . . . thousands! What can one life mean in all of this?"* Moshe thinks (p. 330). But in *The Key to Zion*, is she really lost in God's eyes?

When have you felt lost and forgotten in the midst of thousands? If you believed, like Sarai, that God has not lost track of you in the midst of the crowd, how would your life change?

Chapters 40–42

41. After Gerhardt leaves on his mission of hate, Sarai prepares for her own mission. She musters her courage by remembering, *"Your tomb is still open and empty, is it not, el-Kiama? I will cling to that hope. As You whispered to my heart in the garden that night. I will remember how You, innocent, died for me. How You saw me from Golgotha. And I will follow You. El-Kiama. Resurrection. Yes. It is right that I follow You"* (p. 354).

    Do you believe in the innocent el-Kiama, and that He has died for you? If so, in what ways has your life been impacted? If not, what hinders you from believing in the Savior of Arabs (such as Miriam and Sarai), Jews (such as Rachel and Moshe), and the entire world?

---

42. *"Why should he know the real story? Dov mused. One lie—a little one—to calm the good rabbi's jangled nerves. What can it hurt?"* (p. 356). Have you ever told a lie—even a "little one"—to benefit someone else? When? What was the result in the long run?

---

43. *"He is scarcely a man. So consumed by his hatred is he that he has become hatred. . . . He is the very shadow of death!"* Sarai thinks as she watches Gerhardt's face when he nears his target of destruction (p. 357, 363). Have you come face-to-face with this kind of hatred in someone else . . . or in yourself? How have you come to terms with it?

Chapters 43–44

44. "Hope welled within, and [Rachel] thought she might burst with the joy of it. . . . Rachel was not the same sad soul who had landed on a cold beach in Palestine six months before! Her heart and hope had been reborn. Her life had been resurrected in seeing God's great love for her. He had loved her even in Auschwitz, as He loved all who died there. And now He had brought her from the grave" (p. 376).

    Have your heart and hope been reborn because of God's great love for you? If not, why not open your heart to el-Kiama's love? Why not experience hope and healing for yourself?

    _____

    _____

45. It is Sarai, the abused woman turned courageous because of her belief in el-Kiama, who ends the evil reign of Gerhardt. "In her bright wake, the dark form of evil dissolved" (p. 378). When have you seen good triumph over evil? Share the story.

    _____

    _____

46. If you were Rabbi Lebowitz, accepting a key to the gates of Jerusalem—a key your people have not had since AD 70 (see p. 382)—what thoughts and emotions would you experience? If you were one of the people watching, would such an exchange make you believe or disbelieve the fulfillment of the prophecy in Isaiah (see page 381)? Why?

    _____

    _____

ABOUT THE AUTHORS

Bodie and Brock Thoene (pronounced *Tay-nee*) have written over 50 works of historical fiction. That these best sellers have sold more than 10 million copies and won eight ECPA Gold Medallion Awards affirms what millions of readers have already discovered—the Thoenes are not only master stylists but experts at capturing readers' minds and hearts.

In their timeless classic series about Israel (The Zion Chronicles, The Zion Covenant, and The Zion Legacy), the Thoenes' love for both story and research shines.

With The Shiloh Legacy and *Shiloh Autumn* (poignant portrayals of the American Depression), The Galway Chronicles (dramatic stories of the 1840s famine in Ireland), and the Legends of the West (gripping tales of adventure and danger in a land without law), the Thoenes have made their mark in modern history.

In the A.D. Chronicles they step seamlessly into the world of Jerusalem and Rome, in the days when Yeshua walked the earth and transformed lives with His touch.

Bodie began her writing career as a teen journalist for her local newspaper. Eventually her byline appeared in prestigious periodicals such as *U.S. News and World Report*, *The American West*, and *The Saturday Evening Post*. She also worked for John Wayne's Batjac Productions (she's best known as author of *The Fall Guy*) and ABC Circle Films as a writer and researcher. John Wayne described her as "a writer with talent that captures the people and the times!" She has degrees in journalism and communications.

Brock has often been described by Bodie as "an essential half of this writing team." With degrees in both history and education, Brock has, in his role as researcher and story-line consultant, added the vital dimension of historical accuracy. Due to such careful research, the Zion

Covenant and Zion Chronicles series are recognized by the American Library Association, as well as Zionist libraries around the world, as classic historical novels and are used to teach history in college classrooms.

Bodie and Brock have four grown children—Rachel, Jake, Luke, and Ellie—and seven grandchildren. Their children are carrying on the Thoene family talent as the next generation of writers, and Luke produces the Thoene audiobooks. Bodie and Brock divide their time between London and Nevada.

For more information visit:
www.thoenebooks.com
www.familyaudiolibrary.com

THOENE FAMILY CLASSICS™

✪ ✪ ✪

THOENE FAMILY CLASSIC HISTORICALS
by Bodie and Brock Thoene

Gold Medallion Winners*

THE ZION COVENANT
Vienna Prelude*
Prague Counterpoint
Munich Signature
Jerusalem Interlude
Danzig Passage
Warsaw Requiem*
London Refrain
Paris Encore
Dunkirk Crescendo

THE ZION CHRONICLES
The Gates of Zion*
A Daughter of Zion
The Return to Zion
A Light in Zion
The Key to Zion*

THE SHILOH LEGACY
In My Father's House*
A Thousand Shall Fall
Say to This Mountain

SHILOH AUTUMN

THE GALWAY CHRONICLES
Only the River Runs Free*
Of Men and of Angels
Ashes of Remembrance*
All Rivers to the Sea

THE ZION LEGACY
Jerusalem Vigil
Thunder from Jerusalem
Jerusalem's Heart
Jerusalem Scrolls
Stones of Jerusalem
Jerusalem's Hope

A.D. CHRONICLES
First Light
Second Touch
Third Watch
Fourth Dawn
Fifth Seal
Sixth Covenant
Seventh Day
Eighth Shepherd
Ninth Witness
Tenth Stone
and more to come!

CP0064

THOENE FAMILY CLASSICS™

✪ ✪ ✪

THOENE FAMILY CLASSIC AMERICAN LEGENDS

LEGENDS OF THE WEST
by Bodie and Brock Thoene

Legends of the West, Volume One
Sequoia Scout
The Year of the Grizzly
Shooting Star
Legends of the West, Volume Two
Gold Rush Prodigal
Delta Passage
Hangtown Lawman
Legends of the West, Volume Three
Hope Valley War
The Legend of Storey County
Cumberland Crossing
Legends of the West, Volume Four
The Man from Shadow Ridge
Cannons of the Comstock
Riders of the Silver Rim

LEGENDS OF VALOR
by Luke Thoene

Sons of Valor
Brothers of Valor
Fathers of Valor

✪ ✪ ✪

THOENE CLASSIC NONFICTION
by Bodie and Brock Thoene

Writer-to-Writer

THOENE FAMILY CLASSIC SUSPENSE
by Jake Thoene

CHAPTER 16 SERIES
Shaiton's Fire
Firefly Blue
Fuel the Fire

✪ ✪ ✪

THOENE FAMILY CLASSICS FOR KIDS

BAKER STREET DETECTIVES
by Jake and Luke Thoene

The Mystery of the Yellow Hands
The Giant Rat of Sumatra
The Jeweled Peacock of Persia
The Thundering Underground

LAST CHANCE DETECTIVES
by Jake and Luke Thoene
Mystery Lights of Navajo Mesa
Legend of the Desert Bigfoot

THE VASE OF MANY COLORS
by Rachel Thoene (Illustrations by Christian Cinder)

✪ ✪ ✪

THOENE FAMILY CLASSIC AUDIOBOOKS

Available from
www.thoenebooks.com or
www.familyaudiolibrary.com

CP0064